FILTHY PLAYBOY

ALEX WOLF

SLOANE HOWELL

She's young and innocent. He's tattooed and experienced.

Abigail Whitley transferred to Chicago to live life to the fullest and have fun before settling down.

No commitments. No limitations.

It wasn't supposed to happen.

She never expected Dexter Collins to strut into the office her first day on the job. But how could she not notice his inked-up arms and sharp jawline?

He's smoking-hot, refined, and has a stare that could melt steel.

He's also arrogant, jealous, and possessive.

Before long, their harmless interactions lead to toe-curling in his bedroom.

She realizes there's more to him than she thought, and she's falling--hard.

Just when life seems perfect, business mixes with pleasure and Dexter is, well, Dexter. Nothing goes according to plan.

After a monumental screw up, she's done. Finished with him.

There's just one problem.

When he's not being an ass...

They're fogging up glass.

Enjoy!

Publisher © Alex Wolf & Sloane Howell January 3rd, 2020
Cover Design: Alex Wolf
Editor: Spellbound
Formatting: Alex Wolf

DEXTER

Two things matter in this world—pussy and money.

There's plenty of both on display tonight.

Navigating through PRYSM night club, the bass thumps in my chest when I spot Wells Covington. He's difficult to miss at six-four in his Brunello Cucinelli suit. I head up the stairs.

"Collins!" He tosses me a head nod as I round the corner, like he already knew I was here and expected me right at that moment. He leans over the railing, observing the dance floor from above.

I glance around. The place is anything but optimal for discussing business. This is casual, though. I use the term 'casual' loosely because I'm always on the hunt for a new whale to add to our client roster. Wells is the top of the food chain and Tecker (my brother Decker and his fiancée Tate) would be all up on my nuts if I wrap him up in a nice bow for the firm.

"Hope you haven't been waiting long." I grip his hand firm after I make my way over.

He's constantly back and forth between Manhattan and Chicago. We were tight back at college, then drifted apart. I've been trying to meet with him for months. Our schedules never permitted a get together until tonight. One look at this bastard and I see nothing but dollar signs. It's almost enough for me to ignore all the hot ass strutting half-naked around the club.

Almost.

"Nah. Haven't ordered a drink yet."

"What do you want? It's on me."

He eyes me up and down, grinning his ass off. I know he's about to ask for something ridiculous. "Clase Azul. For old time's sake."

Hmm. He's being nostalgic. We used to chug that shit in Cancun on spring break in college. Last time I saw him he ordered twenty-one-year-old Suntory Hibiki, an eight-hundred-dollar bottle of Japanese whiskey.

"Sounds like a party." I motion a waitress over.

A brunette in tight-fitting black jeans and a vee-cut top saunters our way. One look at us and she grins her ass off. She knows she's just hit the lottery waiting on us. "What can I get you?"

"Clase Azul Reposado. Bring the bottle."

Wells smirks.

"You got it." The girl wanders off through the crowd.

"I'd much rather be having her." Wells looks toward the crowd on the dance floor below.

I follow his gaze to see who he's leering at. I need to make sure he's taken care of tonight. Shouldn't be a problem.

We may go way back, but time has passed. If I can get

our relationship back on a personal level, he'll be more apt to do business with the firm. Being the ultimate wingman is a specialty of mine, and I'm not above making sure he gets to fuck whoever he wants, if it comes to that.

My tie feels like it tightens around my neck and the hair on the back of my neck stands up when my eyes land on his target. She's hard to miss.

Abigail.

Fuck. Why did she have to be here?

Her long blonde curls bounce as she sways her hips to the music and waves her arms up in the air. The bright red dress she's wearing clings tight to her curves.

Of all the women in all the goddamn clubs in Chicago...

It's like the world hates me.

Fuck, she's hot.

My nostrils flare when the asshole she's dancing with grabs her hips from behind. He's pawing all over her, and she doesn't seem to mind one bit. In fact, I think she enjoys the attention.

I'm not used to this feeling—jealousy. It's totally foreign to me. I do my best to tame my reaction, but Wells is a goddamn shark and I'm sure he notices. You don't become a billionaire in your thirties by not reading people like a book, and he's the fucking Tony Stark of hedge funds.

I'm seeing red.

Not good.

Why do I even give a shit? I don't get hung up on chicks. Women chase me, not the other way around.

Abigail is different, though.

3

She's not like the usual women I date—or fuck. She's independent, young, and carefree. No baggage. Which is highly attractive.

Wells grins, suddenly taking more of an interest. "You know her, don't you?"

"Yeah." I let go of the railing after I look down and see the whites of my knuckles. "She works for the firm. Transferred from Dallas after the merger. You don't want anything to do with her, trust me. She's a stage five clinger. I'll introduce you, though. If you want."

A devilish smile forms on his lips when the waitress returns with the tall, slender bottle of tequila and two shot glasses. I silently pray he'll forget about Abigail as I snag the bottle and don't bother with the glasses. I tip it up, and it burns in my throat.

"Well fuck. I guess it's like college all over again tonight." Wells grins and takes a drink straight from the bottle too.

I rub the back of my neck, unable to keep my eyes from darting to Abigail on the dance floor. It's not like we're dating. We've hung out a few times after work, totally casual. Okay, we made out once when we were hammered after a Bears game when she did me a huge favor for Deacon's dumb ass; which he still owes me for.

Still, there's nothing going on with Abby and yet I have this unbelievable urge to grip that guy by the back of his neck and shove his face into a bucket of water. Nothing life threatening, just enough to feel his fear course through my palm.

I want to stake my claim on her like a caveman. Brand her ass with my handprint.

Wells leans over. "No need for an introduction. Plenty of women here tonight, Collins."

"Yeah." I nod. He keeps calling me by my last name. That's a good sign. It *should* make me happy.

None of the women here compare to Abby, though. I glance around the bar and notice she has quite the group of admirers. Every fucker in the place stares at her from afar, and I know exactly what's on all their minds.

They're all pounding booze and watching her shake her ass. The back of her dress rides her thighs, coming dangerously close to showing her panties, if she's even wearing any.

I can't fight my smile, despite the irritation coursing through my limbs. She has this spark about her that lights up the room with energy. She's magnetic, like a tractor beam that reels you in. I get why these assholes are staring, and at the same time, I want to let every one of them know she's off limits.

I take another pull from the bottle when she walks off the dance floor toward the bathrooms. "Be right back."

Wells waves me off with a flippant hand and strikes up a conversation with a leggy brunette.

I take the stairs two at a time to the lower level, losing sight of Abigail momentarily.

The last thing I want to look like is a stalker, so I pull out my phone and do the ol' 'fake call' routine. I shuffle down the narrow corridor toward the women's bathroom, hoping I time this shit just right.

I watch in a mirror and wait for her reflection, then I turn the corner just in time so Abigail bumps into me.

"I'm so sorry. Are you okay?"

I huff out a fake sigh, staring in the other direction. "I'll call you back." I make a show of pocketing my phone and glance up to meet her stunned gaze. "Don't worry about… Abby?"

"Oh my God, Dex!" She goes in for a hug, and I'm pretty sure it's heaven with her tits pressed up against me.

Fuck, I never want to let go of her. I'm close enough to smell her fruity body wash and the effect she has on me is damn near hypnotic.

I have to compose myself and will my cock not to get hard up against her stomach.

"Sorry, I wasn't paying attention." Her hand slides down my arm.

"It's fine."

"What are you…," we both say at the same time.

I hold out a palm. "Ladies first."

"Out with friends. You?"

"Here with a client. Hedge fund manager."

"Cool, well, I should…" She hooks a thumb over her shoulder toward the bathroom.

"Right. Was good to see you."

"You too!" she yells over her shoulder, and I can still barely make out the words as she disappears through the door.

Look at yourself for fuck's sake. What's wrong with you?

We only made out the one time. We were both wasted, and I don't know if she even remembers it. I'd be lying if I said I didn't remember every minute detail of the kiss, though. Not a damn day goes by I don't think about it.

I decide to take a piss, since I'm already down here, so

I walk through the door. That idiot she was dancing with primps himself in the mirror, fixing his hair. The guy is pathetic. He's wearing a fucking Winnie the Pooh shirt and corduroy pants.

I thought this place had standards and a dress code. Fuck.

I cannot believe I seriously have to compete with this ass basket.

I take a piss in the urinal, unlike bitch boy over there who probably squatted in the stall. Afterward, I wash my hands, and he's still there, checking himself out. Of course, as soon as I walk out of the bathroom, he decides to leave at the same time. I open the door and he speeds up to follow, but I let it fall right in his face.

Stay away from what's mine, pussy.

As I walk out, Abigail leaves the women's bathroom at the same time and we nearly collide again, this time not by design.

I catch her in an awkward hug and do my best to try and pull her off to the side, so Pooh Bear doesn't see us.

Of course, he heads in our direction, and I pray for him to do something that makes it acceptable for me to kick the piss out of him.

"Abby, you okay?"

Fuck you for calling her Abby. I call her that.

She's still staring up at me with wide eyes, and I slowly stand her upright.

I don't ever want to let go of her and at the same time my palm twitches with the need to choke this asshole until he passes out.

"Yeah, I'm good." She smiles and it's ridiculously

cute. "This is Dex. He's a partner at the firm and we've literally almost ran each other over twice in the last five minutes." Her head tilts in my direction.

Her friend shoves his hands in his pockets and shuffles his feet around like pussies do. "Oh, well, uhh… Chuck and Barbie got us a table."

What in the holy fuck kind of names are those? Chuck and Barbie? I scoff under my breath where Abigail doesn't notice.

Her hand flies out. "Dex, this is my friend Kyle. He lives in my building."

"Good to meet you." I hold out my hand and resist the urge to crush this guy's metacarpals so he never puts them on Abigail again. It's absolutely *not* good to meet him, at all. He needs to piss off.

He barely squeezes my hand back. It's like shaking hands with a wet noodle.

Jesus.

You can tell a lot about a man by the strength of his handshake and this guy is just as I thought, soft as fuck.

I glance up to the balcony and Wells has two brunettes on his arm, and I'm almost positive one of them is supposed to be for me. He chats them up, but it seems like he's watching me out of his peripheral vision.

Abigail looks at me, and I swear there's a sparkle in her eye. "Okay. Well, I should get back."

"Sure, see you at the office." I watch her go and barely refrain from scowling at Kyle when he glances back at me.

Once I'm back up to the balcony, Wells leans in and his voice lowers. "Don't worry. I found us some ass." He says it like I just struck out and nods to the two brunettes a few feet away.

It makes my blood boil even hotter. If I want Abigail, I'll have her. I always get what I want.

I scan the room and watch Abigail meet up with her friends. Our eyes lock for a moment, but I quickly turn toward the table and sit next to the other brunette.

"I'm Sandra." She holds her hand out and sinks her teeth into her bottom lip.

I take her hand. "Dexter. Call me Dex."

"I've never fucked a Dexter before."

What the hell did Wells just get us into?

He leans back with a satisfied grin.

Sandra smirks and slides her hand up my thigh. Her red fingernails give me a squeeze. Any other night I might enjoy a woman being so direct, but the one I want is across the room with some fuckbags named Kyle, Chuck, and Barbie.

"Let's get out of here," says Wells. "I have the top-floor suite at The Peninsula."

I shouldn't be surprised. That room only goes for eight grand a night. The bastard has a new mansion on Lake Michigan, but it's about a forty-five-minute drive away. I give him a head nod, letting him know I'm on board so we can get the fuck out of here. I'm ready to call it a night even though I'm leaving without Abby. It's still a success. I'll have Wells as a client before the weekend is up so I'm still batting .500.

Like a true asshole, I can't let it go, though. I make a point to parade Sandra and her big tits right past Abigail's table. She needs to know what she's missing out on. I want her to be just as jealous as when I saw her on the dance floor grinding with that limp-handed cock boy.

Instead, she just smiles and waves, like she doesn't have a care in the world.

Goddamn it.

We finally make it outside to the sidewalk.

Sandra leans in close and whispers, "Your place or mine?"

Her friend slides into the back of a black Mercedes with Wells. Of course, he has a car and a driver. Why wouldn't you on a random night out in Chicago?

Man, I *have* to bring his business to the firm.

"Neither."

"Hotel? With those two?" She nods toward Wells and her friend.

"I'm going home, alone."

She frowns.

I lift my chin in Wells' direction. "He has enough dick for both of you. Enjoy yourselves."

Wells smiles, then shrugs. "He's not lying."

Sandra walks over and climbs in.

Wells tells the driver where to take them then turns back toward me. "My life doesn't suck at all and I appreciate the generosity." He pats Sandra on the leg, like she was my possession and I'm sharing her with him for the night. "I'll call you tomorrow."

"Yeah, you will, bitch. Have fun."

He shoots me a middle finger and they speed off down the road.

I glance back at the front of PRYSM once more, then start down Kingsbury street, looking for a cab. Jerking off to the thought of Abigail is a million times better than putting my dick in that thirsty chick.

ABIGAIL

My alarm blares way too early. It definitely feels like a Monday already.

I stretch and yawn.

Staying up late watching scary movies with Kyle and Nick was a bad idea. I know better than to do that when I have to work the next morning.

I rub the pad of my finger over the creases of my eyes. It's like my head just landed on my pillow and I could easily go back to sleep for another four hours, but I roll over and sit up. The minute my feet touch the cold floor I regret not turning the heat on last night. I was exhausted when I got in, and Barbie, the ice Queen, is anal about the thermostat. I think her real name might be Elsa because my room is a damn ice box.

Yes, we're roommates, but it's very much *her* apartment. I needed a place to stay and she had one. No way was I going to move in with some random man in Chicago. Grabbing my bathroom caddy, it's like being back at summer camp. Barbie's a neat freak and bitches any time I leave things scattered about. To be fair, she keeps her stuff put away so I can't really complain.

Leaving my bedroom, I head to the bathroom, but the door's locked.

"Just a minute."

Great.

Chuck, Barbie's boyfriend, apparently stayed over —again.

He's probably in there taking a dump. Talk about lousy luck this morning.

I set my stuff by the bathroom door and shuffle down the hall to the kitchen. I need coffee or I might turn murderous. I grab my favorite mug from the dishwasher.

Opening the refrigerator, I pull out my hazelnut creamer and scowl. I shake the bottle and my face heats. It's empty.

I open it up and tip it upside down over my mug and bang on the bottom.

Not a drop.

If I did this to her I'd have to hear about it for a week. Now, I have to stop off on my way to work and pay a small fortune for what I could've enjoyed at home for free. I press the button for the lid to the trash can with my right foot and toss in the bottle along with my disappointment.

I glare toward the bathroom. I know he's the one who finished it off, and I hope it gave him the coffee shits.

I mentally smack myself. I still haven't taken a shower, and I don't want to go anywhere near where he's been. I need a new roommate. One who doesn't come with an annoying hairy boyfriend named Chuck.

The bathroom door opens and to no one in particular, he says, "Whew. Someone light a match."

This is your life right now. You need to get it together, Abby.

The sound of the aerosol lands in my ears, hissing as he sprays it around.

My nose scrunches in disgust.

Gross.

I hate to skip my shower, but after this, I have to risk it.

He struts past me in the kitchen, looking like a damn yeti in his boxer briefs and no shirt.

Maybe it's a good thing I don't have my coffee, or I might spew it everywhere. I can deal with the hairy, shirtless act, but the rest is a big fat no.

I quickly move down the hall, scooping my caddy on the way to my room and slam my door a little louder than I need to, but screw that guy. I light one of my Bath & Body Works candles and pray it works its magic quickly. Sitting cross-legged on the floor in front of the mirror on the back of my bedroom door, I twist my hair up into a bun. Today will be a light makeup day. A few swipes of mascara and cherry lip gloss. I smooth my eyebrows and pop up to get dressed.

After throwing on my work outfit, I blow the candle out and make a wish. It's a silly ritual that should be reserved for birthdays, but it makes me happy. Plugging my nose, I brave the bathroom long enough to brush my teeth. I gasp for air once I stumble into the living room and manage not to inhale anything toxic.

Once I escape the apartment, I head to my favorite coffee shop down by the L-train station.

Grabbing my white chocolate mocha from the barista, I board the train, throw on my Beats, and crank up *Everyday People* by Sly and the Family Stone.

Just another day in paradise.

MY MORNING GOT off to a shitty start, pun intended, and it seems my bad fortune will carry on through the workday. I've already had trouble tracking down three associates for important depositions. I screwed up and set up two meetings at the same time for Donavan. Fortunately, he hated one of them and rescheduled, then thanked me for the blunder.

That's the totality of my good luck, and I'm starting to think the candle wish from earlier was nothing but a curse.

I walk by Dexter, hoping maybe he can turn around this disaster of a day. "Hey, how was your weekend?" I didn't think he was going to let go of me when we ran into each other at the club, and part of me secretly wished he hadn't.

He barely looks in my direction. "Fine."

Oh my God, what's his deal? The world hates me.

Come on, Dex, just give me that smile of yours once. I need it so bad. I'm drowning over here. Help a girl out. "Do anything fun?" Surely that'll be a good ice breaker to talk about running into each other.

He shakes his head. "Nope." Then, he just walks off, leaving me hanging.

Ugh!

I head back to my desk. I just need to embrace the fact

it's not my day; just get through this one and start fresh tomorrow. I don't have the faintest clue what crawled up Dex's ass. He was so flirty at the club. Maybe Mondays aren't for him either.

I consider us friends in a way. We've met up for drinks a few times after work and it always goes well, despite the intimidation factor because hello, he's a partner. It's never anything too casual. I try to hold back on the flirting and keep the conversations about work considering he's a boss, even though I don't report directly to him. I don't want him to think I'm coming on to him, even though if the roles reversed it might be impossible to resist. He's freaking gorgeous.

He doesn't act like a boss, though. I know for a fact him and Deacon are practical jokers of the highest order and Decker always wants to wring their necks. I think it's cute and fun. They know when to be professional and when they can let their guard down.

I pass by Quinn and she gives me a wry smile, like she knows I'm thinking about Dexter. I know it's just my brain playing tricks, but it feels like everybody is watching me, judging.

The tattoos are the only way I can tell Dexter apart from Deacon. Well, that and he's way leaner. Deacon is big because he played football. Oh, and the scar. Dexter has this scar right above his left eyebrow. It's not huge but it gives him this edgy, bad boy look.

And the kiss. God, I'll never forget it. That whole day was incredible. When Dex told me what he was doing for Deacon, helping him win Quinn back, I couldn't say no. And okay, maybe just maybe, Dexter and I made out in the bar that night to raucous cheers from professional football players.

I don't even remember exactly how it came about, but he just fixed his gaze on me and I was done for.

We were so drunk I don't think he remembers doing it, but I will never forget the way I floated into the clouds when we parted ways that night.

Dex is smoking hot, and I'd be a liar if I said I wasn't attracted to him. Every woman in the office practically drools over him and his brothers. Anytime he's nearby I get this sensation deep in my belly. My heartrate spikes and I feel on edge.

This attraction is insane because I'm not looking to date anyone. I'm twenty-four, just out of school and beginning my career. I tried nursing school for a year but switched to paralegal and I love it. It's the first job I've really felt was meant for me.

No, I need to rid myself of these thoughts of Dex and focus on my job.

At the same time, as I sit down at my desk, I can't stop thinking about his foul mood. I don't know if I'll be able to focus on anything until I get him to smile again.

I need to hit up the breakroom and get my head in the game before I start my afternoon.

Perfect.

He walks in there just as I stand up and stroll that way. He keeps chocolate pudding cups hidden in the back of the refrigerator, practically daring someone to eat them. Nobody in their right mind would do it, but it's cute. He has this boyish charm about him, but he's anything but a boy in that Dolce and Gabbana suit.

No, Dexter Collins is all man and he knows it.

I march over, intent on finding out what crawled up his ass. He's got a big stick up there, and I need to yank it out. I pass by Quinn's desk, and she shoots me this mischievous smirk like she knows exactly what I'm up to. I don't know how to process her grin, so I shove it to the back of my mind.

I don't usually hit it off with women, but Quinn is very likeable, and I could see us being friends. I give her a small wave then feel stupid when I realize she wasn't smiling at me at all. She was looking at Deacon, her fiancé and Dexter's twin who strolls up to her desk.

You're so awkward.

My cheeks pink with embarrassment as I enter the breakroom. Dexter leans up against the dark counter next to the refrigerator. His ankles are crossed, and I can see a hint of his charcoal-gray plaid socks. I didn't take him for a patterned socks kind of guy, but they're perfect with those shoes and that suit. His jacket is draped over a chair, like he didn't want to get it dirty, and the sleeves of his button-down are rolled up on his forearms.

It's arm porn to the nth degree. Ink snakes down his forearms. My chest grows warm. Electricity jolts through my veins along with curious thoughts of what the rest of those tattoos look like under his shirt on his chiseled frame. I blink at the sight, and his gaze meets mine and snaps me out of my daydreams.

I can't tell, but it's almost like he's halfway scowling while he takes an angry bite of pudding.

"You ever going to try something besides chocolate?"

His brows shoot up, but he doesn't reply.

I'm not giving up that easy, Dex. "I went through a butterscotch phase once, but banana is the dom of pudding flavors."

He sighs. "Cool."

What the hell? He'd usually smile at a joke with sexual undertones.

Thought you didn't flirt with him, Abby?

Okay, maybe I do a little. I'd do anything right about now. My brows furrow. "You upset with me or need to talk? I mean, I'm a good listener." I sidle up next to him and give him a bump with my hip. I don't know how much more obvious I can be, and I'm getting nowhere.

"Nah. I'm fine."

I stare down at the floor, like maybe he'll have some pity and actually talk to me. "Don't sound fine."

He drops his empty pudding cup into the trash. He licks the spoon, slowly, for good measure before tossing it in too. And holy shit the way he wrapped his tongue around the white plastic sends a current between my thighs, and for the first time in my life I find myself jealous of a freaking spoon.

He starts for the door, not bothering to look back. "I'm fine. Why you on my case?"

I follow and grip his forearm.

He turns back to me.

I shrug and can't stop the frown that forms on my face. "I don't know. I guess you just seem different. You're not very talkative." The guy isn't usually a chatterbox, but I can always coax more than a few words out of him.

He plasters on the fakest smile I've ever seen. "I'm

fine. Promise." He turns and coolly says, "See ya," over his shoulder.

I frown again. I just want one real smile. It could totally turn around this shit day of mine. "Hey, um, Dex?"

Pivoting slowly, the darkened color in his eyes pins me in place and steals my breath away. He sighs again, like I'm his little sister and he *has* to deal with me. "What is it? I've got a lot of paperwork."

I don't know why I won't let this go. Maybe I'm just competitive and have to get my way. I shrug. "Right... me too. I just..."

He looks like he wants to be anywhere but here right now. I have to look sad, because that's the way I feel inside, and Dex must take notice because he actually attempts a real smile this time, even though I know he doesn't want to do it.

Spit it out, Abby.

"I'm going to The Gage for a drink after work. Maybe we could meet up?" I try to hide the hope in my voice. I know I said he's hot, but that three-letter word doesn't really do him justice. Like the dude could be on the cover of GQ Magazine. I'd put that poster on my wall. And if I'm being honest, I'd so pull out my vibrator and chase more than one big O staring at said poster.

This is bad. Way bad.

I didn't realize how attracted to him I was until just now. I don't need to be having these feelings about Sex...

Shit.

I mean Dexter.

Oh boy.

I let out a breath as he stares me down, and I hope like hell he can't read my thoughts.

His lips curl up into a bit more of a smile, and my stomach rolls in a good way. Maybe my day is turning around after all.

"Sounds fun. I'll be there."

"Grood." *What the hell, Abby?* "I mean, yeah, I was going to say great, then switched to good. You know what? I'll see you there."

This time he gives me a genuine smile, and my whole world lights up.

Then, it simultaneously crashes. I watch him go and already wonder if I should cancel. I shake my head. I'm being stupid. He thinks I just want to hang out, nothing more. Dexter and I can totally be friends.

It's fine.

I'm fine.

There's that stupid word again. I am *so* not fine. I am anything *but* fine.

Stupid Sex...

Hell! Dexter.

I scoff out loud at how ridiculous I am, and I wish my brain would sort itself out. I need some kind of buffer to control myself around him, so I don't get drunk and make out with him again. Or worse, end up in his bed for the night.

Would that really be so bad?

Stop it, brain!

When I get back to my desk, I send a text to Kyle.

Me: Hey, drinks at The Gage after work. Invite a friend.

Kyle: See you there.
Me: Perfect.

If we all hang out as a group, I won't be tempted to flirt with Dex. I'll have at least one distraction I can turn to if he does that smoldering gaze thing at me or rolls up his sleeves and I see his tattoos. This is perfect. I mentally congratulate myself for coming up with it on the fly.

My brain might be cursing me right now, but my body didn't get the memo.

I do know one thing, though.

I got my smile.

DEXTER

Covington must've enjoyed himself the other night, judging by this afternoon's phone conversation. Wish the same could be said for me. I went home alone and rubbed one out in my bed thinking about Abigail. Fuck, the way her tits bounced in my little fantasy as she rode my cock. I don't know if I've ever come that hard in my life.

Then, my thoughts went rogue on me. I couldn't stop wondering if she went home with that pussy friend of hers. I got so fucking mad thinking about it I had to go for a run along the lake at two in the morning. It was cold as tits, and I ended up even more pissed than I was before.

Covington drones on in my ear about the brunettes and the freaky shit he made them do. Fuck, this dude is into some crazy stuff. Something about spreader bars and nipple clamps.

His goddamn sex life sounds like he lives in a torture dungeon. Not my thing, but it's whatever. As long as they were both into it, who gives a shit if they like to put on dog collars and hang from the ceiling while they fuck?

For some godforsaken reason, though, I can't stop thinking about Abigail and that prick friend of hers. It's stupid. It's not my business if she takes some asshole home from the bar, but the thought of her with another man has me all twisted up. I grip the phone tight in my palm and let out a long, frustrated sigh, trying anything to get the tension to leave my body.

Eventually, the conversation comes full circle and returns to business at hand. I'm ready to get out of here. It's been a long and frustrating day, but this is the conversation I've been waiting for, and I can't let all my hard work warming him up go to waste.

"All right, Collins. Give me the fucking pitch. You've worked hard all weekend for this opportunity like a patient little boy."

I laugh. Nothing gets past this guy, no matter how laid back he seems. I can practically hear him smirk on the other end, and I have to appreciate how fucking cocky he is. Some things never change. In fact, some things get worse over time, and Covington is the most arrogant motherfucker ever. I like that about him. "Look, bitch."

He laughs loud enough it booms through the phone. "Oh, I'm going to enjoy this. Fuck, I miss the shit out of you. We spend too much time in boardrooms these days and not enough time at the bar."

"You gonna let me pitch or what, asshole?"

He's dying now. "Please proceed."

I'm like a goddamn sales magician. "I'll cut to the chase and save both of us the time. I head up finance and tax. We specialize in dealings with the SEC and IRS." I tuck my phone between my cheek and shoulder as I exit my office for the day. I told Abby I'd meet her for drinks at The Gage.

"I'm aware. But you know this, so carry on."

Biggest pitch of my life and I can't stop thinking about Abigail.

Fuck. Get out of my head for two minutes, woman!

"I think we should have a discussion about what we can offer you. I know what you're about to say... Bennett Cooper, blah blah..."

He cuts me off. "Absolutely. Let's get something on the books for you to swing by the new place on the lake. We can try out the golf course I have on the property. I'll have my people get in touch and see what we can set up."

My eyebrows raise. "That's it, asshole? You don't want any specifics right now?"

He laughs again. "No, I'm good. Would've set this up over the phone if you'd asked, but it was good drinking tequila straight from the bottle with you."

"Yeah, it was fun."

"Hey, Collins?"

"Yeah?"

"You know I'm not loyal to Cooper. I go where the numbers take me. Everyone else follows. Bring your A game when we set a meeting."

Adrenaline floods my veins and I'm on top of the world. This will be huge.

"Oh, and Collins?"

"Yeah?"

"Full disclosure, I have a meeting already set with Cooper when I get back to Manhattan, to discuss expanding his representation of my new holdings. He's fucking good and business is business. It's not personal, so if you want me, make it worth my time."

Fuck! Fuck Bennett Cooper.

Bennett Cooper is the most pompous prick of all time. He represents damn near every heavy hitter on Wall Street, including Wells right now, and everyone in the industry lives in the shadows of Cooper and Associates. Not for long, after I'm done pilfering his clients.

I need Wells on board, bad. He'll double the firm's revenue. It could mean raises and bonuses for a lot of people, not just the partners. It could be life-changing for a lot of employees around here.

I set my worries aside. Wells will sniff weakness through the phone. "No problem. I welcome the competition."

"That's what I like to hear. Fuck, my life is good."

"Oh yeah?"

"Of course, best attorneys in the world fighting over me. I can't wait to see what the future holds. Better start getting creative. Cooper doesn't fuck around and everyone in New York is aware of you gunning for his clients. I've heard the grumblings."

"They should be grumbling. Maybe he should get better."

Covington laughs. "There ya go. Looking forward to our meeting. Thanks for the eventful weekend."

"No problem. Talk soon, pussy."

I end the call and walk straight toward the elevator.

Fuck. Tecker is in there.

I groan inwardly. I love my brother, but Tate is a tough pill to swallow sometimes, and sometimes she's awesome.

Just depends on the day. I probably get along with her better than any of my brothers, besides Decker, of course. It's my job. I'm the goddamn peacekeeper in the family. Always have been.

My brothers argue and give each other shit better than anyone, but Decker and Donavan have been at it for months. Usually, these little family altercations regarding business resolve themselves within a day or two. I'm going to have to do something soon because they're both acting like petty assholes.

"Just the two people I wanted to see." I smile at Tate. Someone has to combat all the glares she gets from Deacon and Donavan.

"Can't wait to hear this," says Decker.

"Just got off the phone with Covington. Wants me to swing by his new pad and talk shop. Maybe play a round of golf on his new course."

Decker grins his ass off. It's a sly grin. The one that forms on his face when big money is involved.

"Maybe I should go so you don't embarrass yourself off the tee." Tate smiles like she got me. "I'm sure he'll show you his one wood over a nice dinner."

Decker laughs. He loves it when she talks shit to us. This is probably foreplay for the two of them.

I laugh because it was pretty funny, and I can appreciate a good joke. "Tate, for Wells Covington's business, I would wash his balls personally and take the one wood in all eighteen holes."

She grins her ass off. "Nicely-played with the self-deprecation. Always a good defense tactic."

I give her a little nod. "Thank you."

As the elevator makes its way down, Decker attempts to change the subject. "How's the rest of the new client roster shaping up?"

Did he not hear me? I'm about to land Wells Covington. "Fuck the rest of those minnows. I'm doing minimum maintenance on them. Covington is my priority right now."

He shakes his head. "You're putting too much time and risk into one potential client."

"Yep." Tate pops the p when she says it.

Just like that, the lighthearted mood of the elevator evaporates.

Fuck these two. I'm thinking about the firm and all the direct and indirect revenue Wells would bring in. That could be a lot of Christmas bonuses for a lot of employees who don't live in a fucking mansion off Lake Michigan like these two. "Look, I don't tell you how to do your jobs. Don't tell me how to do mine."

Decker's eyes narrow. "I'm the managing partner. I tell everyone how to do their goddamn jobs."

My hands ball into fists. I need to control this anger rising up in me, but I just can't leave it alone. "Then leave your little echo chamber in her office when you discuss mine with me. I don't need her sitting back there making snide remarks."

Tate's mouth drops open. I'm not usually so harsh with her, and I feel a little bad about it, but fuck, I can see why Donavan and Deacon get flustered around her sometimes. She doesn't know where her authority lies.

She folds her arms over her chest. "I'm a partner too, dickhead."

"Yeah, there are lots of partners, yet you're the only one here commenting on things that don't concern you. I run finance. You don't know a damn thing about it. You can go back to leading Decker around by the balls as soon as I get off the elevator."

Decker gets in my face and grits his teeth. "You're talking about the overall wellbeing of the firm. We're not discussing SEC and tax dealings, we're discussing client relations, which all partners are privy to be in on those strategies. And I'm telling you, you're putting all your eggs in one basket and it's reckless. It would create a high concentration on our books from one source of revenue."

"Jesus Christ, what a terrible problem to have. And once Covington brings in more clients, which he would, that risk would disappear. As long as we don't take out idiotic loans against future revenue or buy another fucking building, we'd be fine. He can open up a lot of new avenues."

"Look, I hear you, asshole. It's just my job to be skeptical and protect what we have. Covington is a whale. Dedicate some time to him, sure, but do *not* neglect anyone else at his expense. Is that understood?"

I shrug. "Fine, Dad. Anything else?"

"Yes. Apologize to Tate."

I laugh.

He looks serious.

"Decker, don't..." Tate grabs him by the forearm. "I was talking shit first. I thought it was lighthearted and fun, but the conversation took a turn."

I glance over at Tate. She looks sincere. I know she cares. I'm sure she's dealt with assholes talking down to her ever since she became an attorney. "No, he's right, Tate. Sorry. I shouldn't have made things personal."

"Apology accepted."

Decker glares back and forth at Tate and me. "Fuck, I can't with this place. Bunch of children." The elevator dings and Decker scurries out like he wants far away from everyone.

Tate grins at me. "I think we just aged him five years. He's gonna go gray up top before long."

"Down below too. Ol' silver crotch."

We both die laughing.

"I can hear you assholes!" Decker shoots a middle finger up at us and doesn't bother to turn around.

I DROP by my place to change into something more casual and then head to The Gage.

When I arrive, I find Abigail at a table drinking whiskey. It's weird and, at the same time, I have to smile. I'm surprised to see her sitting alone, and I wonder how many men she's waved off since she got here. Judging by some of the dirty looks as I walk up, I'd say a few.

Eat shit, assholes. She's mine.

She looks up from her drink and smirks. "You came."

Her reaction makes me feel a little assholish. I was pretty short with her at work, but I had a lot going on, and I didn't appreciate being kept up all night with thoughts of her fucking some other guy. It wasn't her fault my mind was being a dick, but still.

"Said I'd be here. Getting started without me?"

"It was a long day, and I *really* needed this drink. Some guy was being a jerk at work."

"Give me his name and I'll write his ass up."

She grins and takes another drink as I slide into the empty seat to her left. I order a Booker's bourbon neat and an intense silence stretches between us.

"So, banana pudding? That's your go to?"

"Hah!" She slaps her palm down on the table. "You *were* listening."

"I was in a mood."

"Because…"

I trace a finger along the rim of the rocks glass. "Not important. Back to this pudding phase. I'm sure butterscotch and banana are fantastic, but chocolate is king. Everyone knows this."

"You ever had homemade banana pudding?"

I shake my head. "No."

"Then, it's settled. I'll make it for you, and it'll blow your mind."

I can think of another thing I'd like her to blow with those cherry-red lips. Wrap them around my cock while I make a fist in her hair.

"Dex?"

I snap out of my fantastic thoughts. "Sorry. What were you saying?"

"I'll make some pudding and bring it to work for you."

"Oh yeah. That'd be nice." Why are we talking about pudding so much?

"Don't doubt my pudding skills. I work magic with bananas."

Fuck.

I'm going to need to adjust my dick if she keeps talking like this. I know she did it on purpose.

"Abigail!"

The high-pitched voice comes out of nowhere and the masculinity held within is questionable at best. What the fuck?

"Kyle!" Abigail waves at him, practically bouncing in her seat.

What. The. Fuck.

Is she trying to piss me off on purpose? Is this payback for earlier at work?

I glance over my shoulder and the bitch from the club the other night pulls up a chair along with two other guys, and the fact I refer to them as 'guys' is extremely polite.

"Hey, man." He sticks his hand across the table.

I leave his hand hanging in the air because fuck him and fuck this.

Abigail's brows knit together. "Dex, you remember Kyle, right? You met at PRYSM, before you left with your friend and a couple of women."

So she *was* paying attention.

"Sorry." I shake my head right at Kyle. "Wasn't a very memorable night."

Man, I need to get out of here. My heartbeat pounds in my ears every time Kyle and his friends so much as breathe in my direction.

And the hell it wasn't a memorable night. I can't stop thinking about her tight body and that clingy red dress riding up her damn thighs. How bad I wanted to bury my face between them and get a taste. I want to fuck her in that dress so bad my balls ache thinking about it.

32

Kyle interrupts our conversation. "This is Craig and Seth. Some of my work buddies."

"You're old enough to drink?" I take a sip of my one-hundred and twenty-five proof bourbon. It slides down my throat and heats up my chest.

"Dude, I'm like twenty-seven." He scoffs and rolls his eyes.

I feel like a goddamn babysitter. I bet they still live at home with their parents. Why in the fuck do I even need to compete with these jerk offs? This is a total waste of my time. I'm better than this.

Abigail.

"Can I talk to you for a minute?" Abigail slides out of her seat and jerks on my arm.

"If you'll excuse me, ladies." I give them a head nod, coupled with a smile, and down the rest of my drink.

Abigail grabs my arm and tugs, leading me toward the bathrooms away from her little reverse harem I've been made a part of. I don't compete for a woman's attention and I'm not about to start now. She invited that fucker who was grinding all over her the other night. That's some bullshit. I thought it would be the two of us. She never mentioned Kyle and his piss pot friends tagging along, or I'd have told her to kick rocks.

"What the heck was that back there?"

I shrug. "What?"

She throws her hands up and gets all animated.

Fuck, she's even cuter when she's irritated. I stare at her lips, and it's hard to concentrate on her words.

"You know exactly what I'm talking about. You're

33

being rude to my friends." Her manicured nail pokes into my chest.

I glance at my watch like I'm late for a meeting. "You finished?" I don't do dramatics and bullshit either. I'm not playing these games. That's what I tell myself, even though I'm clearly entertaining them. It's about to end soon, though. If she wants to have a bunch of pussies fawning all over her and hanging onto every word she says she can have it. I thought she was cool, but maybe I had her all wrong. I'm starting to think she gets off on male attention. Maybe she has self-esteem issues or something, and I hope she gets it worked out if she does, but I won't be part of the solution.

"Somewhere else you'd rather be?"

"I gotta go." I don't wait for her to respond. I stop off at the bar and pay for our drinks.

Jimmy, the bartender says, "And theirs?" He gestures to the three ass clowns.

"They can buy their own. Here, this is extra for you because I'm sure they don't tip for shit." I slide a twenty across the bar.

"Thanks, Dex."

"No prob. See you later."

Sliding quickly through the crowd, I make my exit. Out on the sidewalk I scrub a hand over my face and let out a sigh. Fuck this fucking day.

"Hey!" Abigail comes out of the shadows, ninja-style, like she just teleported in front of me, and flies up in my face.

What the hell?

I stumble back for a second before I catch my balance. "You trying to give me a fucking heart attack? Christ!"

There's a fire in her eyes that turns me on like no other. She's practically seething, her arms flying around all animated as she lets me have it. "What the hell is your problem?"

My eyes widen and I just stare at her. She must be blind as a goddamn bat if she doesn't know what's going on here. "What's *my* problem?"

"Yeah, that's what I said, dickhead." Both her hands go to her hips.

"Dickhead?"

"That's what I said, isn't it?"

Fuck this.

I'll show her the answer to her question.

I close the distance between us and cup her face with both palms, then stare straight into her fiery eyes. Before she can pull away, I slant my mouth over hers and kiss the ever-loving shit out of her.

Her lips are even softer than I remember. I slide a hand down her neck, along her curves, all the way to her ass, then yank her hard against me.

That's my fucking problem. I'm a goddamn man.

I don't play little boy games.

When I want something, I take it.

The kiss is sweet and faster than I'd like but it is what it is. Now she knows and she can quit toying with me like I'm on the same level as those shit birds in the bar.

I'm interested.

Her eyelashes flutter for a moment, and she's in a daze.

She leans toward my mouth, but I pull away, even though it's the last thing I ever want to do.

What I want to do and what I need to do are two different things. I *want* to pull her tight little ass into a cab, take her back to my place, and bury my face between her thighs until she comes so many times she can't breathe.

Abigail stares back at me with her baby blues, seemingly in a trance. I may have kissed her so hard she went catatonic. Her fingers move to her lips.

"*That's* what the hell my problem is." I walk away instead of kissing her again.

I don't look back when I hear my name come from her lips. She can think about shit for a while.

Nope, I keep walking down Michigan Avenue until I find myself at the gym.

I swipe my card and grab the spare clothes I keep in my locker. I need to burn off all this frustration and pent up energy before I do something stupid.

Fuck, she has me so wound up.

I want to take it out on someone, and I definitely don't want it to be her. As enjoyable as it might've been, I didn't want to take it out on her friends either.

Friends.

She really needs to get rid of those guys. You can tell by looking at them they're hanging onto a dream, that someday she'll get too drunk or have a really bad day, and they'll slide in when she's vulnerable and get to put their little baby dicks inside her one time. I know how those fuckers operate. They'll waste months, clinging to someone who has no interest in them, in hopes of taking advantage of them just once. How pathetic can you be?

It was only a matter of time before I blew up on one of them. It's not like I can really blame them for wanting to hang out around her. Abigail is gorgeous. She's funny and a little bit of a goof when she wants to be. She makes me smile.

As I start my workout, my brain settles down and I do what I do best; analyze. There are more than a few problems at play here. For one, she's young. Too damn young for me but I can't help the attraction. She's twenty-four, but she's way more mature than I was at that age. That's not saying much. She's probably more mature than I am now, if I'm being honest.

Another problem; she's one of Tate's Dallas transfers, and I'm sure Tate would not approve, and Abigail probably listens to her more than anyone. I get along with Tate better than any of my brothers, but we both know it's just to keep the peace and for Decker. I'm sure if given the opportunity, Tate would tell Abigail what a player I am if she finds out we're seeing each other. She wouldn't be wrong for doing it either.

I can't help the fact I like women. I like fucking them and I like making them come. It's just what I do. I've never been so fixated on one, though. The more I think about it, the more I realize I haven't even thought about sleeping with another woman since I met Abby.

I throw two twenty-five on the bench press, trying to rid myself of this confusion. I don't have time for it. The biggest client of my life is within reach and I should be devoting a hundred percent of my time to getting that signature on the dotted line.

After three sets on the bench, I hit the treadmill, my

feet racing against my thoughts in a battle to see who'll win as music from my phone filters through my head-phones and pounds in my ears. These Abigail-induced runs need to stop. This shit is bleeding over to work, and I can't have it become a problem. At least this time I won't be cold as fuck and get pissed off all over again, after going on an Abigail run at night. The music is an epic fail. I couldn't tell you the last five songs I listened to. All I can think about is her and how I can still taste her on my lips.

The worst part is, I want to taste her again.

ABIGAIL

IT'S BEEN two days since Dexter stunned me with that kiss. It wasn't a good kiss. It was a smack-you-in-the-face, steal-your-breath-away kind of kiss. It was deep and passionate and forceful, and God, possessive. The way his rough hands and fingers dug into my ass and yanked me into him, like I was his and only his.

Then he just walks away without even looking back?

I've never had a guy kiss me then just leave me hanging. How do I even interpret that? It makes no sense. I don't know what to make of the situation or him.

I've never been one of those girls who gets excited when men fight over her, but I'd be lying if I said it didn't turn me on like no other, how jealous Dex looked. I don't know what he has to be jealous of. It's not like I have feelings for Kyle or any of the other guys. They're completely harmless.

Kyle thinks Dex is a smug bastard, but he doesn't know him the way I do. He doesn't know him at all.

I apologized when I went back inside and said it was a rough day at work.

The more I looked at Kyle and his reactions, the more I tried to figure things out. Could Kyle possibly want more than friendship? No way. He's just a friendly neighbor. He's never once tried to make a move or ask me out or anything like that.

I'm so conflicted right now. I could fall for Dexter, that's for sure. What's not to like about that situation? He's successful, handsome, and charming but he's also older than me and we work together.

I need to step back and just slow down. I moved to Chicago to have fun. Get in life experiences before thinking of settling down with anyone. I've seen so many friends get married right out of high school, settle down, and start having babies, and never really go out and live at all.

There's nothing wrong with that lifestyle, it's just not for me. I want to travel and see the world and have fun before I get married and have those types of responsibilities. I don't want to be accountable to another person right now. I'm in the prime of my life and I want to enjoy it, get everything I can out of every day.

There's only one problem, though. Dexter has me questioning my entire life plan after that dang kiss. That ridiculous, pulse-shattering kiss that threw my world off its axis.

I shuffle my fork through my salad looking for a piece of grilled chicken. I'm eating in the cafeteria today instead of going out for lunch. If I want to move out, I need to save some money. Originally, I was saving for a car, so I wouldn't have to rely on public transportation, but I find I don't mind the train at all. It's actually kind of nice.

What I do mind, is my nutty roommate and her boyfriend. He slept over every day this week.

"You look deep in thought." Quinn slides into the chair across from me. "Mind if I join you?" She has law books with her.

I can't help but notice the huge emerald engagement ring on her finger. It's freaking gorgeous and perfect for her. It makes me want to swoon, just thinking about the night Deacon gave it to her. I still can't believe I smacked Dex in the back of the head. It was playful, like Gibbs on NCIS, but I'll admit, I had a few cocktails in me at the time.

I glance up and Quinn's probably making conversation so she can get out of studying. It's what I'd do. She's sitting for the bar exam soon, and I'll feel horrible for her and Deacon if she doesn't pass. I'm sure she will, though. She's crazy smart and probably the hardest worker I've ever met. I definitely look up to her when it comes to professional conduct. She's always put together and one step ahead of everyone.

"Sure, have a seat."

"Good." She unpacks her lunch. It looks like a container of soup and a sandwich. "So what are you debating with yourself?"

"I'm... I'm not... I was just thinking about some stuff."

"Stuff that had you looking like you were about to murder your salad?" Quinn grins as she crumbles crackers into her bowl of soup.

I don't really have anyone to talk about relationship stuff with. I mean I live with Barbie, but we're not friends. She'd find a way to make the conversation about her. There's Kyle, but I could never talk to him about Dexter. He made his feelings about Dex perfectly clear.

I have to get these thoughts out of my head. "What's the deal with Dexter?" I cringe as I ask the question. Well, it's out in the open now.

"What do you mean? Like as a boss, coworker, friend, or like as in a boyfriend?"

"I don't know." I bury my face in my palms and think maybe the world will disappear along with this conversation. I'm so bad at this. "I don't know anything right now."

"I'm just giving you a hard time." She blows on her spoonful of soup. "Dexter's a good guy. Obviously, he did something, though. Just get it out. You'll feel better."

I still can't look at her. "This stays between us, right?" I'm so terrible at this gossip thing and I have to be super careful. Quinn's not just any girl. She's Deacon's fiancée. As in she lives with Dexter's twin brother. I don't want her running behind my back and spilling this conversation to Deacon. It might get back to Dex.

"You can trust me."

"Okay." I suck in a breath then exhale, because I really want the information she has to offer. "Dexter and I have hung out a few times after work. Nothing major, just grabbing a drink at The Gage, normal stuff people at the firm do. I invited him out the other day to meet up with me and some friends and he was rude to them for no reason."

"Were they guys?"

"Who?"

"The other friends you invited."

"Yeah, why?"

She stares at me like I'm from outer space. "I know you're younger but come on. Men love to piss on everything in the room, to mark their territory. The Collins brothers more than anyone. He likes you. Honestly, the other day I told Tate I thought you guys were secretly dating because he never shuts up about you. Him and Deacon are like this, so I overhear everything." She crosses two of her fingers. "It's the whole twin thing."

"Really? He talks about me?"

"Yeah. I mean, he tries to not make it obvious, keeps it subtle. But he always finds a way to bring you up in conversations."

"Huh." I had never thought about Dex having conversations with his brother outside of work, and I definitely wouldn't have thought he'd talk about me.

"Was that all he did?"

"Well, umm…"

She leans in and grins. "Come on, give it up."

"Well, there was a kiss." My cheeks must be ten shades of pink. I can't remember ever doing this before, talking to another woman other than my mom about a guy. Even that is rare because I've never dated anyone seriously.

"Nice." She slow nods. "Tell me more."

"Okay fine. There have been two, but I don't know if the first one really counts."

"Why wouldn't it count?"

"It was the night at the Bears game, when he got me to take care of your dad."

"So… we both got a little lucky that day, huh?" She jabs me with her elbow.

"Well, we were both hammered. I don't even know if he remembers doing it. We were with all the football players after you'd left. God, it's all so blurry."

"What about the second time?"

"When we were at the bar the other day, he was really shitty to my friends. So, I pulled him aside to ask what his deal was, and he blew me off saying he had to go. I got pissed and ambushed him outside. There was this intense moment and he just kissed me, and I mean he kissed me good."

Quinn nods. "They do that. The Collins boys. They sure do."

I snap my fingers in front of her face when she gets this far-off look in her eye, like she's reliving every kiss ever with Deacon. "We're talking about me here."

Quinn laughs. "Sorry, continue."

"Well, afterward he didn't say anything. He just walked off. No look back. No nothing. I just stood there in a daze. And the past few days he's avoided me, and I don't know what to do or what to say. It's driving me insane."

"Do you like him?"

"I mean… I don't know, I'm so confused. I just… don't like feeling awkward, and that's what everything feels like right now."

"Well, I have experience dating a Collins brother, and my advice is to track him down and make him talk. Yes, they act like boys, but they're calculated. Whatever he's doing, it's for a reason. You have to keep them on their heels."

She makes it sound so easy. I don't even know what I'd say and I'm probably reading way too much into it. He probably just got caught up in the moment.

She looks at her phone. "Oh shoot. We better get back."

I get up to leave and she grabs me lightly by the forearm.

"We'll talk soon. I want a follow up."

"Yeah. Okay. I need to head your way. Decker wants to see me." I gather up my stuff and toss what's left of my salad in the trash.

We walk back to the elevator and get off on our floor.

"I think he's in there alone for another few minutes. Good timing." Quinn nods to his office.

I walk through the doors and Decker's head pops up from behind his computer. "Perfect. I have something for you. Have a seat."

Decker rifles through some folders, and I can't help but appreciate how neat and exact he is about everything. He always gives very specific instructions, and I love these special projects he assigns me. There's always a clear task and a deadline. If I could only have that type of order in my personal life, I'd be in heaven. I always feel like I'm spiraling out of control outside of these walls. The job keeps me centered, like I have a purpose.

He finally finds what he's looking for but pushes it to the side. "Sorry, had to get that separated or it would drive me nuts."

"What can I do for you, Mr. Collins?"

"I need you to do some research. You're the best I've got at this kind of shit."

I nod, my chest swelling with pride. I don't know if anyone, other than my parents, has ever told me I'm the best at something, and it feels amazing to hear it from the managing partner. "Thank you, sir. What am I researching?"

"Not what, who. I need you to have a look at Wells Covington. He's a hedge fund manager. Has a residence in Chicago, but splits time with Manhattan. I'm sure he has real estate there as well."

"Anything specific you're looking for?"

Decker stands and walks around his desk, then leans back against it and folds his arms over his chest. I can't help but notice how much him and all the other brothers look alike. Not just their looks, either, their mannerisms and the way they speak and phrase things. It's like I'm staring at an older, more mature Dexter; like what he'll be like in five or six years.

"I just want to know if he has any secrets. Don't focus on his work and that type of thing. I want to know about his personal life, hobbies, etc."

"So extracurricular activities outside of work?"

"Exactly."

"When do you need this by?"

"Make it a priority. As soon as possible."

I nod once more. "Okay. I'll get started right away."

"Thanks, Abigail."

I stand up and walk out of the office. It's nice to be sought after for special jobs like this, especially from the head of the firm. Plus, the research isn't that difficult. You can find out anything about anyone on social media. They all think I'm a genius at using it. Maybe it's because I'm younger than most of the other paralegals, but I grew up with it and know how to navigate all the platforms.

WHEN I GET home from work, there's a note from Barbie on the fridge.

Please be considerate when you get ready in the morning. I'm on night shift tonight and will be going to bed when you wake up.

–Barbie

Ugh!

She's so annoying. I'm not even loud. She works at the hospital assigning patients to beds or something. I can't remember what she told me exactly. I wasn't really listening. I'm terrible, but it was when I first moved in and I was so tired. She's like a female Sheldon Cooper with a normal IQ. I should leave her a note that says tell your boyfriend to take his morning dump at his own house.

I shove my stuff onto the counter and trudge down the hall after crumpling her note up. I kick my heels off and shimmy out of my skirt and hose in exchange for a pair of sweats and a tee. After letting my hair down, I toss the bra aside since I don't have to worry about Chuck showing up.

My stomach growls, voicing its disapproval of half a chicken salad in the cafeteria this afternoon. I'm starving, but I don't want to cook anything. I should since I need to save money, but it's been a long day, and I just want to curl up on the sofa and veg out while I have the apartment to myself.

Barbie doesn't like anyone eating on the couch. She

acts like it's a five-thousand-dollar leather sectional. It's a Walmart special, but the last thing I want is to be on her radar, then suffer her on the warpath.

I grab the stack of takeout menus from a kitchen drawer and collapse onto the sofa, sinking down while I make a dinner decision. I'm not in the mood for Chinese or Thai. I could go for a pizza, but I know if I get one most will get thrown away, unless I invite Kyle over.

I'm not exactly up for his company tonight and there's really no reason I shouldn't be.

You're lying to yourself.

Of course I am. I know exactly why I don't want his company, and the name starts with a big fat D.

Gah, Dexter is so frustrating. I know we need to talk about that dang kiss. I don't want it to ruin our friendship, though. He's one of my favorite people at work. Okay, he's the best, with his pudding cups and broody stare he reserves for everyone but me, until lately.

Stupid hormones.

I'm about to give up on the menus and just walk to the store when a knock sounds at the door. I don't want to get off the couch to answer but I need to. What if Barbie is expecting a package or something? I'll never hear the end of it.

I begrudgingly stomp to the front of the apartment.

When I open the door, Kyle stands on the other side holding up a bag of fast food.

"Stopped on my way home. Thought you might be hungry." He flashes me a big cheesy grin.

He's so goofy but in a cute way. He is a bit of a dork in his tan Dockers and plaid shirt that's untucked and unbuttoned. He has on a Mickey Mouse t-shirt underneath. He's a manager at some video game store chain his dad owns.

"Is it safe?" He scans the room behind me searching for Barbie. I'm surprised he even comes over here at all after some of the encounters he's had with her.

He only agreed to go out to PRYSM with us because it was so loud he wouldn't be able to hear her talk most of the night.

"Yes. And I'm starving." I wave him in and close the door behind him. I know I said I didn't really want his company right now, but I am so hungry. Plus, it's silly. Kyle's my friend. It shouldn't matter what Dexter thinks. We're not together. I just need to steer the conversation away from Dexter and it'll be fine.

Kyle places the bag on the kitchen counter and pulls out two steak sandwiches and two orders of fries.

"You're the best."

"I always come through."

"This is true." I grab us some plates, cups, and pull a two liter of Pepsi from the fridge.

The two of us settle in on the couch with our food, and I start flipping through Netflix. It's my turn to pick.

Kyle exhales an audible sigh when I make my choice.

"Labyrinth is a cult classic. Who the hell doesn't love David Bowie?"

"You're so weird."

"Says the grown man in his Mickey Mouse shirt."

"Pfft, whatever. I have great style."

I snicker. "Sure."

"You're just used to being around suits all day, like that asshole you're always fawning over."

No, we're not supposed to talk about this. "I do not fawn over Se— Dexter." Damn it! I've got to stop doing that.

Kyle has this weird look on his face.

Fine, I guess we're doing this. I shrug. "What? He's hot."

Kyle rolls his eyes. "Whatever. I don't care who you date."

"I'm not dating him. We work together."

He smiles when he hears that. "Good. You're too good for him."

"I'm not interested in dating anyone. You know that." Even as the words leave my mouth, they sound weak.

"So you say."

I pause the movie and turn to him. "What's that supposed to mean?"

He shrugs. "Nothing, damn. Let's just eat and watch your movie." He bites into his sandwich.

I decide to let it go.

I don't want to argue with Kyle, but the room seems like it just cooled off about twenty degrees. I pick at my food. My mind drifts back to my conversation with Quinn. *He likes you. I thought the two of you were secretly dating.*

"Hey." Kyle taps my knee.

I jolt before I can stop myself. "Sorry. Just have a lot on my mind."

"Yeah. I see that. If you want to talk or whatever..." He scratches at the back of his neck.

I don't say anything because I don't want to talk to him about Dexter.

"Okay, well, I think I'm going to call it a night. I've got some stuff to do."

"Oh, okay. Thanks again for dinner. Next time it's my treat."

"Sounds like a plan." He moves to the door and gives me a wave.

Once he's gone, I turn off the TV and clean up our mess. Last thing I need is a passive aggressive note from Barbie reminding me no food on the couch. It's still too early to go to bed so I pick out my work clothes for tomorrow and treat myself to a bubble bath.

Sinking down in the warm water I try to clear my head and relax. Laying back with my head against the wall, I close my eyes. My thoughts find their way to that damn kiss all over again. Only this time I imagine what might have happened had Dex not walked away. Maybe the two of us would have gotten a cab back to his place or even a hotel room.

Maybe that's what we both need. Just have sex and get whatever this is out of our systems. I play the fantasy out in my mind, picturing Dex leading me into the hotel room, his mouth fused to mine. Trailing my fingers down my neck, I rub and tweak my nipple, touching myself lower and lower as the dream plays out.

I wonder if he would go fast or slow? I bet Dex is a man who goes all out with the foreplay. Takes his time and teases like a maniac. He'd want me begging for it, begging for him. I imagine him sitting there all powerful in his suit, ordering me to get undressed while his broody eyes never leave mine. He just has this vibe about him that is a hundred percent male, pure sex and power. He's older, but not too old, just right. Experienced. That's what he is.

I'm all kinds of worked up after I finish my bath.

When I make it to my room, my eyes flick back and forth between the bed and the drawer where I keep my vibrator. It doesn't take much to convince me I should go ahead and finish what I started.

DEXTER

IT'S THURSDAY, and I'm on my way back to the office after a business lunch that about did my head in. An old friend is going through a divorce and owns stock in several corporations. Both him and his spouse have assets. He wanted my advice about his financial options, and while he's a great guy, he's a total moron when it comes to business. He threw so much money at MLM and other shitty investments. The guy blew through everything and racked up some incredible debt. No wonder his marriage didn't work out.

However, his soon-to-be ex-wife is a trust fund baby with her own healthy portfolio that's managed by competent people. She's worth more than him. He needs her to cover some of his debt. The poor dumb bastard cheated with their nanny. The whole thing is a clusterfuck and emotional as all hell, something money should never be. He's going to be on his ass with nothing. I would feel sorry for him, but he had it made. All he had to do was keep his dick in his pants. The whole situation damn near gives me a migraine.

I'm almost to my office. I think I have some painkillers in my desk, and I plan to eat a couple, sit back, and have myself a nice little stress-free afternoon after that shitshow of a morning.

Turning the corner, I bump into Cole Miller. We go way back, all the way to our days at the University of Illinois. The two of us and Wells were inseparable at college but gradually grew apart as our careers took off. He was a professional MMA fighter for a while and now he owns a nationwide chain of fitness centers. He's a billionaire, but as humble as they come.

He's been in and out of the office a lot the past year. One of his employees took a selfie with one of the members in the background, put it up on social media, then her and her friends started making all kinds of jokes about the woman's weight and appearance.

It blew up and went viral, all over Twitter and Facebook. The member sued his company and now our firm is representing them. Decker's running point on it since media relations is one of his specialties.

"Just the guy I was looking for." Cole holds out a hand.

I take it, and his fucking grip damn near makes me wince, even though I'd never show it. "How's it going? You about to get out from under all that bullshit?"

"Things are shaping up. Decker thinks it'll be dismissed. You guys have worked your asses off for me. Don't think it hasn't gone unnoticed."

"It's what we do. You know this. You were looking for me?"

"I wanted to give you these. Decker mentioned something a while back. Said you're a huge fan." He reaches into his inner jacket pocket and slaps two tickets in my palm for the big MMA championship fight this weekend at the United Center.

Fuck yes. My luck just did a one-eighty. I've been trying to get tickets, used up every connection I could think of, besides Cole, of course. Last thing I wanted was to bother him with a ticket request when he's getting his tits sued off. "Hell yeah. Thanks." I fan them out in front of me. "I've been looking forward to this shit. Didn't want to bother you with it with everything on your plate."

He waves me off like it's nothing. "Don't be ridiculous. Hit me up anytime. It's gonna be a bloodbath. Mandez is a beast."

"I'm sure he is, considering you trained him. Does he have the speed, though?"

He slow nods. "Nice, Collins, you know your shit. And I don't know, but it's gonna be good."

"See you there."

"Yeah." He takes a step toward the conference room. "Gotta get in there and meet with your brother."

"Good luck, man."

We part ways and I smile to myself. It's been a few days, and I do believe Abby has had enough time to stew on that kiss and what she's missing out on. Now, it's time for the next step in my plan. I've seen how this shit works in their little romance movies. Always leave them wanting more. Never look too desperate. The hero always kills when he abides by these principles. I go by her desk, but she isn't there.

Well fuck a goddamn duck.

ABIGAIL

"Hey, Quinn. Is Mr. Collins available? I have some research I was doing for him."

"Yeah. He's not with anyone right now. You talk to you know who yet?" She smirks and tucks her red hair behind her ear.

I sigh and stare off at the wall. "No. Haven't really had a chance." I don't tell her he's still been avoiding me like the damn plague since that stupid kiss. I'm completely over it. That's what I keep telling myself, anyway. No matter how many batteries I've burned through with my vibrator, I'm sticking to it. I'm over Dexter Collins and his little games.

"Better get on it." Her cheeks pink a little and she grins at her computer screen.

"I have work to do." I wave my file at her and smile. Going back and forth with Quinn is fun and helps take my mind off things. Maybe I should have more girlfriends, and the ones in the past have just been unlucky experiences.

"Fine." She fakes a frown at me, like she's disappointed in my response. "I'll let him know you're here. Have a seat." She points to the waiting area for Decker's clients.

I sit down and flip through my papers trying to recall where I've seen this dude before. He looks vaguely familiar.

Quinn picks up her phone. "Abigail is out here. Okay. I'll send her on in."

I meet Quinn's gaze and she waves her hand motioning for me to go ahead.

I know I'm coming back earlier than Decker would've expected, but there's still something about walking into the boss's office that has my stomach in a knot. It's like when you were in elementary school and knew you weren't in trouble, but still had to walk into the principal's office. The room just always seems ominous.

"Got something? That was quick."

I set the file down. "Combed through his social media and online. Nothing criminal or anything. I did find some connections to some umm…" I wince a little because people shouldn't really be judged on this type of thing, but they are. It almost feels wrong bringing it to him, but I know he'll want to know.

"What is it?" Decker leans in, taking a sudden interest.

"Umm, some kinky sex club type stuff."

Decker rubs his chin and twists in his chair, seemingly mulling over what to do. "Take it to Rick. Tell him I want him to dig deep on this guy. I want it all, work and personal."

I nod. It's not my job to question the boss. "Okay. Did you want to read over all this before I…"

"No need." He makes a face that tells me he wants nothing to do with what I found on the Covington dude. "Tell Rick I need this off the record and to keep it discreet. Only the three of us need to know anything."

"Will do."

"Thanks, Abigail. You're killing it. Keep doing what you're doing."

Getting the compliment leaves me on cloud nine. Decker seems pretty cold and all business, but he always gives me compliments. There are so many stories floating around about what an asshole he was before the merger. I wonder if he learned this new technique in a management seminar? Maybe Tate makes him do it. That'd be hilarious. They're so cute together.

At the same time, I feel a little bad about digging through this guy's personal life, regardless of how much money he has. I really need to get over this feeling if I want to succeed at this job, because there will likely be a lot of this type of work in the future.

I leave Decker's office and make my way to Rick's, even though he's never there. I pause and look around before I get to his door, anything to take my mind off this encounter. He's quite possibly the most chauvinistic asshole I've ever met. It's probably why Decker keeps him out of the office on assignment twenty-four seven. As I walk up, I say a silent prayer, begging over and over for him not to be there so I can just send him an email with the instructions.

When I get there, the door is open and he's sitting at his desk reading the Bible.

What the heck? The irony of this situation is almost too much to bear.

And what the hell is going on in here?

He's wearing this all-black suit and hat that makes him look like he's going to an Amish funeral or something. I nearly burst into laughter but manage to swallow it down.

I knock lightly on his door, trying not to grin at his outfit. "Hey, Rick?" I wince, just waiting for him to say something about some new hire's ass or tits. It's par for the course with him.

"Come on in."

"Sorry to interrupt." I hesitate.

"It's fine. Close the door." He doesn't look up from the Bible.

I don't *want* to close the door, but Decker did say this needs to be discreet.

"Right." I close it almost all the way but leave it cracked just a hair. I hold out the file, but he doesn't take it, just keeps reading. "Okay, so Decker has a job for you. He wants you to dig up everything you can on this Wells Covington guy. This is what I have on him so far from my social media research. He said to stress that this needs to be super discreet. You should only communicate your findings to one of us."

He nods toward the desk, indicating for me to leave the file there.

I set it down and quickly take a step back.

"You and Decker. Wells Covington. Got it."

"Great." I turn to leave.

"Hey, what do you know about Mary?"

I stop and have to think for a second. "Magdalene? The

paralegal?" What in the ever-loving hell is going on here? Is that why he's reading the Bible?

"Yeah, the one with the curly brown hair. Didn't you work together in Dallas? You paralegals all talk to each other, right? She ever mention me?"

"We, umm, don't really talk much. She keeps to herself a lot."

"You guys don't hang out and braid your hair and gossip and all that shit?"

I damn near start laughing. Is that what he thinks all the women in the office do in their spare time?

"No, she does a lot of stuff at her church, I think. That's about it, I guess. She's kind of quiet and we don't talk much."

He still hasn't looked up and his lips mouth the words like he's reading Bible verses. "Okay, thanks. I'll let you know what I find out about the asshole in the file."

"Umm… Okay then. I gotta get going." I grab the door handle.

"Yes, he likes you."

I turn back to him. "Sorry, what?"

Still hasn't looked up. "Dex, after the kiss. And Kyle wants more than friendship."

"Excuse me?" How the hell does he know any of that stuff? I've heard he's legendary about knowing everything, but what the hell?

"You heard me." He finally looks up. "I have to go plan for a nativity scene at the church. Peace be with you, Abigail." He walks by and I stand there with my mouth wide open. "And your social media research is always top notch. Great job."

Once he's gone, I scurry out of his office and into the breakroom.

A shiver goes up my spine. That was too weird. And what the hell did he mean when he said Kyle wants to be more than friends? How does he even know who Kyle is? That's absurd. Seems the mighty Rick Lawrence failed in his intelligence gathering, for once.

When I open the fridge there's a package of banana pudding next to Dexter's chocolate ones. I smile but it still doesn't make up for the way he's been so back and forth with me. One day he's kissing me and the next he's avoiding me. Am I that bad of a kisser? No way. I know I'm not. I don't want to sound conceited, but I can kiss above average at the least. He wanted that kiss and enjoyed it as much as I did.

I open up a pudding cup and lick the lid before tossing it in the trash.

"Don't let Dexter catch you eating those." Brenda, Dexter's paralegal walks around the corner. "He had me pick them up this morning. Said they were the most important thing on my to-do list."

"Oops." I grin. That familiar warmth spreads through my veins again. I refrain from telling her I'm almost certain he got them for me. Maybe he did it to be a jerk and eat them in front of me. Maybe I'm searching for a reason to still be irritated with him, because I don't need to be involved with any man right now. Either way it doesn't matter. I'm going to enjoy the hell out of this pudding cup.

"I've never seen a grown man act the way he does over some pudding, but I swear he's obsessed."

"I've noticed."

"Well I won't tell him it was you if he asks." She winks and steals one of the chocolate ones. "If you don't tell him I swiped one too."

"I will take our secret to the grave."

"There ya go. Us girls have to stick together against the evil overlords."

I grin. "Right." I never had any idea what other women meant when they would talk about sisterhood or girlfriends sticking together, but I'm starting to catch on. I've never had a 'tribe' or whatever the cool kids call it these days, but I'm starting to wish I did.

I WALK out the front of the office when my cell phone rings with a call from Kyle. We haven't spoken since things got all tense and awkward. Now, it's even worse after the shit Rick pulled out of his magic hat in his office.

Damn him!

I start to ignore the call, but I don't want to be like Dexter and blow him off. I know how it feels to be ignored, and it's not pleasant. Especially when Kyle's one of the best friends I've had since moving here. Not to mention the fact we're neighbors and he'd be hard to avoid.

"Hey, what's up?"

"Just clocked out. Wanna meet up for pizza and beer with me and Nick before he goes in for his shift?"

No, I want Dexter to talk to me. I don't have anything else to do on a weeknight, though. "Sure. The usual place?"

"Meet you in fifteen?"

"Okay." I end the call.

A text from Barbie pings on my phone the second I hang up.

Barbie: You off work? I need you to do something for me.

I love how she doesn't even ask, just demands things.

Me: Just leaving.

With her I never know what kind of favor she'll ask. Learned that one the hard way. One time I ended up attending a baby shower for some girl I didn't know and had to buy a joint gift with Barbie because she couldn't afford what she agreed to buy off the registry. I'm clearly still not over that.

Barbie: I need jumbo tampons. I'll pay you back.

Me: I can but it'll be a while because I have dinner plans.

Barbie: Can you hurry?

I scrunch my nose at my phone. Can I hurry? Do I look like her assistant? I would be inclined to hurry if she wasn't crazy and the biggest narcissist I've ever met.

Man, she makes me want to punch something, and I am *not* a violent person. Or maybe something else has me on edge and her text is just the catalyst. No, Dexter Collins has nothing to do with it at all. I'm sure of that.

Even my heart knows I'm full of it.

I take two steps, look up, and holy hell...

DEXTER

I'VE BEEN TRYING to track down Abigail all afternoon to ask her to the fight this weekend. She was nowhere to be found. I did notice someone ate one of the banana pudding cups I left for her. Like I said, I know how to deal with women in their own language, *P.S. I Love You* style. Deacon talked some shit about my methods too, until I showed him how it's done. You're welcome, brother. Enjoy one fiancée, courtesy of Dexter.

I hang out by the corner and wait for her to come out of the building because I don't have a clue where she lives.

Finally, I breathe a sigh of relief when she walks out the front door.

"Hey." I step right in her path. It's been twenty minutes and it's starting to get cold as hell. I was beginning to think she caught on to my stalkerish ways and slipped out the back.

Her face lights up and then hardens. "Oh, Dexter, right? That's your name, isn't it? I feel like we met once or twice."

"Come on, Abby. It's been a stressful week."

She continues her little act. "Ohh, you remember my name? Wasn't sure." She starts down the sidewalk.

I can't remember the last time I chased a damn female, but I do it anyway because—it's Abigail. "Hey, just stop for a damn second, woman. Jesus."

She whips around and points a finger at my face. Not in a menacing way. It's more in a *I'm pretending I'm mad at you, so you know not to do this to me again* kind of way. "Just so you know. I'm not making you banana pudding."

I smile really big; bigger than I've smiled in a while, come to think of it. "I'm pretty stocked up on pudding right now, even with someone coming in and stealing them."

She shows me that cute-as-hell grin of hers that says *I'm busted.*

"I've got two tickets to the fight Saturday night. I want you to go with me."

Her grin widens, but she pretends to mull it over. "I don't know."

"Yes you do. I know you ate the damn pudding. This is happening."

She lets out a fake sigh. "Fine. Hot as hell half-naked dudes beating the crap out of each other. Count me in."

My jaw ticks at her comment about hot naked dudes but I refrain from saying anything. "Great. I'll pick you up Saturday. Just give me your address."

"I'll just meet you there. I'm starting to like taking the train around town."

I start to argue but think better of it. She said yes. That's the important part.

"Well give me your number so I can text you the details later."

"Okay cool, Sex... I mean Dexter." Her face goes pale and she can't even look at me.

"Sex, huh?" I grin. It's going to happen sometime, Abigail. Don't you worry your little heart.

She finally glances back. "Shit. Sorry. I meant Dexter. I don't know why your name came out like that. Been a long day for me too. Anyway." She pulls out her phone and calls me real quick so I'll have her number.

I save it in my phone.

She darts off before I can say anything else. "See you there."

"Absolutely." I stand there, admiring her as she walks away.

I can't do anything but smile like a little boy. The way she shakes her ass as she walks down the street; she knows I'm watching, the little tease. I instinctively reach up to pull my hair but stop before she can turn around and see me. The way she said the word "Sex." That tells me a few things. One, I make her nervous. Two, she's been thinking about me...

And sex.

I've got it bad for this girl.

The thought terrifies me. I don't know if I keep pursuing her because I'm obsessed or because the chase is phenomenal. I've never had to work this hard for a woman's attention. Never wanted to, before her.

I need to talk to Deacon. He can help me sort this shit out, and he owes me one. More than one, in fact.

An hour later, I let myself into Deacon's apartment and head directly to the fridge and grab myself a beer. I twist the cap off, fling it in the general direction of the trash can, and down the whole thing.

It tastes incredible. A little Abigail-said-yes celebration chug.

"They went to dinner." Mr. Richards' voice echoes off the walls of the living room.

I walk in and he's kicked back in the recliner watching some documentary about the greatest boxers of all time. He needs a wheelchair to get around because he had a stroke a few years ago, so he spends most of his time in the La-Z-Boy.

Shit.

I always forget Quinn's old man moved into Deacon's apartment when Quinn did.

There goes my game plan. Deacon's probably getting his dick wet in a coat closet somewhere. That's their thing.

"Bring me one of those, kid?"

I snort. "All right." Fuck it, I need a refill anyway.

I grab a couple bottles and join him. I twist the caps off both beers and pocket them, then go pick up the other one I slung on the floor. I know how anal chicks get about leaving shit around the house, and Deacon would love to throw me under the bus for making a mess. Anything to take some blame off his ass.

Never in my life would I have pictured this for Deacon. Totally pussy whipped.

He loves the shit out of her, though, and I suppose

FILTHY PLAYBOY

things could be worse. They balance each other out. Quinn is cool too, so that helps. She's way less intense than the other fiancée in the family, that's for damn sure.

I never saw myself wanting something like this. The whole love and commitment thing. That shit has never been for me.

For a brief moment, I allow myself to fantasize what a life like this would be like with Abigail. Coming home to her every day, waking up in bed next to her every morning. Surprisingly, it doesn't make me want to run for the hills.

I glance around Deacon's apartment to see if much has changed but it's really about the same as before.

Sure, there are some flowers and shit, but it's not too bad. She let Deacon keep all his stuff.

Interesting.

"Thanks, son."

"No problem. You know if they'll be out late?"

"Not sure. You need something important? I can call Quinn and get them back here."

"Nah. I'll live."

Quinn's old man is cool as hell. We have a blast at Bears games.

He looks over at me and his eyebrows rise.

"Okay, so I got these tickets for the big fight coming up and... it's just—" I wave him off with a hand. "It's nothing. Forget it." I shake my head and let out a sigh.

"You got tickets?" He looks like he might come out of his chair. "Lucky son of a bitch."

I laugh. "Yeah."

"Your brother watches football with me, but he's not big into boxing and MMA."

"I love that shit. My buddy Cole hooked me up. He used to fight."

"Cole Miller? Damn, your family knows everyone."

I kick back. Mr. Richards really is awesome. I try to stop thinking about my situation with Abigail, but I can't get her out of my head. Mr. Richards and I fall into an easy conversation about our favorite fighters for a bit. I drink a few more beers with him.

He must sense something is going on, though. "You look flustered, kid."

Flustered doesn't come close to what I'm feeling.

Finally, I decide fuck it. I need to talk to someone. He's here and the dude looks like he knows some shit. He has life experience.

"I DON'T KNOW if I like her or if it's chasing her that's driving me up the goddamn wall." I'm lying on the couch, staring up at the ceiling like I'm in a counseling session when the front door opens and shuts.

Quinn and Deacon walk in.

I don't even bother to stop. "I mean, she's everything I could see myself wanting. Smart, gorgeous, funny... she's a damn challenge. Tits are outta this world." I hold my hands out in front of my chest to make my point. "Know what I mean?"

Mr. Richards nods and grins like he knows what's up.

I shake my head. "She just frustrates the hell out of me sometimes. I think it's because she's so young."

"What the hell is this?" Deacon marches into the living

room. "You should charge his ass by the hour." He looks to Mr. Richards and shakes his head, then stares at me like I'm pathetic.

I shrug like *what the fuck?* "You weren't here. I needed advice."

Deacon snickers. "What's wrong? Still stuck in the friend zone?" A smile plasters across his face. "She's never gonna date you. Way too hot for your ugly ass."

Quinn swats him in the chest. "I fell for you and I'm *way* out of your league."

These two make me nauseous sometimes. They're still in the honeymoon phase of their relationship. Always touching, can't keep their hands off each other. I don't know how her dad puts up with their PDA shit all the time.

"You were *not* out of my league. More like the other way around."

Quinn scowls. "You need to help him. Do I need to remind you it was Dex who saved your sorry ass? You wouldn't have me if it weren't for him."

"She ain't wrong," Mr. Richards says out the side of his mouth, not bothering to turn from the TV.

Deacon frowns but Quinn ignores him and walks over and sits next to my feet.

She turns to face me. "Why don't you work your movie magic on her? One of those grand gestures like the romantic comedies you secretly love." She smirks.

I groan. "I don't *love* those movies. I don't know where you guys got that shit from. I pay attention to them, there *is* a difference."

"You're so full of shit," says Deacon. "We all know you like watching them, just admit it."

"Do not, fucker."

"Boys!" Quinn snaps her fingers. "Back to Abigail."

I sit up. "Abigail isn't like you or other girls. That shit won't work on her. She's too smart." She deserved that dig for suggesting I like those movies. "She'll see it coming from a mile away. It's not her style, anyway. She doesn't get caught up in her feelings. We need to address the elephant in the room. I'm afraid Deacon was right for once. She's put me in the goddamn friend zone. I kissed the shit out of her the other day, and she didn't even seem fazed by it when I asked her out. Said she wants to meet me there and talked about the hot dudes who were going to fight. What kind of shit is that? The guy never gets out of the fucking friend zone. Rarely in the movies, and never in real life. I know things."

"Move over and listen up." Quinn shoves my legs off the couch.

It forces me to sit up.

She takes a seat and Deacon slides down on to the couch and pulls her into his lap.

Could they not touch each other for two goddamn seconds while I'm in a crisis? He leans in, sweeps her hair to the side, and kisses the back of her neck.

I might hurl.

Quinn wags a finger at me. "Listen good because I'm only going to tell you this once in a language you'll understand. Abigail may try to come off cool, like one of the guys, but deep down she's a girly girl who wants the same stuff as the rest of us. All women want romance and to be swept off their feet. We want to be independent and respected, but we also want that take-charge macho shit, even if we roll our eyes at it. You can't be the junior varsity, half-assing everything and expect a keeper to fall in your lap with minimal effort. You gotta step up to the plate and woo her. So, stop acting like a pussy, crying on the couch to my dad and do something about it or yeah, you'll stay in the damn friend zone. If you think that's where you are, that's where you'll be."

Mr. Richards chuckles.

I turn to him. "What's so funny?"

"You, still sitting there. What the hell you doing, son? You heard my daughter. Get your ass up."

I jump up off the couch and look back and forth between all of them, then stare at Quinn. "You know what? You're right. Fuck this." I'm tired of pussyfooting around with Abigail; like she's going to take the train to our first date.

"Of course I am. I'm a woman."

I walk by the end table and sweep a pile of magazines onto the floor. They fly everywhere, making a huge mess.

"What the fuck?" yells Deacon.

"I do what I want, bitches. Dexter Collins runs shit!" I yell the words over my shoulder as I storm to the front door.

I swear I hear Quinn mumble, "What the hell did we just do?" as I yank the door open and walk out.

Fuck this. Abigail *will* be mine.

ABIGAIL

I WALK in the door after meeting up with Kyle and Nick and toss the tampons on the counter. I ate a piece of pizza, but I left early because all I could think about was Dexter. Barbie doesn't even say thank you, and I just walk to the living room, still in my own little world thinking about Dexter.

I can't believe I did that. I said Sex to his face, instead of his name. He heard me say the word—out loud.

How am I ever going to look at him without turning bright pink? This is a Private Santiago code red—a DEFCON one situation. That was utterly humiliating. Now, he'll think I daydream about him and sex.

Well, you do.

That's beside the point!

I'm almost tempted to talk to Barbie but I'm not that desperate yet. This would be one of those rare occasions where I could use a girlfriend. I walk into the kitchen while she hems and haws over some dish she's trying to cook for Chuck. Thankfully, she's taking it to his place.

Honestly, she's not even that bad. We're just a bad match. I think I exhaust her as much as she exhausts me. It's just awkward and uncomfortable. It's a square peg, round hole situation.

I've tried being friends with her, but it's just never going to happen. We're complete opposites one-hundred percent of the time, and not in the good way when friends balance each other out.

We're like a bomb, slowly ticking down to the day one of us explodes.

I lay down on the couch and flip through channels, doing my best to ignore her banging around in the kitchen, while simultaneously trying to rid my mind of me making an ass of myself in front of Dexter.

"Do you know how long to bake lasagna?" The words fly out from the kitchen.

How the hell should I know? I don't want to fight with her, though. "Is it frozen?"

"Uhh yeah. I don't know how to make it myself!"

Her nasal voice is like nails dragging down a chalkboard in slow motion.

I pop up from the couch.

I don't want to make dinner for Chuck, but the sooner I get her ass out the door the better. I'm a terrible roommate. "What does the back of the box say?"

"I don't know. I threw it away."

Jesus. How can she be so anal and picky, and still have no common sense? "Okay." I march to the trash and dig out the box. It looks like a child opened it on Christmas morning. She ripped right through the directions. "It says here…" I fold the flimsy cardboard back together. "Bake it at three seventy-five for two hours."

Shit! Two hours?

"Two hours!" She stomps her foot like a toddler throwing a tantrum. "I'm supposed to be there in an hour."

My mind races for a solution to both of our problems. "Maybe you can bake it until you leave then microwave it the rest of the way? It's already pre-baked, right?"

She huffs out a sigh and stares up at the ceiling, rolling her eyes as if I'm the one who screwed this whole thing up. "I don't know. This is a disaster. It's our three-month anniversary and he said to make something special, but I don't cook. I'm a fraud. I think he might pop the question, but not if I bring him frozen dinner."

Wow, what a way to get engaged, and after three whole months. She thinks pretty highly of herself expecting him to pop the freaking question, but I don't mention she may just be being a little unrealistic. It's difficult, but I manage to fight back a laugh. Who the hell would date a guy who would demand they cook him dinner on their anniversary? Especially a hairy-ass, disgusting slob like Chuck? You have to be Dexter Collins-level hot to make those sorts of demands and have them taken seriously. I'd cook him the best damn lasagna he's ever tasted.

Stop it, Abigail.

My eyes roam back to Barbie and she's staring at me like her entire life depends on me. I can't help but feel bad for her. I don't want to, but I do. "Listen, Chuck loves you. If you're that worried, order carryout and put it in your own container before you get there."

"That's not a terrible idea." She taps her chin. "Yeah."

She nods her head as if she just came up with it. "I like it. You can have this one if you want."

"Okay, thanks." Sweet, free food.

"It was twelve bucks." She stands there, staring like a salesman making a deal and settling on the terms like I didn't just buy her tampons.

Jesus.

I bite my tongue and nod. "I'll Apple Pay it to you later."

"Perfect." She claps her hands together.

I turn the oven on. If I'm paying twelve bucks, I'm definitely cooking this damn thing, and eating every last bit of it. I'm not really that hungry, but I can take it to work and get a couple lunches out of it. Anything to save some money.

That day can't come soon enough, when I can move out.

Barbie grabs her cell phone and taps the screen furiously. "Hey." She looks up. "Thanks for, well, just thanks."

"Sure." My lips move upward and curve into a half smile.

It's almost like we just had a moment and it was kind of nice.

She goes off to get ready in her room.

I pull out a cookie sheet and load the lasagna onto it. My mom would have a coronary. She's all about home-cooked meals from scratch. Buying frozen dinners is a sin in the south. Good thing what she doesn't know won't hurt her.

After the oven preheats and I toss the lasagna in, I

move back to the couch and pick up where I left off, scrolling for something I haven't seen a million times.

Barbie struts out of her room a few minutes later with her hair teased up wearing enough perfume I can taste it in the back of my throat. I let out a small cough as she twirls around in a black sequin dress with a bow on the shoulder. It reminds me of my eighth-grade snowball formal.

"How do I look?"

The snarky side of my brain says ask if she wants honesty, but I settle for a white lie. "Awesome. Chuck will love it."

I wish Kyle and Nick were here to see this but it's probably better this way. I should try to snap a picture, but there's no way to do it without being caught. Instead, I snatch my phone off the coffee table, intending to text them. That would be mean. It's no secret I don't like Barbie, but I'm not that person, so I pretend to check my messages and put the phone back down.

"Don't wait up. I think tonight's going to be the night. Eek!"

"Good luck. I hope it goes well."

Just like that, her face goes ice cold. "I don't need luck."

I fight the urge to roll my eyes. She goes out the door and my phone rings.

"Ugh!" My entire body tenses when I see "unknown caller" flash on the screen. I hope this isn't a work emergency or a bill collector. That seems like the only two possible options.

I really hope it's not work. I'm already in my comfy clothes and the smell of the lasagna isn't half bad.

I slide my thumb across the screen. "Hello."

"Hey, it's Dexter."

It's Sex!

Dexter.

Damn.

I seriously need to break that habit. "What's up?" I frown and wonder why he's calling, and at the same time tingles shiver across my arms and goosebumps pebble all over.

"So, Saturday…" He pauses.

My pulse spikes. Is he going to cancel? I bet I freaked him out when I did the whole Sex thing. He probably just didn't have anyone to go with him. Deacon probably canceled and I was an afterthought and then I acted all weird and got excited for nothing. I bet I was just the first person he saw after he got the news.

"I'm taking you to dinner. Before the fight. And I'm picking you up."

What? The? Hell?

I want to scream my address at him through the phone, but I have to stay calm and play it cool. "Umm… that makes it sound like a date."

"It *is* a damn date. What's your address?"

What the hell is happening right now? His confidence is off the charts. More than usual. I don't know if I could say no if I wanted to. It's so damn sexy. "Dex… I-I… are you sure? 'Cause I mean…" I trail off.

I sound like a babbling idiot. I mean holy shit. Dexter wants to take me out on a date? This is too much to process right now. I thought he only asked me to the fight to try to make up for ignoring me after our kiss. I mean after the kiss I was all about it and had tons of confidence that he liked me, but then he ignored me for several days, and it confused the hell out of me.

"It's happening. Give me your address."

I give in to his demand and shoot off the building name and apartment number before I can stop my mouth from doing it.

"Wasn't so hard, was it? See you at five on Saturday."

The call ends and I stare at my phone in disbelief.

What the hell just happened?

I agreed to go on a date with Dexter, that's what happened.

I promised myself no dating, just casual fun. I thought I could handle this attraction to him but apparently, I can't. I'm screwed. Going out on a real date goes against everything I said I wouldn't do when I moved to Chicago. As conflicted as I feel, I can't help but notice the gigantic cheesy smile staring back at me when I look over at my reflection in the TV screen.

Will it really be so bad? He's hot and successful. If there was a man I wanted to be serious about, it would be Dexter. He's pretty much perfect.

I should find a reason to cancel but I'm too damn excited about this fight. I've always wanted to go to an MMA event, ever since I saw one on TV.

The real question is…

What the hell am I going to wear?

I toss my phone aside and leap up from the couch. Once in my room, I rifle through my closet for the perfect outfit. This would be another time when a female friend would come in handy. About now, I'd settle for Barbie. I laugh at myself and remember the dress she wore to Chuck's. No, maybe I wouldn't settle for Barbie.

I pull out my favorite jeans and spiked heels. I need a new shirt. Maybe I can make a mall run tomorrow after work. I want to wow Dexter. If I'm going to go on a date with him, I need to do it right.

———

LATER THAT EVENING, as I shovel lasagna into my mouth much faster than I should, Barbie bursts through the door in tears. My eyes widen, and I freeze like a deer in headlights, because I know I'm not supposed to eat on the couch. She said not to wait up, though. What the hell is she doing here?

She sobs so hard it sends a shiver through her. Black mascara snakes down her cheeks.

I sit up and nonchalantly slide the plate underneath the couch to hide my crimes against her. "Hey." I drag out the syllable. "What's wrong?"

"Chuck… he… he…" She sniffles and wipes her arm over her nose. At the same time, she kicks her shoes across the room. "He broke up with me. Said we aren't on the same page right now. That things were getting too serious for him. He's too young to be tied down and wants to date other people. Can you believe that asshole?"

I feel bad for her, and at the same time I can't help but feel bad for myself. I'm going to have to deal with this all night now. "No way." She was so excited when she left. Who the hell dumps someone on their anniversary, even if it's a three-month one? You have to be a major-league asshole to make me feel sorry for Barbie. "Here." I pour her a glass of my wine and shove it toward her.

"Thanks." She takes a long drink. "I thought he was going to propose." She smacks a palm to her forehead. "How could I be so stupid?"

Well, I mean… No, you need to comfort her. "He's a dipshit if he didn't appreciate you."

"We should go out and get drunk. Pick up the first guys we see and bring them back here. Then I could accidentally video call Chuck right in the middle of it."

My eyes bug out. *That escalated quickly.*

I pat her on the forearm. "How about we hold off on that? We can watch a movie. There's plenty of lasagna and wine."

She nods. "You're probably right." She walks into the kitchen and eats lasagna straight from the pan like an animal. After a few gulps from the glass, she ditches it and goes straight to drinking from the bottle. After a few more seconds, she lets out a long sigh. "Be glad you're not that pretty."

My brows shoot up.

Did she really just say that? Out loud?

She shakes a finger at no one in particular. "That's what it was. He was intimidated. Scared because I'm out of his league. Be glad you don't have that problem."

I was being nice to her!

I stand up, put my hands on my hips, and shake my head. "I know. You're right." I let out the most sarcastic sigh I can muster to rival hers. "The wine was twenty bucks, by the way. You can Apple Pay me." I walk off and leave her to clean up and be miserable by herself.

To hell with her. I'm not going to sit around and be her punching bag. Screw that. This is exactly why my friends are dudes. I can't stand catty-ass women. I slam the bathroom door a little harder than needed. I genuinely attempted to console her. Hell, I even felt bad for her. I should've known better.

I decide to just call it a night and go to bed early. I want to look extra hot tomorrow at work, no bags under my eyes.

I need to talk to someone, though. I don't want to go to bed pissed off. I should be ecstatic about my date and instead I'm brooding around my room like an angry teenager. There's one woman I can count on, though, and that's my mom.

I walk into my room, flop down on my bed, and call her.

"Hey, Mom."

"You being safe?"

"Yes, I'm at home."

"You still have that pepper spray?"

"Yeah, on my keychain." I can't help but smile every time she nags me.

"I was watching the news."

She means Fox News, obviously.

"Oh yeah?" I grin even wider. Here comes a diatribe about gun violence in Chicago.

"Yep, all kinds of murders in Chicago. All those gun laws are just doing wonders up there. You sure you don't want to take a pistol with you next time you're home? You can ship them on the plane. I was looking at the rules…"

"Mom, I'm fine. I live in a nice part of town." It's not

super nice, but she doesn't need to know that. There definitely aren't many murders around here.

"Oh, well okay. I have it here, if you ever want it."

"I'm going on a date this weekend."

"Oh, sweetie. That's wonderful!" I swear I hear her mutter, "Sure you don't want the gun?"

"I'm really excited. He's super cute." It's amazing how ten seconds of talking to my mom can make me feel like I'm back at home. How it can make me forget about Barbie and all my other worries. Her voice is like being wrapped up in a warm hug. "You need to make a trip up here. I could show you around."

"Honey, you know I can't…" She's scared of flying. It's one of her greatest fears, but I'm determined to get her up here one weekend for a visit.

"You could drive. I could fly home and ride up with you, then ride back to Texas."

"I don't know. I'd love to see where you live, so maybe… Anyway, tell me more about this guy."

I grin. "He's funny, and cute, I already mentioned that, but it's worth saying twice. He has a great job…"

"Will he treat you right? I worry about those boys in the north. They don't have manners like the men down here."

I can't help but notice she called them boys up here and men down there. It makes me smile even harder. She is who she is, and I wouldn't change her for the world.

"He's a man, trust me. And yeah, I think he'll treat me right."

"Okay then. We raised you to make good decisions, so if you're all right with him, so are we. You know that."

I lean my head back on my pillow. "Thanks, Mom. That's all I needed to hear. I'm going to get some rest."

"Good idea. Me too. I'm glad you called and I'm happy you found yourself a hot date."

"Me too."

"I love you, sweetie."

"Love you too. Give Daddy a kiss for me."

"I will, and you stop eating frozen dinners. Cook yourself a damn meal. It'll impress that boy up there too."

How the hell does she do that? Always know everything? I laugh at her intuition, and the fact she called Dexter a boy. "Okay, I will. Promise."

"Goodnight."

"Night."

I fall into my pillow and hug it tight to me. I bury my face in it, kick my legs, and just grin. I'm going out with Dexter Collins, and he's about as far from a boy as you can get.

DEXTER

It's Friday morning and I feel on top of the world.

Tomorrow night, Abigail is all mine.

I feel much better after talking to Quinn. I like Abigail. She's exactly the kind of woman I want.

Quinn's right, I can't do this shit halfway. Not a fucking chance.

Abby deserves the best and that's what she'll get, goddamn it.

I walk into the breakroom and snag one of my puddings. Unwrapping the plastic spoon, I toss the wrapper in the trash. I peel the lid back and lick the excess chocolate from the foil.

When I look up, Abigail struts past the doorway looking sexy as fuck. She has on this charcoal-gray dress that clings to her curves—no jacket. The dress squeezes her tits together, and I groan internally. My thoughts immediately move to yanking her into a supply closet and having my way with her, Deacon and Quinn style.

Can't do it.

It's too soon, and even if I wanted to, Decker installed cameras after word got out about all the extracurricular activities that used to go down in there. Said it was because people were stealing stuff. Yeah right, big bro. I swallow some pudding, and Abigail's eyes shift over my direction. Those baby blues pierce straight through me, and I'm worried I just went from six to midnight in my pants.

She's a damn ten and she knows it. Fuck, I want to taste those cherry lips again.

I pause for a split second to see if she'll walk over, but she doesn't break stride. My eyes roam down to the strappy heels she's wearing. They wrap around her ankles and part way up her calves.

She goes on like business as usual and my heart sinks for a brief moment, but then she looks back over her shoulder with a cute-as-hell smirk.

Yep, definitely hard as a rock. You're so mine.

Tomorrow night.

No work. No jackass friends coming between us. Just her and me.

I can't wait to have her all to myself. I never can seem to get her alone.

I finish off my pudding and grab a bottled water. When I return to my desk, Brenda doesn't look up from the files she's rifling through.

"Decker wants to see you."

I roll my eyes. "Wonderful."

She snickers but keeps toiling away with the files.

I take a few sips of water and stop off in the bathroom.

I take my sweet-ass time, hoping I might bump into Abigail on her way back to her desk.

No dice.

Not all is lost, though. I love making Decker wait for me when he calls these little impromptu meetings, probably to micromanage every little thing I'm doing. He called me in last week to bitch about the way some files were paperclipped together; like I bother myself with shit like that. I didn't have the heart to scold Brenda for it. She works her ass off, so I just took the blame and nodded my head, promising it wouldn't happen again.

I finally stroll on over like I don't have a care in the world. Donavan is here too.

What the hell?

This better not be an ambush about something trivial, but I'd almost suffer through it to see them get along for five minutes. It's about damn time. We're all getting sick of this petty war over some shit that went down with Donavan and Tate. It happened a long time ago.

Business is business, but their two egos are too goddamn big to put it behind them.

Tate walks in and the familiar tension fills the air.

The second she takes a seat, Donavan pops up. "Got work to do." He hauls ass out the door.

I shake my head glancing back and forth between Decker and the door. "Would you assholes work your shit out? You're acting like children. That's saying something, coming from me."

Tate nods her head slowly but doesn't look up from her files.

Decker waves me off with a flippant hand, like nothing

is wrong and he has it all under control. "It's fine. We have other things to discuss. I'll worry about Donavan."

"It's been like six months. I'm losing confidence."

"That's enough. It's not why you're here."

I shrug. "Whatever, Dad. What's up?"

"We need to talk about Wells Covington."

My eyebrows rise. "Umm, okay. What about him?"

"His extracurriculars don't align with our image."

"What the hell does that mean?"

Decker straightens up and adjusts his tie. "He's into some weird shit. Underground sex clubs. BDSM-type stuff. He has a reputation for being a sexual deviant."

"Deviant." I laugh and shrug. "Check out Father Collins over here. Who the fuck cares? I give a shit about the commas on his net worth. So what if he likes his dick poked with toothpicks or clamped off with clothespins, whatever the fuck they do in those places. It's none of our business. He wouldn't be the first or last client we have that's into that kind of thing. Hell, I bet half our roster does shit that'd make your head spin. We've never cared before."

Decker takes a step toward me. "Look, just do yourself and the firm a favor and don't be seen going to those clubs with the guy. The last thing we need is a PR nightmare, especially after just merging with Dallas. You know how the media gets with Deacon and me when they smell a scandal."

Going to a sex club with Covington is at the bottom of my to-do list, so whatever, if it gets me out of this room faster. "Won't be a problem. Is there anything else?"

"You ask Abigail out?" Tate still hasn't looked up from

her files. It's obvious she's as tired of Decker railing on about Covington's secret sex life as I am, and I'm pretty sure she asked the question just to give him shit, because he tries to ignore anything beyond business that happens between these walls.

Decker's hands go straight to his temples like he has a migraine coming on. "Please tell me you didn't. I'd almost rather you be seen with Covington at a sex club." His hands fall and he glares lasers back and forth at Tate and me.

I can't help but snicker at how uncomfortable he is, and Tate looks like she's biting back a laugh as well.

He shakes his head at both of us. "Are we a law firm or a fucking dating agency? Maybe I'll have the sign out front changed. Tell Weston we're switching our focus from law to helping singles find their special someone. Fuck."

Well, he's in a mood today. Better pile it on in retaliation for him giving me shit about Covington. "So, let me get this straight, so I have all the facts… It's okay for you and Deacon to fuck whoever you want at the office but the minute I take an interest in Abigail it's not a good idea?" I turn to Tate. "No offense."

She still hasn't looked up. I swear to God, she has ridiculous multitasking skills. She's probably reviewed an entire contract while carrying on this conversation. "None taken. I think Decker's rule is idiotic. As long as it doesn't affect your work, I don't give a shit, personally."

"It's company policy," Decker groans. "Rules are in place for a reason. What if she decides to sue us for sexual harassment?"

"You're being unrealistic as hell. You put a bunch of

people in a building and have them working together all the time, they're gonna wanna fuck, okay? That's the natural order of things."

Decker shakes his head. "Your intuition is pure fucking Shakespeare, you know that?"

I bite back a laugh. "I'll take that as a compliment."

"You would."

I swear Tate just giggled. I didn't know she was capable.

"Look, Cole hooked me up with some tickets to the fight tomorrow. I'm taking Abigail to dinner then to the fight."

"Fine, whatever. Just don't tell me about it." Decker turns his back. "I don't want to know. It helps me sleep at night."

Tate gives me a thumbs up where Decker can't see her. That's a good thing. I thought Tate might warn Abigail off from dating me. Being nice to her has its perks it seems.

"Then we're hitting up the Sex Dungeon afterward for a little bondage and fire play…"

He points to the door without looking. "Just get the fuck out."

Tate's about to die.

I can't stop snickering as I head toward the door.

"I swear to Christ, between this place and Jenny's teenage hormones, I'm not going to make it to forty."

"I think you'll make it, you're not too far away."

He spins around, his face heats up. "You about done?"

I hold both hands up. "I'm done, I swear."

"Good."

"Might be time to update the will, though. Good to take precautions. Be sure to list me as…"

His face tenses. "Just go." He fights back a laugh and points to the door. "I might be pushing forty, but I'm the big brother and I'll kick the piss out of all of you, including Deacon's fat ass."

I grin and walk out, tossing Tate a fist bump along the way. I'm glad her and I have been getting along better. It just took some time. Giving Decker shit has brought us closer together, and I think it was just the merger and all the emotions that came along with that. We all got started on the wrong foot, but one thing is certain, she's perfect for my big brother. Believe it or not, he has mellowed out a ton since they got together.

AFTER WORK, I head straight to the gym. I may not be a world-class athlete like Decker and Deacon, but I like to keep myself in shape. I was good at sports, but they never interested me much, so I quit by the time I was in middle school. I tried it out, but at the end told my dad I didn't like it. He never took me back to another practice.

"You always finish something when you start it. Honor your commitments and give it a fair chance. But after that, if you don't like it, don't do it. Life's too short to do things you don't enjoy." He told me that when I was ten, and it just stuck with me.

Deacon and I have always been super close, because of the twin thing, but it's weird. We both kind of do our own things to separate us from always being lumped together.

At least I think so. He'll always be my best friend, but I'm my own person.

Deacon was into sports and always looked up to Decker. I was into comic books and stories and art and shit. I'm a daydreamer. I like to get caught up in my imagination, have since I was a kid.

When I walk in, there are a few gym bunnies hanging around the front, but I ignore them. Normally, I might sit back and enjoy the view for a bit, maybe even strike up a conversation, but I have no inclination to do that today.

I haven't for a while, actually. Now that I think about it. Ever since...

Abigail.

Ever since she transferred to the firm, I haven't looked at other women the same way. I never even noticed until recently. She might not realize she's mine yet, but she will.

After my workout, I grab a quick shower and head over to pick up Jenny, my niece. I promised her I'd take her and her friends to some trampoline place. They're almost old enough to drive, and almost old enough to start drinking and doing all kinds of shit that really would send Decker to an early grave. They might even already be doing it. If they want to go to a trampoline place, I'm all about it. I miss her being younger; it's difficult watching her innocence fade. I can't imagine what that's like for Decker. Maybe it's why he's so stressed out.

When Decker became a single dad, us other brothers made it our mission to give him at least one Friday night a month to himself.

It's a tradition that stuck. I love it. She's a good kid.

When she was younger, I'd feed her a bunch of junk then drop her back at home.

He'd get mad as fuck, but hey, that's what uncles do. They spoil the shit out of their niece. I'm not trying to be her parent. I'm a goddamn funcle, and we have fun when we hang out.

Parents have to be responsible, not me.

He always says he's going to pay me back, but the joke's on him. I don't plan on having kids. Being Uncle Dex is fine by me.

I park my car on the street for a minute so I can wait for Decker to back his piece-of-shit SUV out of the garage. Decker traded in his Audi after Tate moved in, and they got matching vehicles. I'll be damned if I park my baby out on the road all night. It needs to go in his garage.

Yes, I'm that douche who treats his car like it's his child. Blow me.

It's a 1970 Chevelle SS and it's a goddamn work of art. I restored it all myself and there's no way I could fit a bunch of teenagers in it, nor would I want to.

"Uncle Dex!" Jenny rushes down the driveway. Her arms wrap around me as she barrels into my chest.

"Hey, kid. You all set to go?"

"Almost. Beth's on her way." She looks at my car. "You have to let me take that to prom in a few years. Please!"

I waggle my eyebrows at her. "Yeah, right. Tell your dad to buy you one. He makes all the money."

"Pfffft. He's already talking about how I need to get a job and pay for my own car."

"Not a bad idea."

"Hey!" She punches me in the arm.

I pretend like it hurt and rub it for a second. "Ow. What was that for?"

"You're supposed to always take my side…" She pauses. "I mean, if you want to be the *coolest* uncle and all that. There's a lot of competition for that title."

I point a finger at her and laugh. "You're a little shit, you know that? You're more like your dad than you think."

We both laugh and walk back up the driveway. I give my car a little glance over my shoulder and tell her with my thoughts that she'll be okay out there until I can get her in the garage.

"Dad ordered pizza for us if you're hungry."

I follow Jenny into the house.

There are three other giddy teenage girls seated at the kitchen counter scarfing down pizza and chugging soda. I can already feel the headache coming on, but traditions are traditions.

"You sure you're up for this?" Tate grins as I walk up.

"I can handle them. Though, I will admit it was easier when they were eight. They'd get hopped up on sugar and crash. They never shut the fuck up once they're teenagers."

Tate laughs. "Well, if you need backup don't call. Decker's taking me to the movies."

"I'll call their asses an Uber if they don't act right, or stick them on the train."

"Jesus." Tate shakes her head. "I can never tell when you and Deacon are joking. So, when's the big date with Abigail?"

"Who's Abigail?" Jenny cuts in. "Uncle Dex, you have

a girlfriend? When can I meet her? Is she pretty? What's she look like?"

There is entirely too much estrogen in my presence. "Easy, killer. I'm sure I have all night to tell you about her."

"Cool."

Decker walks in from the garage. "What's cool?"

"Uncle Dex has a hot date tomorrow night with Abigail."

Decker glares. "I know." He shakes his head like he's trying to rid his brain of the thought. "The truck's ready to go. You need anything?"

I shake my head right back at him and grin my ass off. "How many times do I have to tell you that's not a truck. It's barely an SUV and might as well be a soccer mom van."

His jaw ticks a little, like he's trying to bite back whatever sarcastic remark he's thinking of, because he knows it'll give Jenny a reason to sass his ass twenty-four seven. He finally just shoves Tate's keys into my chest. "Don't call for anything." Then he whispers, "And stay away for a while."

I pat him on the back and toss him a wink. "Don't worry, bro. I got you. Probably been a while. You need to clean the ol' pipes out. I'm sure they're rusty."

"Jesus Christ." He grabs Tate by the arm. "Time to go."

"For real, we'll be fine. Going to the trampoline place then maybe hit up the arcade and ice cream. It'll wear them out."

"Perfect. Thanks. I mean it."

"Yes, thank you," says Tate.

"No worries."

"Beth!" the girls all squeal when their other friend arrives.

Fuck, this is going to be a long night.

ABIGAIL

My stomach flutters. I'm anxious and excited.

"I mean look at Kyle and me. We hang out all the time and it's never been awkward. He's a good friend…"

Barbie rolls her eyes from the chair next to mine as the stylist goes all scissor crazy on her hair.

I brought her with me to the salon, despite her being so damn rude, because I felt bad she was moping around about Chuck nonstop. It was probably a mistake, but she looked so damn happy when I asked if she wanted to come.

I mean, who can't be in a good mood after a nice cut and color?

She glances over. "Because you put him in the friend zone. Trust me, he's sitting there biding his time, just waiting for an opportunity."

What? Why does everyone think Kyle wants to be more than friends? That's insane. He's never once acted interested in me in that way. "Kyle? No way."

I swear if someone wasn't cutting her hair, her nose

would go straight up to the ceiling. "Bury your head in the sand all you want. Just wait until he finds out you're dating the hot lawyer. He's going to turn into a different person. He hangs out with you because you're single. Chuck and I talked about it all the time. We were betting how long it'd be before you got drunk and he made his move."

"What?" I'm already regretting inviting her here. I'm only entertaining this conversation to keep her mind off the breakup, and because I don't want to hear her cry again. I can't imagine myself ever crying as much as she has, but I've never been through a bad breakup. I've never really had a serious relationship. I dated one guy for a few months in high school, but we broke up when he went off to college my junior year. He's married with two kids, and I'm happy for him. In college I dated a bit but never anything hot and heavy. I've definitely never been with anyone I could see spending the rest of my life with. The thought of it sends a shudder through me.

I mean, over half of marriages fail. Why would I ever want to roll those dice? I've seen couples I thought would last forever turn a one-eighty and hate each other after a year.

Maybe that's why I'm so damn nervous about this date with Dex. I've never felt this way about someone else, but I know it's just physical attraction. We don't even really know each other all that well, and I won't just be handing my heart to someone with nice eyes and a little ink snaking down out of their suit.

What if we turn into more? I don't want to end up all sad and pathetic like Barbie.

My usual hair lady moves me back under the dryer for my lowlights while Barbie gets her color done.

She's going darker and I think it's a smart choice. It fits her personality better, makes her seem more adult and serious, which is perfect for her.

While I'm under the dryer, my thoughts return to Dex. There's nothing worse than a date filled with awkward silence. What if we have nothing to talk about? What if I bore him? I'm young, in my early twenties, and he's a decade older than me and has an important job. How could we possibly relate to each other? For some reason, the thought of us not clicking, once we get to know each other, turns my stomach.

Once Barbie and I finish, I rush home to get ready. Thankfully, I shaved my legs this morning when I took a shower. Barbie's going out with some work friends to drink her heartache away, and I'm happy to dump her problems off on them. I did my good deed for the day with minimal confrontation. Score.

With any luck she'll crash somewhere else if things go well with Dex.

Unless he invites me back to his place. Wow, what if he *does* invite me back? What if he wants more?

Should I take a toothbrush? I don't think we'll have sex, but you never know.

Would I have sex with him tonight?

My brain screams no, but my body screams yes. Damn, he has me all worked up again and he's not even here.

Right as I slip on my jean jacket, the doorbell rings.

Shit.

He's here.

I suck in a deep breath, pop a piece of gum in my mouth, and open the door.

Mother of God.

He's dressed casual, and I swear it's even hotter than him in a damn suit. He has on dark jeans and a graphic stretch tee that hugs his biceps and shows off even more of his ink than I usually get a peek at.

His gaze rakes up and down, taking me in. His eyes travel from my peep toe, leopard-print heels, up the legs of my tattered dark jeans, to the bare midriff where my black halter begins. It has sexy straps that cross over my back. There was no wearing a bra with this thing. It's like a black silky hanky that leaves little to the imagination.

My hair is blown out in soft waves that curve around my shoulders. I've got the vintage Pam Anderson look going on, perfect for an MMA fight.

"Wow, you look… incredible."

Don't blush. Don't blush. Why does he make me want to smile like an idiot?

Pretty sure I blush. "Thanks, you look… great too."

Stop being awkward.

"You have a bigger jacket?"

What the hell? "Uh, no."

He smirks. "It's gonna get cold."

I shrug and it's hard to focus on the words with how hot he looks. "I'll be okay, promise."

He shakes his head, then smiles at me. "Texas girls," he mumbles.

He looks different without his suit on. I've only seen him without one a few times. His demeanor is different outside of work, like he lets his guard down and doesn't have to be so serious around me.

As I walk out, the smell of his cologne hits me and makes me want to jerk him through the doorway and climb his ass like a damn tree. I manage to keep my hormones in check and grab my clutch.

"Come on. I know a great place to eat."

I manage not to tell him he can have me for dinner *and* dessert if he wants. "Sounds perfect. I'm starving."

He smirks. It's the sexiest of all smirks. "Good. Was afraid you'd be one of those girls who orders a salad then shuffles it around on her plate." He grins and puts a hand to my lower back and guides me to the elevator.

His hand. It shoots flames up my spine. This is going to be a long night, and I don't mind one bit.

"No way. We know how to eat in Texas."

"Atta girl, Whitley."

We make our way down the elevator, and Dex leads me through the front door.

"Holy shit…" My hands shoot over my mouth. I can't believe I just said that out loud. I seem to do that a lot around him. "Sorry, I just have a thing for cars." There's a Chevelle parked by the curb. It's the mother of all badass cars. It's a dark blue color with white racing stripes. It looks completely restored, like it's brand new.

"What?" Dex shrugs half-heartedly.

"What do you mean *what*? Do you not see that Chevelle?"

"Yeah, I see it every day." He holds up his keys and jiggles them at me.

No way is that his car. How have I never seen it?

Maybe because I take the train everywhere and never go near the parking garage.

"Her name is Betsy and ogle her when I'm not looking. She's all mine."

We walk over and he opens the door for me. I slide in onto the vinyl seats, and damn, it just smells like raw power.

Dex folds himself into the driver's seat. He fumbles for his keys, and I get a better peek at his tattoos as his sleeve slides up his arm. Butterflies go crazy in my stomach as he turns the key and the car rumbles to life.

It's so freaking hot. Like James Dean, *Rebel Without a Cause*, hot. I peek into the back seat, and holy hell, he has the leather jacket and everything.

Dex slouches back in the seat with one hand on the wheel, and I just take a mental snapshot of him while the vibrations run through my body.

It's like we're setting off on a journey together, and I've never seen a man look so damn sexy in all my life.

I really did pick out a great outfit and it's not lost on me that we look like a perfect couple together.

Dex looks over and winks, and before I know it he backs out and we're flying down the street.

DINNER'S GOING GREAT.

We're in this hip little place with a name I can't pronounce and would butcher if I tried, but it's intimate and fancy. It's perfect for a first date. No having to talk over a crowd. We're at a table in the back that's very private. The ambience screams romantic, but not over the top. It's very subtle. A dainty chandelier hangs over our table and we're seated on brown leather chairs that curve slightly toward each other.

He clearly put a lot of thought into choosing this restaurant. Chalk another one up in the win column for Dexter Collins.

"So, what was it like in your house with all those boys? I've always wondered about that."

Dexter laughs and takes a drink of his beer. "Utter chaos. Rough housing nonstop that drove our mom crazy. I don't know how she put up with us. Someone was always breaking something or bleeding."

"So… you're a mama's boy?" I tease him.

Dex picks at the label on his bottle of beer. "What makes you say that?"

Damn, did I say something wrong? God, am I ruining the moment? "Nothing, I just… You made the question all about her. It seemed like you had empathy for her situation, mentioning her raising all those boys, you guys driving her nuts."

He smiles, like he can sense my discomfort. "Can you keep a secret?"

"Sure." All feels right once again when he smiles at me.

"Total mama's boy." He leans back. "There, I said it and I'm not ashamed at all." He pauses. "But seriously, don't tell anyone."

I laugh. He's so relaxed right now. I'm really digging this playful side of him. "I would never." I stare at him long and hard for a few seconds.

"What?"

"Can I tell you a secret too?"

He straightens up. "Absolutely."

"Total mama's girl over here too. I call her almost every night. I told her about you." I fidget with my hands on the table and break eye contact.

His lips curl into a sly smirk. "Only good things, I hope."

"She called you a boy." I laugh.

He frowns.

I hold a hand up. "Oh no, don't worry. She thinks all the men who aren't southern are boys without manners. She's kind of partial to the south."

He reaches out for my hand, and it's like a jolt of electricity flashes through me when our fingers connect. "I'll just have to change her mind, won't I?"

You're blushing again. Knock it off, Abby!

"Tell me more about your mom."

Dex leans back in his chair, and both of us completely ignore the food in front of us. "I don't know, she just always got me, you know?"

I nod, almost furiously. He has no idea how much I can relate.

"Decker and Deacon were good at sports, like my dad. It wasn't my thing." He pauses like he's holding back.

"What is it?"

"Okay, so you know... No, I don't know if I..."

I grip his hand a little tighter. "Tell me. I want to know."

"Well, everyone thinks I love pudding at the office."

I shake my head. "Would've never thought that." Oh

goodie, the mystery of the pudding is about to unfold. I've always been curious what his deal is with it. It's like a ritual for him.

He laughs. "The truth is, that was mine and my mom's thing. She always kept them hidden in the house and told me where they were when I was a boy. It was *our* secret, you know? Four boys and I had a twin brother, so we had to share everything, but it was something just for me. I think it all started when I got this scar." He points to his face. "Crashed on my skateboard when I was young. Decker was supposed to be watching me and I had to go get stitched up. Mom would bring me pudding because it was all I would eat. I was milking it for all it was worth, but it just continued, all the way through high school, and even when I moved out. Hell, sometimes I'd show up to the old house before they moved, when something was bothering me, or I had a problem. She always had them there, and we'd sit down and talk and eat pudding together... It sounds stupid."

I shake my head. "It's not stupid at all. I understand, trust me."

"Well, her and Dad moved down to Florida, and she sends me those in the mail and always has a note with them, telling me what's going on with her and asking me about life. I send some to her with notes from me. It's our thing, still. And I take them to work and keep them up there anytime I have a case that's gnawing at me. It's like I can't think if I don't have them there. It's why I get pissed when people steal them, and why I put a sign on them in the fridge. People think I'm just being anal like Decker, but it really is important to me."

I think my heart might've just melted away. I can't believe he just told me all that, and it makes so much sense. I don't know what I'd do if I didn't always have my mom one click away on my phone.

For some reason, I just sit there, staring like an idiot. I must look so dumb.

"Sorry, I shouldn't have dropped all that on you. You just asked, and I..." He starts to move his hand away, and my fingers tighten around it, almost to the point I might be digging my nails into his skin.

Don't you ever move that hand, Dexter Collins!

"No, thanks for telling me. I'm serious. And I won't ever say a word to anyone else, promise."

Dex nods and snaps out of his thoughts. "What about you? Any siblings?"

I nod. "Yep. I have a younger sister. She was a surprise baby. She's ten years younger than me so we aren't super close. It's weird. I almost feel like half parent, half sibling. I never was great at the whole getting along with other girls thing, but I do miss her like crazy. I never really had girlfriends growing up. I went to a small school in Texas. It was all about football and you were pretty much a cheerleader or you weren't, and I didn't like cheerleading. So, I didn't have anyone, you know, to spill all my secrets to or have sleepovers with. My roommate for instance. I never know how to take her. I can't tell if she's just being a bitch or if she's half joking sometimes when she says things. I think I need to live on my own. I can't wait to find a new place. One that will let me have a dog."

"A dog lover, huh? Totally had you pegged as a cat person."

"No way. Cats are assholes. I want a husky. One with big blue eyes. Growing up I never could have one because my dad was allergic."

"So, you love banana pudding, your mom, and dogs… what else?"

I laugh, and I love that he wants to know more about me. The feeling is mutual. "I don't know if I should tell you this next one. It *is* a first date after all. I won't be mysterious and interesting if I tell you everything."

He leans in like *now we're getting to the good stuff.* "Tell me. Can't leave me on a cliffhanger like that."

I draw out a sigh, just to tease him a little longer. "Well it's bound to come out sooner or later since we work together. I'm Christmas obsessed. Like, I get crazy. Ugly sweaters, decorations, the movies. I love the classics and all the romantic movies that come on the Hallmark channel. Actually, I love pretty much every movie ever made. I can have an entire conversation in movie quotes. But Christmas is my big thing, above all else."

Dex rubs his hands together. "Okay, most important question of your life, Whitley."

Oh no. I hope I don't say the wrong thing. "Is this a test?"

"Yeah, the biggest one of your life." He grins. "*Die Hard*; Christmas movie or no?"

"Definitely a Christmas movie," I say without thinking.

Dex grins like his day just got a lot better.

I try to hide the large breath I exhale. "Thank God I passed the *Die Hard* test."

"With flying colors. Didn't even have to think about it. I like it."

"That could've been a deal breaker for me too."

"Glad we're on the same page."

I nod. "Yep, you got lucky there."

"Oh, *I* got lucky?" Dex laughs.

"You did."

"Did you know Quinn doesn't think *Die Hard* is a Christmas movie? Deacon looked like he was going to die when he told me."

"What? I thought for sure Quinn would be pro-*Die Hard*."

Dexter shrugs. "What can I say? You're better than her already." He glances away, like he's having a little too much fun. "Okay, crazy Christmas lady. I take it you like hot chocolate?"

"Duh! I make the best hot chocolate ever. I learned it from one of my teachers when I was like eight. Every year in my hometown they have a festival. They go all out with a tree-lighting ceremony and Santa parade. It's a big deal."

"You're adorable." He winks.

I fake-scowl. "Shut up. I'm not cute."

"No, you're right, you're a big Christmas clown."

I lightly rap my fingers on the tabletop and try to suppress a grin. Dexter's sweet. He makes me smile a lot, and there haven't been any weird or tense moments. I haven't felt this relaxed in a long time, longer than I can remember. I feel weightless, like I could float off into the clouds. My guard is totally down and that should scare the hell out of me, but it doesn't. Not at all. "Well, I was going for sexy tonight." I say it right as he takes a sip of his beer.

He damn near starts to choke but manages to compose himself. "Well, you nailed it. Trust me."

I'm not usually one to fish for compliments, but I could listen to them come from Dexter Collins all night long. "Don't lie."

"Not a lie. You could dress up like Mrs. Claus and I'd put your poster on my wall. True story."

I laugh at the thought, then heat flushes through my face, thinking about dressing up in a sexy Christmas outfit for Dex. That could be a lot of fun. "Maybe I will sometime. You have to do the classic Chevy Chase rant from *Christmas Vacation*, though. Word for word, Collins."

Dex laughs. "Oh, I'd nail it. You bring Frank Shirley into my living room and I'd tell him what a dog-kissing, brainless, dickless, hopeless, heartless, fat-ass, bug-eyed, stiff-legged, spotty-lipped, worm-headed sack of monkey shit he is."

Oh my God, he just quoted it without even trying. Why is him quoting Christmas movies so freaking hot? "I'm impressed, sir."

I hold up my beer, and he taps the bottle with his.

I don't know if this date can go any better. It's seriously perfect.

I grin. "So, about my poster on the wall? What would you be doing when looking at said poster?"

"It's classified. I could tell you but then I'd have to kill you."

Did he just quote *Top Gun*? "It's not your flying, it's your attitude."

"Nice, you weren't lying."

"You can't stump me. I'll quote any movie. The great ones anyway."

"Tell me something else about you. I could listen to your stories all night long. What's on your bucket list?"

I tap my chin. "Okay, well, I've always wanted to go ice skating. It's not real big in Texas and we lived like an hour outside of Fort Worth. I almost got to go once, though. I begged my dad over and over and he found this outdoor skating rink in the city. We drove all the way there, and I was so excited, but when we got there it was closed for maintenance or something. Dad was furious. Tried to call the manager and didn't get an answer. He apologized to me a million times and looked like he'd let me down. I felt awful for him and told him it was okay. I know he tried his best. But the story is just as good as getting to ice skate. It really showed me how much he cared and stuff, you know? I'm pretty lucky to have two amazing parents."

Dex nods. "Sounds like a great guy. And as far as ice skating goes, well, you moved to the right city for that." He glances to his watch. "Okay, one more Abigail fun fact, then we need to get going."

"That one's easy. Roller coasters. I love them. We used to go to Six Flags every summer and I'd ride them until I couldn't walk straight."

Dex's face pales a little, and he takes a sip of water. "Awesome. Love roller coasters."

He almost sounds like he's mocking me. "What? You don't like them?"

He shakes his head. "No, they're fine."

Shit, did I say something wrong?

Dex signs the air at the waitress and she brings the check over. He tosses some cash on the table and winks at me. "Let's get out of here."

Normally, I'd find a guy winking cheesy as hell, or goofy, but Dex somehow pulls it off. I think it's because he's not taking himself seriously when he does it.

"All right, Collins." I give him an obviously sarcastic wink. "You're one for one so far, let's see how you do next. I'm ready to watch those hot, naked, sweaty dudes pound on each other."

Dex snickers and starts to say something but pauses and shakes his head. "Damn Christmas clown."

"I'm not a clown. Christmas crazy but not a clown." I point at him.

He catches my hand and wraps his around mine. Our fingers interlace like we've done it a million times before.

"Keep telling yourself that..." He leans in close and whispers, "My little sexy Christmas clown."

His hand moves to the small of my back, and I fight the urge to lean into it.

It's so gentle and possessive at the same time.

It's like a warning to everyone around, *she's mine*, but at the same time I'm leading the way. Maybe I'm just overanalyzing this whole situation. That's probably it.

Before I know what's happened, he's draped his leather jacket over my shoulders and we're headed toward the door.

"Sun went down. You're gonna freeze."

I seriously might combust. It smells just like him and his cologne and there's something incredibly intimate about the moment.

Do not sniff his jacket!

I lean into him while we wait for the valet to pull his car around and inhale the intoxicating scent of his cologne once more. It's late October and he wasn't lying. I'm cold through both layers and he has to be dying in just his tee shirt, but he doesn't show it. I've never lived anywhere that gets this cold, but it gives me an excuse to lean into him and let him and his jacket keep me warm. I just hope he doesn't notice me constantly sniffing. He's definitely ticking off all the boxes. I mean, damn. This date is perfect so far.

DEXTER

WE RUMBLE down Madison in the Chevelle toward the United Center.

I can't stop stealing glances over at Abigail. I think she might be more into my car than me.

Things seem to be going too good to be true. I didn't mean to drop all that stuff about me and my mom on her, but she seemed to get it. She seems to just get *me*, more than I thought she would. Some part of my brain kept telling me she was too young, and this date would show me why we're not compatible, then I could get her out of my mind. I mean, I still planned on trying to get laid. Let's not be ridiculous here. The exact opposite has happened, though.

I'm drawn to her, like a moth to a fucking flame, and I don't know how I'll deal with it if this doesn't work out. The feelings are already there. There's a connection that already runs deep and we haven't done anything more than kiss twice.

I keep trying to hold back but it's not working. I don't

want to come on too strong, but every time I see her, I have this unbelievable urge to tell her everything on my mind and kiss the breath from her lungs.

She's so confident and sexy, not afraid to show her true self. The more she talks, the more I want to know even more about her. We get to the arena, and I don't know what to do. I should drop her off up front, but no way do I want to leave her up there alone while I park the car.

Why didn't I think about this beforehand? I should've hired a car and a driver. Then it wouldn't be as intimate, though. I wouldn't have her all alone.

I drive around the block once and my hands tighten around the steering wheel. What the hell am I going to do? She's gonna freeze in her little jacket she's wearing.

Finally, I decide to just go park and then let her use my jacket again. I don't ask because I know she'll refuse it. It's cold as balls out here. The wind cuts through the buildings and it's like daggers on bare skin.

I drape it around her shoulders as soon as we're out of the car.

"Dex, you're gonna freeze."

"I don't get cold. I'm fine." I toss her another wink, but inside I'm shivering my damn tits off. Fuck, I should've worn a long-sleeve shirt. I don't let my teeth so much as chatter, though, because I'm no pussy, and there's no way I'll let her know I'm cold.

She's warm and that's all that matters.

I walk next to her and our hands brush up against each other. If I was cold before, I'm not now. Even the slightest touch sends heat rushing through my veins.

The second time our fingers graze, they interlace, and we hold hands the rest of the way to the arena.

Her hand fits perfectly in mine and she doesn't pull away. By the time we get to the gate, my lips mash together in a thin line because I have to let go of her. The moment we pass through, our hands naturally gravitate back together. We make our way in and head down toward the octagon, ringside. There's media everywhere. Some chick who was obsessed with Decker years ago flies out of nowhere and snaps our picture, damn near blinding us with the flash.

Once her eyes pop out from behind the camera, her shoulders slump and she lowers her head slightly. She was probably expecting Decker and Tate.

Finally, we make it down. Cole wasn't fucking around. We're on the front row next to a shit ton of celebrities and families of the fighters.

Abigail's hand grips mine a little tighter. "Holy…"

"Yeah, it's a different world down here."

She grins back and I pull her closer to me.

"There's Cole. Let's go say hi."

"Okay."

Our heads crane around, taking in the packed arena as we make our way over to him.

My eyes roam down to her. She's so small and petite. "Ready to see some naked dudes kick the shit out of each other?"

Abby blushes and looks away. "Nah."

I raise my eyebrows. "What? Thought that's why you came?"

"No, I came because some cute guy asked me to." Her

teeth sink into her bottom lip.

I want nothing more than to kiss her right now, but it'd be too forward, and we need to go make appearances. It'd be rude not to. "Good answer. C'mon."

We navigate through a sea of people on our way over to Cole.

"You made it. Nice." He holds out a hand.

I shake it. "Wouldn't miss it. Was that 50 Cent back there?"

"Yeah, man. He loves this shit."

"This is Abigail. Abigail, Cole."

He reaches a hand out. "Of course. I think we met at the office. Great to see you again." He flashes his million-dollar smile at her.

I scowl.

Abigail takes his hand in hers, and I really want to smack his damn hand away from her, but I know I'm being ridiculous. "Oh yeah. I remember you. You offered me a discount at your gym." She smiles.

"Hey, filling the place with beautiful women is good for business."

"Well, if you guys will excuse me, I'm going to hit the ladies' room." Abigail turns back to me. "See you at our seats?"

I nod. "Sure."

Cole and I both watch her melt into the crowd.

He turns and slaps my chest. "Holy shit, son. She's hot as fuck."

I narrow my brows. "Hell yeah she is, and she's all mine so don't get any fucking ideas." My words come out

117

on a growl before I can stop them. What is this woman doing to me?

He holds both his hands up and laughs. "Jesus fuck. Calm down, caveman. I got you. Look around. There's plenty of women here tonight." He shakes his head. "I swear to god, you Collins assholes. Quinn led me to a meeting a few months back at the office, and I thought Deacon was going to crush my goddamn fingers when I shook his hand on the way out."

I grin. "We do like our women, don't we?"

"If I couldn't kick all your asses with ease, I might actually be intimidated."

He's got a point. We'd go down swinging, though.

I nod and try to cool it. I don't know what it is about Abigail, but she has me ready to fight any man who even looks in her direction.

Cole straightens up and his brow furrows. "On a serious note, I've been meaning to set up a meeting. I know you handle the finance stuff at the firm, right?"

"Yeah. You need a consult?"

He nods. "Once this bullshit with the lawsuit is done, I'd like to have a face-to-face and talk shop. I'm looking for some angel investors or VC for an infusion. I know a few, but I want to exhaust all my options. Or look at franchising options. We're starting to stagnate and I'm looking for new growth and capital to make that happen, know what I'm saying? Merchandising and product too. I'm looking to do my own bottled water, protein, and workout gear. It's one of the reasons 50 is here, he did the Vitamin Water thing and made millions. Hell, I may even do my own workout equipment if I can get the capital. I'm not above Chuck Norris-ing my ass on some Total Gym informercials."

I'm surprised he hasn't had a sit down with Covington. Maybe he doesn't know he's in town. "Absolutely. Have you called Wells?"

"No, I think it'd be too weird. I don't like mixing friendship and money."

Makes sense. "Okay, well we can run an analysis and I can put you in touch with the right people. With your connections we could get you new capital easy. I don't handle marketing, but we have a department and I can set up a meeting with my cousin Harlow. She just opened a firm in town. In the meantime, just keep networking with all these celebrities. Do them as many favors as they want and get them in your gyms. When the time comes, they'll return the favor. Like Dre and Jimmy Iovine did with Beats. It's free exposure. Send these celebrities and influencers free shit and have them post pictures with it on their Instagram. Make your stuff the next cool thing and stay relevant."

"I like the sound of that. You know your shit. Always have. Speaking of favors, you think Decker would be into some kind of trade for services? I can get your employees a discounted rate at the gym."

"Definitely, he's been on this big wellness kick anyway. It's all the rage in corporate America right now, keeping employees healthy and happy. Cuts down on healthcare costs, which reduces insurance rates. Preventative health. I'm sure you could work something out."

"Great. I'll call the office. Enjoy the fight. And you better get over there. Some asshole is chatting up your woman. Maybe we'll get an undercard fight in the stands before this starts. You might even win this one." He laughs then walks off.

I look over at our seats and Abigail is laughing at something the old man seated beside her says. He looks old enough to be her grandpa.

Fucking Cole.

I hang back a second to watch her. I swear she could make a new best friend anywhere. Everyone is drawn to her. Now, she's striking up a conversation with the guy next to her. I can't see his face because she's blocking the view.

I strut over there toward my woman. Fuck. I'm already thinking shit like that.

It's too soon.

I know it's a first date, but I just want to zoom a hundred miles an hour into the sunset with her.

Her gaze meets mine and she smiles.

My heart squeezes in my chest at the sight. That's a smile that's only for me. There's this sparkle in her blue eyes as I get closer, and I can't remember ever feeling this way before her.

I take my seat and realize she's sitting next to J.B. Pritzker, the Governor of Illinois.

I stand up and shake his hand. "Governor." We've met once or twice at a few functions and at the Capitol building.

"I was just telling your girlfriend here I don't usually come to these things, but I couldn't say no. It's quite the turnout."

Abigail's eyes go big when he says *girlfriend* but

neither of us correct him. Not that I want to. I like the sound of it.

No, if I'm being honest, I *love* the sound of it.

I love that he immediately thought that.

"Yes, sir. Great for tourism and the local economy. Lots of tax revenue."

We have a seat and I take her hand on my thigh, giving her a gentle squeeze.

The main lights go down and colored lasers dance around the arena. Music fires up and Abigail leans into my shoulder. She smells amazing, like strawberries and vanilla.

"Who should I be rooting for? I don't know any of them."

I tell her about each fighter. Of course, she picks all the underdogs. Chicks usually do.

We fall into easy conversation during the undercard fights, and Abigail winces a few times when dudes knock the hell out of each other about ten feet from us. We're so damn close you can see blood and sweat on the concrete around the octagon.

Finally, it's time for the main event.

Bruce Buffer announces the first fighter. "Hailing from the southside of Miami, for Team Takedown, weighing in at one hundred sixty-nine and a half pounds, Callum Black." The crowd goes crazy.

This fight is a big deal.

Cole trained Pedro so I have to root for him.

"And your hometown hero, fighting out of Team Miller, weighing in at one hundred seventy pounds, the undefeated, welterweight champion, Pedro Mandez." The dude is a damn beast.

This will be his toughest fight, though.

Abigail's eyes are trained on the octagon and right now I only have eyes for her. I have to force myself to watch what's going on, because all I want to do is stare at her.

The referee calls them to the center and they tap gloves, then the fight is underway.

Pedro comes in strong, working Black with jabs. He's a striker so he's trying to stay off the mat. He'll have to do that if he wants to win. They fall into the fence locked together.

Abigail is practically bouncing out of her seat as she cheers. She's such an adorable goof. I take that back; she's a sexy Christmas clown.

"This is awesome. Thank you for bringing me. I'm having a great time."

"No one else I'd rather be with."

"Now who's being an adorable little clown?" Her teeth graze her lip.

I lean in about to claim those tempting cherry lips. The crowd roars and Abigail squeals. The moment is lost but I know she felt it too. Fuck she's incredible, and I'm glad to see her cutting loose and having a good time.

"Oh shit!" The words come out before I can stop them. I'm obviously rooting for Pedro. He's Cole's boy. Abigail is cheering for Callum, since he's the underdog.

Callum takes him down, and the crowd goes deathly quiet. Pedro is the hometown boy.

Callum has Pedro on the mat, hammering his head with

his fist, legs pinning him down. He moves with lightning speed and wraps him up in a hold.

Abigail is the only one around us cheering Callum on. "Tap him out!"

Somehow Pedro breaks free and scrambles, rolling away from him. The crowd surges to life.

The bell rings, just when they're about to obliterate each other.

"That was freaking intense."

I look over and Abigail is breathing heavily. Her breasts are expanding and contracting in her halter top, and fuck, I gotta get out of here for a second, before I put on a real show for these people, in my pants.

"I'm going to go grab us a couple beers."

Abigail grabs my forearm and her eyes are dilated, face flushed. "Hurry back, okay."

I smile. "Be back before you know it."

Holy shit.

I need her, right here, right now. It's bad.

ABIGAIL

DEXTER KEEPS his hand on my thigh the whole drive back to my apartment.

The holes in my tattered jeans allow his fingers to brush across my skin, and my entire body is on fire.

I had no idea I'd get so worked up watching grown men beat the crap out of each other. There's just something so manly and primal about it. My adrenaline spiked, and it hasn't come down at all. I'm one-hundred percent sure the reason is sitting right next to me, driving a manly car, looking manly as hell. He had to be freezing his ass off when he gave me his jacket, wearing nothing but that thin t-shirt the whole way, but he didn't so much as shiver once.

It's hard to put into words what walking into a room with Dexter Collins is like. I just feel—safe, invincible even.

Tonight has been perfect. I can't remember the last time I had this much fun. He's a true gentleman, but part of me wishes he wasn't. I keep getting this feeling like he wants to kiss me but he's holding back. There was a moment during the fight when I thought he was going to. I don't get it at all. I've thrown out every signal in the book, short of taking out a billboard ad. I lie my head back at a red light and look at him with my lips parted hoping he takes the hint, but he just grins at me and squeezes my thigh.

"What'd you think about Callum getting knocked out at the last minute?"

"That was freaking insane. I thought for sure my guy was going to win. Pedro looked dead on his feet."

"Yeah, I thought he was done for. He dug down deep for that knockout."

"I wanted the underdog to win, but it was fun either way."

"Honestly, I didn't think he'd pull it off. I thought it'd be close though."

Dexter and his beast of a car rumble down my street, and I don't want this to end. It's been perfect. I wonder if Dex is going to walk me to my door. Is he finally going to kiss me again? Should I invite him in? Why did I not think about any of this until just now? I don't go around sleeping with every guy who takes me on a date or anything, but I'm attracted to Dex and if he wanted to… I don't know. I guess I'll have to see where things go.

I'm like ninety-nine percent sure he's into me, like a lot, but I'm still young and don't know *that* much about guys. Dex and his brothers are mysteries too and intimidating. Maybe he just likes hanging out with me. Which will suck because I really like him more than I should.

The Chevelle rolls to a stop and Dex parks along the

curb. He slides out and holds his hand out to me. Before I know it, his jacket is on me again.

I pull my keys out as we get into the elevator, and I wonder if Barbie's home. Even if he does want to come in, she might ruin the whole damn thing. We get to my door and Dex hasn't even tried to make a move to kiss me in the elevator. Maybe he's just waiting until the timing is perfect. He's been super fidgety ever since we got out of the car.

We pause in front of my door. I wish I could just read his damn thoughts. I want to know what to do, because I want him to kiss me more than anything in the world. I want him to crash into me, and shove me up against the wall, and do whatever the hell he wants. Anything other than staring at me and saying nothing.

He takes his jacket back, and I stick my keys in and twist the knob.

I turn to face him, and his hands are shoved in his pockets like he's scared to touch me after he held my hand all night and rubbed on my leg. What the hell is going on here? "Well thanks. I, umm, had a great time. We should hang out again. If you want to."

His eyes say he wants to eat me alive, the way he's leaned against the wall next to the door, practically searing a hole in my chest with his gaze, but he's still holding back. I feel like a crazy person. I'm going to explode if he doesn't do something.

His jaw ticks and he swallows hard. "Yeah. I had a great time too. See you soon, Abby."

I blink. "Okay, umm, goodnight." I don't know what else to say and I'm not going to act like an idiot and throw myself at him. That would make work weird as hell come Monday, especially if he rejects me.

I open the door and quickly close it behind me.

My entire mood deflates like a balloon. How the hell did I go from being on top of the world to feeling like absolute shit? My heart pinches in my chest. I don't think I realized just how much I like Dexter Collins until right now.

I kick off my shoes wondering what in the hell that was. I sling my purse to the couch as the doorbell rings. My blood heats to a million degrees, and I think I just switched from confusion to rage in two point two seconds.

I swear, if that's Kyle I will punch him in the face if he gives me any lip for going out with Dex. He probably walked past him in the hallway and is coming to give me shit.

It's the last thing I need when my ego just took a beating. I'm not vain, but I know I looked as hot as I could for our date, I gave off all the signs saying I was interested. I dressed sexy. I shaved my legs and trimmed up the rest nice and neat just in case…not that I thought we'd have sex, but I wanted to be prepared. What did I do wrong?

I march to the door and throw it open.

Dex barrels into me and the door closes behind him.

His intense stare is on me and his arms move around my waist. I start to ask what he's doing but his mouth crashes down on mine, and I'm floating. Just floating on the damn clouds, electricity flooding my veins. A wildfire burns through me and funnels down between my legs. My body just—needs, it needs Dex. It's a want so intense I may burst into flames.

Sweet lord can this man kiss too. His tongue thrusts into my mouth and consumes me from within. He pins me to the wall, kissing me so deep and hard it's a good thing he's pressed up against me or I might melt into the floor.

I whisper against his lips, "About time."

"Should've done that a few minutes ago. Wanted to do it all night." His words come out against my lips as a growl.

"I'm glad you did."

His hand grazes my jaw, and his forehead rests against mine. His breath fans over my lips. "Is your roommate home?"

"No. You'd definitely know if she was."

"Good." His lips claim my mouth once more and I don't hold back.

I give as good as I'm getting, running my hand up under his shirt feeling the hard wall of muscle there.

His lips meet my neck and I might just die. "Which way?"

I tilt my head toward the hall and Dex lifts me into his arms, his hands gripping my ass. My legs instinctively wrap around his waist, my arms cradling his neck.

Our mouths remain fused together as he hauls me down the hallway to my room.

Once we're inside, I slide down the front of his body and lift his shirt over his head because I want him to know without a doubt that he can do whatever he wants to me.

Holy crap, I'm about to have sex with Dexter Collins.

Once his shirt is off, I pause for a split-second, just to take him in. The man is beautiful with his razor-sharp jawline, and neatly trimmed stubble. His eyes are a dark blue that could melt steel.

He unties the back of my top and we fall onto the bed together, tongues and fingers moving a million directions. Exploring and touching each other anywhere and everywhere at once. God he's a ridiculous kisser. My shirt comes off and he rubs a hand over my breast, looking at me all sweet but with a wolfish grin that says he's going to devour me.

Man do I want that. I do but this is going fast and it's only our first date.

Now, who's giving off mixed signals, Abigail?

"Wait." I brace my hands against his shoulders.

His eyes widen, but he doesn't look angry that I stopped us, just confused.

"I want this so damn bad, but I don't want to be that girl. I just, I really feel something between us, and I don't want to look back..."

Dex cuts me off. "It's not like that." His hand slides inside my jeans, rubbing over my clit.

I gasp. I don't know if any other man has ever even found it, let alone automatically.

God, he feels so good. Too good. I couldn't make him stop if I wanted to.

He rises up and slides his body down, taking one of my breasts in his mouth. "I just want to make you feel good, Abigail."

His teeth graze my nipple and my toes curl into the mattress.

I can't believe this is happening. I can't believe Dexter

Collins, a partner at the firm, is half naked in my bed, fooling around with me.

I glance down and my God, he might be the hottest thing I've ever seen. His muscles expand and contract at the slightest movements, and I finally see all his tattoos. They roam up both his arms and snake across his chest and back.

Dex trails his tongue down lower, closer and closer to where I need him the most, but I squirm because it's almost too damn intense.

"Relax. Just let me take care of you, Abby."

Even his voice is hot as sin. If he so much as grazes my clit again, I might come undone.

He unbuttons my jeans and slides them down. Next come the panties and oh my god, I'm totally bare in front of him. He leans back on his heels for a moment, and just sits there, staring at me, completely naked.

He rakes a hand up through his hair and his fingers ball into a fist as he stares at me, first my pussy, then my breasts, and then at my eyes. "God, you're a work of art."

Before I can respond, his face is between my legs, and I feel his scruff rub up against the insides of my thighs. He's licking and sucking and nipping, teasing me everywhere. One of his large, rough hands roams up my stomach and he rolls my nipple between his thumb and forefinger.

My legs instinctively try to squeeze together because the sensations are almost too much to bear, but Dex places both hands on my inner thighs and spreads them apart.

He spreads my legs so hard it burns, but in a good way, like a nice deep stretch.

"I've dreamed about this pussy."

Holy shit. He has a filthy mouth.

I've never had a man say anything like that to me. It's still so surreal. Dexter Collins, in my bedroom, talking about my pussy, and I'll be damned if his dirty talk isn't on point.

He keeps teasing and licking everywhere but right where I want his mouth. It's torturous.

"Tell me you want this, Abby."

I look down and his eyes are locked on mine, his mouth inches away from me, so close I can feel his exhales brush across my skin.

"Please."

"Tell me *what* you want." He flicks his tongue across my clit, one time.

Mother of God.

My hands reach out and claw into the sheets.

The only word I can muster is, "You."

I glance down in time to see the devilish smirk on his face.

"Fingers, mouth, or both?"

I don't even know what I say in response to that. It probably sounds like groaned out gibberish. I'm coiled so damn tight and the only thing my body is focused on is the most intense sexual release of my life.

I nod furiously.

Dexter slides one finger in slowly and my back arches off the bed. He's just—intense.

"So fucking greedy, and wet."

I glance back down and he's taking his sweet time,

grinning, like he knows he can make me come any second he wants to, like he's in total control.

"Give me thirty seconds and you'll be bucking these hips, fucking my hand."

Another finger slides in and I'm about to lose control. He pushes them in deep and curls his fingers somehow to hit a spot I didn't even know existed.

My whole body tenses, and I reach up for the head-board, panting out labored breaths. "I'm so close, Dex. You have no idea."

"Want me to stop?"

"I'll kill you." I stare daggers at him.

Dex snickers and his fingers speed up. Just when I think I can't handle anymore, his mouth clamps down on my clit.

"Ohhh, God. Dex…"

Every ounce of energy in my body funnels straight down between my legs. I hold back as long as I can, trying to savor this moment, lock it in my brain for a rainy day with my vibrator, because holy hell it's unlike anything I've ever experienced.

No man has ever gotten me off before.

Dex suckles my clit and does the curl thing with his fingers again, and before I know it, fuzzy stars dance behind my eyelids, and I'm doing exactly what he said I'd do. My hips are bucking against his mouth and hand, and the best damn orgasm of my life rips through my body in gigantic, undulating waves. My ass comes up off the bed, back arched, toes curling. Dex stays latched onto me, riding out the pleasure with me, his tongue relentless on my clit.

My hands fly down to his hair and I grab two handfuls so hard, I wonder if it's hurting him. "Oh God, Dexter." It's the only thing I can say.

Once my hips decide to come back down to the mattress, I feel tingly all over, like I just huffed a bunch of nitrous at the dentist office. Everything is sensitive, everywhere. Dex trails a finger across my inner thigh and goosebumps break out up and down my body.

"There's nothing better than you moaning my name while you get off." Dex leans up and kisses me full on the mouth but doesn't linger. It's like he's trying to make his escape before we both do more than we should.

I can't be bothered to do much of anything. I just want to lie here until I pass out. I feel like I just sprinted a marathon in three minutes.

How the hell did he make me come that fast? I can't even do that to myself.

Dex hops up and pulls his shirt on.

"I really had a great time tonight. Not just because of…" I trail off, already needing to yawn because he just pulled every ounce of energy from my body. Part of me feels bad. He made me feel so damn good and now he's about to bounce. I should at least give him a hand job or something, help the guy out. But I'm so damn spent, I don't know if I could, even if I wanted to.

When he walks back over, I catch a glimpse of the outline of his hard cock against his jeans. God, he's big. Of course he is. And I got him all worked up and now he's just going to leave.

When he makes it back to the side of the bed, I instinctively reach out and touch it.

His eyes roll back for a second, then come down and land on mine. He leans over and his lips brush up against mine. He nonchalantly moves my hand away. "Another time. Tonight was all about you. See you soon, Abigail."

And with that, he turns and walks right out the door.

I listen for him to leave the apartment, then kick my legs and let out a squeal that comes out of nowhere. But, damn. That was just—wow. Dexter Collins has skills. His damn tongue is magic.

I want to just pass out, but I need to get my phone and do a few things before I go to sleep. I grab my robe and wrap myself up in it. I need to take a shower, but I don't want to, because I smell like Dexter after he rubbed all up on me. I check my phone a few minutes later and I have four messages.

Kyle: Hey, where are you?

Kyle: You should come out to The Gage.

Kyle: Barbie and Nick are totally making out.

Kyle: Where the hell are you? I miss you.

I laugh about Barbie and Nick. How drunk did they get?

I should text Kyle back, but my mind is still on Dex. It just feels wrong to message Kyle right now. The worst part is it shouldn't. Ugh, I know it sounds corny as hell, but I don't get why people can't just get along.

DEXTER

I NAB Abigail as she walks outside the office. It's been exactly two days and twenty hours since I ate her pussy on her bed, not that I'm keeping track or anything. "Excuse me? You work in that big building right there?"

She looks gorgeous. I didn't talk to her Sunday and I was out of the office yesterday.

"Yeah. You better watch out. The boss is pretty cute, and he doesn't let us fraternize with strangers."

"Dating the boss, huh? Sounds like trouble."

"Something like that."

"Man, and here I was about to ask you to dinner. Doesn't look good for me."

She hems and haws for a few long seconds, staring up at the sky, pretending to think it over. "Maybe I can pencil you in. The boss had a big evening planned, though."

I slide a hand to her hip, yank her closer to me, and pin her with my gaze. "I'll show you a much better time."

Her eyelashes flutter for a split-second. "Well, I just, that's some offer. I don't know. I mean I was really looking forward to some takeout and all the Hallmark Christmas movies."

"Thought you had a big evening planned with the boss?" I clutch my hand to my heart like I'm wounded.

Abigail grins like an idiot.

I grab her hand, finally ending our little game. "Where you headed? I'll walk you."

She holds a hand out and hails a cab like it's nothing. Must be nice to be smoking hot in a city full of male cab drivers. I've never seen anyone get a cab that fast and now I'm definitely riding with her in case this asshole gets any ideas.

"Right here. That's my cab."

"Perfect. We'll get some drinks then go to dinner. I know a great place."

"Dex?"

"It's gonna happen, so just agree."

She grits her teeth. "You're not gonna let me leave by myself, are you?"

I shake my head slowly.

Her head cranes around and I wonder what she's looking for but don't comment. Finally, she huffs out a sigh and grins. "Fine. Come on. This food better be amazing."

"Don't ever doubt me, Whitley. You're better than that." I open the door for her.

She slides in. "Yeah, yeah. We'll see how you do on my rating scale."

"Wait, you rank your dates?" I slide in next to her, my curiosity piqued. "How does that work?" My thigh brushes up against her leg and my dick takes notice immediately.

"It's a secret."

"How am I doing so far?"

"Meh… I don't know, depends on dinner."

"We both know I'm the opposite of meh."

"Someone's full of themselves."

Someone's going to be full of me if she keeps lacing her words with innuendo. "It's not cocky if it's true."

"Oh really?"

"Yes, really." I fire off the name of the place to the driver. He better keep his eyes front and fucking center. Wells owns one of the hottest new restaurants in Chicago. He told me to stop by anytime I want, and I can't think of a better time than this.

ABIGAIL SMILES over the brim of her wine glass. She's next to me in a private booth. Wells isn't here, but that's not surprising. The hostess seemed like she knew who I was the second we walked in.

"This place is amazing." She gazes around the opulent dining room taking the scenery in. Everything is white. Except for the walls. They're a slate gray, but the tables and chairs are all white. A silver candelabra hangs over the table and there's a red rose arrangement between us with a few tealight candles. Our first date was casual, and now I'm slowly building up the romance, just like in the movies. Can't blow your load and go full-on romantic on the first date.

Of course, I have to give her the obligatory modest reaction. "It's okay."

"Are you kidding?" She grins. "Anyway, I enjoy being wined and dined, sir."

I have to stifle a groan when she calls me 'sir.' Fuck, it's hot. "What else do you enjoy?"

Her tongue peeks over her bottom lip, and I lean forward and kiss her before she can answer the question. Her cheeks bloom a soft shade of pink.

As I pull away, she sits there, momentarily stunned before her eyes open.

"I enjoyed that kiss. I like spontaneous things like that."

I lean in next to her ear. "I'll make a note." My hand slides up her leg. Personally, I'm thoroughly enjoying the way her skirt rides up her thigh.

"Dex." Her word comes out on a sigh, but she doesn't try to squirm away. In fact, it feels like she's fighting the urge to roll her hips toward my fingers.

My mouth remains next to her ear, and I exhale warm breath down her neck when I speak. "I could fucking devour you right here on this table."

Goosebumps pebble down her arms and I feel them along the bare skin of her leg. "You're making things very hard for me."

"That's my line, Abby."

"You're driving me…"

My hand roams farther up her leg, until I'm inches from her panties.

"Insane," she finally huffs the last word out on a labored breath. "And nervous." Her eyes dart around the room, then roll back when I slide my hand a little farther up to where she wants it.

I lean in closer, close enough I could easily brush her blonde curls away and kiss that spot halfway between her ear and collar bone. "Good." I graze her earlobe with my teeth.

A shiver runs through her entire body and she tenses for a brief moment. "Someone could see," she whispers. She paws at my hand but it's a half-assed attempt at best.

We both know what she wants and where she wants it.

I grin against her neck. "Let them see."

"Dex." She pushes against my hand again.

I start to pull it away and she grips me with her fingers, keeping it right where it was.

That's what I thought, Abigail.

"Can I ask you something?"

"No. I'm afraid of what I'll say with your hand right there."

I smirk and continue my line of inquiry. "Have you seen anyone come near us? Since they dropped off the wine?"

Abigail shakes her head.

"There's a reason for that." I hook a finger in her panties and slide them to the side, exposing her pussy under the table.

"Oh my God." Her breasts rise and fall in her top with each of her deep breaths.

I love every second of how bad she wants this, how much she's trying to fight it, but she just can't. She wants me just as bad as I want her. It takes an act of sheer willpower and determination not to bend her over this table, eat her pussy until she moans my name on repeat, and then fuck her so hard she can't stand up straight.

I slide one finger across her clit, and she lets out a light gasp. "Still want me to stop?" Her pussy is so hot and wet I can feel it on my hand. I rake my gaze up and down her face and body, taking in every single reaction, every bit of data I can gather for future use.

"No." The word comes out on a whisper.

"Didn't think so." I know exactly how to make her come all over my hand without causing a scene. It has to be a gradual ascent, like a good symphony. Start slow, then build to the climax. Unlike last time when I just had to prove I could get her off anytime I damn well pleased. I continue to work her, rubbing lazy circles over her clit. It's only a matter of time before she claws at the linen tablecloth.

Her lips part ever so slightly, and I don't need a better invitation.

It's time.

I slant my mouth over her cherry-red lips and push two fingers inside her sweet, hot pussy. Fucking hell, she's soaked, and my dick rages against my slacks, jealous of my fingers.

Pure, untamed sexual energy courses through her body. I can feel it up against me, feel it in my fingers, in the air around us. She's so damn close, but she's holding back, most likely because we're in public.

I press my forehead against hers, so that we're eye to eye. And fuck if I couldn't get lost in her eyes. They're so innocent and helpless as she stares at me, completely vulnerable in the moment. It's a stare that says, *I want to give myself to you, but please don't hurt me.*

Right then, something stirs deep inside me, and it's not

even one-hundred percent sexual. It's just a deeper connection, on a molecular level, a force that can't be described, pulling me closer to her soul.

"Just let go, Abby. You can trust me."

I take two fingers deep and curl them inside her, hitting that deep spot nobody else knows about. At the same time, my thumb strokes over her clit.

Her eyes lock on mine, inches apart, for another brief second. It's like I'm having an entire conversation with her and no words are being spoken. Then, all at once, her hips rise and her hand grips my forearm.

Her pussy clenches and a tremor rips through her body. I move my other hand over her mouth to stifle her moans, our foreheads still pressed together. Her eyes roll back into her head and I ride out the waves from her orgasm.

After one last, quick shudder, I move my hand from her mouth and kiss her full on the lips.

Her whole body relaxes so much, I almost think I need to hold her up, so she doesn't just slide down the booth and onto the floor.

She looks completely sated, just relaxed. Almost like she's in another world right now.

"That was..."

I slide my hand out of her gently and adjust her panties back. "Just the beginning."

"You're dangerous," she whispers, her eyes still half-hooded.

I lean in next to her again. "You're right..." I look her up and down and pretend to adjust a non-existent flight suit. "Abby, I *am* dangerous."

She comes out of her orgasm coma and laughs.

"You're not a bad Maverick. Actually, you're better because you have the height to go with the cocky attitude."

"That's what I like to hear."

"Gonna take me to bed or lose me forever?"

"Hell. Yes."

I almost don't even want to bother with dinner, but I hate to come here and not take advantage. I'm pretty sure Abigail is starving too. I know how long the days can be at the office.

The rest of dinner goes perfectly, just like our first date. We slip in and out of easy conversations like two people who have known each other our whole lives. Right before we leave, she leans over and blows out one of the little candles on the table. Just one.

After dinner, when we get back to her place, I escort her to the door of her apartment. It almost feels like a glitch in the *Matrix* because I just did this a few days ago.

I know she was just quoting *Top Gun* back at the restaurant, and it's too soon, but words can't express how bad my cock wants to know what it feels like to be inside her. It feels right, and if she wants to fuck, I'm not going to say no, but something about this whole thing with her... I don't know. I just want every moment to be special—memorable. I want us to have a highlight reel of memories, including the first time we have sex. This feels like a normal weekday night after a nice dinner.

Abigail presses a palm to my chest when we get to her door. "I would invite you in, but my roommate is home and she's not great company."

I don't want the night to end, but I don't let it show. I might not want to fuck her right now, but I could still eat her pussy and make out with her until the sun comes up. Or just sit around and talk. I just want to be near her.

"Maybe you should come see my place sometime."

She nods. "I wouldn't mind that. I had a good time tonight, Dex." Abigail leans forward and kisses me then pulls back. "In case you chicken out like you did last time."

I nod, smiling. "Oh, it's like that?"

She laughs. "Yep. It's like that, Collins."

I yank her harder into me, digging my fingers into her hips. "Be mindful of your provocations. I fulfill all verbal contracts."

She hooks both arms around my neck. "Why is it so hot when you talk like a fancy lawyer?"

I kiss down her neck. "Why is it so hot when you come all over my hand in a restaurant?"

Her cheeks go pink. "Dexter Collins, my mom would wash your dirty mouth out with soap."

I grin back at her. She's something else, I've never met anyone like her. "I had a great time tonight too, Abby."

"Likewise, sir." She pulls me into her for another kiss, then leans to my ear. "Yeah, I know you like it when I call you that."

I back her up against the door and press into her, my knee separating her legs in her skirt. I kiss down the side of her neck. "You have no idea, Abby."

"I might have an idea."

"Is that so?"

She nods seductively.

"What was that all about back at the restaurant?" I say.

"What?"

"When you blew out the candle. You had your eyes closed."

"It's nothing. It's dumb."

I brush some hair behind her ear. "Tell me. I want to know, even if you think it's dumb."

Her lips curl up into a smile. "I like to blow out candles and make a wish, even when it's not my birthday."

"What'd you wish for?"

She shakes her head. "I can't tell you or it won't come true."

I kiss her on the forehead. "Okay." Then I work my way down, peppering kisses on her cheek and then her neck. She presses her chest into me when I hit the spot halfway between her ear and collar bone.

Always leave them wanting.

I slide my hand up her skirt once more, through her panties, and graze her clit. She's as wet as she was at the restaurant.

Abigail's head looks back and forth in the hall, like she's checking to make sure nobody is going to walk up on us. I slide my fingers through her slick folds, just enough to give her a little tease, then pull my hand out and back away from her.

"A little taste to remember you by until we do this again." I slide both fingers in my mouth and it immediately brings back the memory of going down on her two days and twenty-two hours ago. "Night, Abby."

Then, I walk off.

DEXTER

THINGS HAVE BEEN phenomenal the last few weeks with Abigail.

Except at work. It's driving me nuts. It's like she changes into a different person at the office.

We still haven't had sex. Just more fooling around and light petting, nothing major. She's holding back and taking things so damn slow my balls might shrivel up, but I don't mind.

I mean, I like her. I like her a lot.

She makes me smile and I think about her nonstop. Don't get me wrong, there's nothing I want more than to fuck her, over and over.

But, the timing hasn't been right. I'll wait as long as she wants me to. I want it to be perfect when we finally take that step.

Something just feels, off when we're at work. We don't have that rhythm, you know? That natural melody that carries us along and makes conversations and actions effortless.

I'm on my way back from court when I spot her by herself in the breakroom. My gaze immediately goes to her ass in the black skirt hugging her hips. How does she look so fucking hot every single day of the year? She's wearing black stilettos with animal print on them. My mind immediately imagines her in nothing but those, legs spread on my desk, heels digging into my ass while I'm balls-deep in her.

"You eating my pudding, knowing my mom sends them to me?" I sneak up behind her, wrap an arm around her waist, and move in for a kiss.

The moment my lips graze hers, she yanks away, like she's on fire or something. It's harsh. Super harsh.

I take a step back and narrow my gaze on hers. "The hell is that all about?"

Her eyes dart around. "You can't be doing that here."

I frown. "What? Why? You ashamed of me?"

She glances around like someone might be watching us and lowers her voice. "Of course not. Why would you say that?" She wraps her arms around her waist and hugs herself, like she's putting up some kind of wall I can't break through.

"You're pulling away and looking around like someone might see. You don't want me to meet your roommate. You seeing someone else?"

She shakes her head like I'm an idiot or something. "It's nothing like that. Calm down. I'm just not a fan of public affection."

"Didn't mind in the restaurant."

She whisper-screams, "I don't *work* in that restaurant. I don't want people to think differently of me."

146

I take a step toward her, and she takes a step back. "People are going to find out about us."

Her eyes narrow into slits, and I can't believe she's actually upset about this. I don't get her. We're great together. She wants me. It's obvious, and I feel the exact same way.

She moves to go around me.

Get your goddamn house in order, Dexter. This is ridiculous. You can land 10-figure clients but can't handle a twenty-four-year-old paralegal?

As she walks by, she stops, and her voice softens. "I want to talk about this with you, just not here at the office. Is that okay?"

"Sure. Whatever."

I immediately feel like a dickhead, but fuck that. What if I want to talk about it here? Does she think I just want to mess around and have a middle school romance with her? We sneak off and fool around under the bleachers and then move on when we go to separate high schools? I'm not messing around with her. I want her, and I'm not putting on an act while I'm at work.

I'm not going to walk around and pretend everything is platonic, then as soon as we leave the office where nobody can see she gets to turn into a new person and fuck my mouth and my fingers. That's not how this works. People need to know she's off limits, at least the men around here do.

She frowns, almost looks hurt.

I don't think I have any reason to feel bad, but I do. I don't like it when she's upset. What the hell is wrong with me? Shit.

She starts to walk off, and I narrow my eyes on her. "Hey, Abby." I reach down and grip her forearm, stopping her in her tracks.

Her gaze tilts up to meet mine. "Yeah?"

"This thing here." I motion back and forth between us. "It's real. You can pretend all you want, for now, but you're not fooling anybody. You're mine."

"You're ridiculous." She scowls and stomps off.

I don't even try to hide my amusement. She can be as stubborn as she wants, it only makes my dick harder.

When she turns the corner, I catch her profile, and she's glaring even harder.

Fuck, she makes me crazy.

Now I want to go after her and kiss the shit out of her in front of the whole goddamn office.

Just to show her I can, and I will.

ABIGAIL

UGH!

How is Dexter so cute and annoying at the same time?

He looks so hot in his three-piece suit today, and I have to remind myself it's no excuse for him to act like a damn caveman.

Cornering me in the breakroom and trying to make out with me? What's that all about?

I honestly don't know what I'm more upset about—the fact he damn near groped me at work—or the fact that deep down I really liked it. What the hell is wrong with me? It was so inappropriate and yet I wanted to lean into him, kiss him back.

I shake my head at my ridiculous thoughts. I go out of my way to avoid office drama and politics. The Chicago firm is just as bad as Dallas.

What I do on my own time is my business, and if people want to speculate about that, whatever. But I *will* be professional at all times at work.

People still talk about Quinn and Deacon banging like rabbits in the supply room.

It's not that I don't want Dex. We have great chemistry, and yeah, I feel something there, but I'm not ready to settle down and get serious. I'm just not. I'm too young. He needs to slow down.

Dexter is amazing but the way he spoke to me in the breakroom, it's like he thinks I'm his property.

If I'm honest with myself, though—it's hot. It makes me want him even more.

I have to wonder if I'm actually irritated, or if my brain is just being a dick and telling me I *should* be irritated, and that's what's wrong. I'm so confused about this whole situation.

Dex makes me feel so damn safe around him, and I don't want to want a man to make me feel safe, if that makes any sense?

Gah, I'm so confused right now.

He has me spinning a thousand different directions, like a tornado blowing through my life and scattering things everywhere.

He needs to get it through his thick head that I don't belong to him before this gets even more out of control. I can already see this all playing out. I fall head over heels, he continues this behavior until I'm afraid to even talk to another man without him being petty and jealous. It all culminates with him breaking my heart and judging by the way I already feel when I'm around him, it will take a long time to get over it.

I'm in a really good place right now. Well, other than needing to get a *place* of my own, but still. Professionally,

I'm killing it. Decker hands me important projects and puts his full trust in me. Multiple partners praise me for doing a good job all the time. It's the one place in the world where I have everything in order.

I've made a life for myself here. I feel wanted and respected. I have friends.

Some of them are guy friends and ugh, Dexter has a serious problem with that, I can already tell. I'm not going to ditch my friends and be a jerk because Dexter doesn't approve.

I've been blowing Kyle off ever since Dex and I started this up, dodging him in the hall of my building like a chicken shit. All because him and Dex don't get along. That's not like me. It's not who I am. Even Barbie asked me what crawled up my ass the other day. For her to take notice of something I'm doing means it must be obvious as hell because she lives in her own little Barbie world every minute of the day.

I pull out my phone and scroll through all the texts I've been avoiding.

Kyle: Hey, just got off work. Wanna split a pizza?

Kyle: Drinks after work, you in?

Kyle: Where are you? I knocked earlier. Nick got Chinese if you want to come over.

Right when I'm about to type out a reply, Rick Lawrence knocks on the edge of my desk. He has that same mischievous smirk across his smug face as always. He's such an asshole, and I have to refrain from taking all my frustrations out on him.

What the hell?

He's wearing rosary beads around his neck.

Can the day get any weirder?

"Got a minute?"

I shake my head. "Not really."

"Great." He cranes his head around, looking at the other paralegals. "You seen Mary?"

I fidget with some files, pretending like I'm reading them and about to get up and leave, hoping he'll take the hint and go away. "Did you try her desk?"

"Yeah. Even checked under mine but she wasn't there, where she belongs."

What is it with the male egos in this place?

He stands there, staring at me, like this is an everyday conversation and he's done nothing wrong.

I sigh, because he won't leave. "Haven't seen her. Did you need something, *Rick*?" I think about calling him "Dick" instead, but he'd wear it as a badge of honor and stick around and make it even more awkward. Or actually comment on his dick and send me sprinting to HR.

He leans in toward me.

I immediately lean back because I don't want him near me, and part of me knows Dex might come out of nowhere with a Macho Man elbow drop if he sees another man in my vicinity.

Rick's voice lowers. "Got new info on that secret shit for you and Decker. How would you like to proceed?"

"Can you email it to me?"

"Will do." He takes one final glance around the para-legal bullpen. "You see Mary around, you tell her Rick says hey."

I roll my eyes. "Will do." I'd agree to just about anything to get him out of here.

"Peace be with you, sister." He grins his ass off and kisses the cross hanging around his neck, then makes a cross with his finger over his chest. As he's walking away, he hollers over his shoulder, "You both love your mothers. He loves Christmas too. Stop fighting it. You have a lot in common."

What. The. Hell.

He never turns around, just disappears through one of the side doors.

I swear to God he's a damn soothsayer. If he warns me about the Ides of March, I'm finding a bunker, removing every sharp object, and locking myself in it. Finally, I shake my head and finish typing out my text.

Me: Sorry about the last few weeks. I've been super busy with work and just life. Wanna meet up for drinks later?

Kyle: Wrong number.

The bubbles immediately start bouncing around before I can type out something snarky.

Kyle: Kidding. Drinks sound good. We need to catch up. The Gage tonight?

I lean back in my chair, already worried that it's a bad idea. Dex goes there sometimes. Hell, it's where everyone from work always hangs out.

I shake my head at myself. I can have friends. I shouldn't have to sit here and stew about this. I never had to before. I'm an independent woman and I can do whatever the hell I want. Dex doesn't own me. Worrying about his fragile ego is not my concern.

Kyle's my friend. Nothing more. He's never given me a reason to think he wants anything more than friendship and I'm not going to shit all over him because Dexter doesn't like him.

If he would stop acting like a Neanderthal around him, I think they'd actually get along.

Me: Does 7 work?

Kyle: See you there.

"Do I KNOW YOU?" Kyle grins when I walk up to the bar.

"Stop. I said I was sorry. I was busy with work and Barbie has been nuts since the whole Chuck thing." Most of that is true, but I still feel bad, knowing the reason I haven't been around is because of Dexter.

"You get a pass this one time." He grins at me. "Nick has a table already. I ordered you a shot."

"Awesome, thanks."

The bartender walks over and hands us the drinks.

I take the shot and knock it back. It tastes like heaven after the day I've had.

Kyle loops his arm through mine as we head toward the table. It's Friday night and everyone is ready to unwind after a long week it seems. The place is packed.

"Hey," I say to Nick as I sit down.

"Hey, stranger." Nick gives me a head nod. "Tell me you didn't invite Barbie."

"Actually, she's on her way. I told her I was meeting up with Kyle and you'd be here all alone. Hope you don't mind. She said she thinks you're the one." I give him a smirk as his face pales. "Feeling okay? You don't look so hot."

He glances to the door, looking for Barbie, then shakes his head. "Please tell me you're joking."

I finally can't contain myself and burst into a laugh. Kyle follows suit.

"I hate all of you." Nick takes a huge swig of beer and fights back a grin.

"Okay, yeah, I'm joking, but I do need all the details of you making out with her."

Kyle laughs. "Oh, man, we missed you. We were starting to think your boyfriend had you chained up somewhere."

What the hell? "Boyfriend?"

Kyle sighs. "Dude, the real reason you haven't been hanging out with us. We're not dumb. We know you've been seeing that douche in a suit."

I shake my head. "I never said you were dumb, I just don't have a boyfriend. And he's not a douche."

Nick jumps in. "Oh come on, Abby, we saw you making out with him in the hallway. Thought Kyle was going to cry himself to sleep because you've been ignoring him."

I take a drink of the beer Kyle brought over, then wave a hand out at both of them. "Oh what the hell ever, you guys. Stop trying to change the subject. We were talking about your make out session with Barbie, not mine, and I would hardly call a kiss making out."

Kyle doesn't seem fazed one bit by my attempt to deflect. "So, you guys getting serious?"

Ugh, what is their deal? They're acting like a bunch of girls. I came here to escape thinking about Dexter.

"Look, no offense, but I don't want to talk about him. I

155

want to hear about Nick getting hammered and making out with the ice queen. I'll buy a round of shots for details."

"Deal." They both say at the same time.

"The sacrifices I make for inebriation," says Nick.

"Oh, poor baby." I fake-pout my lips and reach across the table to ruffle his hair.

"You owe me two shots for reliving the torture."

I crack up laughing. "Was it that painful?"

"It was pretty crazy." Kyle straightens up in his chair like he's getting ready for story time.

"Enough, please." Nick shoots me a pleading look. "I'll tell you everything, for shots, of course. But it really wasn't as bad as Kyle makes it out to be."

Kyle stares at him. "Dude."

"Okay, fine." He turns to me. "So, first off, I was crazy hammered. Like, beyond-all-rational-thought drunk."

I nod. "Duly noted."

He looks up toward the corner of the ceiling, searching for the right words. "You know when you had to watch those nature videos in science class, and they show like a boa constrictor swallowing a rat?"

I can barely contain the laughter building in my chest and roll my hand forward like *continue*.

"Kissing her was how I always envisioned that rat's point of view, like what he would see right before the snake swallowed him."

"Keep going," says Kyle.

"Yeah, so we were in a cab when it happened, and the worst part is…"

"Wait for it." Kyle nudges me, already about to die.

"Well, like, right after we, umm, parted ways, so to

speak, she gets this look on her face, like, I don't know how to describe it, but she tilts her head down and projectile vomits all over my chest, right there in the cab."

"Ewwww!" I squeal.

Kyle bursts into laughter. He's so loud everyone in the bar turns to look at us.

"You were right, I didn't need details. Can we please never discuss this again?" I can't imagine how mortified Barbie must've been. I mean, I feel bad for Nick and everything, but damn.

"I'm quite all right with that arrangement." Nick bumps fists with me.

I shake my head, trying to rid myself of the thought of that cab ride. "All right. I'll order shots. What do you guys want?"

"Tequila," they both say at the same time.

Uh oh. This could be a long night and a morning headache. I take a deep breath. "Okay, let's do it."

DEXTER

I PULL up to the entrance at Covington's mansion that sits right on Lake Michigan. He bought the land last year, but I haven't been over since he built everything. The black wrought-iron gates have a solid-gold WC right in the middle, and I'm almost positive it's twenty-four karat.

I laugh to myself. How gaudy can this motherfucker get? It's hilarious because I know he's self-aware and does this shit just for that reason.

The man is a troll one-hundred percent of the time, only he buys companies just to fuck with people and piss them off. I guess when you have "fuck you" money, you can do those types of things. The security camera zooms in on my face as I roll my driver's side window down. I press the intercom button and wait.

"Can I help you, sir?"

I'm still laughing, barely able to get the words out. "Tell Covington to open this monstrosity."

The man doesn't show one hint of irritation. He sounds British too. Of course he does. "One moment, sir."

What the hell? I shake my head and can't quit snickering.

The gates part and I drive up, snaking around a few hills, not believing my eyes. I knew this bastard was loaded but holy hell. When I finally reach the main drive, the house is massive. The front is a mix between brick and rock with floor-to-ceiling windows between that look like they're three stories high. I don't even want to know how he had those fuckers hauled in here. Okay, maybe I do want to know.

I bet he rides around on a Segway with a little helmet barking orders at people.

Decker is out of his fucking mind if he doesn't want this guy for a client. I don't give a shit what kind of kinks he's into. Bet he has a damn sex room ten times bigger than the one in that *Fifty Shades* movie. Yeah, I watched it to get laid. I've made worse sacrifices and Dakota Johnson is hot.

Anyway, what Wells does is none of my business, but I'd be curious to see a giant torture fuck chamber. Who wouldn't want to sneak a peek at that?

I snake around to the side and there's a damn helicopter landing pad. I pass by the eighteenth green of his golf course that's on the property. This guy has it all.

I pull up to the roundabout that circles the front entrance and park Betsy.

The front door swings open.

I exit the car and tuck some confidentiality paperwork he asked me to bring under my arm. Covington has a rocks glass in one hand and a cigar in the other. The British butler guy follows him, but he waves him off.

ALEX WOLF & SLOANE HOWELL

"You like?" He holds his hands out, barely keeping a straight face while he asks the question.

He's in a black silk robe, and all he needs is a few blondes with fake tits on his arm and he'd put Hugh Hefner to shame.

"It's gaudy as fuck and you look ridiculous."

"Good, that means I'm winning at life." He bursts into a laugh. "Fucking Collins, the straightest shooter I know. You're as honest as they come, and that makes you a great friend." He glances over at some lights right off the lake. "Building this pissed off everyone in a two mile radius. It was glorious. Should've seen all the petitions filed."

I shake his hand and he pulls me in close and leans down to my ear.

"From overhead, the house looks like a giant cock and the landscaping is a giant middle finger to anyone flying overhead."

"You'll always be a ten-year-old boy at heart."

"Pissing off people with opulence and some nice pussy are the two things that do it for me. No point in having money if you can't enjoy yourself."

I follow him up to the door. "Indeed."

The front entrance opens into a large foyer with twin staircases that spiral up both sides of the room to the upper level. We pass through a breezeway underneath the staircase. The hall splits three ways and we go to the left to his den. Rich brown couches and a ton of leather-bound first editions throw off a historic vibe. You'd think they'd all be for show, but underneath the shit-eating grins and practical jokes, Covington is a genius. He's a shark and I know for a fact he's read every book in this room, and more than that, understood what the hell he was reading. He's the kind of guy who does keg stands while quoting *Wealth of Nations* and arguing the merits of supply-side economics.

"You like cigars?"

"I don't turn them down."

"Come on." He takes a puff and pats me on the back.

We pass into an anteroom that's a giant humidor. There's a huge display on the wall showing humidity levels and temperatures.

"You've never had one like this before."

"Oh yeah? Why's that?"

"They were a gift."

"From who?"

"Raul Castro."

I raise a brow. "No shit?"

He shrugs like it's nothing. "Had some business in Cuba."

I don't even want to know. I laugh and shake my head. Dude is whack and eccentric as fuck. Of course he only smokes the best cigars in the world.

He punches in a code and pulls a cigar from a drawer, then shuts it and an electronic bolt retracts into place.

He pushes two more doors open and it leads into what I can only describe as the most elegant sports bar in the world. There are flat-screen televisions everywhere, and a giant screen with a projector on one side. They're all tuned to sports, C-Span, and stock market channels.

"I do my best thinking in here, come on." He motions me over to a long bar with a marble top that runs along one side of the room.

I take a seat on a leather barstool.

He opens a box and pulls out a bottle of fifty-year Glenfiddich like it's no big deal. I accept a rocks glass with it poured neat and take a sniff. You can't just throw back a twenty-five-thousand-dollar bottle of scotch, though Covington probably goes through one a week.

He takes his time cutting the end of the cigar and hands it over. "Can't drink that swill you're used to with this cigar. This shit is an experience."

I lift my chin and take a sip. It's fantastic. I can taste notes of vanilla and toffee. I don't know if it's worth twenty-five grand, but fuck it, I'm not buying.

"It's orgasmic, right? Now for the cigar." He pulls out a lighter that looks like a small welding torch.

I decide fuck it, I trust him. I puff as he holds the blue flame to the end.

As soon as I taste the smoke and take a few more puffs I immediately relax.

Look, I'm a man who has a lot of money, an important job—I'm happy. But right now, I feel like a fucking titan, like a peasant made into a king for the day. Covington operates on an entirely different level of wealth than my family does.

We bullshit a bit more and he takes me on a tour of the bottom floor. I keep bracing myself for it, almost a little excited, but there's no sex dungeon in sight, yet. I find myself a little disappointed, but I'm not going to ask him to fucking see it. There's an indoor pool, a bowling alley, two movie theaters, and a gym that would make Cole Miller's dick harder than a diamond in a hailstorm.

Covington pauses randomly, in the middle of a normal hallway. "Did you sign the paperwork?"

"Of course." I pull out the accordion folder I've been toting around.

"Let me see it."

I pull out the non-disclosure shit and hand it over.

Covington looks relaxed, but his eyes work the pages over, a million calculations running through his brain. Finally, he hands it back. "Okay, so look, Collins, I like you. We'll start with a trial run. I'll hand over a few of my newer entities, still nothing to balk at for someone like you. They require quite a bit of start-up administration-type work, instead of usual legal maintenance, so it should net some decent billable hours for your firm. They're a healthy mix of different industries. The rest will remain in care of Cooper and Associates, but that's a temporary situation for now. You outperform, you get the rest."

I know I secretly hoped he'd want to shift everything over but that's a pipe dream. If I was him, I'd do the exact same thing, throw me a wide range of entities and make sure I nailed each one. This is a test; one I will not fail. "No problem. I don't mind kicking a little ass to prove myself."

"That's what I like to hear. Let's go celebrate. You're driving."

Oh shit. Tomorrow is going to be a long-ass day.

Fuck it.

"Let's do it."

I hang out for a bit and Wells gets dressed. He's gone for roughly five minutes and comes back looking like he just stepped out of a GQ spread.

It makes me wonder if he has a personal stylist back there on call to get him ready at a moment's notice.

The two of us walk outside and Wells has to fold himself into the Chevelle. The fucker is like six-four and he's not a twig.

He definitely looks intrigued by the car. "Nice. I like it."

"Restored her myself. Took five years."

"No shit? Why so long?"

"Some of us work for a living, asshole."

He laughs. "I know. Being me is pretty awesome."

I nod. "Pompous motherfucker."

"Always. You ever do any racing?"

"Nah, not since my college days. Got busted and ticketed. Parents were pissed."

Wells nods. "Yeah, that happens when you get caught." He grins and turns to face me. "I never learned my lesson."

This fucking guy. Just when I think he can't get any more arrogant, he outdoes himself.

"We'll go sometime. Friend of mine owns a few stock cars for Nascar and has a private track. You could bring this beauty out there if you want. Open her up a little."

"Sounds awesome."

"What's under the hood?"

"All original, four-fifty-four."

"She purrs like a kitten."

"Damn right she does. Her name is Betsy." I pat the dashboard lovingly.

Wells nods. "Nice to meet you, Betsy. Hopefully, this won't be our last encounter."

We blast off into the night and forty minutes later arrive at The Gage and head straight to the bar. I hadn't planned on coming out at all tonight. I was hoping to convince Abigail to come over to my place for a movie. After the way we left things at the office, I want to make it up to her. I was kind of a dick, but I'm tired of all her mixed signals. Wells called and I couldn't pass up the opportunity to sneak in and meet with him earlier than expected. She didn't act like she'd be up for anything anyway. Maybe it's for the better. Let shit cool down a little.

I lean on the bar while Covington orders a few drinks.

I glance around and quickly jerk my head back.

What the fucking fuck?

Abigail is at a table with those two friends of hers. She's slouched in her seat a little and laughing like an idiot. Her eyes are all glossed over and judging by her mannerisms and the wild way she flings her hands around, she's wasted.

"Gotta be fucking kidding me," I growl. My face heats a million degrees with every second I see her there.

Wells leans over, clearly intrigued. "Ahh, the girl from the club. The one you're falling for."

I whip around to Wells. "I'm not…" I see it in his eyes and can't even finish my sentence.

He knows. Fuck, the whole world probably knows, but Wells *definitely* knows. The fucker can read any situation, probably knew it that night at the bar.

"We've been dating." I pound my drink and set my glass down a little harder than needed.

Wells seems amused, like he's just waiting for something to happen. Like he *wants* something interesting to happen. It's how he is. "Does she know that?"

I fire off a glare in his direction.

It only makes my blood run hotter. Is he testing me? Seeing how far I'll go to defend something important to me? Is it a metaphor for his companies?

He glances over at the table and snickers again, shaking his head. "Christ, Collins. I don't know how to offer you any counsel. My experience doesn't extend to this type of situation. My women don't pull stunts like this." He leans in closer. "What are you going to do about it?"

Just as he says it, Abigail dies laughing and reaches over for Kyle. Her hand drags down his forearm and my hands ball into fists.

"Fuck this shit."

"Atta boy." He leans back, highly interested, as I shove off from the bar.

I glare back at him, scowling. "You can shut the fuck up too."

It only makes him grin wider.

I storm over to Abigail's table.

Lifting her head up, Abigail meets my gaze. "Heyyyy, Dex!" She lets out a giggle and slurs the shit out of her words. She turns to her dumb fucking friends. "You remember Kyle." Her arm shoots out and she nearly falls off her damn chair.

I grab her arm to steady her, then lift her up so she's standing.

Kyle starts to get up and say something.

I wheel around on him. "Fuckin' do something, kid."

He sits back down but glares at me. I glance over and his buddy's eyes are two giant white orbs.

"Sex-Dexter, you need to stop!" Abigail slurs her words again and smacks at my hand.

How can she be this fucking irresponsible? Usually she's the more mature one out of the two of us. I have to remind myself she's only twenty-four.

"I'm taking you home. Grab your shit, let's go."

"No you're not." She points a finger in my face. "You're not my boss." She waves the finger around, trying to finish her thought. "Here, anyway. I'm my own boss. I do what I want when I want. You don't own me, asshole."

I now understand why Decker is always getting migraines dealing with our childish shit all the time. I point to the door. "Go to the car, now!" I bark the words at her.

"Fuck you!" She yanks her arm away from me and moves toward the bar.

"What the hell is your problem, man?" The other guy stands up this time. He must've sat there and worked up some courage.

"You better sit the fuck down, piss pot." I take a step in his direction. "Try something and I'll put you through that goddamn window." I turn and point right at Kyle. "My *problem* is *him*."

Kyle shrugs and leans back, trying to look cool. "She said you guys aren't together, man."

He's pretending to not look scared, but he's practically quaking in his fucking Dockers and Bugs Bunny shit. Who the fuck dresses this ass basket? His mother?

I lean down and get right in his face. "You listen to me and listen good."

He starts to say something, and I grip the collar of his

shirt, just hard enough to choke him a little. I really need to calm the fuck down, but I've had it with this piece of shit. I already know he'll play the victim to Abigail after this, but I don't give a fuck.

"I know the fucking game you're running, and it ends tonight. You pretend to be her friend when we both know what you're really up to. You play the nice neighbor and listen to her problems, but all you're doing is waiting for her to get so drunk she touches that little toddler dick of yours just one time."

His eyes move to the ground, then he glares back up at me. It tells me everything I need to know.

I let go of his shirt and he gasps for air. I point in his face. "Stay the fuck away from her or the only way you'll get laid is up in a goddamn hospital bed."

His buddy steps over and gets in my face. "How about you go fuck yourself. You think you're better than us in your expensive suit acting all tough? Maybe she likes the attention, and did you ever think maybe she wants one of us to take her home and fuck her? She was pretty flirty before you got here. Yeah, really slutty. I wouldn't be surprised if she wants both of us to take her home and…"

I don't hear the rest of his sentence because everything sort of fades off for a second. So much rage consumes me all I see is red and hear people scream and yell.

I ram my forehead straight into his nose and hear the sound of bone crunching against me. Blood spurts down his face.

His voice goes up about four octaves and I'm pretty sure he's crying, but it's hard to tell with the blood running down his mouth. He clutches both palms over his nose. "Oww! What the fuck, man?"

Kyle's eyes go big and he stares up at me. His hands tremble on the table.

Good.

I glare right at him. Fuck it, I already broke his buddy's nose, I'd better squeeze every ounce of intimidation I can out of the moment. "How about you? You want to try to fuck my girl too?"

He shakes his head back and forth so hard I worry he might injure his neck. "Sh-she's all y-yours."

"What I fucking thought."

ABIGAIL

I DON'T KNOW what the hell just happened, but my blood is boiling so hot I can't see straight. You ever get so damn angry because other people are acting like idiots that it sobers you up instantly?

Suddenly, my thoughts are clear as day and none of them are good.

What the hell is Dexter's problem? Oh yeah, he has caveman syndrome. He thinks I'm his property.

To hell with men!

I'm going to have to find a new job. I should've known better than to get involved with someone at work, let alone a damn partner.

Just as I step outside, the cold air socks me in the face, sobering me up even more. People start shouting inside and there are screams.

Oh my God, what just happened? I start back for the door just as Dexter walks out.

His hands are balled up in fists and a vein bulges on the side of his neck. His friend is practically bouncing on the balls of his feet behind him, like he's all amped up on adrenaline.

I immediately recognize the guy from his social media pages when I was doing research for Decker. It's Wells Covington. What the hell does Decker have me doing?

I don't know if I should say something to Dexter about it. Decker was very explicit in his instructions—although now he's on my shit list too, for putting me in this situation. I finally decide it's best to keep my mouth shut; I'm not losing my job to go along with this shit storm of an evening.

Wells follows behind Dex and smirks at me. They stop for a moment and Wells talks loud enough for both of us to hear.

"Thanks for the fun. I'll find my own way home so you can tend to your situation over there." He nods directly at me and heat rushes into my face.

I shoot him a scowl I thought only Dexter could deserve tonight. What an asshole.

My nostrils flare and my nails dig into my palms. "Oh, so I'm a *situation*, Dexter?" I throw my hands up and try to ignore the people now gathering around us on the sidewalk to take in the rest of the show. I spin around and yell at all of them, "What are you looking at? Mind your freaking business!"

"Get in the damn car!"

I start to protest, just because I'm sick of him telling me what to do, until I see the harsh lines on his face. His eyes narrow into two dark, cold slits.

Dexter is being a complete buzz kill.

Yes, I drank more than I should have, but he's not my

father. I can drink if I want to. I don't have to work tomorrow.

I stomp over and get in the Chevelle, just to get away from all the people on the sidewalk. It's so damn embarrassing. I lie my head back on the vinyl seat. More and more people are walking out of the bar and staring around.

Why the hell was he so upset? Okay, yeah, I was drunk, but it's a damn bar and I was with my friends. People from work get hammered there all the time. I've gotten drunk with Dexter on more than one occasion, including the time we made out in front of the Chicago Bears.

But if there's one thing I do know, it's this: I don't like Dexter being mad at me.

As much as I know I didn't do anything wrong, clearly, I did in his mind. My stomach sours at the thought I made him so mad he acted like that. I refuse to take the blame for his bullshit but all I want for now is to get him to calm down. I do know I never want to show my face in The Gage again. It's completely humiliating. I throw my hands up. And of course that's exactly what he wants to happen. He'll be getting his way if I don't go back there, or go out drinking.

Oh God, and there's Kyle.

He already hated Dexter. Did Dex punch him? From the sounds of all the hollering, I wouldn't be surprised. Do I have to choose one of them over the other? Why is Dexter putting me in this position? It's not right.

We need to get on the same page and fast. This type of thing cannot happen.

Dexter parts ways with Wells Covington and walks over.

He opens the door and slides into the driver's side. "Buckle your seatbelt." It's a command, not a request.

I grind my teeth together. "Stop telling me what to do."

"Stop acting like an idiot."

My pulse is running a two-minute mile and I'm about to snap. I whip my head over to him. "You're the one telling me obvious shit, like to buckle my seatbelt."

He starts the car and takes off so fast the tires squeal on the pavement. "I'm sorry for being concerned about your safety."

"You're insecure and concerned about your ego. Those are your only concerns."

He snickers, but the vein on his neck is still bulging and I can hear him breathing heavily. He zooms in and out of cars, his fingers white-knuckling the steering wheel. Classic rock filters through the speakers.

I've never dealt with this type of situation, outside of seeing it in movies and reading about it in books. I've never been in a serious relationship and Dexter is definitely giving off jealous boyfriend vibes. Does he think he's my boyfriend? We've never discussed that. What the hell makes him think he can tell me what to do?

For some reason, everything just filters up to the surface at once and smacks me in the face. Every emotion in the damn book. Shame, embarrassment, anger, hurt. "Take me home." I growl the words at him, as harsh as I can.

A tingling feeling spreads across the bridge of my nose. Tears threaten to fall, burning in the creases of my eyes. He's made me mad enough to cry. That alone tells me something. I care about him. I want to say it's my reputation I'm so upset about, the relationship with my friends, the embarrassment, but I know it's not. I'm pissed at Dexter and it hurts because I want him, and I won't be with him if this is how he is. I just won't.

He shakes his head and gives me what I can only describe as a parental-like stare. "Fine."

I steal a glance over at him and notice a dark crimson blotch on the collar of his shirt. "Is that blood?"

He glances down at his shirt then back up to the road. "Fuck."

"What the hell happened to you?"

"It's not mine."

My eyes bulge and I bare my teeth at him. "What the hell did you do?" Oh my God, is Kyle hurt? Does he need medical attention?

"Nothing, everything's fine."

"Tell me what happened, or I'll jump out of this damn car. Is Kyle okay?"

His face goes red the second I say Kyle's name, but he takes a deep breath before he responds. "Wasn't Kyle. His friend said things I didn't like. My head met his nose. He'll live, trust me. His pride is the only thing wounded."

I shake my head. Hearing it was a million times worse than thinking it. "Take me home *right now*." My jaw clenches and my fingers tremble against my legs. I'm from Texas and I'm used to men getting in fights, but it doesn't mean it's not childish and stupid.

"Getting you there as fast as I can. Trust me." He snorts. "At least I know you'll be safe in your own bed and not acting like a goddamn moron." He grips the wheel even harder.

I scoff. "Classic. Coming from the guy who just head-butted someone in a fucking bar."

"You know what? That's fair." He points a finger at me. "But you were sitting there shitfaced, alone with two dudes who only want to take advantage of you."

"You don't know what you're talking about." He's so ridiculous, this is insanity. "They're my *friends*. At least they *were* until you showed up. I'm sure they'll want nothing to do with me now, which is exactly why you did what you did. Congratulations, you got what you wanted."

"You don't know why I did what I did because your head is up your ass."

"They're nice to me. And I'm nice to them in return. That's how society works. It's called friendship. You should try it sometime."

"Christ, you're so naïve. It would almost be cute if it wasn't so dangerous."

"Well, it's no longer your concern. This isn't going to work so you don't have to worry about it happening again. I won't be with someone who goes around beating up anyone who talks to me."

"Would you listen to yourself? I'm not a fucking animal. I didn't headbutt that douchebag because he was hanging out with you."

"Why'd you do it then? Enlighten me."

Dexter shakes his head. "I had reasons, okay?"

I turn in my seat and glare at him. "No, tell me. Don't hide behind your actions like a chicken shit now."

His voice kicks up an octave. "Okay, fine. Your *friends*

want to take advantage of you. I know this because I was a guy their age once. I know how they are. They're bad fucking news and you're too blind to see it."

I shake my head. "You're so full of shit. You were jealous and went into a rage because I was drinking with my friends. The same way you threw a little tantrum when I didn't want you to kiss me at the office. You're a grown toddler who kicks and screams when he doesn't get his way."

"Oh bullshit, I know that's all they want from you because they fucking told me."

I feel the color drain from my face. More tears come and I don't know what to do because I've never felt this way and they won't stop. My jaw clenches. "You're lying."

His eyes dart over my direction and his glare softens. "I got up in Kyle's face and told him I knew exactly what he was up to and that it was going to end. His buddy got pissed and stood up and told me maybe they'd both go back to your apartment and fuck you, that you'd been all over them all night acting like a slut. That's when I lost it and headbutted him. He was disrespecting you and he wanted to take advantage of you. Look, Abby, there are women across the country getting shit slipped into their drinks by smarmy little cocksuckers like those two every damn day. I haven't punched anyone in ten years. I'm not a violent person. Think whatever you want, though. I knew what they were up to from day one, that's why I've been an asshole to them. They're not your friends, no matter how bad you want to believe they are."

"Maybe I am naïve, but so what? You have to trust me

or this, whatever, between us will never work. You should know me well enough to know I wouldn't go home and sleep with them. I'm young. I moved to the city to live my life the way I want to live it, to have fun."

Suddenly, Dexter swerves the car to the shoulder of the road and slams the gearshift into park. He turns and he stares at me so intensely it steals all the air from my lungs. His gaze is different, and I've never seen him look like this before. It's like he's in pain, on the verge of tears even. He's totally vulnerable right now, the way he was when he told me about his mom and the pudding. His face is a hundred percent sincere. It's so intimate and just, I don't even know how to describe the way he's looking at me. It's a look that says, *I care about you so damn much it physically hurts*. His voice lowers and changes into a pleading tone. "If you want to have fun..." He swallows like he's choking on his words. "Have fun with *me*."

He reaches out with his hand and cups my face and no matter how bad I want to fight it, I can't. There's something about him, some cosmic force yanking us together no matter how much I want to resist. I lean into his hand.

"I want you safe."

"I know, it's just..."

"I don't want to argue. I just want *you*."

My body takes over and I can't even think right now. The moment just overwhelms me, and I think part of me just wants to forget everything that happened back at the bar, but at the same time all I can focus on is the truth I can see in Dexter's eyes. I thought he was just doing the macho, petty jealous guy bullshit, but I can see it all happened because he cares so damn much. And I haven't ever seen him act violent toward other men. In fact, I've only ever seen him be an asshole to Kyle and Nick. Other men have talked to me in Dexter's presence, and he hasn't snapped on them. The exact opposite in fact. Maybe he stiffens a little, but nothing more than that, even when Cole Miller shook my hand, or when I talk to other men at the office. The old man and some of the other guys at the MMA fight flirted with me right in front of him and he just grinned, even though I'm sure it irked him a little.

He must be telling the truth about Kyle, but it's a tough pill to swallow. What a freaking night. Dexter has no reason to lie, and he has no reason to be jealous. I mean, look at him. He could have his pick of the women in Chicago. They'd line up at his doorstep.

I undo my seatbelt, and without a second thought, I slide across the console to his lap. I straddle his thighs and our mouths meet. The temperature in the car doubles instantly. Dexter kisses me deep and hard, but it's full of emotion. There's no denying this connection between us, no matter how hard I want to fight against it sometimes. Caressing his hair, I breathe him in as our tongues roll and dance.

"I'm sorry." Dexter puts both palms on my face and holds me away from him so he can stare into my eyes. "I lost it when he said that shit, but it wasn't jealousy. It was your safety. I just want you safe, even if you end up not wanting anything to do with me."

I nod. "Okay."

His eyebrows quirk up. "Okay?"

"I believe you. Just please don't hit anyone again, even

if they say something about me. I don't like it. I don't like this."

"Okay, I won't. I promise."

Gripping my thighs, Dexter gives me a squeeze. A possessive squeeze that says *I want you and I will have you.* I grind against his cock over his slacks, seeking more friction. All this energy between us from the fight has me so damn turned on I don't even know if I can wait to get home.

I want this. I want *him.* So damn bad it aches.

We finally part and Dexter's half-hooded eyes sear into me. "Two weeks has been a long enough wait, right?"

I nod furiously. "It's torture."

His eyes rake up and down my body as I slide back to the passenger side. Dexter puts the car in gear and floors it back onto the highway.

My entire body heats up and I squirm in my seat.

Holy hell, I'm about to have sex.

DEXTER

I PUT my car in park and go around to the passenger side to open Abigail's door. I hold my hand out to her and the minute her feet touch the pavement, I flip her up over my shoulder and carry her through the entrance of my building.

The automatic front door syncs to the Bluetooth on my phone and opens for me as I walk up. For once, I start to see some real value from that feature. I haul ass through the foyer. I need in my apartment yesterday.

Abigail laughs as I step into the elevator, careful not to hit her head on the ceiling. "Are you going to put me down?"

"Nope. I'm carrying you the whole way, like they do in your little chick movies."

"Hallmark."

"What's that?"

"The Hallmark romances. Those are the best because they're so cheesy it's funny."

"You calling this cheesy?" I smack her on the ass.

She gasps.

When we get to my door, it automatically unlocks with the app on my phone, but I have to actually turn the handle on this one. We walk through the apartment, and I can tell she wants me to put her down so she can look around the place, but there's no time for that. She can get a tour later. I want her in my bed right now.

"I can walk you know?"

"Yeah, but I'm having so much fun."

"You're crazy."

"Crazy about you." I take her straight to my bedroom. Once we're through the door, I flip the lights on and set her down on the mattress. "I need to ask you something serious. And I need you to be one hundred percent honest with me, okay?"

Abigail nods, no longer joking. "Sure, what is it?"

"How drunk are you?"

She looks up at me and pulls her bottom lip between her teeth. "Sober enough to know I've wanted you for weeks." She makes a "come here" motion with her finger.

I don't miss a beat.

She stands up next to my bed before I can make it over, and I kiss her harder than I've ever kissed a woman in my life. At the same time, I unzip her dress and slide it past the curve of her hips.

This is happening.

My mouth goes dry and all my senses are heightened. It's like I'm sixteen again, about to get laid for the first time.

When her dress puddles around her feet, I appraise her from head to toe. She's in a red lace bra and matching panties. I take a mental snapshot because she's just— perfection, inside and out. She uses her foot and kicks her dress across the room. It hits the wall and slides down to the floor.

I reach for the hem of my shirt and peel it up over my head, my eyes locked on Abigail the entire time. She does that sexy shit where she bites her lip again, and if she's not careful I might bite it for her.

"I think we need to take these off." She takes a step toward me and reaches for my pants.

"Agreed."

She fumbles with the button on my pants. I can't remember my cock being this hard, ever. She doesn't even get to the zipper before her hand is down the front.

My head tilts up to the ceiling for a split-second, because fuck, her soft hand on my dick is heaven. My entire body is on fire for her, immolating from within. I want everything, her mouth, her pussy. All of it.

More than that, I just want her.

She's mine.

Her hand is still down my pants when I fist her hair and tilt her head up to face me.

Her eyes widen in shock, then the corners of her mouth turn up into a sly grin. A slight gasp parts her lips and I can't help myself. She needs to know who's in charge in the bedroom, and she doesn't seem to mind one bit. I claim her mouth once more, licking and exploring. Her hand strokes back and forth on my dick, and I groan against her lips.

She takes her free hand and shoves my pants and boxer briefs down my legs, freeing my cock. "I can't believe I just came to your apartment."

I shove her down onto my bed and a soft coo parts her lips. Before she can recover, I spread her legs and stare right at her pussy. "You're about to come in my apartment, repeatedly."

"Holy shit, Dex." She moans when my mouth dives straight between her thighs.

I glance up at her face and her eyes are heavy and sated. They widen when I grip her panties with both hands and rip them apart for getting between me and what I want.

"Holy sh—" Her back arches her tits up into the air.

I reach up and grab both of them, feeling her hard nipples brush against my palms.

I lick all around her pussy, tracing an outline around the edges, just enough to tease her relentlessly. She instinctively tries to close her legs, and I dig my fingertips into the insides of her thighs and keep them spread apart. I exhale warm breath over her clit and lick all the way up her slick folds and end at that sensitive bundle of nerves.

Goosebumps break out all over her tan skin, telling me I'm doing my job correctly. Just when she's about to come, I pull away, put my hands on the backs of her knees, and shove them up to her shoulders. It lifts her ass from the bed and angles her pussy straight up to my face.

Before she can say or do anything, I dive back down and stroke her clit with the tip of my tongue.

"So. Close." The words are barely audible over her labored breaths.

I lean back and fist my cock, then rub the head back and forth over her clit to feel how wet she is.

She stares up at me and our eyes lock. I watch every expression on her face, note every muscle in her body that tenses when I touch her a certain way. Her body is perfect, and I plan to master it, learn every way possible to give her more pleasure than she's ever had in her life.

"How close are you?"

"God." She drags out the syllable. "So close, please."

"Good, beg me to let you come."

"Please, Dex. I want it so bad." Her words come out on a whimper.

I use my thumb to rub lazy circles around her clit, then line my cock up and barely push the head in, back and forth. "Not yet. I want to feel it with my cock." I reach for my drawer and pull a condom out, then roll it on, my hand never leaving her.

"I'm on the pill."

For some reason I frown. Fuck, how does she make me so damn jealous? Why is she on the pill? For whose benefit?

She shakes her head immediately like she can read my thoughts. "I just started two weeks ago, after our first date." She looks away, damn near blushing. "Just in case."

Euphoria shoots through my veins at her admission. I stare back at her, the head of my dick lined up with her warm, slick entrance. I wanted our first time to be special, and while earlier in the evening wasn't my finest moment, I can't think of anything more special than her, here in my room, saying these things to me. Not to mention that moment in the car, on the side of the road. I just cracked.

Something stirred deep inside me and I couldn't hold back my feelings.

I gesture toward my open drawer. "I bought these two weeks ago too, just in case." I hope she doesn't think I'm just saying that, because I'm not. It's true. I lean over to her and our mouths lock. I still can't believe how soft her lips are, how phenomenal she tastes.

I want nothing more than to just shove into her and fuck her so hard she can't walk straight, but I don't. I slide into her and, oh my God, I'm falling, falling hard. She's hot and tight, but having sex with her feels more like a warm hug than just a reason to get off. We fit together perfectly.

Her legs spread apart, and I push deeper and kiss her harder, rocking back and forth. Our foreheads meet and her eyes flutter. She bites her bottom lip between her teeth and soft moans escape her lips each time I push farther into her.

I slide a hand down and circle her clit with my index finger while I push in and out, harder and faster, ramping up in intensity. "Look at me when you come. I want to see *you*."

I'd be lying if I said I hadn't fantasized about fucking Abigail nonstop, since the first time she walked into the office and was introduced with the new Dallas transfers. In my mind, I bent her over, pulled her hair, spanked her ass. Made her go to her knees and beg for my cock in her mouth.

But right now, it's so different. We're not fucking, we're making love and it's perfect; the perfect moment. I feel so connected. Maybe it's because I've told her things

I've never told anyone else. The world just feels right when I'm inside her.

"Dex." Her voice snaps me from the moment, just being submerged in the experience of her wrapped around me.

"Yeah?"

"Please let me come."

"Okay. Come for me, baby."

She nods against my forehead once more, and I watch her eyes as they roll back in her head. Her entire body tenses and I speed my finger up on her clit and drive into her as deep as I can. She clenches around me and it feels so damn phenomenal words can't describe it.

"Oh, God, Dex…" Her words trail off when she bites down on my collar bone.

Fuck, it hurts so damn good. Something about it awakens the primal part of my brain, when men evolved to hunt and conquer. I want to own her, every fucking inch of her body. My hips speed up as the orgasm crests through her body and her low groans turn into audible moans.

"Oh God. Oh God."

I'm about to blow, so I pull out and stare at Abigail, nostrils flared, trying to keep my own orgasm at bay. Her eyes widen and they're two parts excitement one part nervous; the perfect ratio.

I dive down on her pussy again and lick and suck, my fingers digging into her hips, yanking her up against my mouth. Her hands fly out and my sheets rumple between her fists.

I take two fingers in deep and hit the secret spot inside

her while my tongue lashes at her clit. At the last second, I flip her onto her stomach and pull her ass up into the air.

"Oh my God."

I fist a handful of her hair and lean down to her ear. "What's that? Want me to stop?"

"No." She damn near barks the word at me. "Don't you dare."

I grin against her neck. "Good answer." I line my cock back up with her from behind. "Are you nervous?"

She nods toward the headboard. "A little."

I push into her and tighten my fist in her hair. "Good, you should be. I'm going to fuck you so hard you feel me inside you a month from now."

"Holy sh—"

I speed up my hips, pounding into her from behind. Her pussy is so wet it streams down her thighs onto the sheets. "So. Fucking. Tight." I groan out the words.

I expected Abigail to be more submissive than she is, but she's not. Her hips buck back into me and she gives just as good as she takes. It's hot as shit. I don't know how much longer I'll be able to last.

"God, Dex, don't stop."

I let go of her hair and grip both her hips, yanking her back into me as her words fuel my hips forward. The sound of our skin slapping together echoes through the room, and I wouldn't be surprised if she has bruises on her ass tomorrow from my hips crashing into her.

I don't want to finish too early, not before she gets off again, so I pull out and spread her ass with my palms. I dive into her pussy from behind and fuck her with my tongue, licking and sucking.

Abigail let's out a squeal and covers her mouth when it comes out. I lean back and slam back into her and resume where we left off.

"Again. Soon." It's all she can manage to get out.

I know exactly what she means, she's about to come again. I reach forward and wrap a hand lightly around her throat and pull her head back toward me as I drive into her over and over. I slide my free hand around the curve of her hip and reach down so I can stroke her clit while we crash into each other.

"Shit, Dexxx."

The orgasm rolls through her and she clamps down on my cock so hard I can't hold back now. I ride it out long enough for her to finish, then pull out and yank the condom off. I don't know what comes over me, but I have this unbelievable urge to mark her, brand her as mine.

My hand flies over my cock, stroking furiously and my balls tighten. I splay my fingers across her upper back, shoving her chest down to the mattress. It angles her ass up in the air. I hold my cock inches from her and grunt. Every muscle in my body contracts at once, and I shoot hot spurts of come all over her ass, then lash her hot cunt with the rest.

When I'm finished, I can barely breathe. I pant uncontrollably, trying to catch my breath, then stare down at my orgasm as it rolls down her thighs. It's fucking perfect. She's mine. The proof is right there.

She stares back at me, a huge smile on her face. "That was amazing."

I nod. "Yeah." That's all I can say at the moment. I feel like I'm floating on the clouds. Like the strongest narcotic just shot through my veins. It was far and away the best sex I've ever had in my life.

Finally, I shake my head to snap out of my euphoric daydream. "Shit, sorry. Hang on." I get up and walk off to the bathroom, then return with a towel. I stop halfway into the room and just stare at Abigail.

Her long blonde curls drape over her shoulders and frame her perfect face. She's still on all fours, ass up in the air.

"Dex?"

I shake my head again. "Yeah?"

She laughs and glances around. "You gonna clean me up?"

"Shit, yeah, sorry. I was just... I don't know." I walk over and bend down, then drop a soft kiss right on her cherry-red lips. "You're just perfect. I can't stop staring at you."

Her eyelashes do the flutter thing again. "Thank you." I swear she blushes at the compliment.

I grin and move back to clean myself off her.

"Why are you grinning?"

I shrug. "Nothing. Just you blush at that compliment, but two minutes before you were throwing that ass back at me and begging me to fuck you harder."

Now, her face turns full-on pink and she buries it in the covers. "Oh my God. You're not supposed to say stuff like that. I'm so embarrassed."

I can't stop laughing. Once she's cleaned up, I crawl into bed with her and kiss her a few more times, then push a few wayward strands of hair from her face. I swear I could stare at her blue eyes all night. I slide a palm onto her cheek and cup her face in my hand.

She leans into it and does a long, slow blink, like she's about to pass out.

"Don't ever be embarrassed. You're gorgeous and it was hot as hell."

"It was?"

"Fuck yeah." I slide my hand under her chin and lift her face up so we're eye to eye. "Don't be afraid to tell me what you like and what you don't. I want to make you happy, out there." I gesture toward the wall. "And in here. I'd try anything for you."

She grins. "Anything, huh?"

My eyebrows rise. "Within reason, of course."

She taps her chin, pretending she's deep in thought. "Well, I mean all of it was perfect. It started so sensual and slow, and that was amazing. And then you got this look in your eye and I thought my heart was going to beat out of my chest. It was all a blur after that, but it was incredible."

"Anything else?"

Her cheeks turn pink again. "Okay, come here."

I lean in and she pulls my neck over so that her mouth is next to my ear. She licks slowly up my neck to my ear and whispers, "I really liked when you pulled my hair."

I grin like the devil. "Good." I snake my hand up into her hair and give it a light tug. I smile against her lips and say, "I like pulling your hair. And I like you saying my name when you come on my dick."

"You have the filthiest mouth I've ever heard."

"Get used to it, Christmas clown."

She smacks at my chest. "Maybe I will. I kinda like that too."

We both laugh and she curls up against my chest. I stare around the room and up at the ceiling as she falls asleep on me.

I could get used to this. Going to bed and waking up next to Abigail every morning. I kiss her on the forehead. I don't want to go to sleep. I don't want this night to ever end.

ABIGAIL

GROANING AND STRETCHING, I come to and look around the room. The smell of fresh coffee wafts into my nose. I smile as memories of last night play through my mind. I spent the night with Dexter.

Holy crap.

And we had sex. Not just any sex, but like the whole spectrum from making love to hardcore banging, for lack of a better phrase. Phenomenal freaking sex.

The ache between my thighs reminds me just how good he was, and his words filter through my brain. *"I'm going to fuck you so hard you still feel me inside you a month from now."*

I squirm in his bed just thinking about it. He wasn't lying. He has magical powers. I'm convinced of it.

My cell phone beeps from somewhere in the room. I rub my eyes and slide out of bed. I help myself to a t-shirt from Dex's drawer and find my way to his bathroom. I go through the motions of washing my face and brushing my teeth with my finger. It's not the best method but I don't want to have horrible morning breath if he kisses me. It should work.

I find my purse on a chair along with my dress. Pulling out my phone, I scroll through my missed texts while the sound and smell of bacon frying sweeps into the room.

Kyle: Wow. That guy is a fucking asshole.

Kyle: He headbutted Nick.

Kyle: Do you even give a shit?

Kyle: Did you really go home with him?

Kyle: Nick saw you get in his car.

Kyle: I don't know if we can hang out anymore if you're going to date that guy.

I shake my head. He's not sure if we can hang out? I don't even know how to respond to that. I don't like ultimatums, and I believe what Dexter said. It hurts like hell, but I feel like Kyle played me like a fool.

I was nice to him. I genuinely thought he was my friend. I don't know what to do. He's still my neighbor and it'll be impossible to avoid him until I can move out. I'll just have to nod and smile in the hallway until I can find a way to deal with it somehow.

I stop in the living room and cover my mouth when I glance in the kitchen. Dexter is completely naked, dancing around and singing, using the spatula as a microphone. He pauses during the chorus, between flipping two eggs, and does a little helicopter twirl with his dick, then goes right back to cooking.

Laughter erupts from somewhere deep inside me. I don't even know how I laugh that hard, but I can't freaking breathe.

Dex sees me and shoots me that boyish grin of his,

then shrugs. "Tha fuck ya gonna do?" he says in some kind of Boston accent.

I shake my head and finally manage to control myself. To his credit, he stops dancing after he sees me. I wonder if he's embarrassed he got caught and is playing it cool.

I walk over as he puts everything onto two plates. He's acting so sweet. I can't believe he cooked for me, and I'd be lying if I said he didn't look incredibly hot while he did it, dancing and everything. He reaches up into the cabinet for something and muscles upon muscles ripple. He's not huge like Deacon, but he's lean and cut. The ink comes to life all over his torso as he moves around, hell, even when he just breathes.

I finally get a look at his tattoos and they're so interesting. It looks like some ancient Greek buildings, like the Acropolis or one of those things, along with a few philosophers. There is writing. Then some music notes fill in the background along with a few more sayings in what looks like Latin.

"What do your tattoos mean? I've never seen anything like that."

He turns around slowly and does a three-sixty to let me get a look at them. "They're everything that makes me, well me."

"Elaborate, sir."

"Well, I have stuff that symbolizes the Hammurabi code, the Old Testament, Lady Justice. Because I'm a lawyer and it's a huge part of my life. Then I have the musical notes and work from some of my favorite artists, then the double helix DNA structure and some binary code. It's all sort of an amalgamation of me trying to reconcile science and art, the subjective and the objective. Those are things I struggle with internally."

"Well, aren't you just a riddle, wrapped in a mystery, inside an enigma."

"Nice, Churchill. One of my favorite quotes." He eyes me for a long moment, like we're still figuring each other out.

I do a fake little curtsy. "I know things on occasion. So, what'd you cook for me? I'm starving."

"You know I was actually planning to surprise you with breakfast in bed. But this is good. Less crumbs on the sheets."

I walk up, trying to look as sexy as I can, and wrap my arms around his waist. "You cooked for me." I peck him on the cheek. "I don't care where we eat. That's enough for me."

His rough hands dig into my hips again. "Is that so?"

I press a finger to his lips, silencing him. "I have a much better idea." I drop to my knees on the dark, hardwood floors. My knees may hate me later, but Dexter is worth it. Eye level with his cock, I smirk up at him.

His brows shoot up. "Food's gonna get cold."

I wrap a hand around the base of his shaft and stare at it. Wow, it's even bigger than I remember. "Not *my* breakfast." I flick my tongue out, swirling it around the tip. "You were saying?" I bat my lashes at him, sliding my fist up and down him.

His eyes roll back and he groans. "Breakfast can fucking wait."

Dex is big and thick. I take him into my mouth, and I can't fit all of it. I suck my cheeks around him, even harder, just to hear him groan again. It's so damn hot, knowing I can have that effect on him. I wrap my hand around the base and stroke him in a circular motion as I take him in and out of my mouth.

He fists the back of my hair, and I have to fight the urge to lean back into his hand.

Why the hell do I love him pulling my hair so much? It feels incredible, especially when his knuckles press up against my scalp. He holds my head in place, and before long, his hips start to move, slowly at first. I swirl my tongue around him and after a few seconds he's thrusting into my mouth.

I stare up at him with wide eyes and love how he's about to lose control. Tears burn at the corner of my eyes, but it's only fair. He's gone down on me twice and I haven't done anything just for him.

The tighter he squeezes his fingers in my hair, the harder he strains to hold my head in place—it's just raw, and possessive, like he never wants to let go of me.

"Fuck, Abby."

I want to smile at his reaction, but it's impossible with his thick cock in my mouth. The way his face tenses, screws up tight, like he's about to release sends a shudder through me. I love knowing I can get him off this fast. It means I'm doing something right.

It's only like my third time total doing this, but I've watched enough porn to know what guys like while I got myself off with my vibrator.

I stare up at him once more and his jaw clenches.

He moves to pull out of my mouth, and I latch onto him and shake my head back and forth.

His eyes widen. "Fuck."

I want to taste him. I want to make him as happy as he made me, and there's something about girls swallowing that just does it for guys; so I've heard anyway. I have no clue what I'm in store for, because I've never done it, but I don't show it. This is his fantasy and I want to do it for *him*.

His hand tightens in my hair and the burning against my scalp has my senses on high alert. He grunts. "Shit, Abigail."

His cock twitches and he comes in the back of my throat. I gag for a quick moment but do my best to just leave it in my mouth and keep my throat in check.

My fingers dig into his ass with my free hand, and his whole body tenses. His ass and legs are rock-hard, and I keep stroking him as he fills up my mouth.

Finally, he pulls my head back from him and stares down at me.

This is the moment of truth, Abby. Just be sexy. Be sexy.

Our eyes lock, and I open my mouth and show it to him on my tongue. His eyes widen again, and I close my mouth and swallow it all like a shot of tequila, just as quick as possible.

Not gonna lie, it's not awesome. But, it's not the worst thing I've ever done.

Once I swallow, I open my mouth and stick out my tongue at him, just like the girls always do in the videos.

He's grinning like an idiot, his eyes bugged out. "Holy. Fucking. Shit."

I smile at his reaction. For some reason, all I want to

do is make Dex happy and he's smiling like a little boy again. My heart warms and comes alive at the sight.

"That was some next level shit. So fucking hot."

I take his cock in my hand. "Oops, I think I missed some." I clean the rest of him up with my tongue and he's still rock-hard.

He could easily have sex with me for another thirty minutes, especially after I just got one out of the way with that blowjob, but I'd hate to ruin breakfast for him. He worked so hard on it.

Maybe afterward. God, I hope so.

Dex scoops me up by my arms and lifts me to my feet.

He immediately goes for a kiss and I pull away. "Gross, I just…"

"I don't give a fuck." He puts both palms on my cheeks and plants a kiss right on my lips. I don't know what it is, but it's hot once he does it. Like he doesn't give one shit, he just wants to kiss me and that's what he's going to do.

He walks to his bedroom and slips on some boxer briefs, then walks back out.

I can't help but stare down between his legs. He's still hard and it's corralled against his thigh.

He catches me looking. "Later."

"Huh?" I mumble, still in a trance just staring at his sculpted body.

He glances down at his crotch. "There'll be more fun later. We need to eat. Need some energy so we can fuck like rabbits later tonight."

Why tonight? Why not all day? I shake my head and grin back at him. "Okay, Dickens."

He does the worst British accent I've ever heard. "Thou est well versed, is he not?"

I burst out laughing and dig into my omelet. Damn, this dude has skills in the kitchen too. Mushrooms, onion, cheese, and sausage—it's perfect, everything I like. I sip on my coffee.

"Listen." Dex sits down, taking up the stool next to mine. "I know I might have overreacted a bit last night."

I put a hand on his forearm. "We don't have to do this right now. I'm actually enjoying myself."

"No." He shakes his head and puts his fork down. "I don't want shit between us. I don't want things like last night happening again." He wags a finger back and forth at us. "This is serious to me. I'm serious about you and I want to do it right, clear lines of communication."

I set my fork down. "Maybe you overreacted a little."

His brow furrows.

"Those were my friends. Maybe they still are, maybe they aren't anymore, I don't know yet. But, if you want to be with me, Dex, you need to trust me."

His jaw clenches a little tighter and he starts to say something, but I cut him off.

"I know my limits, okay? I'm an adult."

Dex's fingers tighten around his fork. "I just want you to be careful. You don't know guys like I do. There are a lot of assholes just looking for someone to get drunk and take advantage of. And I know you're smart and you think those guys are your friends, but they aren't. You wouldn't believe the types of cases I've seen. The women we represent and the shit that's been done to them."

"I know. I get it. I appreciate you having my back and

looking out for me, but I have to know. What exactly did you say to them? I have messages this morning saying we can't hang out anymore."

"Good. Fuck those guys." He shovels a forkful of egg into his mouth. "I'm sorry if I made you uncomfortable. Or made things difficult for you, but I'm telling you." He huffs out an irritated sigh. "Yeah, I could've handled it differently. I was pissed." He points the fork at me. "Someone needed to give them a kick in the ass. Even if they didn't try something with you, they'd pull it on someone else. You're better off without them. And that Nick guy deserved what he got. I won't apologize for wanting to protect you. If you're pissed at me about it, fine. I can live with that, knowing you're safe."

"I'm just… I don't know, it does put me in an uncomfortable position."

Dex mumbles, "Better than you getting hurt."

"Okay, well, can you just not headbutt anyone else? Please?" I grin to try and lighten the mood.

"I would never do that to anyone who respects you. And I promised you I wouldn't do it again. When I promise something, I follow through, always."

"Okay. Fair enough. But for the record, I will have to have a conversation with them at some point. They're my neighbors and I have to figure out what to do."

Dex glares at his eggs. I know this a tough pill for him to swallow, but to his credit he doesn't blow up like he did last night. Through gritted teeth he says, "Fine."

"You know I mean without you present, right?"

His lips mash together in a fine line and he looks like he wants to explode, but he finally nods. "I understand."

It's almost funny, but it's really not. He's trying, though, so I have to give him that. I finish my food and my coffee. While Dex finishes eating, I walk over and start on the dishes.

He comes up behind me. "You don't need to do that. I have a cleaning lady."

"I want to." I lay my head back on his shoulder as he wraps his arms around my center. "Thank you for breakfast. This is nice. I feel so domesticated."

"Don't get too comfortable. I ain't put a ring on it yet." He laughs.

I smack playfully at his shoulder. "Jerk. I'm trying to say I'm enjoying spending time with you."

He squeezes his arms tighter around me. "I know. It is really nice. Amazing actually. We work together pretty well."

"Oh yeah? Me doing the dishes while you cop a feel?"

He moves my hair away and drops a kiss on my collar bone. "If I copped a feel, you'd know it."

I snicker. "Totally believe you."

"I don't think you do." His hand works up under the shirt I'm wearing and he squeezes my breast.

His hand feels so damn good. It burns a trail of flames up my skin, every time he touches me. When he presses against me, his hard cock rubs up against my ass.

How the hell does he take me from zero to horny faster than his car runs the quarter mile?

"I'll be right back."

I don't want to let go of him. Don't want him going anywhere. "Where you going?"

He whispers, "Protection," in my ear. "Just a sec."

My nails dig into his thigh and pull him back to me as I grind my ass up against him. Shit, he feels so good right there. "I told you, I'm on the pill."

His eyes widen. "You sure?"

I nod.

What the hell is wrong with you, Abigail? My body rationalizes it, but my brain isn't sold. In fact, it's screaming "No!" with big red warning signs. "I'm sure."

Before I know what's happened, Dex shoves me over the counter and yanks the t-shirt I stole from his drawer halfway up my back. One of his large hands kneads my ass, and then out of nowhere he smacks it. The stinging pain radiates up my spine, but it doesn't hurt. It just burns in the most delicious of ways.

I've never been spanked before, but a coo parts my lips and I think I actually enjoyed it. What is this man doing to me?

"What are you doing, Dex?"

"Wanted to see my handprint. It looks amazing."

Before I can get another word out, he's inside me. I'd never truly been filled until I was with Dex. His cock is thick and stretches me in ways I've never been stretched before. I back into him and moan out my approval.

"Fuck, Abby, you keep doing that and this is going to be over fast."

I smile at the counter. He pushes into me harder, each thrust more and more intense until I'm throwing my hips back into him as he pounds into me. It feels so much more intimate when it's bare, skin to skin. I don't know how to explain what it's like being with Dex, but we just have this connection that hums between us on a microscopic level.

I'm so close, and he keeps pushing me higher and higher until my vision starts to blur. Right when I think I can't take it anymore, one of his hands grips my hip, and the other goes straight to my hair.

Damn, when he pulls on my hair, I think I'd do anything to make him happy. It's heaven, pure heaven.

"You gonna come on my dick?" He grunts out the words.

I nod against his hand. "Very. Soon."

When he reaches around and strokes my clit, I lose control. My legs quiver and my body quakes. I clench around him. There's nowhere in the world I want to be but in this moment as the orgasm rolls through my limbs like an electric current, buzzing through my veins.

Once I release, I feel like Jell-O, like I might melt into a puddle on the floor. Dex slips out of me and picks me up, carrying me toward the table.

I half giggle, still in a partial orgasm coma. "Where are you taking me."

"I want you on top of me." He yanks one of the heavy chairs from the table with one hand, moving it like it's nothing.

He sits down and pulls me to him, so that I'm straddled over each of his legs. I stare into his eyes as I lower down onto him, watching his face the whole time.

I trace the curve of his jawline with my hand as I take every inch of him.

He's so deep. Deeper than deep. The angle of his cock hits my spot perfectly, and a small shudder rips from the base of my spine up to my neck and goosebumps pebble all over my skin.

"That's it, fuck me, Abby."

Between his mouth and his cock, I'm already on the verge of another big O. I wrap my arms around his neck and ride him up and down.

He has that young boy look about him again, like he's so excited I'm riding him like a roller coaster. He has these flashes where he's so cute and innocent sometimes.

"Fuck, it's so good when you ride my dick like that. You have no idea."

And then he opens his dirty mouth and all innocence is lost. I nod against his forehead. "It's just as good for me, I promise." I smile at him until he thrusts up and hits my spot again. "Shit, right there. God, Dexter, don't stop doing that." This time my hands grip his hair and it's like someone possesses my body, because I ride him harder and faster. "Don't. Ever. Stop."

Before long, my ass is clapping on his thighs and I can feel my wetness stream down into his lap, but I don't care. It feels incredible. I don't know if I've ever been this wet before.

"Abby, fuck. I'm so…"

An orgasm hits me at the same time and I bite down on his shoulder because it's too much to bear all at once, the intense feeling pooling low between my thighs. "Holy shit, Dex, Dex…"

I seize up on him, clamping down as another one rocks through me. At the same time Dex's cock kicks deep inside me and he lets loose. Hot jets of come shoot into the depths of my pussy and it streams out around the base of his shaft and down my legs.

I stare into his eyes and get lost for a second. I don't

want to get up. I don't want to do anything but sit there and feel him inside me, feel this connection between us I've never experienced before. It's just so *real*.

Finally, our foreheads touch and we grin like big cheesing idiots at each other.

"That was incredible." He cradles my cheek in his palm like he did last night.

I lean into it and close my eyes, nuzzling his hand. "Agreed." I nod, unable to form any words. "We should probably go shower."

"Okay, then I have to go in and work for a while this afternoon."

I can't hide the frown on my face. I don't want to do anything but stay here with him.

As if reading my thoughts, he says, "You can stay here if you want, but we need to go by your house tonight or sometime tomorrow morning."

"What for?"

Dex waggles his eyebrows. "It's a surprise."

DEXTER

ABIGAIL STAYED over at my place last night too, and we fucked nonstop until we passed out. It was incredible. She's so damn young she might wear me out, but I'll go down fighting.

We cruise by her apartment this morning so she can grab warmer clothes.

It's cold as tits outside.

There's no way she'll go for it if I told her what we're doing, so I keep telling her it's a surprise.

Finally, we pull up to Harry Caray's Tavern on Navy Pier.

She looks over at me with a quizzical glance. "A bar? At this time of day?"

I shrug. "It'll be fun. Trust me."

As soon as we walk in, she freezes, and her shoulders tighten. She starts to turn around but I nudge her toward the table. "You're fine. Just smile."

Everyone else is already here, sitting around with beers

wearing their Bears gear. Deacon, Decker, Tate, Quinn, Cole Miller, and Mr. Richards.

"About time," says Decker.

Abigail turns to me and glares. She lowers her voice where nobody can hear. "A heads up would've been nice."

Deacon must've read her lips or something because he turns to Cole and says, "Shit."

Cole grins as Deacon pulls out his wallet and hands him a twenty.

I point at both of them. "What's that all about?"

Cole says, "Bet him a twenty spot you wouldn't tell her she was hanging out with the family."

Deacon shrugs at Quinn. "I didn't think he'd be that big of a dumbass."

Abigail laughs at that then turns to me. "See, you should've told me."

I stare at her like she just sprouted three heads. "You wouldn't have come."

Abigail sits there, thinking over what she wants to say. "Okay that's true, just…" She motions with her head like *can we please speak out of earshot of everyone*?

I follow her over by the bar.

"Seriously, what are we doing? I work with most of the people at that table."

"Oh stop. It'll be fine. This isn't work. You already know everyone except for Mr. Richards. He's good people. It's not like they don't already know about us."

"You told them?"

I shrug. "Well yeah, they're my family. I tell them everything. Especially Deacon."

She finally sighs. "Okay. I just wish you would've warned me."

"Come on, it'll be great." I squeeze her hand and she doesn't protest as I pull her along to join the group.

Tate smiles, trying to lighten the mood a little, and latches onto Abigail. She hands her a Bud Light from one of the buckets in the center of the table.

"I see you stopped being a bitch." Quinn hands me a bottle.

I glance down and Mr. Richards gives me a thumbs up. When nobody is looking, he holds his hands out from his chest, suggesting Abigail has a nice rack and he winks. I shake my head. I did the same thing to him when I had Abigail help out getting him to the Bears game after Deacon royally fucked up and had to win Quinn back, and then again during our little counseling session on the couch.

I excuse myself while Abigail chats winter work outfits with Quinn and Tate.

I walk down and have a seat next to Mr. Richards.

"Don't worry, son. She's a great date. I should know." His gaze moves over to my girl.

I laugh. "Yeah, you would, you old shit."

He dies laughing. "I'm happy for you, kid."

Decker smacks me on the back, a little too hard, and speaks through his teeth. "*So*, this is happening." To his credit he doesn't reach for his temples like he's about to have an aneurysm.

"Yeah. Get used to it. I like her a lot."

Decker sighs. "All we need are some cameras in the

office and for Donavan to start nailing interns and we can film the fucking Jerry Springer show."

"He's already fucked like three interns." I turn to Deacon. "Or is it four?"

"Might be four," says Deacon.

"And we already have the cameras ready. Just have to go in the supply—"

"I fucking hate all of you." Decker bites back a grin.

A waitress brings out our food. It's chilaquiles and some bean dip.

I turn to Decker and lower my voice. "Donavan not coming?"

Decker takes a long drink of a beer and glares at me. "Fuck, man. Please don't start. I'm actually enjoying this, and Jenny is off with her friends right now. I'm trying not to worry about that. I know they're talking to boys and shit."

"Will you just talk to him? Fuck man, it's brutal not having the whole family together. The holidays are coming up."

"I know, okay. I fucking know. It's just…" His jaw clenches. "Look, I've been trying, the timing just hasn't been right. It's not my job to kiss his ass and be his mother. He's acting like a baby, because he is a goddamn baby."

"I know you're marrying Tate, and I expect you to have her back a hundred percent, Decker." I shake my head. "It's a tough spot but it's family too. So, apologize or whatever you have to do, even if you don't mean it. If Mom and Dad still lived here, this shit wouldn't be happening, and you know it. So work it out as if they're here. Find a compromise. Does he even spend time with Jenny anymore?"

"He calls. They talk on the phone and he's picked her up a few Fridays but doesn't speak to me much. Just the bare minimum. From what I can gather from Jenny, he doesn't say anything about me, but I don't press her about it. I don't want her caught in the middle of anything. It's just me he's freezing out."

"Well, good." I nod. All of us are close with Jenny. We all helped raise her.

"You happy now? I want to enjoy my Sunday."

I grip his shoulder. "It'll work out. Don't worry, we're pressing him as hard as we're pressing you. It doesn't all fall on your shoulders."

Decker looks over at me. "At the risk of sounding like a total bitch, thanks. That means a lot."

"And don't worry about Jenny. She might be dealing with teenager shit, but she's a great kid. The attitude is normal."

"How the hell would you know?" Decker laughs.

I shrug. "I don't but I thought it'd make your anxious ass feel better. Eat a goddamn Xanax like an adult, fuck."

"There he is. You were acting too mature there for a moment."

We clink our bottles together and I look down the table.

Abigail blends in perfectly with the group just like I knew she would. Tate and Quinn are doing their best to make her feel welcome. She glances at me and smiles. Fuck, I can get lost in that smile.

Decker turns to me and Deacon. "So hey, I meant to

tell you two. Mom and Dad are flying up for Thanksgiving. We're doing it at my place."

"Awesome." Man, I can't wait. It sounds corny as fuck, but I love everyone getting together at the holidays, especially when Mom and Dad come into town. All of us do. It gutted me moving Mom to Florida. I miss her constantly.

I grin over at Abigail and can't take my eyes off her.

"You two getting serious?" Cole nudges me with his elbow.

I do my best impression of Kip from *Napoleon Dynamite*. "Yeah, man. She accepted my friend request on Facebook, so I guess you could say things are getting pretty serious."

He dies laughing. "She have any single friends?"

"A roommate from hell."

"Crazy, huh?"

"From what I hear."

"I don't know, I like 'em a little nuts. Psychos are good between the sheets."

"Not this kind of crazy. You don't wanna go there, man."

"Go where?" Abigail asks as she walks to our end of the table.

"Nothing," we both say at the same time.

"Mmhmm." Abigail stares.

We finally finish off our food and drinks, then everyone files out the front door.

There's a charter bus parked in front.

"What's that?" asks Abigail.

I nudge her. "To take us to the game."

She shakes her head. "I should've known."

"Yeah, you should've." I lean down in her ear. "Don't worry, we've already made out in front of the team once, so it won't be a big deal when we do it again."

She pinches my arm.

"Ow, woman!"

"You deserved that." She walks in front of me, swaying her ass. "You coming or what, clown?"

I run up behind her. "You're the Christmas clown, not me."

"Mmhmm, let's go, *clownboy*."

AFTER THE GAME, the charter bus takes us back to Harry Caray's, and I drive Abigail home. I don't want to, but the weekend is almost over, and we have to work tomorrow. It was awesome spending the last two days with her. I'm a little behind on some work I need to do, even after going in on Saturday, but nothing major.

As I walk her to her door, that Kyle prick leaves his apartment. Abigail tenses up immediately. I swear to God that smarmy bastard probably sat there and watched out his window like a loser and timed it so he'd leave right when we walked up. I know how dipshits like him operate.

He stares at the ground and ignores us as he power-walks by.

Good. I want that son of a bitch to be afraid to even talk to Abigail.

She stays tense until he's in the elevator and the door closes.

I grab each of her shoulders. "You okay?" I glance

around at her dilapidated building. She really does need to move out of this shit hole. That would solve all my problems. I know Abby, though. She'd never let me pay for it or accept any kind of help. I'll think of something to get her out of here.

She shakes her head. "No. Yeah. Totally fine. I was just worried he might say something to piss you off."

"He pisses me off by existing, but you don't have to worry about anything happening. I promised you."

"Dex?" She stares at me like I'm full of shit.

"I would never do anything." I hold up both hands and mumble, "In front of you."

She pushes at my shoulder. "Stop, you're terrible."

"I'm fine, okay. I don't get pissed off very often. That was a fluke deal. Bad timing and his friend said the wrong thing. That's all." I push her up against the wall next to her door. "I meant what I said about my promise. Though I do feel like Johnny Lawrence, not allowed to touch Daniel Larusso until the tournament."

"That makes you sound like the villain."

I scoff. "Uhh, Johnny was the hero. Daniel was an arrogant dickhead."

She laughs, then her eyes lock onto mine. "I had a really great time this weekend." She strokes my jaw with her petite fingers.

"You could have a great time with me tomorrow night at dinner too?"

She grins. "I'll think about it. I can't always let you get your way, though, you know? Have to keep you on your toes."

"Yeah you can." I move in for what is supposed to be a

quick kiss, but it turns intense in a hurry. "You drive me crazy."

Abigail grins against my lips then bites the lower one. "Ditto."

The moment is nice, and it's hot as hell. If she keeps looking at me like that, I may have to kick the door down and haul her to her room, because who has time to use a key?

Out of nowhere, the door to her apartment flies open.

"There you are." This chick's voice is as nasal as a voice can get.

What the hell? Just be nice. "You must be Barbie." I hold out my hand. "Dexter."

Her nose goes up in the air. "Funny. Abigail's never mentioned you."

I can't help but snicker. Jesus fuck, Abby wasn't kidding at all.

I flash her a smile. "No worries, you'll be seeing a lot of me."

Abigail shakes her head, and I lean in for one more kiss, right in front of Barbie.

I squeeze Abigail's hip. "Call me later before you go to bed."

"Okay."

"Barbie." I give her a weird salute. "Say hi to Ken for me. Night ladies."

As I walk toward the elevator, I hear Barbie pissing and moaning about a guy named Nick.

I wonder if it was her boyfriend I headbutted in the face? Interesting.

I glance around on my way down the elevator. Yeah, I

have to get Abigail the fuck out of this place. She deserves way better.

On the way to my car outside, Kyle creeps out of the shadows and saunters up the sidewalk. He's such an idiot in his little Pokémon t-shirt. It looks like something one of Jenny's friends from school would wear.

He starts toward me but abruptly stops and scowls when he sees me.

I sigh. Fucking perfect, just what I need. I know he's been out here waiting on me. Guys like him never learn and they don't handle rejection. They're dangerous for women. I've seen it a million times.

Stay calm.

The last thing I need is this twerp mouthing off and me sticking my foot up his ass. Shoving his hands in his pockets he shuffles awkwardly.

I can't believe how pathetic he is. Who raised him? If he wasn't such a conniving little asshole, I'd feel sorry for him.

I try to ghost him, just walk right past.

But, he turns around the second I walk by. "Hey!"

I stop and exhale a large breath. Silence would've been too easy it seems. "What?"

He shakes his head in the most condescending fashion possible and snorts. "Women are all the same."

I laugh at that one and eye him up and down, knowing exactly what he means by it. "It's not the women who are the problem."

I turn and walk off.

"The hell is that supposed to mean?"

I toss up a middle finger without turning back. "That

means you're the problem, Kyle. And don't go near Abigail or I'll rip your legs off and kick your ass with them."

I glance back in time to see his eyes get big, then he power-walks all the way back to his apartment.

I get in my car and rev the engine then pull out onto the road. The entire drive to my place I try to think about Abigail but can't get that smarmy asshole out of my head. I have to get Abigail away from her roommate and that guy. What did she get herself caught up in? The people in her life give me anxiety, and I rarely have to be around them.

At my apartment, I go through the motions of getting everything ready for the week. I check my calendar and get my schedule up to date. Brenda's always on top of things but I like to double check. I hate being caught off guard with last-minute changes. Nothing irks Decker more than incompetence, and I don't need to give him any more petty reasons to fuck with me over the Wells Covington situation.

After a quick shower, I crawl into bed just in time to get a text from Abigail.

Abigail: I had a great time today.

Me: Me too, miss you though.

Abigail: Wow, did you just say something sweet?

Me: I have a problem over here.

Abigail: What's that?

Me: Cold bed and my dick is lonely.

Abigail: There's Dexter, I was wondering who was texting me. And poor little guy, hope he'll be okay without me.

Me: Nothing poor or little about my dick.

Abigail: SMH. I wasn't being literal.

Me: Sounded literal. Afraid I'll need to prove myself again. Come on over.

Abigail: Some of us have to be at work on time.

Me: All right, then. No more pudding and a spanking is in order.

Abigail: Hmm, I may need to misbehave more often.

Me: Careful, Abby. You're making my poor little dick hard.

Abigail: I'm sure he misses me. What are you going to do to him?

I stare at the message. Shit, is she really going there? Fuck it. I'm not passing this up.

Me: It's not so much what I'll do to him as what I'm going to think about while I do it.

I can't get the image out of my mind of her squirming on her bed, touching herself as she reads my messages. I need to perform at my best here.

Abigail: What are you going to think about?

Me: Bending you over the bed, and spanking your ass just to see the outline of my hand.

Abigail: Then what?

Me: Tease all around your pussy with my tongue, until you beg me to touch you.

Abigail: Maybe I'm already touching myself.

Fuck. She has me so wound up I might explode. I stare down at my lap and my dick is pointing up at the sky, the only thing on my mind is feeling Abigail's tight pussy wrapped around it.

Me: You're definitely getting spanked for that.

Abigail: That a promise or a threat?

Me: Both.

Abigail: While you figure it out, I'll be here all alone with my vibrator, dreaming of being punished for my insubordination.

A close-up photo comes through of her slender hand shoved down the front of her white lace panties.

Fuck texting. I try to Facetime her, but she rejects the call.

Me: Pick up the damn phone, woman!

I'm so hard it aches as I stare at the picture.

Fuck it.

Two can play at this game. I send her a picture of me fisting my dick. Obviously, I angle the camera just right so it looks gigantic. Minutes go by and there's no response. I try to call three times and it just rings and goes to voicemail.

You dirty little girl, Abigail. I can't believe this.

I'm going to think up some way to get revenge, as soon as I finish jerking off to her picture.

ABIGAIL

"Oh hey! What's up?" I stare at Mary as she hovers near the edge of my desk. We don't usually talk much, even though I've worked with her longer than anyone here.

She transferred from Dallas at the same time I did. From what little I could gather, it was to do some work for her church up here.

She has on a terrible brown sweater that completely washes out her complexion. It's paired with navy blue dress pants and black leather flats. She could be so cute and adorable if she'd let me dress her or take her shopping, but I don't want to be rude and suggest it.

She fidgets, reaching up and fumbling with the rosary beads around her neck. I don't know how she survived the interview process because she's incredibly shy. She knows the law like nobody's business, though, and is always putting together presentations for partners. We call her the Power Point wizard.

"I was just over near the partners' offices and Dexter

needs you. Said it's urgent. I hope you're not in trouble. He seemed really mad."

"Did he now?"

She grimaces. "I don't think he's had any coffee. He was grumpy." Her voice drops down low and she glances around to see if anyone is listening. She makes a twisted-up face and does her best Dexter impersonation and reenacts the whole scene for me.

I bite back a laugh. I can picture it all playing out in my mind perfectly. "Thanks for letting me know. I'll go see what he wants."

"No problem." She smiles and goes to her little cubicle. "Good luck," she whispers as I shove my chair back to go see what Dexter is up to.

This better be work related.

I walk over to his office and stop in front of Brenda. "Hi. Mary said Mr. Collins needed to see me."

"Yeah, go on in. He's waiting." She waves me forward.

I smooth my hand over my skirt before knocking on the door. I don't want to just barge in even though she said to.

"Come in." His voice is smooth and deep, and I feel it reverberate through my body. I blink a few times. Things are different now. We've spent the night together more than once. We've been intimate.

I take a deep breath and walk in.

"Close the door." He says it like it's a request, but we both know it's an order.

I close the door behind me.

I don't know why, but for some reason I lock it too. Okay, I know exactly why I lock it. Because I know exactly what Dexter is up to and I don't want to look intimidated. I want to look confident and sexy. The lock clicks and the sound of the bolt echoes through the room. Or maybe I just imagine it did. It sounded so loud inside my head I could swear the whole office heard the noise.

You're being paranoid.

I gingerly step toward Dexter who still hasn't looked up. "You wanted to see me?"

I can't read him. He's emotionless, staring down at some papers on his desk. "Come here."

I shuffle forward and start to take a seat in front of his desk, but he shakes his head at me with that devilish smirk.

"Abigail, I said come here. You're over there. I want you over here."

I sigh. "Dex."

His voice goes low and he speaks slowly, enunciating each syllable. "I said come here. *Now.*"

Something flashes in his eyes, a primal hunger that ties my stomach in a knot. He has his damn jacket off, and the whole sleeves-rolled-up thing again too. I think he does it on purpose to torture me. Does he just accidentally look this hot and commanding, or does he practice it in the mirror at home?

My feet urge me forward though my head screams no. I know what he wants to do and it's completely inappropriate. "I've told you. Not at the office."

"Don't make me get up."

I want him so bad I can't see straight. My entire body is on fire. I know I locked the door and nobody can see in here, but still.

I shake my head at him but bite my lower lip at the

same time. I shouldn't tease him because it's so not cool, but it's like my actions are completely separate from my brain at this point.

"It's gonna be worse." He starts to get up and I walk over to him.

I can't believe you're doing this.

Every time I think Dex can't turn me on more than he has before, he proves me wrong.

"What are you going to do?" I inch my way around his desk.

He doesn't respond and my heart is about to redline its way out of my chest.

As soon as I'm in front of him, he reaches out and snatches my forearm. I don't even know what happens, because it's all a blur, but suddenly I'm bent across his lap and he has me pinned down with one arm.

Holy. Shit.

I'm on fire inside, and for two different reasons. I'm so into this, but it's so wrong. "We're at work." I hiss the words out at him, knowing it's only goading him even more.

His hand slides up the back of my thigh and scorches a trail of fire up my leg. "Why'd you lock the door then?" His voice comes out all gravelly.

Warmth spreads through my veins and I soften to him automatically. I have no answer. "I… I don't know."

"Strike one." His firm hand squeezes my ass over my skirt. It feels so damn good I have to bite back a soft moan in my throat. I'm so damn weak for him, not myself at all when he's around.

"Don't lie to me."

"I'm not."

"Strike two."

"What are you talking about, strikes?"

"Too much talking. Strike three." Dexter yanks my skirt up and his strong fingers knead my ass over my panties.

My eyes dart around the room, making sure all the shades are drawn. If someone saw this, I would never be able to show my face in this office again. "What the hell, *Dexter*?" At the same time I say the words, I close my eyes because it feels so damn good.

I squirm in anticipation because I know he's about to spank me and ever since he did it the first time at his apartment, I've wanted him to do it again.

He shakes his head back and forth. "Fight this all you want. I told you what was going to happen."

"I fell asleep," I say in the most innocent tone I can muster while his fingertips dig into my ass.

"Is that so?"

"Uh huh." I nod my head.

"That's the story you're going with?"

"Yeah."

He laughs. "Okay, maybe I'll let you off the hook this one time."

Disappointment washes over me at once. He's such a tease.

His hold loosens for a second, and then his hand grips my hair.

Whack!

The pain radiates from my ass straight up my spine, and God, it stings so good. I let out a gasp.

"That one is for lying. Tell me the truth, Abby."

"I-I did." I can barely get the words out because I'm so damn aroused and out of breath.

His palm rubs over me, like he's warming me up for another one.

Whack!

"Okay, okay!" I grin and huff out a breath. "Fine. If you must know…"

"The truth this time. I'll know if you're lying."

I crane my neck around and fake-scowl back at him. "I got… distracted."

"How?"

My cheeks must turn a bright shade of pink. "I, umm, I was taking care of myself."

"You finished without me?" He growls the words and nips at my ear lobe. His tongue traces the shell of my ear.

Holy shit. The sex at his apartment was phenomenal but this dominant, possessive side of Dexter is heating me up in all kinds of new ways I didn't know I enjoyed until just now.

"I like these." He runs his fingers along each one of my garter belts that ride halfway up my thighs. He snaps them against my skin one at a time, like he has all day to mess with me.

I yelp.

"Shh. Don't want anyone hearing you alone in here with me, with the door locked and the shades drawn. What would people around the office think?"

"Oh my God." I exhale the words.

His hand slides over my mouth while his free hand continues to massage my ass. He continues to take his time, enjoying playing with me like I'm some kind of toy put here for his amusement.

I bite his palm but it's useless. He only tightens his grip.

One. Two. Three. Four.

The swats come in quick succession and I gasp into his palm.

The outline of his hand throbs on my ass, and I feel the heat rush back into my rear.

Dexter releases his palm from my mouth, and I look over my shoulder at him. My eyes narrow on his.

"Want a few more?" He smirks.

"What if I do?" I mumble.

I'm at his mercy and it's impossible to resist him, and judging by the look on his face, he knows it.

He leans down to my ear and growls, "That can be arranged."

"I'm gonna get even for this."

He smirks. "We'll see." He pats me on the ass, gently this time. "Oh, we'll see about that."

"Don't threaten me with a good time." I slide down from his lap, then make my way up and straddle him. Grabbing his hand, I suck two of his fingers into my mouth getting them good and wet.

His gaze pierces through me and his breaths grow ragged at the sight. His eyes go half-hooded.

"Touch me, Dex." I lean next to his head and lick around his ear. "Fuck me with these fingers." I push his hand down between my legs. "I've never been this wet for you before. See for yourself."

As his fingers rub up against me and he feels my heat, his eyes roll back. "Fuck, Abby. I won't be gentle."

I grind against his hand. "I don't want you to be."

He grips my panties and yanks them to the side.

I wrap my arms around his neck. "Please, I need it so bad."

"This what you want?" Dex forces two fingers inside me.

Holy shit. It hurts so damn good.

"You want to fuck my fingers while you're at work? Like a dirty little office slut?"

Oh. My. God.

I can't believe he just said that, and I can't believe how much I liked it.

I nod and purr against his lips. "I've been bad. I deserve to be punished."

His thumb slides up to my clit and he does exactly what I asked for, pumps two fingers in and out. "Yes, you do." He cups me in his palm and squeezes hard, digging his fingers into me. "This pussy is mine. Nobody touches it unless I say they can. That includes you. Is that understood?"

"Yes."

"Say it, Abigail. Tell me who this belongs to." He grips me harder and digs his fingers in.

I whimper through a shaky breath. "It's yours."

He shoves two fingers back in me and his thumb moves back to my clit.

I'm so close already, it's not going to take long. Before I know it, I'm riding his hand while he stares into my eyes. My center coils tight like a spring and I'm on the edge, so damn close. An intense heat funnels between my legs and I gasp in his ear. "Let me come, please."

His free hand massages my breast through my top, then he pinches one of my nipples so hard it yanks my mind out of the clouds.

"You have my permission to come on my fingers like a little whore."

And I'm done for.

I buck and thrash on his hand, every muscle in my body constricting and contracting as the orgasm fires through every nerve ending in my body. "Oh God, Dex."

"Yeah, say my name. Tell me who owns this." He shoves his fingers in deeper.

I shudder a few more times. "Dexter Collins, it's his."

"Goddamn right it is."

I exhale a huge breath. Once I'm finished, I stand up in front of him and straighten my skirt.

Dex stares down at his tented slacks, then back up at me.

I pat him on the shoulder. "Sorry my little office manwhore, I need to get back to work."

"What the fu—"

I'm already almost to his door before he can stand up and turn to face me.

I smirk. "Told you I'd get even." I unlock the door and open it halfway, then turn back. "Maybe I'll make it up to you later, if you take me to dinner."

He smirks his ass off right back. "You're in a lot of trouble."

"A lot?" I grin.

"That's strike twenty-three. Better pack a fucking lunch tonight, Whitley."

A tingle rips up my spine at the thought of what he'll do to me. Mission accomplished. My entire day is going to be amazing now, anticipating tonight.

"See you later, Mr. Collins." I sway my hips as I walk out the door.

I STEP off the train and head a block toward Dex's apartment, hurrying as fast as I can. It's difficult carrying the casserole dish with me. I had to rush around my apartment while Barbie whined nonstop while I made it.

I pray it's a sufficient peace offering because I have no idea what Dex will have in store for me when I get there. I left him hanging and even felt a little guilty, but it's so much fun. I've never played these little sex games like this. It's so hot. When he finally gets what he wants, it'll be that much better for both of us. That's what I tell myself, but secretly, I worry I pushed things too far. Somehow, he just makes me feel so damn comfortable and sexy around him, that I'm not afraid to do anything I want. The more I think about it, the more I think that's the way it should be.

I love how confident he makes me feel in the bedroom, or the office, when the doors are locked and nobody can see, obviously.

I walk through the front of the building and hop on the elevator up to his floor. When I get to his front door, I ring the doorbell.

The door opens but nobody is in front of it.

"You're late." His voice echoes through the entryway, but I still don't see him anywhere.

"I brought…"

"Get your ass in here."

My heartbeat kicks up about twenty notches.

I take a few tentative steps through the door and I feel a presence slide in behind me. I start to turn.

"Don't fucking turn around, Ms. Whitley."

My breath hitches. "So, we're keeping things formal are—"

Something wraps around my face, cutting off my sentence, and I realize it's one of Dexter's silk ties from work. He covers my eyes and ties it off in the back, a little more forcefully than needed.

"What's this?" He takes the dish from my hand.

"Umm, h-homemade banana pudding."

There's complete silence and I can't see. It's a little disorienting to say the least.

"Dex, what are you doing?"

His finger slides up to my lips. "Shh. You just do what the fuck I say, understand?"

This is so freaking intense. I don't know if I should be scared or elated. Does he have one of those red rooms in his apartment I don't know about? I don't know how I'd feel about *all that*, but something inside me really wants to see where this goes.

"Follow me." He takes me by the hand and leads me down the hall.

At least, that's where I think I'm going. I have no

earthly clue where I'm at in his apartment at this point. He turns me into a room then releases my hand.

"Stay there."

I do as he says, then hear him set the dish down on something.

I hear his feet on the wood floor as he walks back over. His hands go to the buttons on my jeans and instinctively I squirm.

He grips both of my hips and digs his fingers in. "Hold still, or you'll only make this worse for yourself."

For some reason I can feel the grin on his face, like I can sense that he's enjoying this immensely.

"Would that be so bad?"

"Probably not." He pops the buttons on my jeans. "For me, anyway."

He slides my pants down and I kick my heels off then step out of them. Next, he grips the hem on my top and lifts it slowly over my head.

"Fuck, your body belongs in the Louvre."

"Thank you, sir."

He hisses out a breath. "You have no idea what it does to me when you call me that."

His hands roam my body, caressing and massaging every square inch of me up and down, until I feel his face right in front of mine and his warm breath plays across my lips.

He doesn't kiss me, though. Just teases the hell out of me like he might do it.

I'm already wet for him. My panties are soaked through.

He slowly inches me back with nothing but his hard

frame pressed against my chest until I run into what I assume is the bed. I jolt at the sudden impact.

His hand slides up my stomach to one of my breasts and he grips it tight over my bra, then all at once, his fingers splay across my chest and he shoves me backward.

Panic rips through my body while I fall until my back makes contact with his mattress.

I pant uncontrollably, my heart racing. "Holy shit."

I hear him walk around the bed as I scoot to the middle.

"Lay down." His voice booms through the room.

I do exactly what he says because holy hell is this hot. My senses are dialed up to eleven. Sound, smell, touch… Everything is so intense.

He takes one of my hands in his and ever so delicately, I feel him slip something around my wrist and he ties it off. Then as my brain processes what he's doing, he yanks my arm back and ties me to the bedpost.

"Oh wow, I've never been tied up before."

"Good." He leans over in front of my face, so that I can feel him inches from me. "I'll be your first for everything from here on out." There is zero uncertainty in his voice as he says it.

He does the same thing with my other arm and both of my legs, until I'm stationary in the center of his bed, all four limbs stretched out, in nothing but my bra and panties.

Dexter climbs up on the bed. I feel his weight shifting around on the side of me.

"Look at this fucking body." His hand glides along my ribs and he traces a finger down my shoulder. "So helpless. Nowhere for you to go."

I squirm but it's no use. I can't move at all.

"I could do whatever the fuck I wanted to you right now, Abigail."

Be sexy. For the love of God, be sexy and turn him on more right now.

"Do it then." I spit the words at him.

He snickers. His hand travels over both of my breasts. "I could fuck your tits." His fingers slide up and he shoves two of them in my mouth so hard I nearly choke, but his words remain calm and composed. "Could fuck this pretty mouth."

Oh my God, I might die.

His hand slowly makes its way down my stomach and he cups me in his palm. "This pussy." Two fingers slip down lower and he presses them hard up against my ass.

I squirm on the bed, but oh my God, it feels kind of nice.

"So fucking dirty. Look at you. You're enjoying yourself." He applies even more pressure and I hear his breath go ragged. "I could definitely fuck this ass. I could shove my cock anywhere it'll fit in you."

My thoughts race, but I don't even have time to process all the filthy things he's telling me because his hand slides up around my throat.

It's extremely possessive, but he doesn't choke me, just grips tight enough for me to know his hand is there. I gasp out a breath because I don't know how much longer I can stand all this anticipation.

"Don't worry. I have you for the entire night. I think I'll take my time."

His hand slides down to my breast and in one violent

motion he yanks the cup down, exposing me to the air. My nipples harden at his touch. He reaches over and yanks the other down the same way. Ever so slowly, he leans down and grazes my nipples with the tip of his tongue.

I shudder and fight against the restraints for a quick second, before I relax again. I want to grab his head and put it between my legs, but I can't do a damn thing all tied up like this. It's agony.

His hand slides down and he caresses my pussy over my panties. "Look how wet you are, Abby. You get off on this dirty shit, don't you?"

"No." I shake my head. "It's not doing it for me."

He doesn't fall for it at all. Just snickers. "Sure. Sure. You fucking hate this, don't you?" He slips a finger inside my panties and rubs it over my clit. "Yeah, look how fast you're breathing. I can hear your damn heart racing. You definitely want me to stop."

My hips betray me and lift against his hand.

"So responsive." Then, his finger slides down farther and he presses it up against my ass again.

This time, I roll my hips and push my ass up against his hand.

He snickers again. "Just like I thought. You want to be my filthy little whore, Abigail?"

I nod furiously, unable to play this game anymore. "I'll do whatever you want. Just don't stop touching me, please."

He immediately gets up off the bed and it's like I can feel it when his presence is gone.

I writhe against my restraints. "Dex, please. I'm so

close. Come back, I need it." Hell, I'd settle for straddling his damn pillow at this point and trying to ride one out.

His door closes and he leaves me there. Dude freaking leaves me alone, tied up to his bed!

"Dex! Dex!" I keep shouting.

He makes me wait for a good three minutes, then walks back in. I only know because I hear the hinges on the door and then his feet on the hardwood floor.

"I'm going to *kill* you when you let me up."

"Highly doubtful. You'll be begging for more, trust me."

"You wish." I hold my head up as far as it'll go, trying to get a sense of where he is.

It's completely silent.

His hand grips my hair and yanks me down to the bed. I gasp as his knuckles dig into my scalp. How did he get over here so quickly? I didn't even hear him.

He leans over, and I can feel his mouth inches from mine. "Your pussy is wet. Your body tells me when you lie."

I start to say something and oh my goodness.

Something ice cold makes contact with my nipple and the delicious chill tears through my limbs.

What the hell is that? It feels like a spoon flipped upside down.

He rubs it over both of my nipples, and it feels so damn amazing.

Then, he slides the curved part down my stomach. When he gets to my pelvis, he pulls my panties halfway down my legs.

Holy shit, he's not…

He does.

He rubs the back of the spoon across me, then presses it down on my clit.

Never in my life did I think a man would get me off with a spoon, but Dex has me damn near there and he's barely even touched me.

He rubs the spoon in small circles all over me.

His fingers trace a line up my jaw, and then he pulls the tie back from my eyes.

When my eyes adjust to the darkness of the room, I spot Dex next to me, completely naked.

He has the pudding I brought, and he scoops some out and makes a show of savoring his first bite, right in front of me, with the spoon he just rubbed all over me.

It might be the hottest damn thing I've ever seen in my life.

He licks it, taking his sweet time, curling his tongue around it. Then, his eyes land on mine and he heats my entire body with nothing but his stare. "Best fucking pudding I've ever had in my life." He scoops another bite and shovels it in his mouth. "Tastes like bananas." He leans down to my ear. "And *you*."

My chest heaves up and down with deep breaths, watching him eat the damn pudding right in front of me. I need him so damn bad right now. My body is in flames. I ache just watching him, and when I think it can't get any hotter, he spoons some pudding out and dumps it right above my pussy, then spreads it around slowly with the spoon, his eyes never leaving mine the whole time.

Next, he does the same, right on each of my breasts. Then each side of my neck. He smears pudding on the insides of my thighs and makes a little trail from my breasts down to my stomach.

"That should be enough. I have quite an appetite."

His fan is on above us, and I can feel the chill everywhere he has the pudding on me.

He takes his sweet-ass time, walking over and setting the dish on his nightstand, along with the spoon. The wait is killing me. I writhe on the bed, covered in the pudding I hauled ass to make after work. It might be the best peace offering of all time.

He moves the tie back over my eyes until everything goes black again. "I'll be back shortly, and I'm going to have you for dessert."

I don't know how much more I can take. It's excruciating.

He walks off and he's gone for like another five minutes that seems like an hour. This time, I don't even hear him come again. I don't know what's happened until two hands spread my thighs apart as far as they'll go and then it happens all at once.

His tongue makes contact with my skin and he laps up the pudding from the insides of my thighs, constantly grazing the edges of where I need his mouth, but not making direct contact.

I move against the restraints in agony, trying to get him to speed up but he doesn't. "I can't hold it, Dex, you have no idea."

"Don't fucking come until I'm finished. Or I'll leave you tied up all goddamn night."

I nod furiously. "Okay."

I can do this. I can do this. There's no way in hell you'll last until he's done. It's impossible.

Dex ignores my pussy, once he's done with my thighs, and hovers over me up to my neck. He cleans both sides of it with his tongue, and I fight the urge to arch my chest up into him. His hard cock drags across my stomach, and I know he just got pudding all over it. I can feel it smeared up to my chest.

"You made me make a mess." His hand cups my jaw and his fingers squeeze my cheeks until my mouth forms a big O. "Gonna need you to take care of that for me."

I nod, eager to do anything to relieve myself of this torturous foreplay that I secretly want to never end.

He presses the head of his cock to my lips, and I open immediately and take him in.

Sure enough, as soon as he pushes into my mouth, I taste the pudding all up and down him. I'm not one to be outdone, and I want to be sexy for him, so as soon as he pulls his dick away from my mouth, I say, "Your balls too, sir."

He groans, loud, and breaks character for a brief moment. "Fuck, Abby. You're killing me."

He lowers his balls and I lick and suck each one of them, until I'm sure I got every speck of banana pudding off them.

Dex hovers back down and licks across both breasts. He bites down on my nipples and sucks until I'm writhing in agony.

"You're gonna have to hurry. I'm not going to last."

He spreads my legs apart and his tongue connects with

my clit. I buck my hips as hard as I can at him as he fucks me with his mouth.

"Please, Dexter. Please." I drag out the last word on a whimper. My hands grip his headboard, and I'm about to shatter into a million pieces.

"Okay." As he says it, he shoves his thick cock inside me, and I come undone all over it. "Fuck, Abby." He groans the words as I clamp down on him and have the most intense orgasm of my life.

In my limited sexual experience, there have been self-induced orgasms, regular Dexter-induced orgasms, and then *this* orgasm. It's on another plane of existence.

My mind is a blur, my arms and legs trembling, my entire body seizing as I writhe against the restraints. His headboard thrashes against the wall, banging loud enough anyone in a three-block radius might hear. I squeeze around him while my hips buck uncontrollably.

"Dexter." I groan out his name.

I'm in a fog, floating around on the clouds and it's like a strong drug flows through my veins down to my finger-tips and toes. I don't know how long it lasts, but it's pure euphoria. Fuzzy stars firework in front of my eyelids. After a few long seconds, hell, it might even be minutes, my brain returns from a temporary fog and I crane my head around, the room still completely black.

I shake my hands and legs, panting uncontrollably. "Get this shit off me, now."

He slides the blindfold down and his eyes widen when he sees me, and he furiously unties all the ties. The second my arms and legs are free I dive into him and knock him onto his back. Before he can recover, I straddle him and put his cock back inside me. I start rolling my hips, riding him as hard as I can.

"Fucking hell." His eyes roll back then narrow on mine.

Before I know it, he's flipped me to my back and he's on top, pumping into me. I'm not even sure I know what happens after that, but we're a mess of tangled arms and limbs. Dex fucks me so hard, I come again without notice and my whole body spasms underneath him.

"God, Abby, fuck." He grunts and groans. His whole body stiffens, and he comes deep inside me. It's like it never ends as he fills me up so much it streams out around his cock and down my thighs.

We both pant heavily, staring into each other's eyes, then we both grin at each other.

He lingers above me for a long moment and brushes a wayward, sweaty strand of hair from my face. "You're mine." It's the only two words he says and then he collapses onto my shoulder and nuzzles into my neck, his arms wrapped tight around me.

Yep. He's not wrong.

ABIGAIL

IT'S BEEN EXACTLY four days since the pudding incident. That's what I'm calling it, anyway, and it's been impossible to think about anything else.

I gather all the information Rick Lawrence gave me on Wells Covington. I haven't looked at any of it yet and Decker asked for it ASAP. I glance down at the top page and see his picture. His dark eyes stare back at me, and for some reason it sends a shiver up my spine.

It's probably because he was there the night Dexter and I had the huge fight. I think he just reminds me of a shit memory, but I can't help the effect his picture has on me. He stood there and basically cheered Dexter on, jumping around, voicing his approval. Asshole.

I still wonder why Decker is looking into his background. He's done it for a few other clients, but they're usually criminal cases, not for potential financial clients. It seems weird but I'm sure Decker has a reason. You don't build a firm this size without being smart and careful.

I'm sure Dex knows about it by now, but I don't like

talking about work when I'm with him. I get enough of that here, and we have plenty of other things to do. Not to mention when you bring up money or work with Dexter, he gets that shark look on his face, like it's all that matters. I love possessive Dexter, but I like a nice mix of that guy and the boyish one who tells me about phone calls with his mom.

I do my best to remain professional at work, well, other than the time he spanked me in his office, but other than that, my willpower has kept me in check since. He's always trying to sneak kisses and touch me in front of people whenever he gets the chance, and I still have to tell him to knock it off.

I hurry to Decker's office to get the file to him. He's about to leave for the day and I want to catch him before he takes off for the weekend. I heard Tate mention something at lunch about them going away to do wedding plans and she was sneaking out of the office early. When is their wedding, anyway? It must be coming up soon, but they still haven't announced a date, even though they already did the bachelor and bachelorette parties. Tate's was back in Dallas a while ago. I went home that weekend and went out with them.

When I get to Decker's office, he walks out the door with Tate.

I put myself right in their path. "Hey, Mr. Collins, I have that uhh, project you had me working on." I glance around because I'm not sure Tate is supposed to know, and I like to follow instructions to the letter when I get an assignment.

"Is it top secret or something?" says Tate.

Decker ignores her. "Thanks. Great work." He snatches it from my hand.

"Enjoy your weekend."

"You too." Tate winks at me like she knows something I don't.

I watch them leave totally smitten with one another. She teases him about the file, he whispers something in her ear, and she laughs. Decker is a complete hard ass. Tate too, but something about the two of them together, they mellow each other out. The man is head over heels in love with her. I see it in the way he looks at her when he thinks no one is watching. He looks at her like Deacon looks at Quinn and like—oh my God.

It's the exact same way Dexter looks at me.

I don't know why the thought hits me right then, on a Friday, in the middle of the office. But it slams into my chest like a Mack truck.

I suck in a breath. Holy shit. I mean I don't think Dexter is in love with me. That's crazy, but he definitely *likes* me a lot. I know the look and I'm stupid for not recognizing it sooner.

When I get back to my desk, Dexter is waiting for me. I take a seat as he leans over the cubicle. "Hey, you. What are you doing?"

He has that boyish grin on his face and gives me that look I just saw on Decker when he stared at Tate. "Don't make any plans for tonight. I have a surprise. Pick you up at seven."

I don't get a chance to contest because he immediately turns and struts down the hall.

Okay, I sneak a look at his ass when nobody is watching. Just one though.

Damn, it's a fine ass too.

DEXTER

I swing by my apartment and grab a quick shower before my date with Abigail. For some reason, moments of clarity always come to me in the shower. It's where I do my best thinking outside the office. It's usually about work, but not so in this case.

I'm either nuts or I'm fucking falling in love. I never go this above and beyond planning dates for women I'm with. I may help my brothers out when they need it, because they're clueless and I'm awesome, but I make fun of them for doing this shit.

What does that mean? I know I'm not in love with Abigail. It's too soon and falling in love is for pussies. I do love burying my cock inside her, though. Thank God she's on the pill because I've been reckless. Coming inside her like an idiot; I just can't help myself. The moments are so intense and it's just… It's never been like this with anyone else. There's a connection there. A force I can't pull away from.

I can definitely see a future with her. I know she has

reservations about getting serious with anyone. She's mentioned it multiple times, and it heats my blood anytime I hear her say it.

You'd have to be blind to not see we just work together. We fit. She may be young and not want to settle down, but I know she feels it too. It's more than lust. I thought that was all it was at first, and once I fucked her, I'd have it out of my system and want to move on, but I can't. It runs much deeper than getting her into my bed. It's bone-deep, and I feel the pull every goddamn day. I just want to wake up and see her face. It's painful when she's not around me.

I shoot Abigail a quick text to let her know I'm on my way. When I arrive at her building, I spot her watching for me in her window. I take the stairs two at a time instead of the elevator.

She opens the door before I get there, and I walk right past her.

"Dex, what the…"

"You need an overnight bag."

"Oh." She grins before the recognition sets in. "Ohh." She draws the syllable out this time.

Her roommate rounds the corner in a robe, then shrieks when she sees me.

"Abigail, why the hell is he—"

I hold up a hand. "Save it. I'll be gone in two seconds. Go back to your room."

"You don't tell me what…"

I glare right at her. The stare I reserve for opposing counsel and my worst enemies, back when I used to try criminal cases right out of law school.

She immediately turns on a dime and walks to her room.

"Holy cow. How did you do that?" Abigail gawks at me like I'm some kind of magician.

"Doesn't matter. Hurry up before she changes her mind and comes back out here. I want to stay in a good mood."

"Good idea." Abigail rifles through her armoire and grabs a few things and shoves them in a bag. "You *have* to teach me your Jedi ways, Obi-Wan. It would drastically improve my standard of living."

I reach out a hand. "Join me, and together we can rule the galaxy as… Shit, that doesn't work, does it?"

She shakes her head like I'm an idiot. "Was that some weird attempt to get me to call you daddy?"

I burst into a laugh. "No, actually, I'm not much of a fan. It's weird."

She nods. "Agreed, I'll never call you that."

"Thanks." I kiss her on the forehead. "And, I don't know if the death stare can be taught. It's just a natural talent."

She does this fake glare at me, a terrible imitation of my courtroom scowl.

I can't stop laughing and hold out my hand again. "Come on, crazy. Let's go on an adventure."

She looks around and giggles like a girl sneaking out of her parents' house late at night. "Okay. Let's do it."

We both run down the stairs, even though there's no hurry, and exit out into the freezing cold night, laughing like kids.

I didn't think I could ever have this much fun again. It's even better than I thought, like playing hide and seek with my brothers when we were little at my Uncle's house outside the city.

I open the passenger door for her and take her bag and stick it in the trunk.

I return to the driver's seat. "You ready?"

Abigail smiles. "Hell yes. Barbie is a nightmare, alternating between raging and crying."

"That bad?"

Abigail rolls her eyes and groans. "You have no idea. I don't know how women do this whole girlfriend thing. I'm exhausted."

The hairs on the back of my neck stand up at attention. "What?"

She reaches for my forearm and laughs. "I didn't mean, like *girlfriend* girlfriend, I mean like, being friends with a girl. I don't mind being *your* girlfriend at all."

My heart warms immediately. We've never really discussed our relationship status. We just sort of went from zero to sixty in a matter of weeks. I keep glancing over at her and smiling.

"I have something on my face?"

I shake my head. "No, we just haven't really talked about, *us*, you know? You called yourself my girlfriend."

"Oh." She looks away. "Was I being presumptuous?"

I squeeze her hand tight. "Hell no. Not at all. I loved hearing you say it. I've been so caught up in work, and, well, you…" I shake my head and my jaw clenches. "I didn't do it right. Fuck." I glare out the window. "I should've asked you. It should've been a thing. It feels like it should've been a big romantic…"

"Dex?" She shakes my arm.

I turn to her and can't help the shame coursing through me. "Yeah?"

"The answer is yes, okay?"

I don't think I could want to kiss her any more than I do right now, but instead I decide to tease her a little. "Yes what?"

She fights to hold back a smile. "You know *what*, you big idiot." She smacks me on the arm.

I can't take it anymore and the first thing that pops in my head is to tell her I love her.

Whoa! What the fuck?

My palms get slick on the steering wheel and my shoulders stiffen.

"You okay?"

I look past her and play it off. "It's nothing." I try to shake the thought out of my head. If I was driving alone, I'd roll the window down and shout it right out of my head. I smile. "We're gonna have fun tonight. Deal?" I hold out my fist.

She bumps it and her smile returns. "Deal."

"You're gonna love it."

"I'm excited." She's practically bouncing in her seat.

Abigail is so beautiful. I'm so damn lucky. I'm going to prove to her this shit is real between us. She might say she's my girlfriend, but that lingering tension is still there, like she's going against her own wishes. I need to get rid of that quick before it poisons things.

"Do I at least get a hint?"

"Nope. But trust me. You'll love it."

"All right."

A few minutes later I pull up for the valet.

Abigail glances around. "A hotel?" Her eyes widen and she mumbles, "A very *nice* hotel. Holy…"

"Yeah."

The valets open both our doors. One of them takes my keys and opens the trunk.

We walk inside and get checked into our room. The valets carry our bags and lead us up to the elevators and into the suite.

The phone rings and the manager tells me everything is set while Abigail walks around, scoping the place out. It's not the top floor like Wells normally reserves, but it's nice as fuck. It's a corner suite with fantastic views of the city.

"This is incredible, Dexter."

"Haven't seen anything yet." I hold out my hand. "You ready?"

"Almost." Her arms go around me and she brings me in for a deep, passionate kiss. After a few long seconds, she lets go. "Okay. Now I'm ready."

I swat her on the ass playfully as she walks toward the door.

We take the elevator up to the rooftop.

"This way." I take her by the hand, and I'm so excited I'm damn near shaking.

"Oh my God, I love how excited you are. You look like a little boy on Christmas."

"I don't want to build up the hype too much, but you're going to love it."

The wind whips up from between the skyscrapers. "Where are you taking me? It's freezing!"

"Don't worry. You'll warm up fast. Come on." I think I might be more excited than she is.

Right when we're about to turn the corner, I stop us. "Hang on, I'm not sure you're ready. Maybe we should…"

She flies right past me. "Dexter Collins I'm going to —" She stops on a dime as soon as she sees it. Her hand covers her mouth for a second, and then a tear slides down her cheek.

Oh God, did I screw this up? Maybe it was too much.

She's practically shaking, and I don't know whether I should turn and run for the hills or what. I slowly walk over to her with caution in every step.

She looks over at me and smiles so damn big through the tears. She waves me over to her, and I jog the last four steps.

She wraps her arms around my neck. "Oh my God, it's… You…" She leans up and kisses me, then pulls back. "I can't even talk I'm such a mess right now."

I spin her back around to face it and wrap my arms around her from behind.

"I can't believe you did this. How…"

"I know the manager. Come on, follow me." I take her by the hand.

Abigail can't peel her eyes away from the rooftop ice-skating rink. Tall skyscrapers shoot up all around us and evergreen Christmas trees form a perimeter around the outside. They're covered with red bows and Christmas decorations.

We get our skates all laced up, and I hold out my arm. "You ready? Got the place to ourselves for the next few hours. Did I do good or what?"

"Yeah, you… It's just perfect, and you surprised me, as usual." She cranes her head around, taking it all in. "It's amazing." She looks like she might cry again and wipes at the corner of her eye. "No one has ever done something like this for me before. Not for a date."

I take her hands in mine and look down at her. "I know I have some rough patches to work on. I'm not perfect." I gesture out toward the ice. "This is just the beginning."

She hooks an arm in mine and she can't stop grinning. I don't think it could get any more perfect, but once we're out in the open, ever so slowly, large snowflakes start floating down all around us. If this isn't meant to be, I don't know what the hell is.

We get to the edge and I help her onto the ice. Her knees wobble and shake.

"Easy. I've got you." I grip her waist and guide her until she gets balanced.

Abigail laughs. "I look like a newborn calf finding its legs."

I shake my head. Southern girls. "I'll have to take your word for it."

She looks totally relaxed; despite the fact her legs are working overtime to keep her balance. "They look just like me; awkward."

"You're doing great, come on."

I lead her around the rink slowly.

She keeps looking over. "Seriously, Dex. Thank you for this. It's so much fun. I had no idea this is what we'd do."

"I have more planned tomorrow."

"What more could there be?"

"You'll see." I skate off and cut around the ice a couple

times, then head over to her and spin around backward, grab her hands, and pull her along with me.

"Okay, hotshot. Now I'm impressed. Where'd you learn how to do that?"

"Everyone up here can skate. It's like playing football down in Texas. I played some hockey when I was younger. My mom said I needed a healthy outlet to burn off energy and take out some aggression."

"I could help you with some of that aggression."

My cock strains against my zipper when she says stuff like that. "Don't be a tease. I still owe you one more. We're not even yet."

"I have no idea what you're talking about." She feigns innocence. "We're totally even."

"Oh, Christmas clown. Don't act all innocent. You know exactly what you did. Got me all worked up on two different occasions and then ghosted me." I slow to a stop, pulling her to me for a kiss.

"I would never. I'm a southern lady." She uses a fake southern drawl that's way over the top.

Truth be told, it's kind of hot. I wouldn't mind her doing it again.

Our lips meet, and her mouth parts, inviting me in for a deep kiss.

It sets me on fire inside. I need her, like now. Once we part, I give her a smirk. "We better calm down, don't want to melt the ice."

"Okay, that was corny." She shakes her head, laughing.

"I thought it was pretty smooth. Kissing me, is like…"

She puts a hand on my chest. "Just stop, Dex. You're embarrassing yourself."

I yank her into me and lift her up off the ice. Our mouths connect again, and I twirl us around in a slow spin while I kiss her. It's fucking incredible. Maybe the most perfect moment of my life with the Christmas trees and skyscrapers and snow falling all around us.

After we part, I cradle Abigail in my arms and skate us around for a few laps. She nuzzles up next to me and she just looks—safe, like she feels right at home. It's amazing. I could do this shit for hours.

Finally, out of nowhere, she says, "Keep this up and I'm gonna suck your dick so hard you can't breathe."

"What the…?" It takes me by surprise and my feet fly out from under me.

All I can hear is the sound of Abigail shriek and then her laughing as she comes down right on top of me.

"Are you okay? Are you hurt?" I scramble to try and get up, but she straddles me and pins me down.

She's dying laughing. "I'm sorry, I just…" She mimes what just happened, with half sentences that make no sense, and she laughs so hard reenacting it she can't breathe. "You were just, so… And then I said…"

I nod, trying to hold in a laugh. "You don't say shit like that when someone's skating you around on a block of ice."

She's damn near hyperventilating. Her cheeks are bright pink. Finally, she collapses onto me and we're lying there on the ice, like a couple of fools, me on my back and her on top of me.

Before I can think, I say, "I'm falling for you, Abby."

I expect her to take off so fast she leaves a vapor trail

behind. But, she doesn't. She presses her lips to mine for a long second, then sighs. "I know."

I flip her over and tickle her ribs. "Seriously, you're gonna Han Solo me like that?"

She's laughing so hard she can barely breathe again. "Yeah, I mean, we were on the ice and I started thinking of carbonite then Harrison Ford and it just kind of…"

I stop tickling her for a second, then push a strand of hair from her face. She stares up at me with those baby blue eyes that could stop a man's heart. "I'm falling for you too, Dex. Hard." She looks away. "It's bad. It scares me."

I cup her cheek in my palm. "Why?"

She puts her hand on mine and leans into it. Fuck I love when she does that. She's so vulnerable right now, her feelings totally exposed. "Because you could hurt me. Like, you could really hurt me bad."

I shake my head. "I'll never hurt you, Abby. I promise."

She stares at me. Her face hardens, then she reaches up and cups my cheek. "Please don't make promises you can't keep."

"I'll never break that promise. I won't."

She nods. "Okay."

I still can't tell if she believes me or not, but I don't care. I won't ever break her heart, so I have nothing to worry about. We're perfect together.

"Come on. You're getting cold. Let's warm up with some hot chocolate." We skate over to the benches and change into our shoes, then go into the heated lounge.

I had hot chocolate brought in from Lavazza and Chicago-style hot dogs from Hot Doug's, both the best in the city.

"Jesus how many marshmallows you put in there?" I laugh at the mountain toppling over the brim of her mug.

"What are you talking about? So sue me. I like a little hot cocoa with my marshmallows." She flings one at me.

"God, you're adorable." I scoop whipped cream off the top of mine and dollop her nose with it.

"You're so dead for that." She doesn't wipe it away.

"Did I ruin your makeup?" I grin.

Her mouth drops. "I'm not wearing makeup."

I squint. "You sure?"

"Yes, I'm sure."

I look down at my cup. "They're going to fire you from being the Christmas clown if you don't keep your makeup on."

"Oh, now you're really a dead man."

"Yeah right, come here." I hug her into my side and kiss the top of her hair. "You ready to go to our room?"

"That depends."

"On what?"

"You gonna stop being mean to me?"

"Oh quit playing the victim. You love it." I squeeze her hip and slide my palm up under her sweater.

"Holy sh... Your hand is cold."

"So warm me up then."

Abigail stares up at me with a goofy grin.

I kiss her once more and slide my hand up farther and tweak one of her nipples.

She pulls back and nods. "Yep, let's go to the room."

ABIGAIL RUSHES around the hotel room, throwing clothes on, even more excited than she was last night. "I didn't know there would be a Christmas parade. Are you freaking serious? It's not even Thanksgiving yet."

Every year they have the Magnificent Mile Christmas Parade and tree lighting ceremony. It's the week before Thanksgiving this year, but when Abigail told me how crazy she gets for Christmas I knew I'd have to take her.

"I'd never joke about Christmas." I glance off at the corner of the ceiling. "Not around you anyway."

"Damn right. You better not when I'm not around either. It's not a joking matter, Collins." She wags a finger at me with fake anger. "I don't know why I put up with you."

I hold up my hand as I count the reasons on each finger. "You like to fuck me. I take you on amazing dates. I make you feel wanted. I pay attention to details."

"Damn you're good." She laughs. "I noticed you listed me getting to fuck you first."

"It *was* in order of importance, yes."

She shakes her head. "You're so damn cocky."

"I know." I smack her playfully on the ass. "Get dressed or I'm going to chain you to the bed and eat your pussy all day."

She shrugs. "Can we compromise?"

I quirk an eyebrow up. "How so?"

"You can do what you just said, as long as we're at the parade on time."

My cock goes hard at the thought and I smile at how cute she is. "I suppose your needs can be accommodated."

She smiles, but then scoots back on the bed when she sees the hungry look in my eyes. "Uh oh. What did I just agree to?"

"You wanted this, Abigail." I crawl up over her and use one of my ties to bind her wrists together over her head. It's not as good as having her completely subdued like she was in my room, but it'll do. I roll her tank top up over her shoulders and neck, leaving it over her eyes like a blindfold.

"Dex!" She squirms beneath me.

"Be still." I drag my tongue between the valley of her breasts, pinching both nipples between my fingers.

I slide farther down her and rip her panties in half because they get in my way.

"Hey, I liked those."

"You'll like this more." I flick my tongue across her clit and her thighs squeeze around my head.

Life is good.

I could stay buried between Abigail's legs the rest of my life if she'd let me. I'd get down on my knees and worship her pussy every damn day.

It doesn't take long and she's moaning out my name as an orgasm rocks through her. When she's done, I pull her shirt back down.

"Okay for real, now. We need to hurry."

"What about you?"

I love how considerate she always is. Like she always wants things to be fair. But I love going down on her. I love making her feel good, even when I don't get anything out of it. I really don't mind it at all.

"Don't worry about me. We can take care of me later. This weekend is about you."

"Hey, Dex?"

"Yeah?"

"I'm falling a little more."

I smile. "I know."

ABIGAIL

THIS WEEKEND HAS BEEN TOO good to be true, and we're still not done yet. It's Sunday, and I'm definitely falling for Dex and I don't know how I feel about that, other than the fact that I can't help myself. You don't get to pick and choose when and who it happens with, the heart just knows when it knows.

It's scary how much I like him. Ninety-five percent of the time, he's too good to be true. He took me freaking ice skating and then took me to the Christmas parade and the tree lighting yesterday. The way Dex looked at me under all the twinkling lights... He says he's falling for me, but it's more than that. He's fallen already. I just know. I feel it deep inside me, and if I'm being honest with myself, I'm right there with him.

My two biggest reservations are how he handled the Kyle/Nick situation, and that he's demolishing my plans. Finding myself a Dexter Collins was not supposed to be in the cards for three to five years max, according to my life plan. I always stick to my plans. If I set out to do something, I do it.

It's so hard to make that adjustment. What happens after this happy phase when things get serious? How will Dex handle a high-pressure situation when things aren't all sunshine and rainbows? These are things I need to know, regardless of how well put together he seems in his professional life. That doesn't necessarily equate to personal life where the emotional stakes are much higher.

I'm reckless around him. I'm on the pill but I should still make him wear a condom and I don't. The worst part is I know he'd do it for me without question, and I don't even ask him to.

I look over the red sparkly dress he gave me in the mirror one more time. He told me to put it on and get ready to go to dinner. It fits perfectly. How the hell did he pull that off? Did he go through my closet when I wasn't looking and find my size?

I smooth my hair over my shoulder and apply some lipstick and mascara. This is as good as I'm going to get, but I don't think Dex would care one way or the other.

I walk out of the bathroom and do a little twirl for him. "How do I look?"

"Gorgeous." He helps me into my jacket. "There's a car waiting for us downstairs."

We get down to the lobby of the hotel and there's a limousine and a driver. When he said a car was waiting, I thought he'd called us a cab. I glance over at him all dressed up in his Marc Jacobs suit and Saint Laurent dress shoes. He looks refined with his perfectly slicked-back hair, like he just stepped out of a magazine. All these dates and the way he looks, if Mom ever meets him, she's going to eat her words. He is *all* man. I know she always pictured me staying in Texas and marrying a local boy like she did, but she never seems to judge my life decisions. If she was here, she'd be pushing me toward him.

She's old fashioned and thinks the man should take care of the woman. I like that to some degree, but I'm much more modern. I like having a job and making my own money, making my own way. It's empowering. I don't like being dependent on anyone. Even if this works out with Dex, I'll still always feel that way. Staying at home and taking care of kids and a house is not for me. That doesn't mean I don't like it when he gets all forceful and takes charge, though. It's just a situational thing.

We climb into the back where a tray of champagne flutes and strawberries await us.

"Where we going?"

"Another surprise." He feeds me a strawberry to silence me.

We ride a little ways and I sip some champagne. The car comes to a stop. I try to look out the window, but Dexter stops me.

"No peeking. Just trust me."

"I do trust you." I try to steal a glance over his shoulder. "The suspense is killing me, though."

He shakes his head. "Looks like we're doing this again, since I can't trust you to keep your eyes closed." He sighs, grinning the whole time, and pulls his tie off and wraps it around my eyes.

"Damn it, Dex."

"You only have yourself to blame."

"Fine."

He finishes and I hear the car door open. I get that tingly feeling all over my body because there's no clue what he has planned this time. I could end up naked or in the middle of a football stadium, I just don't know.

Dex leads me from the car then swoops me into his arms, cradling me. I hook my arms around his neck and inhale. I smell water and the sound of boats.

"Ohh, are we going on a boat?" I move to take the blindfold off.

Dex sighs. "Would you stop? You're ruining this shit. I'm doing a whole thing here… Just, okay?"

I smile. I love when he gets all frustrated while he's trying to be sweet. "Fine, grumpy."

He ignores me and keeps walking for a while. Finally, he gently slides me down his chest and spins me around. My back to his front. "Keep your eyes closed, promise?"

I nod.

He lifts the blindfold, but I keep my eyes closed since I did promise him, and I know he put a lot of effort into this.

"Okay, open your eyes."

I slowly open them and stare out at the water surrounding us. "Holy shit," I whisper.

"Right?"

"This is a yacht. Like not even a yacht." I spin around. "This is a damn mansion on water." I turn and get a glimpse of the Chicago skyline and the harbor.

Dex hugs me as the boat slowly eases farther out in the lake and the skyscrapers melt into the horizon behind us. "This is just… wow. How did you? It must cost…" Why am I always bringing up how much everything costs like an idiot? It's so rude, but I'm not used to being spoiled like this. I didn't grow up with much, but we were always happy and that's all that matters to me. It's so nice, though. All of this. I won't lie.

"Easy, killer. It belongs to a friend."

I start to ask if it belongs to Wells Covington, but I think better of it. Tomorrow is the start of another work week and I don't want to talk about work. I just want to live in the moment.

"What are you grinning like an idiot about? I can see it on your face."

I turn to him, trying not to laugh. "Nothing. It's nothing."

"No, spit it out, Whitley. You're giggling like a schoolgirl."

"Okay." I take his hand. "Follow me." I take off running down the deck and he follows behind. I head toward the very front of the boat.

"Oh God."

I turn back and laugh at him. "What?"

"I know what you're doing. You're out of your mind."

My breaths become labored because this freaking boat is big as hell and it's taking much longer than I thought it would to get to the end of it. "You're doing it with me, Jack!"

"My name is not Jack! And that movie sucks!"

"Don't ruin my moment, Collins!"

I swear I hear him mumble, "Fine," as he chases after me.

When we get to the very front of the boat, I hold my hands out to the side, just like in *Titanic*.

Dex wraps his arms around me and I can barely keep a straight face because I know he thinks we look like idiots.

"Jack, I'm flying!"

I don't have to look back to know Dex is smiling; I can feel his chest rising and falling with laughter.

"If you ask me to draw you like one of my French girls, you're getting a stick figure and then I'm fucking you while you're still naked."

I lean my head back on his shoulder. "My boyfriend is so romantic. Jack would draw me perfectly." Finally, I turn back to him. "And what do you mean that movie sucks? It might be the most romantic film ever."

"Maybe for you."

"Why don't you like it?"

His eyes bug out. "Because all the men die, Abigail!"

I can't stop laughing at how serious he looks, like he's really thought this all through. "Yeah, but he loves her."

"Yeah, and she gets to live and bang other dudes the rest of her life while he freezes to death." His hand flies out and he points at me. "And she had room on that thing!"

Finally, we both stare at each other and then burst into laughter.

"Look, I'll do whatever I can for you, Abby. But you're scooting your hot ass over on that board and we're both floating to land if this yacht goes down."

I hook my arms around his neck and plant a kiss on his lips. "Deal. And thanks for indulging me, for a while anyway."

He drops a sweet kiss on my forehead. "No problem, babe. And for the record, I would draw you as good as I could, but nothing would do you justice."

"Ohh, he recovers just like that. Very smooth, Mr. Collins."

"Come on, we're going to freeze to death out here." He leads me by the hand, giddy with excitement and takes me inside to meet the captain. It hadn't even dawned on me other people would be on the boat to operate it, and I just acted like a fool in front of everyone. My cheeks are pink the entire time Dex introduces us and it's not from the freezing wind outside.

Once that's done, the chief steward gives us the grand tour. I can't get over the size of this thing. People actually live like this. It's mind blowing. There're several bedrooms, an office, media room, fully staffed kitchen with a private chef, who happens to be cooking us dinner, I'm told.

The intricate woodwork detail in the bar is out of this world. I feel like I'm on an episode of *Lifestyles of The Rich and Famous* or *MTV Cribs*. We used to watch those shows at home and talk about what it'd be like to actually live in those houses or have all those cars.

This whole world is so alien to me. It's like I'm floating overhead watching this fabulous dream play out.

There's a guy behind the bar making me a drink as Dexter sips on a beer.

"So, how did I do?"

I cup his jaw. "At the risk of sounding ridiculously cheesy, so, sounding like you…"

He laughs.

"You've taken my breath away more in the last two days than anyone has my entire life. I don't know how to repay you for this weekend."

"Easy over there, Texas. Not everything is a business exchange. You don't owe me anything." He flashes me that million-dollar smile. "Just be happy." He cups my face again, like he always does. "Just smile for me every day. It's all I want." He kisses the corner of my mouth. "You're worth more than any of this."

How does he make me forget the damn world outside of us exists? I love the fact he's so damn confident, and not afraid to say cheesy things to make me smile. He makes it hard for me to keep my walls up. I'm playing Russian roulette with my heart, but even if I get burned, these experiences almost make me think it'll be worth it. We're past go and I've collected the two hundred dollars anyway. If he hurts me now, it's going to destroy me. I have no choice but to drop my guard and plow forward.

I accept my drink from the bartender and take a sip. It's like heaven in my mouth. "This tastes like sex with you."

Dexter laughs.

"I'm serious, it's incredible. They should call it Dex sex."

He flashes me a blank stare then raises his brows. "Guess you foreshadowed the drink the first time I asked you out."

"Stop! That was so embarrassing." I smack at his chest. "Was mortified the rest of the day when I did that." I hold up my drink. "You should have one of these, though. A Dex sex."

"Wouldn't want to masturbate at the bar. It's not civil, Abigail."

I damn near spit the liquor out and choke for a second. We're both dying laughing when the steward returns to show us to the dining room. He leads us to the upper deck where a candlelit table is set up in a room with a glass dome ceiling and fireplace. Off to the side there's a hot tub and a small pool.

"In the summer this celling retracts."

"I could get used to this."

"Don't." Dex cracks up.

I return his laugh with one of my own.

"I'm serious. I'll do whatever I can to impress you, but I'll never have this kind of money."

I reach for his forearm. "I don't care. I'd be happy in a shack with you, freezing cold with no heater."

"Okay, Texas." He laughs. "You've never been through a Chicago winter with no heater, obviously."

"Oh, and you have, Mr. Designer Suits?"

It's meant as a joke but Dex's jaw clenches a little. "Yeah." He doesn't say it mean or anything, but I can tell it bothered him.

"Dex, I didn't… It was just a joke, sorry."

He winks. "It's okay. I know."

I set my drink down and stop eating. "Don't do that, babe."

"Do what?"

"The guy thing where you pretend like I didn't just hit a nerve in your wisdom tooth with an ice pick."

He rubs his jaw. "Fucking hell, woman. Could you find a little less direct metaphor?"

I grin and shrug. "I am who I am."

He finally says, "Fine, I just… People always assume we grew up rich, because we have the firm and everything, but it wasn't like that. We weren't poor, but for a while our

267

parents lived paycheck to paycheck. One year, they didn't pay the gas bill on time and we were without heat for three days, in the middle of winter."

"I can't imagine. That must've been awful."

"Actually, it was kind of nice. We all huddled in the middle of the living room in sleeping bags. I don't know. I thought it brought me and my brothers even closer together. Mom took care of us. We had a space heater and we went to school during the day. I thought it was going to kill my dad, though."

"Why?"

He traces the rim of his glass with his index finger. "It was the only time in my life I've seen him look ashamed. Like he couldn't provide what his family needed. Family is big with him and he's traditional, old school. Like it's his job to take care of everyone, you know?"

"I know exactly what you mean. My parents are the same."

"My mom talked about getting a part-time job and he wouldn't have it. He got a second job after that and I guess, maybe that's why I'm closer to my mom. Dad wasn't around as much then. When he did have time off work, he was always taking Decker and Deacon to sports stuff. I don't knock him for it. He did the best he could, you know?"

He hasn't really opened up this much to me since our first date, so I want to keep him going.

"I love hearing about you and your mom and your dad and your brothers. It's so hard to picture you all as kids."

"We were ornery little shits. Always playing pranks, getting into trouble." He smiles like he's reliving his childhood. "We fought nonstop, but if anyone outside the family started any shit, we all finished it. Like we could fight with each other, but once an outside party jumped in, we ganged up on them and made sure they never did it again."

"I think that's a universal family code. I don't know much about it, but my friends were that way."

Dex sighs. "It's why I'm so worried about Decker and Donavan."

"Why would you be worried?"

Dex takes a drink of his beer. "That's right, you weren't here when the shit went down before the merger was finished. Did they not talk about it in Dallas?"

"I guess not. What happened?"

"Well, Donavan... ehh, that's not fair. None of us were really on board with the merger. No offense."

"I heard whispers about that from some partners, like everything wasn't going smoothly. Tate reported back to Weston but people talked."

"Well, Decker didn't tell any of us about it and had already signed a letter of intent before discussing it with anyone."

"Really? Wow."

"Yeah. Me and Deacon were opposed but came around. He did it to free up some time to spend with Jenny. Which was great. It really has been best for everyone. Last year I wouldn't have been able to date you like this. I rarely had nights off. But Donavan just snapped, out of nowhere. Didn't like it. Wasn't having it. He's always been that way, goes against the grain. I think it's because he's the baby and always feels like he has to prove himself. They can be in the same room now and be civil, but if Tate comes around, he's gone. Him and Decker rarely speak. He won't even talk to Tate. Donavan hates her."

"You know, I noticed they'd give each other dirty looks when they pass, but I kind of keep my head down at work. I just want to do a good job and be taken seriously."

How did we end up talking about work? I guess it was inevitable we would have to do it at some point. I should get used to it. I need to get this rolling before he ends up bringing up Wells Covington. I don't know what he knows, and I don't want to be put in a position between him and Decker, and I wouldn't put it past Decker to keep it from him. Especially after hearing how things went before the merger.

"So, you were saying about them not getting along." I roll my arm forward like *continue*.

"Long story short, Donavan tried to sue one of Tate's clients, knowing it was her client and knowing it would cause a conflict of interest while merging the firms. She told Decker. Decker squashed his lawsuit behind his back. They had a huge blowout and things haven't been the same in the family since."

I glance out at the lake. "Wow."

"Yeah, anyway, enough about that shit. They'll work it out. They have to. He's marrying Tate. There's no chance that won't happen. Donavan will have to get over it, eventually. If he makes a scene at the wedding, my dad will kick his ass so hard he won't sit down for a week."

"I think I like your dad."

"He's a great guy. I wish they still lived here, but they're really happy in Florida."

The stars shine above us and I feel like I'm at the top of the world.

I look down and realize I've taken about two bites of food. I'm just so enamored with Dex and hearing about him as a boy. I glance over at the pool. "That hot tub looks amazing."

"Better put it to good use."

I eat a few more bites and finish off my drink, then Dex and I go change into bathing suits. I don't know how he found time to get me a bikini and in the right size. He must've spent a lot of time planning this, like he does with everything. I'm really enjoying how calculated he is. He must be a shark as an attorney if he puts this much effort into his work.

I think he likes me in red because my dress is red and the bikini is red too. I make a mental note to wear more of it.

I can pay attention to details too, Dexter Collins.

Dex sneaks up behind me and runs a hand over my ass. "I don't know if we're going to make it to the hot tub."

"Why's that?"

"All I want to do is watch this bikini fall to the floor." His hand glides up my back and with an expert twist of his fingers, my top comes undone from around my neck and falls in front of me. The red triangles fall to my waist and his mouth crashes into mine. I climb him without even thinking, legs wrapped around his waist.

Dex kisses me deep and our tongues roll in unison, like we've done it a thousand times before. Warmth pools between my legs. Thoughts of the hot tub fade away as we fall to the bed.

We're nothing but a tangle of limbs. He yanks off my bottoms and flings them against the wall. Dex sucks a nipple into his mouth and I let out a low moan and rake my nails through his hair. He knows just how to touch me. Which buttons to push to drive me wild.

I use my foot to shove his shorts down his hips, wanting nothing but him, inside me. His stiff cock pulses between my legs. It's so close and I need it closer. The tip parts my lips, teasing me just enough to drive me mad.

I groan in his ear. "I need you, Dex."

"You have me." He guides himself into me, thrusting in long, deep strokes.

I hook my ankles around his backside, pulling me up into him, angled just right to feel him deeper. Dex's forehead presses up against mine and our eyes lock.

It's so intimate and perfect. He doesn't choke me or spank me this time. He's tender and loving and it's exactly what I need in this moment. His hands stroke my cheeks and rake through my hair, until he's kissing me deep and soft. It's so sweet, I don't ever want him to let me go. I don't ever want to be apart from him.

He hits my spot perfectly and I shudder beneath him, right on the edge, where he likes to keep me.

His hips speed up a little and he hooks an arm in the crook of my knee and pushes harder.

"Come for me, babe."

I nod against his forehead and he takes me higher, higher, higher, until I'm breaking apart beneath him.

"It feels so damn good when you come while I'm inside you." He thrusts a few more times and then his eyes roll back as he groans and blows deep inside me.

Once we're finished, we're both reduced to heavy pants. He collapses to his side on his back, and I snuggle up next to him, resting my head on his shoulder.

His hand caresses my hair. "You're my world, Abby."

I nuzzle into his shoulder, loving how safe he makes me feel.

He rolls to his side and his palm rests on my cheek. "I mean it. I love you, Abigail Whitley."

Holy crap! Dexter Collins just said he loves me!

I should be scared out of my mind right now, but I'm not. I'm not because it's Dexter and I can see he means it with every fiber of his soul. And the scariest part is, I love him too. I love him so much. To hell with my plans, when you find the right person, you just know. And I just know. We were meant to be together from day one. I could feel it then, and I feel it now, I just wouldn't admit it to myself.

"I love you too, Dexter Collins."

I wish I had a camera to capture the smile on his face right now. He looks like I just made him the happiest man on earth. I take a mental snapshot, because I never want to forget the way I feel and the way he looks.

He reaches over and puts my hand on his chest, right over his heart. "You own this. It's yours. And as long as I'm breathing, I'll fight every day the rest of my life for you."

I blush. What else can you do when the man of your dreams says something like that to you?

He reaches over and lifts my chin so I'm looking right in his eyes. "I mean every damn word. You can trust me with your heart. I promise."

We kiss once more and then I snuggle back up on his shoulder.

This is all too good to be true.

I EASE out from underneath Dex, wondering what time it is. There's a cart at the end of the bed with breakfast on it. I grab a mug and pour myself a coffee then start looking for my phone.

I find my purse and blink when I see the time. Oh no. "Dex." I put a hand on his shoulder and shake him.

He stirs, mumbling under his breath as he squints and glares at me. "What?"

"I don't mean to panic but how the hell are we getting to work?"

"You worry too much." He smirks and rolls out of bed.

My eyes naturally roam south, where his thick cock swings between his legs like a pendulum. Dex sees where my gaze is trained and grins. "Didn't get enough last night?"

My cheeks flush. He woke me up in the middle of the night with his face buried between my legs. "Stop distracting me. How are we getting to work? We're on a boat in the middle of the lake."

"Stop stressing. I took care of everything. It's covered." He yawns.

"Okay, well get your dick covered too, or we won't make it there in time and I need my job."

"Fine. You're no fun."

We both scurry around and get dressed. I stare out the

window and it doesn't look like we've moved an inch. "We haven't gone anywhere. The boat's not moving."

He grins like he's amused with the whole situation. "Will you stop freaking out? Come on."

I've never been late to work a day in my life and I don't plan on starting today. "Umm, okay." I take his hand and follow him up some stairs.

Then, I hear it. *Whop whop whop.*

Dex opens a door that leads out to the helicopter landing pad.

I can't help but feel a little like a Bond girl, going on crazy adventures with a suave man in suits.

The cold air whips all around us as we walk hand in hand over to the chopper. The pilot takes our bags and puts them in a compartment, then makes sure we're both buckled in. Once everyone's secure, he straps himself in and we lift off.

I can't stop going back and forth between me and Dex, looking out my window then leaning across him and looking out his. The yacht turns into a speck on the horizon.

"Enjoying the view?" Dex asks, laughing his ass off at how excited I am.

I've never flown in a helicopter before, not that it matters *how* we're flying. "I really am the worst. You always want to give me the window seat if we fly on a plane. This is even worse because of windows on both sides."

He smiles and takes a sip of coffee that I have no idea where it even came from. He looks like he's done this a million times. "I see that."

I give him a smack at his chest, then gaze out the front of the helicopter where the Chicago skyline grows bigger and bigger as we head right toward it. It's so beautiful. My eyes roam back and forth between the lake and Dexter.

Chicago is growing on me, fast. It's starting to feel like home, and I know it's a beautiful city with amazing food and culture and nightlife. But, part of me knows Dex is the biggest reason I have these feelings. He's anchoring me to his city, and I clearly don't seem to mind one bit.

The helicopter makes a large loop around the city, giving us a view of downtown from all angles. I wonder if the pilot did it to be nice and show us the city, or if it's because of some air traffic rules from O'Hare. Regardless, it's incredible. Finally, we hover the pier, and the pilot drops us off right where the yacht picked us up yesterday.

Once we're in the limo again, I curl into Dex in the back and fall asleep until we arrive at my apartment. Dexter carries my bag and walks me to my door, lingering long enough to kiss me. When we're done, he gives one of my breasts a quick squeeze. "One for the road."

I shake my head and can't stop cheesing like an idiot as I watch him walk to the elevator.

I can't believe this is all happening. It's totally surreal.

DEXTER

ABIGAIL SNUGGLES up next to me on the couch. There's nothing better than having a fire going and wrapping my arm around her. It's perfect.

I talked her into staying in at my apartment tonight. I ordered takeout because it's colder than fucking Hoth outside. She giggles when I pull out a tauntaun blanket I ordered when I saw it on a Facebook ad. You can unzip it, crawl inside, then zip it up around you.

We share one container of twice-baked spaghetti I ordered from a place down the road on DoorDash. The fireplace crackles and spits a few sparks when I adjust the logs. The night couldn't be more perfect. We watch two girly Hallmark Christmas movies even though it's still not even Thanksgiving yet. Multiple glasses of wine are had by both of us.

I shake my head at her after the last movie, even though I know this will work in my favor in the future. I know these movies like the back of my hand. "You have to admit the plots are almost identical. There's always a catastrophe that robs her of her Christmas spirit, and the hero always has some tragedy that's caused him to lose hope in humanity and become a loner. He springs into action and his name is always Nick and her name is always something like Holly. He does something monumentally stupid that seems unredeemable, then makes a huge gesture and begs for forgiveness. They share a wonderful PG-rated kiss, Christmas is saved, the end."

"Wow." She laughs. "You've really done your homework on this." She takes another drink, finishing her third glass of wine.

"I want to see one where they break up. Or it looks like they're about to kiss and make up and instead he fucks her brains out. Or one where it doesn't work out and he just lives his days hating Christmas even more. It'd keep me on my toes, not knowing if the happy ending was coming or not."

Abigail glares. "It's not romance if they don't end up together."

"Okay, well how about one where *she* screws up and has to beg *him* to take her back for fuck's sake? We need more equality in Christmas movies."

"Eww, no. Nobody would watch that."

"Why? It's the same shit, just gender reverse the plot."

"Because, Dex." She grabs my chin and gives it a shake like I'm a puppy who just got caught digging. "The hero has to mess up and redeem himself. It's the natural order of things. Women don't do stupid stuff like men do."

I laugh. "Oh really?"

She shrugs, biting back a smile. "Yep. We're perfect

and you guys need to beg for our affection. That's how the world works."

"I'll show you how the world works." I tickle her ribs then plant a kiss on her mouth.

"Mmm, show me more." She purrs the words against my lips.

Abigail switches the channel and a rerun of Jeopardy is on the TV.

I slip my hand between her legs. "I'll take Abigail's pussy for five hundred, Alex."

She smacks at my chest. "You're terrible."

"You like it."

"You're not wrong. But you know what I like even more?"

"What's that?"

She slides down to her knees, situating herself between my legs, and fumbles with my zipper. "Your dick."

"I do not mind this at all." My head falls back against the cushion.

Abigail tugs my pants down. "You did so well, indulging me in my cheesy movies. I feel I should return the favor."

I lift my hips as she slides my pants down to my ankles and my hard cock springs free. She strokes her hand up and down my shaft and I already feel like I might pass out. She drives me crazy with even the slightest touch. I'm addicted to her. Every time she walks out of the room withdrawal sets in. When I'm with her, all I can think about is burying myself inside her.

"Mmm, I missed you." She smiles at my dick, fist wrapped around my shaft. She kisses the tip, her eyes locked on mine, savoring every second she gets to tease me. Her lips part and she slowly slides me into her mouth.

My fingers go straight to her hair and I make a fist. Abigail sucks me deeper, swirling her tongue around me.

When she takes more of me, my eyes roll up to the ceiling then land back on hers. Her hand grips me at the base and she pumps up and down while taking the rest of me in her mouth.

It's so fucking good, but I want her pussy. I'll go crazy if I don't get it soon.

I tug her head back, sliding myself from her soft lips. "Need you naked, now." I stand up and make quick work of undressing her and then myself. I lay her on the couch, ready to eat her pussy until she hollers my name then fuck her senseless. I'm about to dive in right when my phone rings.

"Shit."

"What's wrong?" Abigail glares at me like *don't you dare answer that right now.*

"It's my mom. I have to take it."

She covers herself up like my mom might see then nods. "Okay."

"I'm sorry." I hold up a finger. "Just give me a second." I grab my phone off the coffee table. "Hey, Mom." I could say it nicer, but my balls ache like a motherfucker.

"Hey, Dex. We're gonna be there in a few days for Thanksgiving."

"I know. I'll see you then." I keep my eyes locked on Abby while I try to get Mom off the phone.

She starts in on some story about what her and Dad did today.

"Now's not a great time, Mom, can I call you back?"

"Why, what's going on? Are you working late?"

I never lie to my mom but I'm not about to tell her my girlfriend is spread eagle in front of me, covering her tits with her hands. "No, no, nothing like that."

"Well I feel like I never get to talk to you or any of my boys for that matter. Deacon is always busy with Quinn or her dad. Decker is always running around taking Jenny to something or sneaking away with Tate. I just love Tate, she's perfect for him." She yells in the background. "Yeah, Tate. Decker's fiancée! That's what I said. Decker and Tate. Deacon and Quinn. I said it right, you don't know what you're talking about."

"Mom!"

"Yeah, honey?"

"You gonna talk to me or Dad?"

"Oh, yeah, sorry. Did you get the pudding I sent?"

I grin, then look down and remember everything I did to Abigail with the pudding she made me. It's ridiculously awkward talking to my mom with Abigail's pussy staring me in the face. "Yeah, I got it. It was great. Thank you."

"You already finished it? I'll get you—"

"Mom, I'm not done. I just had some and it was great so far. Anyway…"

"I miss seeing you. You know I don't play favorites, but still… You'll always be my little Dex, even with the tattoos and the suits."

"Mom, I love you. You know this. But I—"

"Deacon said you have a new girlfriend. Why am I

hearing it from him and not you? You used to tell me everything. Is something going on with you?"

I sigh and I think Abigail can hear Mom through the speaker because she's covering her mouth and trying not to laugh so hard it's shaking her breasts. And if I don't stop staring at them, I'll have to mute Mom and put them in my mouth. "Of course not. I meant to tell you, I've just been…"

She feigns being upset and teases. "For years I want you boys to settle down and get your lives in order. Then you all get girlfriends and forget all about the woman who gave birth to you."

I laugh. "I still call you all the time."

"Yeah, yeah. Can't even tell me about your new girlfriend."

I glance down and Abigail is still grinning her ass off like she's enjoying this more than my mouth.

"Have to hear all about it from your twin brother. Maybe I should be sending him pudding in the mail."

"You're being a little dramatic, don't you think?"

She laughs. "I'm so excited for Thanksgiving. I'll have everyone together again. All my boys."

"We're excited too." Deacon and I haven't had the heart to tell her Decker and Donavan are barely talking. We both keep hoping it'll resolve itself before she finds out.

"Well anyway, I expect to meet her on Thanksgiving. Is she coming to Decker's?"

"No. She's probably going home to spend time with her family. She's from Dallas. Can we talk about it later? I really need to go."

Abigail raises a brow at me.

I shrug like *I'm so sorry*.

"Well, ask her what she's doing."

"What?"

"Ask her."

"I will, okay? I'll call her as soon as I get off the phone."

"Dexter, it's not polite to lie to your mother. Just go ahead and ask her right now."

"What lie? You want me to call her then call you back?"

"No, I know she's right there. It's the only acceptable reason you'd have for hurrying me off the phone at this hour." I can't fight back a smile. She knows me too well. I should know better.

Abigail's grinning from ear-to-ear when I glance at her.

"My mom wants to know what you're doing for Thanksgiving?"

She leans forward, like she's talking directly to my mom instead of relaying the answer to me.

I finally just sigh and put it on speakerphone.

"Hi, Mrs. Collins. I was planning on staying in town. My roommate is going to her family's house, so I figured I'd just volunteer at a shelter or something."

"Oh no. That's not happening, sweetie."

I mouth "I'm sorry" to Abigail over and over, but she seems amused. I don't know if it's because of my discomfort or because my mom is well, Mom.

Mom shouts into the phone and it blares through the speaker. "Dexter, you're bringing her to Decker's for dinner. That's final. And you know when I say final that's it."

"If she says yes will you hang up?"

"Yes."

I glance to Abigail and shrug like, *this is the only way we're getting rid of her right now.*

Abigail grins wide and looks at the phone. "I'd love to, Mrs. Collins. Thank you for thinking of me."

"You're welcome, sweetie. And you let me know if my boy is anything less than a perfect gentleman. I'll drag him out of the room by his ear if—"

"Mom!" I holler the word before I can stop myself.

Abigail dies laughing.

"Okay, I'll leave you two alone now after Dex does one thing. He knows what it is."

My eyes roll up to the ceiling then land back on the phone. "Sorry for lying, Mom."

"That's a good boy. Can't wait to meet you, Abigail. Love you, Dex."

"Love you too." I say the words as fast as possible and Mom laughs right into the speaker before it cuts off.

I grin at Abigail as I move back between her thighs. "You're in for a treat."

"I'm so nervous."

My eyes widen. "Why? I've eaten your pussy half a dozen times at least."

She smacks at my chest. "I mean about meeting your entire family at Thanksgiving. Were you talking about going down on me when you said I'm in for a treat?"

I smirk. "Of course, what else would I be talking about?"

She laughs and shakes her head at me. "You are the most arrogant—"

I dive down and flick my tongue across her clit.

"Phenomenal man on the planet."

I grin against her slick wet heat. "What I thought." I lick the length of her slit, then go back to focusing on her clit. "Don't be nervous. It'll be fine. You'll love my parents."

"Mmhmm. Oh, God. Whatever you say. Just don't stop what you're doing right now." Her fingers tighten in my hair as her hips grind against my face.

I take two fingers to the hilt and curl them up to her favorite spot. Her greedy pussy squeezes tight around them. I make a 'come here' motion inside her, hitting the mark over and over again while my tongue works lazy circles.

Abigail makes this cute whimper sound that tells me she's about to come.

"You want me to keep going or you want my dick?" I glance up at her.

"I need you inside me."

I shove off from the couch and pick Abigail up. Her legs wrap around me and her hot, wet pussy grinds against my shaft. We make it halfway to the bedroom and I can't take it anymore. I slam her back up against the wall and it knocks a picture frame to the ground. Fortunately, it doesn't shatter everywhere.

"Can't wait." Before she can respond, I shove my cock into her. Her head smacks back against the wall.

Before I can stop myself, my hips are a blur, bouncing her up and down on me as I thrust deep into her. She bites down on my shoulder, like she always does when she's about to come.

"Fuck, Abby." I groan out her name just as she clamps down on me.

My cock kicks and I shove her down on me, as deep as humanly possible before I blow inside her sweet cunt.

Her forehead falls onto my shoulder. A few seconds pass and her eyes drift up to mine. We both turn and look down the hallway to my bedroom.

Through rough pants, I say, "We almost made it."

She nods in agreement. "Almost."

"There's always next time."

"Indeed, sir."

ABIGAIL

I'm on my third outfit change this morning. I don't know what I was thinking agreeing to go to the Collins family Thanksgiving. What if I screw up? What if the food I made is terrible and gives them all food poisoning? What if I make a complete ass of myself and say the wrong thing or do the wrong thing? What if Dexter decides he doesn't like me as much as he thought he did?

Thanksgiving is for family. Everyone will be there. It's too much.

We haven't been dating *that* long. I mean, we're both obviously in love, but it's still too soon. I told him I loved him too early and now I'm about to lose my sanity.

You're psyching yourself out. Stop being ridiculous.

I glance at the clock and wonder if it's too early to start drinking. It's a holiday. Day drinking is acceptable. At least I think it is. I need a Xanax because my anxiety is off the charts. I almost wish Barbie was here to talk me down from the ledge, but she left last night to stay at her parents. They live about two hours away in Indiana.

Pull yourself together, Abby.

Dexter is going to be here soon and I'm a damn mess.

My cell rings and I pick it up. "Hey, Mom. Happy Thanksgiving." Perfect. I should've already called her. If anyone can get me through this, she can.

"Hey, sweetheart. I wanted to check in on you. Did you make plans?"

"I'm going to Dexter's to meet his family and I'm freaking out a little, to be honest." I yank a casserole dish out of the oven with the phone clutched between my cheek and shoulder.

"It'll be fine, baby girl. Just be yourself. They'll love you."

"I wish I was at home with you and Dad. I should be there."

"Nonsense, you're coming home for Christmas and that's enough for us."

"Thanks, Mom." There's a knock at the door. It's probably Dexter. "Shit," I mumble.

"Abigail Louise!"

"Sorry, Mom. I just. I'm all over the place. I gotta go. He's here. I'll call you tonight if it's not too late when I get in."

"Okay. I love you."

"Love you too." I end the call and open the door.

It's Kyle.

We haven't spoken since the night at the bar when Dex headbutted Nick.

"Wow. You look great."

I glance down at the tan wrap sweater dress I settled on

288

and raise an eyebrow. "Umm, thanks. What are you doing here?"

He scratches the back of his neck and rocks back on the heels of his feet. "I know things have been weird, but I wasn't sure if you had plans or anyone to spend Thanksgiving with. Barbie told me she was going to her parents last night and I just wanted to invite you to go down to the mission with Nick and me." He holds up a hand. "If you want to. I'm sure you made plans already."

"I appreciate the invite, but I'm actually waiting on Dexter. We're going to his brother's. His parents are in town."

"Meeting the family." He mumbles something else I can't hear under his breath. "Sounds like things are getting pretty serious."

I glance down at the floor, I don't know why I feel so ashamed. I don't know why I feel any kind of way. Kyle and I are friends, at least I think we are, but I won't sit around and listen to him badmouth my boyfriend. I can do whatever I want.. "Yeah. We are."

He kicks at an imaginary rock. "Cool."

"I really like him. I'm sorry if you don't get along, but he's going to be around. If that's going to be a problem…"

"I just miss hanging out with you. I still want to be friends. We just won't talk about your boyfriend, okay?"

"Sure." I agree even though I know it'll never be how it was. Too much has changed and even though Dex head-butted Nick, I don't know what Kyle said in the bar. I just don't want to be rude. We'll see each other in passing and say hi until I finally move out, then I'll probably never hear from him again. It makes me sad, but I love Dex and I just need to keep the peace a little while longer. I already have half a security deposit saved up and I'm sure my parents will give me money at Christmas time, even though I tell them not to.

"Guess I'll see you around then."

"Yeah, see ya." I close the door and pull a few other dishes out of the fridge and set them on the counter. I made pecan pie, caramel drizzle cheesecake, and banana pudding for Dex, plus sweet potato pie because even if they made it you can never have enough, and I don't know if they make it right up here.

A few minutes later, Dexter shows up. He kisses me good and deep, grabbing my ass in the process.

"What's all this?" He motions to all the dishes on the counter.

I pace back and forth, trying to calm myself down. "I'm an idiot. It's so dumb. I just didn't know what to make and where I'm from you don't show up empty-handed when someone invites you over."

"This all looks amazing." He starts to dip his finger in my pudding.

I smack at his hand. "Don't you dare touch that food, Dexter Collins. I slaved all night making these for your *family*. Not just for you." Wow, we sound so domesticated already, and it's actually nice. It warms my heart and makes this whole thing easier. We just work together.

"You're gonna make me fat if you keep cooking like this."

I wag a finger at him. "Well keep your fat fingers out of it, okay?"

He holds his hands up in surrender. "Okay, Betty Crocker. Damn."

When I look away, he gets a finger full of pudding and shoves it in his mouth, grinning his ass off.

I scowl at him. "No more for you today. You're in a timeout."

He grabs me by the hip and yanks me into him. "Abigail, you love me because I don't give a shit about rules. You did this to yourself."

I shake my head at him. "I *will* tame you."

He laughs at that. "For real, though. That pudding is amazing." He leans forward into my ear. "I'll have to get a spoon from my brother's house, for later."

He always knows how to make me blush.

WE GET to Decker's and the moment we walk through the front door his daughter, Jenny, and Tate snatch the food I brought and take it into the kitchen.

A woman, who I assume is Dex's mom, launches herself at us, hugging us both tight. "You must be Abigail. Let me get a look at you." She holds my hands and pulls back assessing me from head to toe. "Gorgeous." She drops my hands and smiles, then turns to Dexter.

She's a thick woman. Tall, like an athlete, but very graceful. She's wearing this goofy sweater that reminds me of Dexter's sense of humor, and I start to see where he gets his silliness from. There's a cartoonish turkey on the front in a suggestive pose and it says 'Pour some gravy on me' above it. I think we're going to get along just fine.

291

"Jesus," Dex mumbles.

She smacks his arm. "You watch your mouth, Dexter Harrison Collins."

I glance up at him. "Harrison?" I grin.

"She says it's after the president, but we all know she had a crush on Harrison Ford when I was born." He turns to her. "Because there's no way she'd name me after a president who died a month into his term, right, Mom?"

She giggles and gives him a big hug. "I love you, baby boy."

"Love you too, Mom."

She takes me by the hands. "Now, Abigail, has Dex cooked you breakfast yet?"

"Oh my God, yes. And it was fantastic."

Quinn and Tate walk up about the same time.

Quinn says, "Deacon cooks amazing breakfast too."

Tate nods, like she's in a trance. "So does Decker."

"You're welcome, ladies." Mom grins at all of them. "I taught all my boys to cook breakfast and told them that's the secret to keeping a good woman, because I always wished *someone* would cook breakfast once in a while." She flashes a dirty look across the room like she's looking for her husband.

He's oblivious, talking to someone else.

All the boys turn around, suddenly interested, and Dex glares in a playful way. "Wait, that was just a trick to get us to cook?"

"Dexter Harrison Collins, the girls are talking. You mind your business."

"Someone's in trouble." Donavan laughs and walks up behind us. "I heard the middle name come out."

She wheels around on him. "Don't you start getting mouthy, Donny, or I'll go around the room asking why you can't keep a woman happy like my other boys. At least they have someone to cook breakfast for." She shakes her head and looks at me again. "Four boys and only one grandbaby to spoil. You see what I'm dealing with here?" She turns to Deacon. "You should think about getting your sperm tested."

Decker damn near shoots whiskey out of his nose. "Mom!"

Quinn turns bright pink and smiles up at Deacon. Deacon's eyes bulge and he freezes up.

I've never seen the Collins brothers look so nervous in my entire life. They usually walk around with scowls while employees scurry around trying to look busy.

She turns back to me. "You and Dexter are going to make beautiful babies. I know these things."

I try not to gape at her, but holy crap we just started dating. Babies? I don't even know if I want kids, but there's no way I'm going to admit that here. My face must say it all.

She smiles and runs a hand across my forearm. "I'm not trying to scare you off. I'm just armed with a mother's intuition."

An older man walks into the room and damn near takes all the air with him. He has on a collared shirt with a sweater pulled over it and looks like he could've stepped out of a Calvin Klein catalog. He looks regal and stately, with silver hair slicked back perfectly. He leans down and pecks Mrs. Collins on the cheek. "Give the girl room to breathe, honey. Let them get their coats off before you start counting future grandchildren." He turns and holds a hand out to me. "Nice to meet you. I'm David." He leans in close. "The father of all these little shits running around here."

Great, another D name to remember!

I laugh. "It's nice to meet you both. Thank you so much for having me."

"Don't mind Donna. She gets excited about grandkids. We have Jenny, but she's older and chasing boys around now."

Decker glares in his direction when he hears it but doesn't say anything.

I follow Quinn and Tate into the kitchen and politely make my escape from the family craziness for a few minutes.

"I'm so glad you came." Quinn smiles.

"Thank fuck you brought pecan pie," Tate mutters, eyeing my desserts. "Man, I miss the food back home. And my mom's cooking. And Daddy's fried turkey. They don't do Thanksgiving for shit up here."

I laugh. She's probably right. You can't beat Thanksgiving in the south. "How do you and Decker handle holidays with your families in different states?" I ask because I'm curious, but I also want to see what the future might be like for Dex and me.

"We're flying down in the morning. We couldn't leave knowing that his folks were coming from Florida. Did you see Jenny invited her boyfriend? Decker's shitting bricks but trying to be nice. It's hilarious."

I follow Tate's gaze to the dining room where Jenny

and a boy are seated next to each other looking at something on her phone.

"Oh, she went for the bad boy right out the gate. Well played." He has dark shaggy hair that lays to the left side and his bottom lip is pierced. He's wearing a hat turned backward. Decker is in major trouble.

"Right? Boys did *not* look like that when I was in school. Just saying," says Quinn.

"Amen to that." Tate grins. "All we had were jocks and country boys. Trucks full of shoulder pads or rifles. No angsty artists and tortured souls in leather jackets."

"Babe, come here I want you to meet someone." Dex practically yanks me into the other room and thrusts me in front of a man who looks almost identical to David Collins, and a young woman, maybe mid-twenties. Wow, she's beautiful. She has tattoos up her ripped arms, just like Dex, and jet-black hair with icy blue eyes. "This is my uncle, Damian, and my cousin Harlow."

I hold out my hand to both of them. "It's nice to meet you."

They're both super nice even though Harlow looks like she could beat the hell out of anyone in the house. She's seriously intimidating, the way she carries herself, but she's as nice as can be and stunning.

Dex can't stop singing her praises; they must be really close. "She works in digital marketing. She's been killing it too, ever since she graduated. Just started her own firm here in Chicago."

"Speaking of that, I wanted to talk to you. We need to set up a meeting."

"What for?"

"Work."

"Might want to talk to Decker about that, if it's about marketing…"

"Look, you hire my firm for the financial services division. I'll have you kicking everyone else's ass and make you look like a fucking hero at your firm."

"Harlow, language," says Damian.

"Oh fuck that. We're all family."

"What kind of shit do you do?" asks Dex. "I don't handle marketing much. Haven't studied it since undergrad."

"I'm sure you pussies probably have billboards and other lame shit, sponsor events, things that get you a bullshit ROI. I'll install pixels on your website, launch Facebook and Google adword campaigns. Highly targeted with warm audiences to get your ads in front of the right eyeballs."

Dex looks like a deer in headlights but shrugs. "All right, fuck it. Let's get something on the books."

Harlow smiles. "You were always my favorite cousin." She dives into Dex and wraps her arms around him. "My pitch kicked ass, didn't it?"

He kisses her on top of the head; they look more like brother and sister than cousins. "Kicked all the ass."

She leans up and whispers something in his ear, and he stares right at me and grins wide. I want to ask Dex what she said, but Decker walks into the room.

"Okay, we're ready to eat. File in, ya bunch of animals." Decker's voice booms through the house.

Everyone moves to the dining room to find their seats.

Their dad says a prayer over the food and then everyone jumps up to go fill their plates.

I lean over to Dexter. "What'd Harlow whisper to you?"

"That I'm lucky you didn't go to college with her when she went through her phase."

I damn near choke on the water I was taking a sip of.

The four brothers start for the food, looking like ravenous wolves, and their dad glares right at them. They freeze in their tracks, and I'm starting to see where they get their commanding presence from. Hell, he stared at them and I shrank back in my seat a little.

He turns to the rest of us. "Ladies, go ahead." He turns to the boys and I hear him grumble as we walk by, "Act like you have some damn manners."

After everyone fills their plates, I sit next to Dexter, and Donavan takes a seat on the other side of me. Jenny and her boyfriend sit at the kitchen island on barstools, secretly holding hands where they don't think anyone can see.

The food is fantastic. Tate baked a ham. She said she marinated it in Coca Cola. Everyone eats and makes small talk at the table.

Dexter's parents crack me up. I was expecting them to be more, I don't know, not how they are. They're both really down to earth, but Mr. Collins seems like he's mellowed out a lot from how he probably was. He definitely fits the hard-worker personality type. Man of few words, but when he does speak, it matters, and everyone listens.

One thing I do notice, that sends a warmth spreading

through my veins, is that he looks at his wife the way I've seen the Collins brothers look at all of us. I think the way a man treats a woman is learned behavior; his experiences watching his parents interact shapes the way he'll be one day. Mr. Collins might look hard and no-nonsense, but his face lights up, even when his wife tells an embarrassing story in front of him. He changes when she walks into the room, and that's really what it's all about, having that effect on the man you end up with.

"It's just a beach we go to. It's no big deal." Dex's Mom says it proudly, and all the color drains from the boys' faces.

I lean over to Tate and Quinn, because I was daydreaming, waxing poetical about how I think Dex will treat me. "What was that? About a beach?"

Tate grins her ass off. "They go to a nude beach."

Mr. Collins shrugs when all the boys, his brother, and Harlow look at him like there's no way he'd ever do anything like that. He takes a huge bite of turkey. "Don't knock it 'til you try it. It's quite liberating, actually."

"Jesus Christ, like I don't get enough of this shit at work," Decker mumbles and buries his face in his palm.

DEXTER

I LOOK over at Abigail and can't stop grinning like a complete idiot. She fits in like she's been coming to these things for years.

Mom walks up while I'm spying on her helping with the dishes. "I know that look." She bumps me with her hip.

I inhale a huge breath. "So, what's the verdict?"

Mom narrows her eyes, then she puts her arm around me. She says, "Are you kidding? You haven't brought a girl to meet us since high school, and that was for prom."

"I'm nervous. What if I screw things up? What if I hurt her?"

"If you're concerned about hurting her, you won't."

"I don't know."

"Dex, look at me."

I turn to face her.

"You're not perfect, kiddo. Nobody is. You're gonna screw up." She gestures toward the kitchen. "She's gonna screw up. It's how you deal with the screw-ups that defines

ALEX WOLF & SLOANE HOWELL

the relationship. If you love each other, nothing is irreparable."

"So… verdict?"

"If she makes you happy, she makes me happy. But I do like her. So you can relax. You and your brothers are so high strung. I worry about you boys."

I bend down and kiss her on the forehead. "Thanks. I'm glad you like her."

Mom bumps me with her hip again. "Noticed she made you pudding."

"Yeah, sorry, I know that's our thing, and I told her about it. I kinda felt like I betrayed you a little."

"Don't apologize. I'll keep sending it. I like that you want to share our little thing with the woman you love."

"Really, I thought, I don't know. Thought you'd react different. Like maybe, I don't know, like she was moving in on your territory or something. This is all new to me. I've never felt this way before."

She gives me another hug and does her best to get her arms all the way around me, like she always does. She whispers, "You'll always be my little boy. But I can relinquish being the number one woman in your life with grace. That's how it's supposed to be. I'll always love you, no matter what."

"I love you too." I look out at Abigail. "I love her. So much it hurts."

"I know." She winks. "Moms always know."

I smile as she walks off and Dad wraps her in his arms. They sit back, watching everything unfold in front of them. When I glance back to Abigail, I wonder if that'll be us someday, watching all our kids as adults.

"You boys got any other women around the office for Donavan?" Dad grins his ass off. "Looks like he could use some pointers."

Donavan rolls his eyes. "You guys keep this shit up and I'm leaving."

Mom glares. "Language, son. There are ladies present."

"Sorry, Mom. I forgot Deacon was here."

"So you could ask me for my number, big boy?" Deacon laughs.

Without thinking, Donavan says, "Fu—" He looks at Mom. "Uhh, screw you guys." He shakes his head and mumbles. "A-holes."

"A-holes. Well done on that one," says Deacon.

I can't stop laughing. "Hey, Abigail has a crazy-ass roommate. I can hook you up. Just let me know." I slap him on the back, and apparently he's had enough because he yanks me into a headlock and down to the floor.

We go at it like we're ten years old all over again. Decker and Deacon take bets on who will tap out first and egg us on.

"You see how they act?" Mom says to Tate, Quinn, and Abigail. "I raised a bunch of animals. Boys! Knock that crap off!"

We get up and I dust myself off. "Totally won."

"Like hell you did."

"All right, that's enough." Dad gestures toward the hall. "Let's go to the study. I brought cigars."

"He was *not* talking to you." Decker holds his arm out in front of Jenny's date as he starts to follow.

Fuck, that kid has balls.

I glance back to the kid and shrug. "Sorry, ol' smoke crotch isn't any fun, is he?"

Decker glares lasers at me.

I hold my hands up. "Hey, just saying. The ol' rug is getting a little silvery up there."

"I'm not Donavan, I'll lay your ass out for good."

"Please. Snap those brittle bones like twigs if you come at me."

"All right." Dad looks back to make sure Mom is out of earshot. "Knock the shit off."

We get into Decker's study and Dad leans against the desk after passing out cigars and lights his first. The rest of us follow suit.

Dad has that serious stare on his face, like he did when we'd get in trouble as kids. Fuck. I have no idea what this is about, but it's not good. An ominous feeling fills the room.

He glares back and forth at Decker and Donavan and points a finger at each one of them. "Front and center, *now*."

They both glance at each other and for a brief moment in time, we're kids again and not high-powered attorneys. They both know what's up.

"What the hell is this?" says Decker.

"Boy, I will knock your fucking dick in the dirt you talk to me that way again. This shit has gone on long enough. You're lucky I didn't fly my ass up here a long time ago. Your mother has been a wreck for months. You know how she gets when you're not getting along."

We all stare at him like we can't believe they know.

"Yeah, she knows. That woman knows everything

going on with her boys at all times." He stares around at all of us, pointing his cigar. "This is family. You don't have anything but each other, and you'd better not fucking forget it. This shit gets aired out and resolved *right now*. I won't have your mother endure another minute."

Donavan stares at Decker, then at Dad. "He merged the goddamn firm without discussing it with us first. I have to share my criminal law department with a bunch of incompetent assholes out of Dallas. Then, he took Tate's side over mine with a client and fucked up—"

"Enough." Dad turns to Decker. "Well?"

"The shit wasn't personal. It was business. I built the firm. I run the firm. I make the decisions. Nothing changed other than a lighter workload for all of us. Excuse me if I didn't want to be a piece-of-shit absent father to my only daughter. I was thinking about Jenny when I made the decision to merge the firm and now the bonuses are bigger and the hours are less for everyone."

Donavan looks away, shaking his head when he mentions Jenny. "I get the dad stuff, but fuck, man. You let Tate waltz in here like she owned our damn firm, boss people around, all because you fell in love with her."

Decker shakes his head. "It had nothing to do with my feelings for Tate or you for that matter. You're my brother and I'll always have your fucking back, always. But when you're wrong, I'll call you out on that shit. I have to. At work I'm the boss, and family shit comes second. As soon as we walk out the door, it's family first."

"It sure fucking felt like you were picking her over us."

"Look, maybe…"

Dad glares at Decker.

Decker holds up both hands. "Okay, I maybe could have communicated things better. It was never my intention to piss you off. I knew you'd throw a fit and I'd have to deal with all of you for months to get you on board and I didn't have that kind of time. Every minute I didn't get with my daughter was torture for me, don't you get that? But regardless of your feelings for Tate, that lawsuit was petty as fuck and you know it. It was a frivolous loser. You wanted to tank a nine-figure business deal because you were up in your feelings. I couldn't have that. Too many jobs on the line and people who aren't in our family would be affected by it."

Dad turns to Donavan. "Donny?"

He shrugs. "Okay, maybe the lawsuit was bullshit. And yeah, it did hurt when you ignored us for a woman. I'm glad you found someone and I'm happy for you, I just…" He sighs in frustration. "It was our thing. The firm. It was ours. Our name was on the wall and now it's gone and we'll never get it back."

Decker's glare softens. "Isn't it better, though?" He raises his shoulders like, *come on, man*. "It was just a name on a wall. It doesn't take away who we are or where we come from."

Donavan looks away. "Yeah, I mean, I guess it is. I just… I wish you'd done it differently and I'd have been on board, maybe. But fuck, why does your fiancée…"

"She's the way she is because she won't get any fucking respect if she isn't. You know this. We all know how women associates get treated. Fuck, we're all guilty of doing it. Do you know how many times she's begged me outside of work to reach out to you? That she *hates* being a wedge between us. It keeps her up at night. Do you know how many fake promises I've made to reach out to you to try and resolve this? I've just been too damn proud to do it and no time ever seems like the right time. You know how I get." A tear slides down Decker's cheek. "It's why our fucking wedding has been delayed, because she refuses to marry me while I'm pissed off at you! You don't know her. Not like you think you do."

"I-I didn't know she felt that way."

Decker finally cracks. He walks over and puts a hand on Donavan's shoulder. "Look, maybe we can talk when we get back to the office after Thanksgiving. If you want a more managerial role all you have to do is say something. I think you'd be great for it and I have a ton of shit on my plate I'd gladly farm out if I could."

Donavan's eyes light up, but he tries to play it cool. He nods. "Yeah, *maybe*, I'd be interested in something like that."

Decker glances to Deacon and me with his eyebrows raised.

At the same time, we both hold our hands up. "Fuck that," says Deacon.

"Yeah, you guys can have that stress." I grin.

Simultaneously, it feels like a weight just lifted off all our shoulders. Like every burden in the world just removed itself from the room. For the first time in months, it feels amazing to have them getting along. It just took Dad putting his foot down.

"You two know what to do." Dad waves his cigar hand between the two of them.

They both hug it out and they're actually smiling. It feels surreal. I didn't think it was possible at this point.

"Work your problems out from now on." Dad throws an arm around me and Deacon and moves us in closer to Decker and Donavan, almost like a football huddle. "I don't want to see this shit happen again. You're fucking Collins's. That's not a light responsibility, I raised you better than that. Honor, integrity, respect. You have responsibilities and duties to your family. I'm proud of all you boys. You've all amassed more than I ever dreamed for you when I was working two jobs to get you all the way to college while your mom took care of you. It's the only thing that got me through it, knowing I was providing, and your mother was making sure you didn't kill each other, so you could have better lives than we did. So you could accomplish everything you wanted." He leans back and takes a puff off his cigar. "Respect and love for your family is the glue that holds it all together. We have a role to play and when one cog in the wheel isn't functioning right, it's up to all of you to get off your asses and fix it." He turns to Donavan and me. "Tate and Quinn are already part of this family because your brothers have made promises to them." He turns to Deacon and Decker. "And when a Collins man gives his word, he follows through." He grits his teeth and gets that angry-as-hell look on his face that sends a shiver up my spine. "Tate and Quinn are to be treated like you would treat your mother. They are to be protected at all costs and they will *NOT* be disrespected in any fucking way. Or if I hear about it, I will fly up here and kick every ass in this room personally. Is that understood?"

"Yes, sir," we all say in unison.

He smiles. "Good. There will be peace in this family, as long as I'm breathing. Now, let's finish this little get together with me sharing a cigar with my boys. It's been too fucking long."

"Amen to that," says Decker.

I grin. "Where do you keep the whiskey in here?"

"Great idea, son. I like the sound of that."

Decker and I pour everyone a glass and things go right back to normal, just like that. No more fighting, no more tension.

We laugh and joke and bust each other's balls. It's perfect. I glance over at Dad, laughing and cutting up. I haven't always agreed with him on everything, but he's a good father and I hope I can be somewhat like him one day, with the things that matter anyway. I could imagine it eating me up inside if my sons weren't getting along, whether they're rich or poor. Some things are more important than money and status, and he's right, at the end of the day, the people you love are all that matter.

"This is how family is supposed to be." Dad stamps out his cigar in an ashtray, wearing a satisfied grin. "I don't know about you fucking clowns but I'm ready for some dessert. Tone down the goddamn language in front of the ladies. It bothers your mother."

We all file back toward the kitchen when Decker puts his arm across my chest. "We need to talk shop for a second, while I've got you here."

"Dude, it's Thanksgiving. What the hell? Can't we forget about business for a few hours and enjoy everyone getting along?"

"It's about Covington."

"Seriously? You're still on that shit? Let it go. I already secured part of his business, and I'll have it all by the end of the quarter. It'll be a big fuck you to Cooper and all those pompous pricks in midtown Manhattan."

He shakes his head. "Not gonna happen. I had Rick look into him."

"You what? What is the goddamn deal? You don't do this type of due diligence with any other white-collar clients."

"You don't know what I do. There's a lot I don't tell you guys and there are reasons for it."

"Why are you trying to fuck this deal in the ass? Where Covington goes, the money follows. Do I need to spell it out for you? This is what you pay me huge bonuses for. I can't do my goddamn job with you hamstringing me behind my back."

"Will you just cool your temper for two seconds and listen to me? Jesus Christ."

I wave an arm out. "Well go on. You're going to anyway."

"I run a clean house. I had Abigail and Rick both look into him. It's all bad."

My face heats up and it's not good. I can already feel the rage building in my chest. "Abigail knew about this?"

"Shit." Decker looks away then back at me. "You two weren't really, *serious*, when I put her on it. And I told her to only report to Rick and me, nobody else."

"Why the fuck wasn't I read in? I'm the one dealing with him." He's always pulling this clandestine shit and

I'm sick of it. And him and Abigail are keeping secrets from me?

"It was need-to-know and your emotions are clouding your judgment. Look, your buddy owns a few corporations with ties to cartels and organized crime shit. They're money washing operations. He also owns a large portion of a shipping company, and we think they may be involved in human trafficking."

"Does it tie back to him? *Legally*?" I have to put an emphasis on that, because he's speculating right now.

"None of it ties back to him, legally, but I don't want him on our roster. Do you really want your name associated with that shit?"

"Fuck you. Our criminal law department defends murderers. Do you want our name associated with *that*? Money is money and we don't know for a fact that he's doing any of that shit, or if he's aware of any of it. He's at such a high level he looks at spreadsheets and data. He owns interests in thousands of companies. I know him personally. You're biased because he likes all that BDSM shit and you're looking for a reason to fuck this deal up." I shake my head and all I can think about is how Abigail didn't say anything. "No. I know what's motivating this. Fear. You're pulling this shit because you're afraid of ruffling feathers in New York. Cooper has you scared like a little bitch."

He gets up in my face. "I will say this once and it's final. Fuck Bennett Cooper. And Covington is done, so get him out of your thick fucking head and move on."

"Fuck you. He's my client. I've been working on this for months if not years. It's happening. We don't need to know about any shady shit he has on the side. We have plausible deniability. When did you become such a fucking saint? Tate put you up to this or something?"

He points a finger in my face. "Don't bring my fiancée into this because you're pissed off about being wrong and because I gave your girlfriend an assignment. Business is business and she was just doing her damn job. Covington's not to set foot in our fucking offices until I say so."

"Fuck this. I don't need it. Not from you. Not from anyone." I throw a shoulder into him as I storm out of the study.

ABIGAIL

I'm in the kitchen helping Tate serve dessert as the guys stroll in from the study with Mr. Collins leading the way.

Donovan and Deacon fall in behind him and grab a plate.

"This pudding is amazing." Jenny beams at me and gets a second helping.

"Thank you." I turn to Deacon. "Where's the other half of you?"

He shrugs. "I don't know, he stayed behind with Decker for a minute. Maybe something with work?"

"Holy… this pecan pie reminds me of home," says Tate, trying to make idle conversation, but I see her keep glancing toward the study too.

I slide into a seat next to her where nobody else can hear. "Thanks again for having me. I know Decker wasn't thrilled at the thought of Dexter and me. I hope it's not a problem. I don't want to cause tension in the family."

"Oh, trust me. Whatever is happening in there right

now… It has nothing to do with you. All these boys like to act tough, but inside they're all softies. You just have to be around them outside of work to get to the good stuff. I think they're at each other over a potential client."

My stomach drops and I wonder if this is to do with the file I gave Decker about Wells Covington.

Finally, I see Dexter and I know the look on his face immediately. I've seen it once before and it wasn't a good outcome.

Decker storms in right behind him, looking just as pissed off, if not more.

"Oh shit," Tate whisper-sighs the second she sees them.

Dexter doesn't slow down at all as he marches past me. He shoots me an angry scowl and goes straight out the front door.

"What the hell?" I look at Tate.

Decker goes to the fridge and yanks the door open so hard I'm surprised it doesn't fly off the hinges, then takes out a beer.

I stand up. "I'm going to go check on Dex."

Quinn steps in my way. Her eyes are wide. "Don't. Trust me. Whatever it is let him cool down and work through it. If you go out there it'll be worse. Seriously. Him and Deacon are exactly alike."

"I'd listen to Quinn," says Tate.

"No." I shake my head. "He can be pissed at Decker all he wants but he has no business treating me that way. I didn't do anything."

I grab my coat from the hall closet and find him

outside pacing on the sidewalk. "What the hell happened back there? You don't just shoot me dirty looks and walk out on your family and me with no explanation."

His hands are trembling and not from the cold. "Just let me be, Abby. Fuck! I just need five minutes."

I shake my head. "No, if you want us to work, you talk to me."

He points a finger in my face. "You mean the way you came and talked to me when you were doing research on my friend?"

Shit. It *was* about Covington. "I was doing my job. What my boss told me to do."

"Horse shit! You knew Decker was working behind my back, but you said nothing. Not one word. You knew about Wells. You saw us at the bar, you knew who he was so don't act all innocent now. You went behind my back with my brother to sabotage me." His hands ball into fists and his face is bright pink. "Were you even going to tell me at all?"

"Oh, can I speak now? Or would you like to keep screaming at me like a child throwing a tantrum?"

"I told you to leave me alone for five minutes and you didn't listen. What you see is what you get."

"I didn't know what was going on, *Dexter*." I point at him. "This is why I knew we were a bad idea." A tear slides down my cheek as I say the words, because I knew this was coming. I knew something like this was going to happen. "I told you we wouldn't be able to keep business and personal separate, but you kept at me, kept pressing, until I gave in and now look at us. Is this what you wanted? You're breaking my heart right now and you promised me you wouldn't."

"Just doing your job?" He scoffs. "Rationalize it and play the victim all you want. You betrayed me. You didn't come talk to me. You hid things from me and now you act like it's my fault. I don't need this shit."

I'm not going to sit here and be his punching bag. I don't have to put up with this. Not from him. Not from any man. Maybe my mom was right, and he is just a boy, throwing a hissy fit, all up in his emotions like women supposedly get.

"Yeah. My job."

"That's what everyone around here says. I'm just doing my job but when I'm the one doing mine, I get fucked."

"I didn't do this to you."

"Right. You just fed the information to Decker during the day and fucked me at night. You know what, Abigail? Why don't you go back in the house with my brother and enjoy the holiday. He's the one who pays your fucking bills. Business is business, right?"

Tears burn in my eyes as he climbs in his car and squeals the tires, leaving a trail of smoke behind them.

I cover my face with my hands and the back of my throat burns. He just left me here, knowing I'd be alone with his family after what just happened.

I don't know if I've ever been so ashamed in my life.

I wipe the tears from my eyes.

Fuck you, Dexter!

I start toward the end of the driveway with my phone in my hand, because there's no way in hell I'm going back in that house after what just happened. It's too humiliating.

The front door opens, and Tate and Quinn come rushing out. They probably heard Dexter peel out of the driveway like an idiot.

"Just come back inside, please?" Tate wraps her arms around my shoulders.

I shake my head. I can't. And if I see Decker, I might blow up at him and lose my job. "I'm fine. I'll call an Uber. Really."

"I'll drive you home," says Quinn.

I can't even look at her, I just nod.

"Just let me tell Deacon and grab the keys. Did you bring a purse?"

"I'll grab it." Tate gives me another squeeze on the shoulder.

I sniffle and try to dry my eyes on my sleeve where they can't see. I'm a mess, crying in front of all my coworkers.

A few minutes later, I'm in the car with Quinn.

She turns the radio down. "You don't have to talk about it if you don't want." Her gaze and tone softens. "But I'm here if you need me. Those boys can act like idiots sometimes."

"I appreciate the offer, but I'm fine, really." I'm not fine. I'm anything but fine right now. I can't be with someone who doesn't respect me. The only good thing about today is that Barbie is at her parents' house, so I can't explode on her and end up homeless.

Quinn pulls down my street in front of my building.

"If you need anything call me. We can grab lunch one day next week."

"Sure. That'd be great." I know it won't happen, but

Quinn is nice, and I don't want to be a bitch to someone who doesn't deserve it. I know her loyalty is with Dexter. She's engaged to his twin brother. Anything I say to her will get back to him.

She drops me off and I walk inside. The apartment is quiet and cold. I turn the heat up and sulk down the hall to my bedroom and change into sweats and a t-shirt. I put on fuzzy socks and twist my hair up into a messy bun.

Finally, I settle in on the couch and watch the Hallmark Movie Channel with a pint of sea salt caramel ice cream.

I'm halfway into my movie when someone bangs on my door.

I don't want to answer. It's most likely Dex and he's either here to be a bigger asshole or to get on his knees and grovel. I don't have the patience for either of those scenarios tonight.

I do walk over to the door though, my curiosity getting the best of me. I look out the peephole and it's Kyle.

I open the door and he takes one look at me, then pulls me in for a hug. "Are you okay?"

I shake my head. "No, my life is shit right now."

"What happened?" He takes a step inside and I close the door. "Were you crying?"

I look in the mirror and my eyes are still red as hell. "No. It's… I'm fine."

"Did he do this?"

"I don't want to talk about it."

He hems and haws for a second, but surprisingly he doesn't mention Dexter again. "Well, come to the apartment. We have chocolate cake and shots. Nick brought a bunch of food from his family's get together. We're just chilling. Don't sit here all alone on Thanksgiving."

I glance around my apartment. He's right. I shouldn't have to sit here all alone, miserable. "Okay." I grab my keys and leave my phone. "Just for a bit, though."

DEXTER

I'VE DRIVEN AROUND AIMLESSLY for about half an hour trying to cool off. I know I shouldn't have exploded on Abigail the way I did. I was pissed at Decker mostly. Yeah, I'm upset with her, but I shouldn't have taken off like I did and left her alone at Decker's house. If she would've just given me five fucking minutes by myself, it's usually all I need to cool down. But when I'm like that and people don't leave me alone, I say and do hateful shit. She wouldn't stop pressing and I just lost it.

I don't know what I'm doing. I'm too mad to see Decker right now, but I need to at least go back and drive Abigail home. Then she can tell me she never wants to see me again and scream in my face or whatever she needs to do. I'm in the right frame of mind and won't act like a maniac this time. I deserve it, whatever she does. Who knows what the hell everyone else is saying to her about me.

Fuck!

I turn my car back around and head to Decker's house

as much as I don't want to. I pull up and leave the Chevelle running in the driveway and jog to the door. Tate comes to the front and glares like I'm the world's biggest asshole.

That's fair.

She steps outside and lowers her voice like someone might be listening in on us. "She's not here. What the fuck is wrong with you, Dexter?"

I inhale a deep cold breath. "I don't know. Your goddamn fiancé was acting like an idiot and he had Abigail running research projects on Covington behind my back, telling her not to report to anyone but him. I'm sure you were read in on it, but Wells is my friend. Not just a client. And he had my girlfriend investigating him and nobody told me shit."

"Did he now?"

"What, you didn't even know?" I shake my head. "Fucking figures."

"I'll handle Decker. Just go patch things up with Abigail. She was really upset."

"I told her to leave me alone for five minutes, she didn't listen."

Tate points a finger up at my face. "Listen up, short stack. It doesn't fucking matter who started it or who didn't do what or who was wrong. You assholes get to rule the workplace with an iron fist, women rule everywhere else. Get your shit together, snapping at her like that. You're the man, now go apologize. Those are the goddamn rules of the universe if you like to get laid and be with a badass like Abigail. So suck it up."

"Where is she?"

"Quinn drove her home."

"Thanks."

"Hey, Dex?"

"Yeah?"

"Please work things out with her. She really loves you, and you two are perfect for each other."

I walk back to my car and say over my shoulder, "I'll do my best."

When I'm back in the Chevelle, I grab my phone and dial Abigail. There's no answer. No surprise. She's no pushover. It's one of the many things I love about her.

I drive straight to her place but there's no answer when I call again from the car.

I make my way up her stairs, dreading every step, wondering what the hell I'm going to say. Finally, I stop in front of her apartment door.

I knock.

No answer.

I knock again. "Come on, Abigail. I know you're there."

A door down the hall opens and that prick Kyle walks out of his apartment. He spots me and has a smug grin plastered across his face.

Don't say shit to him, Dexter. Don't do a damn thing or you'll never get her back.

He takes a few steps toward me. "She's not home."

"How the fuck do you know?"

Damn it, just be civil to this prick. Turn the other cheek.

He smirks at me. "Because she's in *my* apartment." He

hooks a thumb behind him. "And she doesn't want shit to do with you."

I shake my head at him. "You're pathetic. Your manipulation bullshit won't work, kid. Go fuck yourself."

"I might fuck someone else who's sitting on my couch. Because I'm not lying."

To hell with being nice.

"I'm getting sick of your shit, you smug little prick." I start toward him, fist clenched.

His eyes get big. "I'm calling the cops if you don't get the hell out of here." He yanks his phone out of his pocket.

"You don't own the building. I'll bring a sleeping bag and camp out in the goddamn hallway if I want to, dipshit."

"No, but you're walking toward my apartment threatening me."

"I don't need to threaten you before I kick your ass. Now get out of my face before I punt you out a fucking window."

"Fuck you." He flips me off, but damn near stumbles over his feet as he backs up toward his door.

"Kyle? Where'd you go?" Abigail steps out into the hallway in her damn pajamas with a beer in her hand.

I don't know if I've ever felt so fucking stupid in my life. I thought for sure he was lying. No way would she be in his apartment. Less than an hour and she already ran off and started drinking with him. Everything in my body aches, all over. My heart feels like it was just ripped out of my chest. I keep waiting for anger and rage to consume me, but it doesn't. It feels like my body might collapse on itself. I have to get the fuck out of here.

Kyle stands there with a cocky, 'I told you so' smirk on his face, and I've never felt so emasculated.

I shake my head right at her. "Unbelievable."

"Dex?"

"I can't believe I came here to apologize. Enjoy your evening."

"Dex!"

Her word hits me in the back and I just keep walking.

To hell with everything.

ABIGAIL

I can't stop crying and I don't remember ever being this upset in my life. Dexter was a total asshole, but I can't get the look on his face out of my head. I didn't make him mad, I hurt him. The worst part is I don't know if I should feel bad or not. I don't know how to feel.

Yeah, I probably shouldn't have come to Kyle's, but I was so upset, and I just didn't want to be alone. I know how it looked to Dexter but it wasn't what he thinks. He'd never listen to me if I tried to tell him and I shouldn't have to explain myself anyway. He's supposed to trust me. He's the one who blew up and acted like a damn idiot. If he hadn't done that, I wouldn't have been back at my apartment all alone, eating ice cream.

Kyle walks up with two full shot glasses. "Here, it'll help."

I shake my head. I shouldn't even still be here, but my feet feel like concrete and I just can't move. Nick is in the bedroom playing some video game so I'm all alone with Kyle in the living room.

Get up and leave.

Kyle plops down next to me. "More for me then." He takes both shots, back to back. When he's done, his eyes dart over to me. "You're better off."

"Don't. Please. I need to go."

I start to get up and his hand moves to my thigh.

I glare down at it. "What are you doing?"

He leans up. "Oh come on, you deserve better than him. Someone who knows how you should be treated."

I shove his hand off me. "What the hell are you even saying?"

His jaw ticks. "You know what I'm saying. You have a guy right here in the same hallway who cares about you and you're off messing around with some asshole twice your age."

"He's not twice my age and you're supposed to be my friend." I stand up. "Dexter was right. What did you say to him that night in the bar?"

He remains silent, sitting there, brooding.

"I'm out of here."

When I take two steps, Kyle leaps up from the couch.

"Of course you are, you fucking tease. Go on, run back to him. It's what you bitches do best."

My face heats up and every muscle in my body constricts, partly because I'm pissed at Kyle and partly because Dexter was telling the truth and was right. I was stupid not to listen to him. I wheel around on Kyle. I want to say mean things to him, but I don't want to stoop to his level. I'm tired of being angry today. Everything hurts. My heart aches for Dexter. A real friend would be comforting me right now and not because they wanted to get me drunk and get laid.

"You're pathetic."

"Don't, Abigail. Just stop with the whole pity thing." He waves a finger up and down. "It doesn't suit you. You're just like all the pretty girls in high school, running after the hottest dude you can find, even if he's a total prick to you."

"It's true, I do pity you, Kyle. You know why?"

"Why?"

"Because you were nice to me when I moved in. I liked you and Nick. I thought you were actually my friends. And if you'd asked me out on a date before Dexter did, I would've said yes. You were too insecure to even try. But now, I wouldn't pour water on you if you were on fire. Have a great Thanksgiving."

I storm out while he stands there, staring at the ground.

You did the right thing.

I could've gotten into a shouting match with him, but what would that have done? It feels so much better knowing I was the bigger person. And I wasn't lying. I would've gone out with him, but now I won't, ever.

Now, I just have a broken heart I need to get over. I'm so done with relationships, for a long time.

ABIGAIL

IT'S BEEN two weeks and Dexter and I haven't spoken since he saw me in the hallway. I know it didn't look good, but what the hell? It wasn't what it looked like and I'm not going to chase him down and apologize when he's the one who acted like an idiot.

It's been tense and awkward at work. I go out of my way to not cross paths with him. Not because I don't want to see him. I do. I miss him like crazy, but it's just not worth it. He hasn't even said he's sorry and I'm sure he won't. All he'll remember is seeing me in the hallway and forget everything he did before that. I need to get out of this city. I don't want to be at work around Dexter and I damn sure don't want to be around Kyle or Barbie.

It'll take some time to get used to being single after Dexter, but once I'm over it, I'll be happy again.

Any time I do happen to see Dexter, it's like I don't exist. He doesn't glare, doesn't look frustrated, just carries on like I'm nothing to him.

I can't believe I put myself in this position. He

promised me he wouldn't do this to me. I don't know what to do.

Living with Barbie has been unbearable. She's back to being a total bitch. She hates the world thanks to Chuck and wants to make everyone as miserable as she is, not that she didn't before, but it's worse now.

Tate and Quinn have reached out multiple times, but I'm just not good at this stuff. I don't want to talk about my problems with them. I know where their loyalties lie.

I wouldn't expect anything less, either. They're both engaged to his brothers. If I was in their shoes, I'd report back everything I heard. It makes me feel so out of place. I can't wait to go home to Texas for Christmas. It's my favorite thing in the world and I refuse to let Dexter ruin it for me.

I turn the corner and catch him walking a female client to the elevator. My heart sinks when I see his hand at the small of her back. I'm sure it's nothing. He's probably just being polite, but it's like a knife to the heart. That was something I thought he only did for me. Every feeling I have is amplified by a thousand any time he's near me. Just seeing him hurts.

He smiles and jokes like nothing is wrong in his world and I feel like I'm slowly cracking. Like my entire life might just crumble down any second. I hate it. I hate this. I hate being in this office breathing the same air as him. I hate feeling this way. Being angry and still wanting him. I want out of my head for just five minutes.

I exhale a long breath and do what I should have done two weeks ago. I march to Decker's office.

"Is he in there?"

Quinn nods. "I'll let him know you're here." She picks up her phone. "Abigail is out here. Do you have a minute?" She hangs up the phone. "You okay?"

"I'm fine." I plaster a fake smile to my face and hope it's convincing.

"You sure?"

The pity in her eyes has my skin crawling, but I know she's just being nice. "I'm good."

"You can go on in. He's waiting."

"Thank you."

I walk in.

Decker leans back in his chair and looks intimidating as hell, but I square my shoulders and push all my anxiety away.

"Abigail." He gestures to the seat in front of his desk. "Look, I'm sorry about—"

"It's fine. It's done. That's not why I'm here."

His glance turns quizzical. "Okay, so what can I do for you?" He's being way nicer than usual, which tells me he knows he fucked up, but he probably won't apologize.

I don't want him to anyway. I meant what I said. I just want to forget it ever happened. I don't want to hold grudges or blame anyone. I just want to put this all in the rearview mirror.

I take a seat. "I was, umm, I don't really know how to say this, but is it possible for me to transfer back to Dallas?"

"Is this because of Dex?"

I shake my head. Of course it is, Decker, Jesus. How can you run this firm and be so blind sometimes? "No, I just miss home. I want to be back near my family." I'm sure he probably sees right through the lie. If he doesn't, he's oblivious.

"You sure it's not about Dexter and the Covington thing?"

I really don't want to get into this again. It'll bring back too much pain. "I don't know, Mr. Collins. Probably some of it. I do miss my family. I just feel awkward, like I don't belong here."

"You're a great employee. I had really high hopes for you. Have you talked to him?"

"No." I have to choose my words carefully. For all I know he's recording the damn conversation. "There's not really anything he can say or do. Things just didn't work out between us."

He glances off at the ceiling, then his eyes fall back on mine. "If that's what you want then I don't see why not. I'm sure Weston would love to have you back. Do you have any work that needs transitioned?"

"No. I got everything wrapped up. I was going home to visit for Christmas before any of, well, you know... It should go pretty smooth."

"Okay, well, when do you want to go back?"

"I'm leaving for Dallas tomorrow. It would make it easier if I could just stay there."

"Wow. Okay, I'll call him this afternoon. You sure you're okay? You've thought about this?"

I nod. "Yes, sir."

"Okay, well I'll make the call."

"Thank you, Mr. Collins. I really appreciate the opportunities you gave me here. I learned so much."

"The pleasure was ours, even if we only had you a short time."

I turn to walk out.

"Abigail?"

I stop and face him. "Yeah?"

"It's Decker, okay?"

I nod. "Okay, thank you, Decker." It feels so weird calling him by his first name, but I don't want to be rude and I really do appreciate everything he's done for me, professionally. I could stomp a hole in his chest for mixing business with my personal life, but I love my job and going off on him in his office would be stupid. It would be something Dexter would do and I'm better than that.

I walk through the door and let out a deep breath. I'm not going to cry. I'm doing the right thing.

As soon as I look up, Dexter is standing right there.

Shit.

DEXTER

I HEAD toward Decker's office. I need to talk to him about Wells Covington. He's going to get on board or I'm finding a new job. He's making a monumental fuck up, the way he's handling this. I've had to meet with Rick twice already to go over stuff when I've had far more important things to be dealing with.

It already destroyed my relationship. It's not going to ruin me professionally too. I've had to meet with clients and work a ton the past two weeks. I still met with Covington twice, but I'm not about to tell Decker that.

I know I should apologize to Abigail, but I don't know what to say to her, so I bury myself in work, meeting with potential clients. I tried to reach out a couple times and my calls went straight to voicemail. I sent two texts and they went unanswered.

I need to clear all my work off my plate and then I'll deal with her before she leaves for Christmas. If there's one thing I know about her and me, it's that we need to cool off. I can sit down and talk to her now that all the anger is out of our systems and at least give her something to think about while she's there. I can't do two things at once and be in two places at once and it's driving me insane.

As soon as I walk up to tell Quinn I need to talk to him, Abigail walks out of his office. Fuck, it's too soon. I'm not prepared to say anything, but I have to say something.

She eyes me and tries to speed past, but I step in her way. "Hey, I really need to talk to you. I've been slammed with work, but I tried calling a few times. I just really want to sit down and talk face to face. Please?"

She shakes her head. "Don't bother. It's too late for that."

Before I can respond she just walks past me.

What the fuck? I didn't yell at her. Can she not even talk to me now? I know I screwed up, but she was at that asshole's apartment and I didn't even blow up on her. I kept my cool.

I keep glancing back and forth between Decker's office and Abigail walking away and I want to scream. My whole life is out of order and I'm going to die if I don't get all this shit figured out soon. Fuck it, she needs to cool down a little more apparently. She looked like she was about to rip my head off. I'll just wait it out another day or two. She can't stay pissed-off forever.

Or can she? That's what worries me. Fucking women. They know how to hold a grudge. Jesus.

I walk into Decker's office.

The second his eyes come up from whatever he's reading, he lets out an exasperated sigh and holds up a hand.

"Not more personal shit. I can't fucking deal with it right now."

My eyebrows rise. "What?"

"Yeah, your little girlfriend was in here wanting a transfer back to Dallas. She's my best researcher out of all the paralegals and she wants out of here, because of you. I'm sure you're coming in here to stop it from happening. I can't deal with all this shit. Not right now."

I swear my heart stops beating. All the air sucks out of my lungs, and then my face heats to a million degrees. It's even worse than at Thanksgiving. And fuck Decker for wanting to blame all of this on me. He's guilty too.

Decker turns around and his eyes widen when he sees me. "Just calm down for a minute, okay?" He takes a step toward me.

"She's not fucking going anywhere." I haul ass toward the door.

"Dex! Get your ass back…"

I fly out of the room before he can finish his sentence.

The whole office is a blur. People try to say shit to me, but I don't hear a word. I sprint down the stairs and out the front just in time to see Abigail slide into a cab.

"Fuck!"

Everyone on the sidewalk turns and stares at me after I scream the word. My head is on a swivel, craning around, and I see the parking garage. Thank God I drove today. I take off running through the street and a couple cars screech to a halt and lay on their horns, but to hell with them. I fish for my keys as I slalom between a couple pillars in the parking garage over to my car.

It fires up and I haul ass out into Chicago traffic. The

skyscrapers float by overhead and the engine rumbles under my feet as I zoom in and out between cars, going as fast as I can through downtown.

At the last second the car in front of me slams to a halt while the light is still yellow.

"Fucking pussy, go!" I beat on the horn.

A middle finger flies up and I halfway start to unbuckle my seatbelt, but I can't chase Abigail down and tell her to stop being an idiot from a jail cell. So, I just sit there, breathing heavily, brooding.

What the fuck? Yeah, I was an asshole but you're just going to up and move across the country over it? Why the hell did I have to fall in love with a twenty-four-year-old? This is the type of shit they do. The sky is falling anytime someone makes one little mistake. It's not like I fucked someone else. I can't even think about anyone else but her and she won't give me the time of day?

You were a dick, man. It was a major screw up. Don't rationalize it. You need to calm down.

I want to do anything but listen to my brain right now, even though I know I should. My fingers grip the wheel. I shouldn't be going to talk to her right now, not like this. It's what got me in trouble the last time, but I can't help myself. I just want to grab her by the shoulders, shake her, and make her listen to reason. I want to promise I won't ever fuck up like that again. My heart just aches. I've never experienced anything like it.

It's my fault. All my fault.

I just want to scream at the top of my lungs.

I don't think you can ever really appreciate how much you love someone, until they're taken away from you.

Finally, the light turns green and I fly down Abigail's street. I catch a glimpse of yellow and her getting out of the cab, just as I pull up. I throw the Chevelle in park, right in the middle of the road because I don't give a shit about a car or a job or anything else. I just want her.

I rip open the door to my car and take off running to cut her off before she can make it inside her building. Horns blare and people shout all kinds of shit because my car is blocking the road, but I don't pay any attention to it. I run up the steps and grip her forearm and spin her around.

Her eyes go wide at first, then narrow in on me. "Go away. I don't want to talk to you right now."

I throw my hands up. "Seriously, Abby. We need to talk."

"It's not the time. Like I said, not right now."

"Oh, would tomorrow be better, when you're in Texas?"

She grits her teeth. "I said not right now. I don't want to talk to you."

"You're acting like an idiot."

Her face tenses. "Me! I'm an idiot? Are you kidding me right now?"

I shake my head. "You're not going back to Texas. What's wrong with you?"

She shoves a finger in my face. "You don't tell me what I can and can't do. You're not my father. You were supposed to be my partner, but you're not anything to me anymore!"

Her words are like a slap to my face. Fuck, it hurts so damn bad.

She stares down at the concrete. "I didn't... I didn't mean that, Dex. I'm just hurt, and…"

"Well, you said it. I'm here. I'm trying. I wish you'd just talk to me. I just need to hear your voice or be around you or something, I don't know."

She looks up and there are tears in her eyes. Her voice lowers an octave and her words slow down, like she's having trouble getting them out without having a break down. "You left me. At your brother's house, with your whole family, on Thanksgiving. And I work with all of them. They're my bosses. Do you have any idea how humiliating that was? Do you really have any idea? You acted like a child. In fact, all of you act like children. And that's saying something, considering it's coming from a twenty-four-year-old who is actively trying to have fun and be irresponsible at this stage in her life."

I nod. "You're right. I know."

She reaches out and grabs my forearm.

I just want to hold her so fucking bad and make a million promises to her, but I can't. She won't let me. And I can't really blame her when I step back and look at everything I did. I broke the one promise I made to her. The one that mattered the most.

"I really, really love you, Dexter. It's why this is so hard. If you were any other guy, I wouldn't even talk to you. I had an amazing time, being with you, and I'll never forget it. But I can't be near you right now. I just… can't." Her voice cracks a little. "It physically hurts, so much, even being in the same building as you. I have to go back home and get away from this place. I'm sorry."

Before I can say anything else, she turns and walks

through the door. I want to run after her, but I don't. Seeing her in that kind of pain was the worst thing I've ever experienced. I don't want to make it worse.

I finally make my way back out to the car. I don't know what to do. I've never felt the way I do right now.

It feels like my life is over. Like there's nothing worth living for.

DEXTER

It's a week before Christmas and I can't concentrate for shit. Work sucks. I see Abigail everywhere, even though she already left for Texas like a week ago. Life is dull, colors are drab. Going for runs, working out, driving along the lake in the Chevelle—none of it helps. All I think about is *her*. I see Christmas displays everywhere and I just want to light the fucking things on fire.

I should throw myself into work and focus on managing this Covington situation, but I can't think. I finally got Decker to listen to reason for two fucking minutes and we're assessing things with Covington on a day-to-day basis. It's the one highlight of the last week, but even that feels insignificant. I think he only did it because he felt bad. That's how he apologizes for shit, by not being an asshole about something for two seconds but leaving it open-ended so he can still get his way.

I barely eat anything. Can't sleep. I want her back so goddamn bad. All I think about is her meeting some asshole in Texas. Smiling at some other guy at one of those

338

line-dancing bars where they ride bulls and shit, whatever they do down there. He has a big belt buckle and talks like a fucking moron with his pussy cowboy hat. The entire scenario plays out in my mind over and over. It's fucking torture, and I did it to myself.

I'm sure she's probably doing the same thing as me, judging by her reaction outside her apartment. I'm sure she's talking to her mom and lamenting ever giving me the time of day. But in my brain, she's moved on with someone else, because the mind is a dick like that.

How could I have been so stupid? I pushed her away and acted like a total asshole.

I head up the elevator in Deacon's building. I know him and Quinn are off doing some stupid romantic shit and it reminds me of ice skating and the yacht. The whole time Deacon told me about his big plans for Quinn tonight, my heart squeezed tighter in my chest and I damn near had a panic attack. I managed to escape without him noticing. How? I have no idea.

Mr. Richards is home, though, and he's a good listener. At least last time I talked to him I ended up going and asking Abigail out. It turned my luck around and fuck if I wouldn't try anything right now. I'm desperate. I've never been superstitious in my life. I've always left that to my idiot brothers, but here I am. I'd go see a fucking psychic at this point if I thought there was an inkling of a chance of it working.

I walk through the door without knocking, like I own the place, and he's faced toward the TV in his electric wheelchair.

"Come on in, son."

"How do you know I'm not here to rob the place?"

"I figured you'd be here sooner or later. Quinn told me what happened."

I shrug. "Fair enough."

His hand points to the couch, but his eyes never leave the TV. "Well, lie down. I'm thinking about starting a side business, imparting wisdom to all you pompous rich bastards."

I snicker. He's probably right. It'd make Decker happy if he could take care of all the personal shit around the office. I walk over and lay down on my back, staring up at the ceiling. It really does feel like a counseling session all over again.

I don't even wait for him to ask, I just launch into it. "I messed up, bad, Mr. Richards. Got pissed off about some work stuff. I mean, it was a huge deal, but it wasn't her fault. I just got so damn, angry, all at once. And I never get pissed. I'm always the one keeping the peace with everyone else, staying neutral, level-headed and all that bullshit. Like fucking Switzerland or whatever."

"Yeah, you Collins brothers do get angry like that under certain conditions."

"What? Really?"

He nods slowly, still staring at the TV. "Yep. You guys are a weird bunch when it comes to your damn women. Always fucking it up, flying off the handle." He does that whistle thing that trails off.

"This was about work, though."

"Involves your women when it happens. Deacon did the same thing, didn't he? He ever blow up about 'work shit' before then?"

I think back. "No. Never." Interesting. I never put two and two together. I mean, I know Abby was involved, but I just thought it was work-related because I always compartmentalize everything. Abby and I rarely ever even talked about work. When Deacon blew up it was because Quinn was involved too.

"Look, son. There's nothing wrong with being passionate about your woman. Fuck, you should be, otherwise what's the damn point? It's why some places have rules and it's definitely an unwritten rule that you shouldn't date people at the office." He shakes his head. "Stupid, though. You can't help who you fall in love with."

"Yeah." I sigh.

"So she went back to Texas?"

"Yeah, she's gone."

The old man snickers.

What the fuck? Doesn't he see me pouring my damn heart out here? I don't make it my business to share my personal life with just anyone.

"Something amusing? What the hell? I'm dying over here."

"Oh cut the shit. You ain't dying."

I sit up on the couch. "Is this some kind of mindfuck you're pulling on me right now? Of course I'm dying."

"Men overseas are dying, away from their families, wishing they could hold the people they love. You're acting like a pussy. Talking instead of doing. Feeling sorry for yourself. And I must say." He finally turns and eyes me up and down. "It's not a good look."

I halfway want to punch his ass, but he's in a damn

wheelchair for fuck's sake. Not to mention, I can't really argue with him. I *am* feeling sorry for myself.

Before I can say anything, he says, "Maybe that's a little harsh, but you're thinking about this thing all wrong, kid. When Deacon fucked up, what'd you do? He was probably looking the exact way you are right now, wasn't he?"

I hold my face in my hands. "Yeah, he was in bad shape. A fucking mess."

He spins his chair around. "Well, what did you do? You were on the outside looking in. That's how you need to approach your little problem here. You smacked him around a little, I'm sure, to get him out of his own head. Then you guys came and took me to the Bears game, Deacon begged and pleaded until she couldn't say no. He refused to let her go. He made his move. He did something instead of crying on a couch about his problems. Why aren't you taking your own advice right now? You watch all those damn romance movies and shit. Wasn't that how you came up with it?"

Jesus fucking Christ, I could kiss this old bastard.

I jump up to my feet. "You're right. I've been caught up in my emotions like a little bitch, wallowing in self-pity. I'm not a damn woman like Deacon."

"Well, I wouldn't exactly put it like…"

He sounds like he's in a tunnel a million miles away right now. My brain is spinning, scheming. Concocting a web of ideas like John Nash in *A Beautiful Mind*. The light bulb goes off. "Fucking hell." I shake my head. It's all so obvious now. I can still have her. I snap my fingers and point right at him. "The over-the-top redeeming gesture. I need one, bad. And it needs to be way better than Deacon's because he's a bitch and I'm the pioneer of this shit."

Mr. Richards laughs. "Well, hell, there ya go, son."

"Gotta get out of here. I have work to do. Thanks, Mr. Richards."

He waves me off with a hand and goes back to watching TV. "Anytime, kid. Good luck."

I haul ass toward the door and damn near barrel over Deacon and Quinn as they walk in.

"What the fuck, bro?" Deacon yanks Quinn to the side so I don't level them to the ground.

"Outta my way!" I grin at both of them. "I need a dry-erase board and some markers. Gonna draw up a plan that shits all over yours."

They both stare at each other as I haul ass to the elevator.

"What just happened?"

Deacon shrugs. "I think he's going after Abigail."

Quinn clutches her chest. "Finally. I wish I could be there. I bet it's amazing."

Deacon grins at Quinn. "Bet mine still ends up being better."

The elevator doors open, and I step in and turn back to them. "You wish, dick breath." I hold up a middle finger at him as the doors shut.

ABIGAIL

IT'S Christmas Eve and I've sulked nonstop for the last twelve days since I got back to Dallas. Weston told me I didn't have to start until after the new year, and to enjoy a break before I came back to the firm.

I glance around the room and I should be happy right now. It's freaking Christmas, my favorite time of the year. Dad's legs are shot out perpendicular to the floor in the recliner and his snores echo through the house. He has a Dallas Cowboys blanket draped over his Longhorns hoodie because Mom keeps the house cold and he just deals with it and never complains. I smile at him. I know it drives him up the wall, but he always shrugs and says, "Happy wife. Happy life."

Mom's in the kitchen, baking a turkey she'll use for turkey and noodles tomorrow. It's our tradition. My sister is back in her room, doing God knows what. She's fourteen and at that angsty teen stage where she listens to her headphones all day and wants nothing to do with anyone. *National Lampoon's Christmas Vacation* is on the TV and all I can think about is Dexter quoting it word for word on our first date.

I start to laugh at the thought, then stop myself. Part of me wishes Cousin Eddie would drag Dex to the house so I could give him my own version of a Clark Griswold Christmas diatribe, but the rational part of my brain knows I need to just mope around for a bit longer and then forget about him.

Dexter.

My favorite Christmas movie is on, the house smells amazing, and yet all I can do is think about him. What's he doing? Who's he doing it with? I know he's probably with his family but all I can seem to imagine is him finding someone else and moving on already. She's probably older, more mature, more beautiful, more experienced in the bedroom. Better for him.

You did the right thing.

I know my brain is right, but my heart doesn't agree one bit. Why does this hurt so damn bad?

Mom walks into the living room and gives me the obligatory *I'm sorry you're in pain, sweetheart* look. "Honey, why don't you come help me in the kitchen? Take your mind off things."

I shrug. It can't make anything worse.

I sulk into the kitchen behind her and she reaches into the very back of the fridge and comes out with a bottle of wine.

"Mom!" My eyebrows rise.

She waves me off like it's nothing, but then peeks around the corner to make sure Dad is still asleep. "It's this or the gun. Which one do you want to use to fix this problem of yours?"

I can't tell if she's joking or not. Finally, I nod at the bottle. "The wine, please."

"Nothing wrong with it on a holiday." She pauses and points a finger at me. "In moderation of course." She pours us both a glass.

This is hilarious. I've never seen her drink a day in her life. I wiggle my eyebrows at her. "So, does Dad know you like to get all sauced up?"

She glares. "I do *not* get all sauced up." Mom stops and sighs long and hard. "Look, nobody is perfect. Not me. Not your dad. Not you. And not your boyfriend you're getting over, okay?"

I nod.

"It's hard to watch you going through this, especially since we just got you back home, and because I know how much you love Christmas."

I feel like I might tear up. This is the part where we finally talk about everything, like we always do, and for some reason my throat is scratchy, and I don't know if I can get any words out to my mom. And we talk about everything.

"This is a part of life though, sweetie. Everyone has their heart broken by someone. It might sound, I don't know, insensitive, but I promise you something…"

"What's that?"

"It's going to make you a stronger woman. It will hurt and you'll cry, and I'll be here every step of the way to comfort you, but you'll eventually look back at it, learn from it, and it'll lead you to the man who ends up with your heart one day." She walks over and pulls me in close to her chest.

I finally break. The tears start to flow as she smooths down the back of my hair.

"Mom, I know I'm still young, and I didn't plan on meeting the right guy for a long time." I sniffle and bury my face into her shoulder. "I just… For some reason, I just knew he was the one. I don't know how to explain it. He just got me. And I got him. We were just… right."

Her grip tightens around me, and I know she's having murderous thoughts about Dexter right now. It's what I'd do if someone caused my child any emotional pain. "If he loves you the way you love him, he'll come crawling back. Trust me, they always do."

"I don't think so. He would've done it already. He's older and has a good job. He won't have any problem moving on. It was stupid. I think I just read too much into it." I can't believe I'm in my kitchen, crying to my mom over a guy. I've never been that kind of girl. I can't believe Dexter Collins turned me into this.

I wipe away at my tears and pull back.

Mom grabs her glass of wine and glances out into the living room at Dad, then back at me, and her voice lowers. "You never tell another living soul what I'm about to tell you, okay?"

I take a sip and nod. "Umm, okay."

"Your dad screwed up really bad once too, back at the very beginning. It was our first anniversary and you weren't born yet. Our *first* wedding anniversary, and he stood me up, didn't show. Who the hell does that? I could still wring his damn neck. We were supposed to go to dinner. His friends got tickets to the Cowboys and Giants game. He went. Didn't tell me he was going. Didn't say anything about it."

"Oh. My. God." I almost want to laugh because it's so Dad, and it was so long ago, but I bet she was furious when it happened.

"Yeah." Her eyes bug out. "I sat at the restaurant and he never showed. We didn't have cell phones yet. I had no way to get hold of him. I just sat there, seething, then crying, turning my wedding ring over and over on my finger, wondering if we were going to work. So, I went to Grandma's. He got home. Didn't know where I was. Didn't know what was going on." She pauses and looks like she's getting worked up about something that happened more than twenty-five years ago all over again. "Geez, that big idiot, I swear. It was our first anniversary as a married couple. Anyway, so, he shows up at Grandma's at almost midnight and bangs on the door."

"Uh oh."

Mom nods. "Yeah. Right? At your grandma's house. Your father is a lot of things, but he does not lack testicular fortitude, at all. We made it a point to never argue in front of you girls, but we're not perfect at all. We can have blowouts with the best of them when you kids aren't around, still do on occasion. So, anyway, he's upset. I'm even more upset and the dummy doesn't know why, and I have to finally tell him. Things get really heated. He's telling me to stop acting so dramatic and being stupid. I tell him to just go home. I don't want to see his dumb face and I'll come back to the house when I don't want to tear his head off."

This is so surreal. I can't even picture them arguing like this.

"And I sat up, and I cried to your grandma, looking the same way you look right now. She pulled a bottle of wine from the back of the fridge and shocked me the same way I shocked you just now when I did it. That bottle's been sitting back there waiting for this moment for years, honey. I bought it the day you went on your first date, knowing this day would come at some point."

I laugh and cheers her glass, somehow feeling a little better because I know the HEA is coming soon. "So, what happened with you and Dad?"

She smiles toward the living room, the smile she reserves just for him and nobody else. "The big goof didn't even make it until the morning on his own." She laughs and leans in. "He was back within an hour, begging and pleading and apologizing."

I almost want to swoon. Good for Daddy.

"Look, Abigail, the moral is, if you screw up in a relationship, you own it. You ask for forgiveness. That's all you can do. I don't know all the details of what happened with you and that boy up north. But I know you're a good judge of character. We raised you to be. If he's any kind of a man, he'll be back, and he'll fight for you. If he doesn't, you don't need his sorry ass." She covers her mouth. "I swear, this is why you shouldn't drink. This stuff turns you into a heathen."

I laugh and cheers her glass one more time. "Thanks, Mom. You're right." I reach for her glass. "Should probably let me have this then, so you don't turn into more of a heathen."

She smacks my hand away playfully. "I didn't say it was a bad thing to be a heathen once in a while. I've waited years for this wine."

We both laugh.

Dad's snores eventually echo into the kitchen while I help Mom with some of the side dishes. She just shakes her head and keeps baking. "Maybe I should've stayed at Grandma's house forever."

A WHILE LATER, we're still in the kitchen and the doorbell rings.

I look up from a mixing bowl. "You expecting company?"

Mom shakes her head. "Not at this hour. Maybe it's Lorraine next door. She's baking too and all the stores are closed. Probably needs something." She continues to knead a pie crust. "Can you grab it? My hands are all doughy."

"Sure."

I push away from the counter and walk past Dad. He's still completely out of it, probably asleep for the night. *A Christmas Story* is on the TV now and I curse myself for missing part of it.

As soon as I open the door, about ten carolers start singing *We Wish you a Merry Christmas*. My face lights up for the first time in weeks, since I left Chicago. It's my favorite Christmas carol of all time because it's so simple and to the point.

The carolers are adorable too. They're all boys and girls ranging in age from about six to twelve.

I stand there, basking in it, just remembering why I love the holidays so much and being with my family. I glance back and Mom, Dad, and my sister are fanned out behind me, smiling at the carolers. Mom must have rustled them up and hauled them to the door.

When they sing the verse about figgy pudding, they part in the middle and Dexter rises from a knee and starts toward me.

Figgy *pudding*. Of course, he planned out every damn detail.

Mom's hand grips my forearm and her fingers are trembling. Not in a protective way, but in a way that says *oh my God, what did I tell you?*

I don't even have to look back to know she's grinning like an idiot. It looks like a scene right out of the Hallmark Christmas movies.

As much as I want to stare at Dexter's face, and read every single one of his expressions, I can't, because he's holding a Husky puppy with the brightest blue eyes I've ever seen. My brain tells me I should scream at him to get away, do something. Tell him off in front of everyone. Let him know how stupid he is for what he did. I should do anything but gush at the puppy in his arms, but I can't.

It's the most beautiful dog I've ever seen in my life. If any man on this godforsaken planet knows how to buy my affection, it's freaking Dexter Collins. Ugh!

"Merry Christmas, Abby."

I fold my arms over my chest. All I want to do is grab that puppy from him and bury my nose in its fur, but I know I can't just let Dex off the hook like that. He hurt me, bad. He can't buy his way out of it by flying to Dallas with the cutest puppy in the world, but it might get me to listen to him for two seconds and no more.

I can't be bought, and I don't know if I want to forgive him anyway. I already moved across the country because of him.

"Dexter, I…"

He cuts me off. "Look, Abby, I was an idiot. I know there aren't words that can make up for what I did." He glances down at the ground, but then angles his gaze back up at me.

I can see the shame written across his features. He looks like he genuinely feels remorse, but it's still not enough. I was doing my job back in Chicago and I won't apologize for it. My career means a lot to me and I will always work my ass off. That's how my parents raised me. I didn't keep any personal secrets from him.

He hands the dog to my mom and I immediately want to snatch it away from her, but I don't. All I can do is stare at Dexter. He has that little boy look about him again, the one where he shows me his vulnerable side. It's the Dex I fell in love with.

Then, he does something I don't expect. He takes both my hands and drops to his knees in front of me. Why does it feel so good when he touches me? Why does it send warmth rushing through my veins and make me want to forget all our problems and rush into his arms? I've missed him touching me so much.

"I'm not perfect, Abigail. I never will be. I'm an idiot. I do stupid things all the time and I won't promise I won't screw up again. I should've never made that promise to you in the first place. But I'm begging you. Please, I want another chance. I was always content being on my own, doing whatever I wanted, until I met you. You deserve the truth and the truth is, I'm going to screw up again. And again. But what I will promise you is that I'll always come back, and I'll always apologize, and I'll always make it up to you."

A tear slides down my cheek. Everything hits me at once, all the pain and all the happiness. Dexter just makes me—feel things, emotions I didn't know I had inside me. "Dex, I can't…"

"Yes you can."

I look away because staring at him like this in front of me is too much to bear.

"Abby, look at me."

I glance back to him and his eyes are glassy, tears forming in the corners. His voice cracks when he tries to speak. "I'm miserable without you. I can't eat. I can't sleep. My whole world is gray. There's no color in my life without you. I'm blind, stumbling around, lost."

If I wasn't turning into a blubbering mess before, I am now. "I just can't, Dex. You hurt me so damn bad."

He uses his shoulder to wipe away some of his tears. "I know. I don't know much, but I know I hurt you and I know I screwed up. I know one other thing, though."

"What's that?"

"I know I love you." He glances down. "I'm down on my knees, in front of your family, risking the worst rejection of all time, begging for you. I've never begged a day in my life. It's the hardest thing I've ever had to do, but I'd beg for eternity just for one more chance to show you how much I love you. I'm not going away, not now and not ever. I'll fight for you every day the rest of my life if I have to." He shakes his head. "I just need one more chance. Please don't leave me. I'll do anything."

I glance back at Mom and she has a hand over her mouth like she can't believe she's seeing what's taking place in front of her. Dad's smiling, like he can relate to Dexter's predicament. He's clearly been in that position a time or two in his life. It makes me smile on the inside. What would their life have been like if my mom hadn't forgiven him over and over? Dexter is a good man. I know it in my heart. I know he means what he says. I could see myself spending the rest of my life with him, and when I picture it, I'm always happy. It's the best life I could hope for and I really want that. I really want him. My life is also gray without him in it and I hate wallowing in all this pain nonstop, and it doesn't feel like it will ever go away.

"Abigail Whitley, come back. We want you to move in with us."

My head whips back to Dexter. "We?"

He gestures toward the puppy. "Me and Max."

My face softens when I see the dog, because how can it not? "You named him Max? After the dog in the Grinch?"

Dex nods. "Yeah, but we can change it. You can name him whatever you want…"

I shake my head. "No!" More tears stream down my face. "No, it's the perfect name for him."

"Abby, please. Just give me one more chance." He stands up and holds my hands in front of him. "Take a leap of faith with us. We won't disappoint you."

I glance back at Mom and she has tears in her eyes. She's snuggled up with Max and nodding her approval. I glance to Dad and he's practically a mirror of Mom.

"Oh for fuck's sake, take him back before I do," hollers my sister. It's one of the few sentences she's uttered since I've been home.

"Hey! Language! There are children out here." Mom scowls at her.

I can't fight the smile that spreads across my face.

I turn back to Dex and rush into his arms.

I think it takes him by surprise because he almost stumbles backward, but his big, strong arms wrap around me and for the first time in weeks, I feel safe again. I feel like I have a body of armor around me and nothing in the world can hurt me.

His hand caresses my hair and he pulls my face into his broad chest. "Thank God, Abby. Just, thank you." He kisses the top of my head, over and over, then puts his palms on both my cheeks and angles my face up to his. "You won't regret this."

Before I can say anything, his lips meet mine. He doesn't overdo it. I assume it's because we're in front of my parents and he hasn't even formally met them yet, but I can tell he doesn't ever want to let go.

And I don't want him to. I lean into him and resist the urge to melt into a puddle on the ground. After a few long seconds, he pulls back a few inches and smiles so damn big it could light up the whole block. "Good to have you back, Christmas clown."

I want to give him a smack to the chest, but I can't fight back my smile. "I haven't been much of a

Christmas clown lately, but I'm sure I'll turn it around soon."

"Abby?"

"Yeah?"

"I'll always do my best for you, I promise. I'll give it everything I have."

I nod. "So will I. Promise."

"I guess I'll let go of you now."

"What? Why?"

He tilts his head toward Mom. "I know there's someone you want to meet."

I immediately jerk away from him once I remember. "Max!" I rush over to Mom and snatch my new puppy out of her hands so hard she gasps. "Oh, how's my new big boy?" I shake my head at him and do the silly baby-talk faces at him. His head tilts to the side like *is this lady serious? Is this my life now?*

I hug him close to me and pepper his snout with kisses, then bury my nose in his fur, all the while grinning up at Dex. "Bribery won't work on me again."

"I know." Dex smirks as he pulls out his wallet and hands a twenty-dollar bill to each of the kids standing around.

They all take their money and take off running to their parents out by the road.

He turns and grins. "Totally, can't ever bribe you again."

"Oh, it's like that?" I laugh. "Good to see you're still as cocky as ever." My eyes widen when I remember I've forgotten my manners. Mom is going to kill me later.

"Crap, I'm sorry, Dex. This is my mom and dad." I glance back. "And my sister."

Dex walks over and shakes hands with Dad. He holds his hand out to Mom and she yanks him in and wraps her arms around him. Dex's eyes widen, but he quickly recip-rocates. She leans up and whispers something in his ear that sends pure panic across his face. Then she says some-thing else and that mischievous grin of his appears.

"Yes, ma'am." He nods.

Holy cow. I've never heard Dexter say "ma'am" before, like ever. He definitely learns fast. He starts toward my sister and she immediately backs away like *don't touch me.*

"Uhh, nice to meet you." Dex holds his hand up in an awkward wave.

"Good job with all… *that.*" She waves her arm out at the scene in front of her then takes off back for her room.

Dex mumbles, "Um, thanks, I think," to her back as she walks away.

"Come on. Come on. Let's get out of the cold." Mom ushers us in.

"Give me just a second." Dexter walks out to what must be a rental car. He turns back and sees us waiting on him. "Go on inside and get warm, I'll be right there."

I walk in next to Mom, hugging Max so hard to my chest I worry he can't breathe but I don't care because I already love him so much. He's the best dog in the world. I keep him away from Dad since he's allergic, but Dad doesn't complain. He just keeps smiling at me.

"Well, I like him. The boy grovels like a champion."

Mom laughs and gives Dad a pat on the back. "Could give you a few pointers."

"I'd take 'em. No stranger to screw-ups. It's why you love me."

"I don't know if I'd go that far." Mom scoffs. "Best just stay out of trouble, mister."

Dad holds up both hands and goes back to his recliner.

Max and I sit down and he sprawls out and rests his head on my lap. When I stop petting him to adjust myself on the couch, he whines and shoves his snout back into my hand.

"Aww, are you co-dependent on mommy already? That's a good thing, because I love you so much. Yes I do." I scratch him behind the ears.

"God, what have I done?"

I look up and Dex is standing there, staring at Max like a jealous lover, probably wondering if he's ever going to get any attention. He has a bag of dog food cradled in one arm and some puppy toys in his other hand.

It's so freaking adorable how sad he looks.

I pat the cushion next to me. "Don't worry, there's plenty of me to go around."

Dex doesn't hesitate and rushes over to sit down next to me.

Max glares right at Dex the second he slides a hand on my thigh. He even growls a little while he does it.

Dex's eyes go wide.

"Someone's protective already, isn't he?" I scratch behind Max's ears to show him I approve of his behavior. "Such a good boy."

"Third wheel Dex. That's my new nickname. I can see it already."

I reach up and scratch behind Dex's ear with my other free hand. He makes a show of closing his eyes and leaning into it the way a puppy would.

Everyone laughs, even Dad. "Know your place in the pecking order, son. That's what I always say."

I scratch a little harder behind Dex's ear and he starts kicking his leg out in the air.

Mom dies laughing.

I look around the house, and it just feels like Christmas again.

It's perfect.

My two boys, my family, and the holidays. What more could I ask for? It's the perfect happy ending.

I glance over at Dex. "Hey, remember that time you asked about my wish? After I blew out the candle at the restaurant?"

"Yeah."

"It came true."

He smiles for a brief moment, then stares blankly. "Wait, that we would end up together, or you would get your dog?"

I scratch Max behind the ears and pet his sweet little head. "Guess you'll always wonder about that, won't you?"

EPILOGUE

Dexter

Three Months Later

"You excited?"

Abigail nods, practically bouncing in her seat. "Freaking giddy."

We're on our way to Six Flags Great America for Employee Family Appreciation Day. The firm does it every year and it really is a lot of fun. They rent out the whole park and we get it to ourselves. Abigail hasn't shut up about it since she found out about it last month.

"I can't wait to ride Goliath. I looked all of them up online. It reminded me of the Texas Giant back at Six Flags Over Texas. That one was always my favorite when I was a kid. I like the wooden roller coasters the best. They have this vintage feel to them and really toss you around."

I shake my head at her. "Just glad you're excited."

I love going fast in my car, but heights aren't my thing. In fact, I'm terrified of them. I've ridden a roller coaster once when I was about eleven, and that was enough for me. It was the worst experience of my life.

My stomach has been in a knot for days, actually, but I don't have the heart to tell Abigail I don't want to ride roller coasters with her. Plus, I'm no pussy. I'll never tell her that. I just have to man up and do it. Hopefully, my brothers don't say shit to her.

We arrive and pull into the private parking lot up close. For once in my life, I wish the place was packed with people, so we'd have to wait in line and wouldn't have time to go on that many, but only the people from the firm and their families are here.

I park the Chevelle and we walk in holding hands. To take my mind off the damn roller coasters, I focus on the past few months with Abigail. It's been fantastic. Her and Max moved into my place and it's awesome. Max is a total mama's boy. He's always crawling up in her lap and nudging me away from her. I still take his ungrateful ass for walks in the park sometimes. He's a really good dog and we've bonded some, even if I do have to fight for Abigail's attention on occasion.

Work was the one thing I was worried about, but it's actually been great. Since Abigail does mostly research stuff, we're always working on different cases. She always has the craziest stories. There's not a lot of weird shit when it comes to finance, unless Decker is looking into Covington's sex life.

We're still on a trial run with Covington and I'm taking care of his legal needs for a few of his smaller entities. It looks promising now that Donavan is a managing partner too. He's not nearly as conservative as Decker. He doesn't give a shit about the firm's image, just the bank account. The situation with Covington will change soon. I can feel it. I've been knocking shit out the park and already restructured his companies and saved him seven figures in income and capital gains taxes. He knows what that means if he gives me the reins on all his holdings. Bennett Cooper is about to eat a dick, and then I'm coming for the rest of his big-name clients.

"About time!" Decker glances at his watch and shakes his head.

I can't tell if he's just giving me shit or serious, probably a little of both.

Tate nudges him with her elbow, telling him to knock it off. "Hey guys!"

Abigail walks straight over to her and they start talking about the Six Flags back in Arlington and how Jenny already ran off with her boyfriend, probably to make out somewhere.

Decker glares right at them when they bring up Jenny.

"You look nervous as shit," says Deacon.

Quinn walks over to the girls to get away from us. I don't blame her. I'd do the same probably.

Mr. Richards wheels himself up. "Lucky sons of bitches, I can't ride shit. Anyone wanna take my seat and let me have theirs? I used to love roller coasters."

"Shit, I would if I could," I say to him.

"Sure you wanna go through with this?" Decker gives me a sly grin.

I slowly nod.

"Way to sell the jury. Let's go, pussy, before you change your mind."

I gesture toward Goliath, the big wooden fuck towering into the sky. "She wants to ride that one. Better make it that one."

Decker and Deacon both look up at it as Donavan walks up.

"He's really gonna do it?" says Donavan.

"That's what he says," says Deacon. "We'll see."

"Anyone tell Abigail about the last time he rode a roller coaster and pissed his pants, then had to walk through the crowd?" Decker's about to die laughing.

I wheel around on all of them. "Nobody is saying shit, assholes. It's not gonna happen this time. I was like eleven."

"Sure, maybe we should grab you one of those souvenir drinks to take with you. You can 'accidentally' spill it in your lap, Miles Davis." Deacon's cheeks are at full capacity and pink as shit, like he might explode any minute.

"Probably the best plan on short notice. I doubt they sell Depends around here," says Donavan.

My middle finger comes up before I can stop it.

"You guys coming or what?" Abigail hollers from twenty feet in front of us.

"On our way, babe." I turn to my brothers. "Do what you're told and keep your mouths shut. Got me?"

"Yeah, yeah, little bro. We won't let you down." Decker throws an arm around my shoulder, and the rest of us follow suit.

Other than the gigantic roller coaster in my future, this

day is perfect, this moment right now. It's like we're kids again, arm in arm, walking through the amusement park. I'm so glad Decker and Donavan put their shit aside back at Thanksgiving. Life has been a million times better, once Abigail took me back anyway.

We get to the roller coaster and the girls walk up to get on.

I take a deep breath and try not to look up at the fucking thing.

"We're all set. You sure you're good?" says Deacon.

I nod.

I'm not fucking good at all. I should've eaten a goddamn Xanax earlier. I want my mind to be clear, though.

I walk in front and the guys fall in behind me. Abigail is in the front seat waiting. Perfect.

I climb in and hear the muffled laughter behind me from my brothers, but my stomach is in my throat and my palms are sweaty as hell. Front seat. Front row view, all the way down.

Abigail's hand slides into my lap and she squeezes my leg. "You okay? You look really pale."

"I'm fine." I do my best to smile at her. I really am excited about today, but roller coasters are like my biggest damn fear. I really should get off this thing.

Abigail looks so carefree and happy, though. I'd never ruin this for her. She's ecstatic, practically bouncing up and down in her seat.

The worker guy walks up to the platform and he looks nothing like an engineer or someone who would be qualified to work this thing. He's a fucking pimple-faced teenager. My fingers grip the bar in our lap so hard my knuckles turn white. My whole body is tense.

You can do this. You can do this. God, you're such a bitch, saying you can do this over and over.

"So, uhh, yeah dude, keep your hands in the car and hold onto the bar at all times. Here we go."

That's it? What the fuck? I'm going to die.

My body involuntarily starts rocking back and forth and it's like the sky is falling in on me, like I'm in the trash compactor in *Star Wars*. Black spots dance in my vision like I'm about to black out.

"Enjoy the ride." The kid hits a button and a buzzer sounds.

Bolts retract and we start rolling.

"Oh shit." Fuck, did I just say that out loud? "Oh shit." Yep, definitely said that one.

"Babe, are you okay?" Abigail leans over and puts a palm on my forehead. "You're sweating, like bad."

I nod furiously. "I'm fine, babe. I promise I'm fine."

"No, you're not. I'm going to holler for them to stop this thing. Look at you."

I grip her forearm. "No!" I nod again for the thousandth time. "I'm fine. I promise."

"Babe, what's going on? You keep saying you're fine. Over and over."

Deacon leans forward from the seat behind us. "He's scared shitless of roller coasters. It's basically his biggest fear in life."

We go around a turn and a chain jerks us up the steepest fucking hill I've ever seen in my life.

"Oh, Dexter." Abigail wraps me up in her arms.

I feel like the biggest bitch in the world right now, but I don't give a shit what I look like. It feels good when she squeezes me into her. I didn't realize how bad I was shaking until she hugged me. I turn into a stuttering asshole and I can't stop myself, no matter how bad I want to. "I-I-I'm okay. I promise."

"Stay away from his lap." Deacon laughs from behind, then says, "Ow!"

I assume Quinn smacked the shit out of him.

"What?" says Abigail.

"Nothing." I glance over at her. "If you don't know how much I love you, now you do." I shoot a glare back at Deacon and see how far up we've already gone. "Oh fuck."

"Look forward. Don't look down, Dex."

I glance over to make sure she's looking straight ahead, and I turn back and raise my eyebrows at my brothers. We're almost to the top of the hill.

They all flash me a thumbs up.

"It's all good, brother!" Decker hollers.

Okay. It's gonna be worth it. Another five minutes and it'll be done.

We start to crest the hill and Abigail looks over at me. "I'm so sorry. I would've never asked you…"

I shake my head. "Don't be sorry. Don't worry about me. Just enjoy this. I'm serious."

She gives me a worrisome nod, then holds her hands up.

And fuck, fuck, fuck, fuck, we're at the top.

The roller coaster stalls out for a split second. I look around and the view would be gorgeous from an enclosed room or an airplane, but not with my torso hanging out in the damn open.

We slowly pull forward, heading down the hill, and I think my heart might explode it's beating so fast. Then, it happens…

We roll over the edge and my stomach leaps into my throat. I close my eyes and say about ten million prayers in the span of two seconds.

My body vibrates all over the place while Abigail and everyone else screams their asses off. We fly down the hill, then through a tunnel and once we're at the bottom, relief washes over me and I open my eyes. I can't believe I didn't pass out.

"Oh fuck!" I scream.

Just as everything gets a little calm, we're yanked up a second hill. I was so focused on making it through the big one I didn't bother to think about the rest of the roller coaster.

"Fuck! Fuck! Fuck!"

The thing tosses us back and forth, jarring my neck and my back all over the goddamn place. I grip Abigail's leg so hard I worry I might be cutting off her circulation. It's two minutes of hell. That's exactly what the fuck it is. By the time we come to a stop, I exhale a gigantic breath I didn't realize I'd been holding.

Abigail leaps out of her seat, and I slowly stand up and make sure I didn't, in fact, piss all over myself again. I hobble out of the fucking death trap from hell and Abby spins around.

"Oh, babe, I'm so sorry." She dives into me and hugs me.

I wrap my arms around her. "It wasn't that bad."

She glances up at me and flutters her eyelashes the way she always does, like she's swooning over a romance movie. She leans up and pecks me on the cheek and whispers, "Thank you." Then, she leans back and stares for a long second. "You're never going on a roller coaster with me again."

I laugh as Decker, Deacon, and Donavan walk past and smack me on the back. "You didn't do too bad," says Decker.

I snicker. "Yeah, right. You know what they say about facing your fears?"

"Yeah."

"It's total bullshit. I'm never getting on one of those things again."

They all start laughing and we walk off.

Everyone falls behind Abigail and me and I grin my ass off at Deacon.

He gives me a fist bump on the sly, when nobody is watching. "It's done."

I nod at him.

"Oh my God, the pictures!" Abigail starts toward the little kiosk where they sell the photos of people going down the first big hill. You know, where everyone is making stupid faces and screaming their tits off on the big displays, then you can buy them for like fifty bucks.

We walk up and Abigail is bouncing up and down. "I can't wait to see your face in this picture, Dex. We're blowing it up and framing it on our wall."

I snicker. "Thanks, babe. You always got my back."

She leans up and pecks me on the cheek. "You know you love me."

"Yeah, yeah. Go on, check them out." On the inside my heart is still beating like a damn hummingbird's wings.

She's grinning so wide her face might get stuck that way. I love how happy I just made her. I've pretty much forgotten about all the anxiety from the ride, but my stomach is still all twisted up.

I take a few deep breaths as Abigail stares at the photo screen.

Her hand shoots over her mouth and tears well up in her eyes. I walk over to see my brothers didn't let me down. I look at me in the photo first, and it looks like I'm about to vomit everywhere with my eyes squeezed shut. Abigail has her hands in the air screaming and smiling.

Behind her in the photo, Donavan holds up a sign at the rear that says, "Abigail."

Next is Decker and Tate, holding one up that says, "Will you."

Then Deacon and Quinn are holding the last one that says, "Marry me?"

I already have the bright blue box out of my pocket, and I drop to a knee next to her. I open it up and reveal a princess-cut Tiffany solitaire in a platinum setting. She's still staring at the photo on the screen, her whole body trembling, tears streaming down her cheeks.

She turns and glances down to me on the ground, then looks around at everyone else. Tate and Quinn have their hands on their chest. My brothers are all grinning, along with Mr. Richards. Jenny flashes me a smile while her boyfriend stares down at his phone.

"Oh my God," says Abigail, when she sees Mr. Richards has a leash and Max is sitting on the ground next to him, watching us. She whips back around and stares down at me.

"Abigail Whitley, I love you more than anything. There's nothing I want in this world more than to ride the roller coaster of life with you. Will you marry me?"

She nods so hard she might break her neck. "Yes! Of course, yes!"

I take her hand and slide the ring onto her finger, then stand up and pick her up in my arms. Her legs wrap around me and I kiss the softest lips I've ever felt.

"Someone's chopping a damn onion out here," says Tate.

"Are you chopping it by Decker too?" says Donavan.

"Oh fuck off, I'm not crying," says Decker.

I grin right at Abigail and press my forehead against hers. "I love you. I always will, no matter what."

"I love you too." She shakes her head.

"What?"

"I cannot believe you rode that damn thing, knowing what it would do to you."

I glance around at our family and friends, then turn back to Abby. "Worth it."

"You're always full of surprises."

"Speaking of surprises, hold that thought." I glance around the corner of the roller coaster, set Abigail down, and yell, "Did you get it?"

"Wait, what?" Abigail's head flies around.

"We definitely got it!" Mr. Whitley hollers with his

phone in his hand as Mrs. Whitley comes sprinting over, barely able to control herself.

"Mom!" Abigail takes off in a sprint and the two of them damn near tackle each other to the ground.

Mr. Whitley walks up in his Texas Longhorns shirt and shakes my hand. "Congratulations, son. You did good."

"Thank you, sir."

He tightens his grip on my hand. "Take care of my little girl."

"I absolutely will, sir."

He walks over and starts up a conversation with Mr. Richards, probably about dad stuff.

My brothers, Tate, and Quinn walk up. Tate and Quinn both hug me at the same time. "You did so good! We're so proud of you."

I give them a little squeeze then shrug them off me. "All right. All right. I'd love to remember this last part, but we can all forget about the minutes leading up to it, right?"

"Oh fuck off," says Deacon. "That ain't happenin'."

I laugh when Jenny nearly tackles me and wraps her arms around my waist. "You're the coolest uncle," she whispers.

I drop a kiss on top of her head. "And you're the coolest niece. Best ever."

"Congratulations, Uncle Dex."

"Thanks, kiddo." I turn to all of them. "You guys did great. It was perfect. Thank you."

Quinn shakes her head. "You really are a master at the over-the-top romantic gestures. You could write this stuff in Hollywood, you know?"

I buff my nails on my shirt. "I have a particular set of skills."

"Damn right you do," says Tate.

I glance over and Abigail is talking to her mom a million miles an hour and keeps showing her the engagement ring.

We all turn to Donavan at once.

I smile big as hell. "Looks like you're up next, asshole."

Donavan smirks. "Not a goddamn chance. You bitches are gonna hate me the rest of your lives, while I'm out doing whatever the hell I want, and whoever the hell I want."

I see Abigail in my peripheral vision, smiling her ass off. "Nope, got everything I need."

"Me too." Decker wraps an arm around Tate.

"Me three. Fuck that was lame as shit, but you know what I mean." Deacon wraps his arm around Quinn.

Donavan shakes his head. "Whatever, let's go get hammered and celebrate."

"Sounds good." I walk over to Abigail and her mom.

"Oh, Dexter, I'm so proud of you." She goes in for a hug. Once she has me in tight, she whispers in my ear, "We have a lot of guns, boy."

I laugh, but secretly I'm a little nervous. I'm not quite sure if she's joking or not.

"I can't believe you got her here. I've been trying to get her to come visit for like a year."

"You know when I was away on business last Wednesday?"

Abigail nods.

I shrug. "It was family business."

Abigail's eyes widen. "You went down and picked up my parents and drove them here?"

"Yeah." I smile. "They're staying for the week then we're going to rent an SUV and drive them back. Stay for a few days in Texas. I have a little work to do at the Dallas office. Then we'll fly back out of DFW. Already booked the vacation time at work for both of us."

Abigail flies into my arms again. I don't think I'll ever get tired of making her happy.

Fuck, my life is awesome.

THANK you so much for reading Filthy Playboy, we hope you loved it! Be on the look out for Arrogant Playboy, book four in the Cocky Suits Chicago series. It is set to release on March 20th, 2020.

Made in the USA
Monee, IL
27 January 2020